THE SKELETON KEY

Praise for the Keys and Guardians Series

"Jacklyn is a perfect lead with her sharp wit and just a touch of cynicism balanced with a healthy dose of self-deprecation.
- Indies Today

"Manzano absolutely kills it with characterization in this novel. She makes it so very easy for her audience to picture each of the characters right down to the sounds of their voices…[she] left me no option but to hang on to the edges for dear life and turn pages as quickly as I could."
- Ms. J Mentions…

"The Order of the Key…has enough tropes and traditions to feel familiar and comfortable in the genre, but at the same time enough twists and nuances to read as something fresh and exciting. The characters are tightly drawn, each with their own motivations. The "good guys" and "bad guys" don't blend into amorphous lumps. Even the villains are the heroes of their own stories, at least in their own minds…I highly recommend The Order of the Key for readers of fantasy, urban fantasy, and paranormal fiction, and I am excited to add it to my classroom library to share with my students."
- Jennifer L. Gadd, Teacher and MG Author

"The old saying, 'power corrupts but absolute power corrupts absolutely' rears its ugly head among the members of the Order and the Head of it…various characters in the story were so duplicitous that it was hard to tell the good ones from the bad ones. And that made for a tremendously complicated storyline which was a kick to read. Guess you can call that depth of character. I call it fun!!"
- G. Themann

Indies Today 2020 Finalist
Author Shout Recommended Read 2021
Page Turner Awards Long List

JUSTINE MANZANO

THE SKELETON KEY

EVENTIDE BOOKS

Eventide Books
Visit the website at www.JustineManzano.com
Second Edition: December 2024

Print ISBN: 978-1-965476-06-2
Edited by Jennia Herold D'lima
Cover Art by Celin Chen
Layout by Celin Chen

To Logan,

For showing me just how strong parental love can be.
I'd lift a car for you.
Just...please don't make me have to.

ONE

KYP

Kyp Franklin pressed a yellow sticky note to his bedroom window before he climbed out into the crisp night air. His movements were careful, controlled. He avoided brushing the edges of the sill as though the sounds of his clothing sliding across the paneling would be enough to alert his housemates to his plans. They'd never allow him to go alone if they knew his intentions.

The note was only there to ensure that, should he meet his unfortunate demise at his destination, they would know where to find him.

The trellis screeched when his booted feet touched down upon it, and he winced. The last time he'd climbed out this way, it hadn't done that. But then, the last time he'd ventured out of his third-floor window had been over a year ago. He'd been on his way to meet Jacklyn in the woods. He'd been happy. Blissfully unaware that the worst of his troubles were yet to come.

Kyp climbed down, painfully aware each of the handholds he grabbed had once been held by Jacklyn as she snuck from her room to meet him in the woods.

He should have headed straight to the car. He had something important to accomplish, and he needed to leave before anyone realized he was missing. Instead, he allowed his feet to follow his memories. They led him down the winding paths between the trees. He kicked thick branches aside and let his fingers run across the rough bark of the trees he passed.

And there it was. It had been a year since he'd last been to the willow tree. The last time he'd been with Jacklyn, when they'd made love. And then, before twenty-four hours had passed, she'd been gone.

Not dead as he'd believed at the time, but gone.

For a moment, looking at the base of the tree, he could almost see her, beckoning for him to come sit with her.

He missed her. Missed sitting beside her. Feeling the weight of her head on his shoulder. He had an eidetic memory, but the ghost of her within his mind wasn't the same as her actual warmth.

He knew she'd run for a good reason. She'd left to be with her father, Raymond, to get far away from his Mother's reach. Far from the place where her sister's blood had stained the floor.

But Mother was gone, the constant threat of her return the reason behind dozens of wild goose chases since her disappearance on that fateful night when their entire world changed. He knew she would return, and this time he refused to be caught off guard.

This time, he would be the aggressor.

Up until this point, none of his leads had panned out. Flights of insanity, his housemates had called them. They were tired of the game, tired of the danger it put them all in. But it had to be done. Triggering traps she had set for them, pressing any information out of those who knew where she'd gone. It was necessary. Because if she got the drop on him, the Order would be back at her command. She'd already sacrificed hundreds of human lives to interdimensionals in her time leading them, purely to maintain access to her own power. He couldn't allow that again.

Even if his allies would hinder him out of concern, he *wouldn't* allow it again. This time, he knew his lead was good. This time, he would find her.

When he'd tapped out all of his contacts, he'd gone to his free agent hacker friend, Zane, for something credible, only to discover she'd been hired by Ray and Jacklyn. She warned him to stay away from them, as if he hadn't been the one to tell Jacks to run before it all went to hell. But then she'd given him the lead.

Kyp couldn't begin to parse out what the hell it meant that she'd still trusted him with a lead, and the frustration of it spiked in his veins. He channeled it until he felt the potential energy sparking at his fingertips. He was sick of feeling this way. Impotent. Out of control. No matter how hard he tried to make things change, he ended up a victim of his circumstances, of other people's rage.

It was damn time he let his own rage make the decisions.

He sucked in a cool breath and breathed in a memory.

Jacklyn sat at the base of the tree. "C'mon, Kyp. Hurry up! I'm cold."

His own voice echoed in his ears. "You can generate your own heat."

"Yes, but I'm pretending I can't for the benefit of cuddles!"

Laughter. The kind of hearty laughter he hadn't released in ages.

I love you, *he'd thought, but he was terrified to say it. What if he scared her away? What if the admission made her awkward, took her lightness and laughter away from him?*

The cold in his chest from the brisk air and the fear of abandonment made him ache then, as it did now. Only this time he throbbed with it, releasing his pain in a torrent of telekinesis that rumbled the ground beneath him in a straight line between himself and the tree. The earth undulated beneath and as the tree groaned, Kyp remembered why he'd left his room in the first place.

Crap.

He took off at a run, pushing himself until he made it to the parking lot along the side of the estate and into the crappy old car he used for low-key missions. He'd barely closed the door when he heard the tree crash down.

If a tree falls in your backyard, does it make a sound that wakes everyone in your frickin' house?

He started the car and hit the gas.

So much for a clean escape.

For most of his life, Kyp had given off an air of being in control. People expected it of him, believed he kept his emotions reined in tight, that he could push them into neat little compartments and choose not to address them. The last couple of years had proven that supposition incorrect. In actuality, his emotions were snarling beasts with clenched muscles, ready to strike.

His heart was black and numb, a muscle that had been still for too long. What had once been a full house now only contained himself and his Guardians, Cass and Drew. Though he may have alerted them to his escape attempt, he couldn't regret knocking that damn tree over. At least he'd felt something. Pins and needles, but the heart he'd been struggling to silence for the sake of his search was awake again.

Righteous anger was at least an emotion, even if it wasn't a welcome one.

As he approached his destination, Kyp took a second to glance in the rearview mirror and nearly laughed at what he saw. Stringy, greasy hair from shoving his hands through it, trying to settle his demons. Shadowy black stubble in patches across his jaw. Bruised skin beneath his eyes, the whites marred with red, highlighted by the sallowness of his normally bronze skin. Proof of the nightmares that consistently disrupted his sleep.

He'd fit right in where he was headed.

At one time, his destination had been a home. Now, the yard was covered with overgrown grass and weeds, the off-white paint grimy and pocked. Some of the siding had pulled free from the house. *Death to the Elite* had been spray painted on one side in bright red. The windows were boarded, and even the boards looked decrepit. Entire roof shingles were missing. The door was a thin slab of wood, balanced on rust-colored hinges.

Kyp parked his car and stepped out onto the street, taking a moment to focus his Aegis, the collection of enhanced abilities he'd been born with, on his target. Zane's tip had been right. Mason Deckard was inside.

Need pulsed through Kyp's veins because it pulsed through Mason's. Kyp's mind connected with his, and the manic nature of his thoughts made Kyp's stomach churn. All Mason could think about was his next fix. Kyp understood that level of single-mindedness. It reminded him of his own inability to focus on anything but plotting to take down his mother before she could do any more damage, and the thought sent shivers down his spine.

A deep breath of icy air burned as it filled his lungs. He didn't knock on the door before entering. People didn't knock when they belonged.

The inside of the house was worse than the outside. He gagged at the stench of mold mingled with urine and excrement. He wanted to wash his hands aggressively with every step he took further inside. The paint on the walls was so chipped he could hardly tell what color they had once been. Graffiti spattered the walls in random bursts. Names and curses and phrases took the place of family photos.

Someone rushed from a room in the back, and Kyp stood his

ground, forced himself to act natural and calm, despite his blood slamming through his veins.

"Kyp?"

Kyp's eyes closed. This could not possibly get any worse. "Marcelo."

Marcelo was the only Sirin he'd ever bothered to have a conversation with; he had come to the estate to find out if Kyp would be continuing Mother's agreement with the interdimensionals. Kyp had proudly informed him that, as the new leader of the Order of the Key, an organization that hunted interdimensionals before they could kill and eat humanity, there was no way in hell he intended to provide him and his kind with unlimited access to dinner. Marcelo had been surprisingly mellow about being rejected.

Marcelo released a laugh like car tires spitting out gravel. "What the hell are you doing here?"

"Why does anyone come here? You *know* why I'm here."

"Bullshit." Marcelo wrapped his clawed hands in Kyp's jacket and shoved Kyp back against the wall so hard his teeth chattered. He snarled, releasing a fetid burst of air that heated Kyp's face.

Kyp had seen needle-teeth like his tear flesh from bone. It took all he had not to add to the stink of piss in the place. He'd seen far worse than Sirins, but it was something about their intelligence combined with their monstrous nature that made them considerably harder for him to stomach.

"You thought you could come here and try to close us down?

Are you insane? I don't sense the others, where are they?" Spittle flew from his lips as he spoke.

There was nobody else, and his plan required Kyp to be unarmed and stacked with cash. If Cass and Drew knew what he was doing, they'd say he'd lost his mind.

Maybe he had. Something about cleaning the blood of someone he'd known since she was a baby from his kitchen floor and holding the lifeless body of the girl he loved in his arms had made him a little unhinged.

He supposed he couldn't blame Jacks for staying away.

"You don't sense them because I came alone," Kyp answered, as cool as he could manage. "Right now, I have no quarrel with you. You only have one thing I want."

Marcelo's garnet-colored eyes widened slightly and he let him go. "How the mighty have fallen. Unzip your hoodie."

He did. "I didn't have far to fall. You've met Mother."

"Yeah, she's a real beast, that woman." Marcelo straightened his round sunglasses and adjusted his fedora. As always, he looked ridiculous. "You well and truly look like shit. What happened?"

Kyp slapped his billfold on the small table by the entryway with a bit more force than was necessary, causing the table to wobble back and forth, the wood creaking like it would shatter.

"Okay, okay." He counted the money inside and grinned, likely ripping Kyp off, but Kyp didn't care. Once Marcelo was satisfied, he handed over a black zippered pouch from behind a broken wooden panel on the wall. "Don't kill yourself in the back.

That would be a little too much cleaning for me. And you know I won't be able to resist launching into a rousing rendition of the Death-Bringer Ritual. I'm zany that way."

The Death-Bringer Ritual meant permanent death, not the death/return game Keys like Kyp normally endured. The one thing a Sirin had against the Keys that made them more trouble than any of the other interdimensionals that plagued them. Sirins could speak, and that meant Marcelo was capable of performing the Ritual and making sure Kyp never came back.

"No honor among thieves, Marcelo?"

Another chuckle. "Ain't no such thing, my friend." He held out an arm. "Right this way."

The stairs cried out with every step they climbed, and Kyp half expected them to collapse underneath his feet. The floorboards on the upper level didn't look much safer. Marked and faded doors lined the hall. One of them was just for him.

"Not quite a five-star hotel, but it does the job." Another laugh. For a murderer, this guy laughed a lot. "You know the rest of the payment for this?"

"A pint of blood. Give or take a few drops." Kyp waved the pouch at him. "This makes it even yummier, right?"

If Marcelo doubted Kyp's reasons for being there, he didn't let on. "It's all yours." He slid out of the room and closed the door behind him.

The room was filthy, and the cot inside was likely flea-ridden, with stains in the center that could have been… anything. Kyp's nose twitched in disgust. It was hard to keep his mind from running through all the ways he was likely to get an infection just by standing there.

He ran his fingers across the vinyl pouch. So tiny, yet filled with the power to make someone forget. Kyp wished he could forget. He didn't *think* anything like what was in that pouch would help him.

He threw the pouch on the cot, wiping his hands frantically on his jeans, as though that would clean the thought from his mind.

They said Mind Keys eventually went mad. Mother certainly had.

This wasn't what he came here for. He closed his eyes and hoped the rats that were surely in this place wouldn't sneak up for a bite or two when he wasn't looking.

Reaching deep into his center, he drew from his Aegis and pushed past the minds of monsters and humans that surrounded him, searching for the signature he'd sensed earlier. Kyp hadn't sensed Mason Deckard's energy signature since he was ten. Mason had been cast from the Order for exactly what he was doing now—injecting drugs and allowing interdimensionals to feed from him.

Mother herself had cast him out when she'd discovered his habit. And now she was working with him again. Funny how fickle Mother's loyalty could be.

The answers to his search were one flight of stairs away.

With a steadying breath, Kyp inched his way out of the room.

Keeping his back against the wall, he moved up the stairs, trying to avoid potentially creaky floorboards.

He stopped with his hand on the doorknob. Last chance. No going back now.

He opened the door.

Mason Deckard was a burly mountain of a man. He sat on the floor with his back facing the doorway, a dingy t-shirt stretched across his expansive shoulders. He rocked in place, blissed out on the same substance that was in the pouch.

"Go ahead. Take your payment." His voice was strained.

What could make a person agree to this?

When he tried to understand, he felt a pull like a vacuum, his Aegis connecting him to Mason's very open mind. It was like walking into a cloud, the contents leaking in through his ears and fogging his brain, and rather than pull information from Mason's thoughts, he pulled the effects of the drug into himself. Kyp choked with horror as the vomit-spotted rug morphed into sand beneath his feet.

He knew this beach. It calmed his racing heart. Jacklyn and Ray were playing there. He just had to find them. He stepped forward to search for them, but he tripped.

Before he could regain his bearings, Mason's fists balled up the front of his sweatshirt and he was snapped out of the vision and back into reality. Perhaps coming here without a weapon was foolish.

Mason rammed Kyp's face with his fist, the impact tilting

Kyp's world. He hit the floor face first. Mason, whose Aegis was strength, was currently impaired. It would have been much worse if he wasn't. As it was, if he took another hit like that…

He tried to stand, but Mason kicked him in the stomach before he could get his feet under him. Air rushed from his lungs, and he slumped to his knees, gasping.

The floor shifted, and he was on the beach again. The heat of the sun beat down upon Kyp's head. Ray sat on a bright orange towel. His elbows rested on his knees and water pooled beneath him. The lenses of his sunglasses reflected the searing light in the sky, and he smiled widely. Ray passed him a blue plastic pail and a shovel, as Jacklyn, five years old and full of life, buried herself under the sand with her bare hands.

"Sand's not gonna bite, son," Ray said with a laugh, and pointed at Jacklyn. "The lass has the right idea, yeah?"

He should protect himself. But the beach was there, he could smell it.

The stench of the carpet fibers snapped him out of his hallucination. He didn't know when he landed face first on the floor, but he rushed back to his feet. Mason must have been caught up in memories as well because he swayed, eyes unfocused, a creepy smile forming a fissure across his rock-like face.

Kyp took the opportunity to launch a punch into Mason's gut. He should have run away instead, because the punch brought Mason back to reality.

His focus now razor sharp, Mason twisted Kyp's arm behind

him and slammed him into the wall. One of his giant paw-like hands came down on Kyp's head, pressing his cheekbone against the peeling paint. Something in his shoulder popped and burned like fire.

"Do you know how many people would pay to see you dead?" he growled against Kyp's ear.

"Lots," Kyp mumbled.

"I'm gonna kill you for free, you little bastard." Mason threw him to the floor and rained punches and kicks down on him. He tried to fight back, but Mason was too strong and every one of his swings was met with two more from Mason. A red mist of pain filled his senses. He barely knew where the hits were coming from anymore.

He'd been dealt worse deaths.

Glass shattered, and Kyp's eyes slitted open. Mason's feet stumbled to the right, then to the left, and the strikes finally stopped coming. He went down, shaking the floor beneath him, and the rumble shot slices of pain into Kyp's skull.

Twin sai were buried deeply in Mason's bloody eye sockets.

Cass.

She dropped onto Kyp, forcing his breath out with a painful gag. Her face was inches from his, and cold fury shone in her amber eyes. Gripping his hoodie in both hands, she yanked him up into a seated position.

"We don't have a healer! Why would you do something this crazy when you know we don't have a damn healer!" Her voice was high and tight, and her hand swung back as if to punch him. She dropped it, punching herself in the leg instead.

She leapt to her feet, stabbing a finger at Mason. "Look what you made me do! And I'm gonna have to do worse. I can't just leave you like this. It'll take you months to get back to fighting shape." Her face broke, and he knew the tears coming down weren't a sign of sadness—they were from frustration.

"Kill me," he whispered. "I'll come back in fighting shape."

"I know. I hate you," she hissed.

She didn't. Most of the time, Kyp knew that, even though it was difficult to believe.

He tried to move, but pain made his vision black over. He was in the middle of a Sirin drug den, alone with Cass, and he couldn't move. He couldn't protect her. After she had killed for him.

Killed a person. Not a monster. A human being. For him.

Her job is to protect you.

The memory of Mother's voice in his mind. Telling him Guardians were beneath him. Meant to serve as protectors, their lives expendable. He knew better.

Jacklyn had taught him better.

"Okay." Cass' voice shook. "This is what I need you to do."

The door squeaked open and Cass tensed, ready for an attack.

"You have got to be kidding me." Marcelo. The door closed behind him. He puttered around the room for a moment, outside Kyp's view. Not being able to see the Sirin was nerve-wracking, but Cass was tracking Marcelo with her eyes, movements slow, like a wildcat.

"Girl I Don't Know, get him standing."

Cass glanced between the two of them but did as he demanded. She yanked at Kyp's shoulders, and he hissed. His brain sloshed around inside his skull.

Marcelo's arms crossed tightly over his chest, one eyebrow quirked. "I knew you'd try something." His jaw worked. "But I didn't expect this. He was one of yours, wasn't he?"

"No." Kyp barely waited for him to finish. His voice sounded wrong, slobbery, and his mouth was numb. "He wasn't one of yours, either. He's something else entirely."

"You don't appreciate shades of gray," Marcelo said.

"People like my mother, like Mason Deckard. They're worse than you."

Marcelo placed a hand on his chest, red eyes softening with humor. "You wound me."

"Our kind is food for yours. That's nature. Can't help it. Mason, though, is a parasite."

"Was." Marcelo punctuated the word with a nudge to the side of Mason's head. "Anyway, allow me to get the crown prince out to the car. We'll say he had a bad trip, and he needed help leaving."

"Stay back," Cass warned, putting a hand up and scrambling between them.

Pain spiked in Kyp's head and he groaned.

"Look, kid," Marcelo said. "I'm trying to give you a hand."

"I said stand *back!*"

A rush of unexplainable warmth whooshed by Kyp. Marcelo shouted. Cass had set Marcelo on fire. The odor of burning flesh choked Kyp and swears ripped through the otherwise quiet room.

Cass winced and dropped to a knee beside where Kyp remained on the floor, attempting to push himself fully to his feet. They both knew what she'd done would draw unwanted attention.

"I can't lift you on my own," she said. "Work with me. It's going to hurt, but frankly, I don't give a crap."

He had to be hallucinating. Her voice sounded like Gana's.

"You're angry with me. I get it."

"I don't think you do." She yanked him to his feet, pulling on the arm Mason had dislocated. Kyp bit his lip so hard, fresh blood dribbled into his mouth.

"You set the room on *fire*?" he slurred. He sounded worse every time he spoke. Brain damage? This was bad. He peered at Cass through swollen eyelids.

Her face softened. "Jeez, Kyp. You really are a mess."

"Thanks."

"Please don't talk. You sound gross." She glanced out the window. "I can't climb out while supporting you. Can you get down on your own?"

Kyp looked over the edge, the world swaying as he gripped the window. Cass's car was pulled onto the sidewalk below. A glance over his shoulder revealed Marcelo had almost put out the fire.

"I can't. Push me out."

"No." She sounded like Cass again.

He jerked a thumb backward in Marcelo's direction. "Push me. I'll come back."

Cass swallowed, her eyes darting from Marcelo to Kyp and back again. "I hate you so much."

She shoved him through the window. The last thing he saw as he descended toward the concrete sidewalk was Cass climbing out after him.

A moving car. Cass was the driver, a filthy white and blue baseball cap pulled down over her eyes.

"How long was I down?" He shivered and cleared his throat.

Coming back from the dead was an awful process, and not a speedy one. It had been late afternoon when he'd arrived at the den. Now it was dark out. How long had they been in the car?

"I've had to refill the gas." She didn't look at him.

"Why didn't we go home?" Kyp shifted in his seat.

"I called ahead." She tapped her hand on the steering wheel. "Drew said I wasn't allowed to come back home with you like that."

"What's going on?" It wasn't like Drew hadn't seen him banged up before. Something was up. But he was still weak, still half-numb with the chill of death, and he couldn't put the force he wanted into the question.

"You'll see soon enough."

"Tell me."

"You're not my boss anymore, remember?" Cass said. "I'm not your protector. You made that clear when you snuck out of the estate, away from the wards, away from our protection, and went off on a mission of your own."

"One I failed. I still don't know where Mother is."

"Lavinia will show up. And when she does, you can't be in some Sirin drug den without people who will fight by your side. Drew's pissed too."

"Really?" Kyp snapped. "Drew wasn't even a Guardian when the role meant unquestioning service, and he's still that self-sacrificing?"

Cass didn't answer for ten full minutes. Kyp had just gotten comfortable staring out the window at the lights streaking by on the highway when she decided to speak again.

"It took you months to find a new recruit you could live with and now you're complaining about Drew?" She turned into the estate driveway and slowed the car to a stop. "Take that hoodie off. It's covered in blood and we have a visitor."

A visitor. Who could it be? Jacklyn? Ray?

He stumbled out of the car, not waiting for Cass. He'd never limped so fast in his life.

"You are so predictable!" Cass shouted after him.

"No, wait!" he heard Drew shout as the door to the estate swung open before Kyp.

Andrew Clayson, their newest member, sighed and slumped against the doorframe. He flashed Kyp a helpless smile. Tall and lanky, with rich brown skin and light eyes, he had the build of a swimmer, though today it was hidden in overly baggy clothes. He pulled his glasses off and wiped the lenses clean on his sweatshirt.

Cass gasped. And Kyp stopped short.

Because standing in front of him was a girl. She couldn't be more than five years old. Short brown curls haloed her face, and her eyes were a piercing brown. With her rounded and rosy cheeks, she looked downright cherubic.

And also, familiar.

"Hi." Kyp knelt in front of her and looked her in her eyes. "I'm Kyp."

"But..." She looked at him, eyes wide, face screwed up in confusion. "You're just a kid."

"I'm twenty, actually." He hoped to keep the tremble out of his voice. "Totally an adult."

"Not old enough," she insisted. "Is there another Kyp here?"

Kyp frowned. What was a little girl doing here? Why would Drew allow her in? His heartbeat ran ragged in his chest as he stared down at her, his palms slicking with sweat. This couldn't be possible…

"I'm sorry, kiddo. I'm the only Kyp here."

"Well, then." She straightened her t-shirt. "Kyp Franklin, my name is Jaina Elizabeth Franklin."

Kyp's breath caught in his throat.

"I'm your daughter."

TWO

JACKLYN

Music shook the brownstone's foundation, waking me out of my barely existent sleep. For the entire year I'd lived there, this was my alarm clock, set off every morning by my father, Raymond Madison. It was part of a training regimen he used to run when he lived at the estate. When Kyp unlocked my memories of him, the grin on his face when he'd turned up the stereo with me hitched high on his hip had been one of my fondest memories.

It didn't have the same effect anymore. Then, it had made me giggle. Now, it mostly made me want to kick him in the teeth.

I rolled out of bed and pulled myself together, putting on a jogging suit, sneakers, and a headband to push my hair back from my face. That would do until it grew back.

Reactions to the worst losses of my life:

1) Left the boy I loved in the dust like I didn't even know

him.

    2)   Threw myself into my work.

    3)   Learned to kill with efficiency.

    4)   Cut all my hair off.

I missed my hair. And the boy. But the rest I was cool with.

What I wasn't cool with was the crap I was going to get when I went downstairs. Ray may be starting the day like everything was normal, but it wasn't. Not after yesterday.

I had good days where I could bounce out of bed and work out with my father and our two new Guardian friends, Zane and Austin. On those days, I was proactive. I went out and fought interdimensionals, and sometimes, I caught humans wrapped up in dirty dealings, and I eliminated them too. Because evil was evil. On days like those, I got on flights and sealed rifts all over the world with the help of my team. Things got done. More than I had gotten done in my time at the estate.

But I also had my bad days. Days where Ray's wake-up call didn't help. Days where I couldn't leave my bed. Days where I tried motivating myself to do anything at all, even shower. Those days, Ray brought me meals in bed. His not-girlfriend, Zane, popped her head in to update me on our investigations. Austin, my best friend in this place, would sit on the floor beside my bed, providing either fun stories or a shoulder to cry on.

Then there were days that started well, only to take a header into a bottomless pit. Yesterday was like that.

A group of Sirins got the drop on me and Austin. It was ugly, in a way it could only be for us—Austin and his self-healing Aegis, and me with that and more as a Body Key. Torture only does so much when you heal quickly. I made a decision to get us out. Was it a dark decision? Sure. Was it the wrong one?

Well, Austin was still alive, wasn't he? I couldn't regret what I'd done.

I wouldn't.

I bounced down the stairs, ready to go for a run to work off my aggression, ready for any challenge the others would present.

My team was waiting for me in the foyer.

"Mornin', Birdie," Ray greeted in his Irish brogue. He'd spent his early years in Ireland and had never shaken the accent. I hoped he never did. "Feeling a mite less suicidal today?"

I ignored him and looked at Austin instead, stretching my lips into the ghost of a smile. Austin smiled back, though it didn't reach his teal blue eyes. He bumped his shoulder into mine when he noticed me looking.

"How you feeling?" I asked.

"Same. Better'n yesterday." Austin's Texan twang was pronounced, a sign he was fighting down something bitter.

"Good." I straightened my headband. "We're all here, so I'm only going to say this once. I did what I had to do to get us out alive. I didn't do it because of... everything. I did it because I was injured and I wouldn't have recovered in time to get us out safely."

"Hanging yourself was necessary?" Zane tossed her straight

black hair over her shoulder. She looked impeccable in her spandex activewear. "Having Austin use a Ritual to bring you back faster was necessary?"

"Look, it was that or let Austin die waiting for you two to rescue us. They could have done a Death-Bringer Ritual on me to make sure I was dead, too. Or they could have tortured us until one of us cracked and told them where our base is." I shrugged. "It was a Hail Mary play, but it was the play I made."

"A Hail Mary play." Ray's mouth was a straight line. "That you happened to have the materials for? They got your knives and your guns, but not the damn Arvokian herbs and activator for that particular Ritual?" There was no twinkle in his eye. None of the fun dad he'd been trying to play since I'd arrived, to counteract the trauma and the painful miscarriage I'd suffered. He even attempted to be "Fun Dad" when I told him the boy he'd helped raise, Kyp, had been the father of my baby. Somehow, this was what made him drop the act.

My Hail Mary had been a necessary evil. But maybe I had been running on a combination of depression, lack of sleep, and anger. Maybe I always was. And maybe I'd been a bit curious about the Ritual I'd asked Austin to do, because it was the Ritual Kyp's mother tortured him with for years.

It was hellish. The pain of returning before my body was ready was like someone had torn my soul free and stuffed it where it didn't fit. My body ached, my insides burned, my brain was sluggish and detached.

Lavinia had been responsible for my sister Gana's death. She had beaten and terrorized me. I'd already made it my life's mission to kill her. But feeling what that forced return Ritual felt like, knowing she'd put Kyp through it repeatedly, made me hate her even more.

"I told you, it was a necessary risk." I spoke through gritted teeth. "One I'd foreseen. I've been carrying the supplies with me for a while. Now, can we get moving?"

Ray looked at Zane. She gave him a small nod, then glanced at Austin. Austin's shrug was almost imperceptible.

I knew that look. I knew what it meant. They were going to drop it. And then they were going to monitor my every movement, like a broker during a stock market crash.

My heartbeat ratcheted up. I didn't want anyone watching me too closely. If they did, they'd see I was holding on by dental floss and sheer will.

"C'mon," Ray said. "Let's go for a run."

We headed through the heavy-duty security doors into what had once been a basic vestibule. Now there was a security setup built into the left wall, with a full fingerprint ID station and a retinal scan required for entry. A computerized lock served as a striking decoration on the inside doors. From the outside, it looked like an ordinary brownstone.

It all helped me feel safer. That, and being off the radar. There weren't even wards surrounding the brownstone.

I'd finally learned how to quiet my Aegis. It had taken a lot of moving around. Ray and I lived on the road for an entire month, fighting off interdimensionals and hitting the road again before more could show up. And while we traveled, Ray taught me. Then, when Austin came along, Zane had done the same for him.

Because the estate was a training ground, and because those at the estate trusted the Arvokians, they were willing to use the wards to hide the estate. But we were in hiding. Ray couldn't afford to trust the Arvokians to hide him, and neither could I. Not after an Arvokian had betrayed me. If we put wards around the brownstone, whichever supposedly allied Arvokian had told Lavinia I'd raised an inquiry about her leadership would know where to find me, and it wouldn't be long before Lavinia did as well.

I pushed my way out through the green double doors with enough force to make the wispy linen curtains covering the large panes of frosted glass in the center blow back and brush my face.

The air outside was crisp and refreshing. I closed my eyes and inhaled deeply. The cold of the air in my nose was better than any caffeinated wake up.

I walked down the stairs, gripping the wrought iron banister tightly. It was something real to hold on to. The brownstone was beautiful; the city, even more so.

I stepped off of the stairs and drank in the skyscrapers, the honks and shouts of traffic, the scent of roasting coffee and grilled sausage. The only thing more beautiful was the city at night, radiant and bustling; the city that never slept.

We had a kinship in that way.

I started at a light jog. The others trailed behind me, none getting too close, which was good because I wasn't in the mood to be approached. My shoulders remained rigid; I was eternally on guard, awaiting disaster. Joining the Order had taught me a valuable lesson—life was little more than a series of battles to fight. You just kept fighting, though you never won.

"It's lovely out here today," Ray said, catching up with my pace. "A good day to clear your mind with a good run, yeah?"

Austin and Zane were only slightly behind, exchanging whispers.

So much for being unapproachable.

"Sure is," I said. "But you're not talking to me because you want us to clear our minds. You're here to press the issue."

"I'm not," Ray said. "I'm here to talk to you." Minutes passed in silence.

"Okay, let's hear it." I didn't actually want to hear it. Ray wasn't always the most sensitive when it came to training. Or emotions. Or much of anything.

He took a deep breath, and not because he was running too fast. Running barely affected him. Just like me. It was a part of our Aegis. No, he was gearing up for whatever he was about to say.

Dread rolled in my stomach and crawled up my throat.

"I was going to suggest we revisit the conversation we had when you first got here." Another few steps in silence. "I think we should contact the Order."

My breath hitched, and I stumbled. Energy crackled in my veins, the surge moving from my core and zipping to the tips of my fingers and the soles of my feet.

I released the hold over my Aegis. And I ran.

People crowded the streets as the clock ticked toward the start of the workday, and I weaved in and out between them. I flew past shops, cars, neighborhoods, feeling weightless. All that existed was the jolt of my feet hitting the pavement, the music of my pulse pounding in my ears, the huff of my breath.

"Birdie, enough." My father stepped in front of me, just before the walkway of a bridge I hadn't realized I'd been running toward.

The High Bridge. The only pedestrian bridge that led back to the Bronx. My home.

The one I'd left to join all of this.

Ray had been in New York City all my life, while I was there growing up without a father, with Gorvhans closing in, with no idea of what I was. A twenty minute drive away. He'd been staying away to protect me from Lavinia. And yet…

Now there wasn't any home to go back to.

I stopped running.

My arms flopped. Pins and needles danced along my cheeks and lips. My legs wobbled.

"I shouldn'ta said it," Ray said. "I knew it was a bad idea. I never shoulda brought it up." His eyes pleaded with me, but I remained numb.

Gently, almost timidly, he reached out and wrapped his fingers around my forearm.

"We'll go home now, yeah? No harm, no foul."

No harm, no foul.

I nodded and let him guide me back the way I came.

When I returned to the brownstone, I stalled at the scene I was met with.

Austin and Zane watched me, clearly waiting for an explanation. How long had I been gone? It must have been a long time. The walk back hadn't exactly been short, and my legs ached.

"I'm cooking lunch today." It was how I used to appease my little sister when I'd screwed up. "Pasta with meat sauce." Her favorite meal.

I nodded, like that made the statement an official declaration. Ignoring the eyes on me, I headed for the stairs.

Austin caught me by the elbow as I moved past him. "You feelin' alright, girl?"

"No."

I continued up the stairs to my room, and this time, I didn't let anyone interrupt me. I took my phone from my pocket. *Damn.* It was already ten a.m. We'd left at seven.

I sighed and set an alarm for a quarter to twelve, in time to make lunch. Kicking my sneakers aside, I crawled under my blue bed covers.

The wall was painted a dull taupe. I welcomed the tears that blurred my vision, so I no longer had to look at the same three mistakes the painters made, the ones I always caught when I stared at the wall and attempted to abandon the thoughts in my brain. The tears created sticky streaks along my nose where they had wended their way over my face. I focused on the flaws in the paint job. I tracked them as though they might change.

Sometimes, I stared into space until I lost myself. Sometimes, I needed to think just to breathe.

One minute, I was doing something functional, and the next I was staring at blood soaking into my clothes, my limbs numb.

Sometimes I was like that for hours.

Sometimes it hurt to come back.

The whole time, I replayed all my past choices in my head.

What if I hadn't opened my damn mouth to Lavinia?

What if I'd accepted her every word?

What if I'd never come to the estate?

What if I'd turned Kyp in when he'd first come to me?

What if I'd given Lavinia the damned Skeleton Key she wanted so badly?

What if I'd died that night in the alley?

Would Gana be eating pasta and meat sauce today? Would Mom?

I'd been surviving for the whole year. Surviving, but not living. Vengeance and protecting what I had left kept me from imploding. I grasped at sanity like a drowning woman lost in a churning sea would grab onto a flotation device. Thinking about my family would only poke holes in what was keeping me afloat.

But even when I thought that, I'd close my eyes, and I was

surrounded again by the sterile white walls of R.D. Livingston's clinic, warm medication pumping into me from an IV, Livingston's kind voice in my ears. It was only my third visit, but he'd always been very nice to me, even as I grimaced at my discomfort with the whole situation.

He had looked me in the eye and swallowed hard, like he had to struggle to get the words out. They couldn't save the baby. I had barely even realized I was pregnant, and the baby rebelled, jumping ship.

They left me. The important things tended to leave. Or I left them.

"Jacks? Jacklyn?" The words sounded like they were under water, drowned out by the white-noise hum in my ears.

A hand landed on my shoulder, and I was grounded, back in my body, and jumping out of my skin.

"Sorry, lass." Ray winced. "Didn't realize you were in one of those."

He said it the way he always did. Like I was breakable.

My alarm rang. Quarter to twelve. I had been staring at the wall for nearly two hours, and it felt as if no time had passed at all.

Ray gingerly lowered himself to the side of the bed and turned off the alarm. We both knew I wouldn't be cooking anything today.

"Are they mad?" I asked, despising how shaky my voice sounded.

"They" were Austin and Zane. Zane was a hacker, but also a technomancer, which made it even easier for her to find her way through computer systems. She had been an Order contact for ages, tech support that had never wanted to pick a side, until Ray begged her to help protect me. Austin was a fresh-faced boy with a body like a pro football player. A frickin' mountain with a kind soul and a streak of vengeance in him. He hated what the Sirins had done to a small-town girl back in his home state of Texas. The Sirins figured nobody would miss her. But Austin did. He'd tried to take them on, and had the scars to prove it. Then he'd sought out the Order. Loudly. We scooped him up before Lavinia could. There was no sign Kyp had even noticed Austin's clumsy search.

Zane and Austin were good people. They were my friends. The past year had practically made them family. And if I kept going on like this, I was bound to scare them away.

"No," he said. "If they were, I'd give them each a sound beating. We're worried about you."

"Are you okay?" I don't know why I asked. I always spoke before I thought, but these days what came out was as much a surprise to me as to the people I spoke with.

He barked a laugh. "You're asking *me* that?"

"You didn't answer."

"Hell no, I'm not okay. I'm scarred down to my bones on a good day, and I've been terrified for you every day for the past year. And I'm terrified for Kyp, too. I know you don't want to hear that, but, as much as I'd like to protect you, you both need to get back to reality."

My stomach twisted. "Why? What happened to Kyp?"

Ray sighed. "He fumbled another mission. Nearly died. Cass had to kill our lead to protect him. We may be back to square one if this doesn't bring Lavinia out of the woodwork."

My heart squeezed painfully. "Kyp doesn't fumble."

"I didn't want you to worry, but he's been fumbling a lot lately. This time was a disaster. Zane sent along a lead we had that might help us track her down."

He didn't have to say who he meant by "her."

"You sent him a lead on Lavinia?" I asked shrilly.

"Yeah," Ray answered. "And he went alone."

My throat went dry.

"It's something we've been doing for a while now. Zane contacts Cass, the same way Kyp had Cass reach out to Zane when he needed identification documents for you, back when he was trying to get you to run. We kept the middle-man between us so nobody catches on. It's perfectly natural for Cass to need to contact Zane. Better to keep it looking that way."

"And you didn't think you should mention that to me before?" I snapped.

"No, because I like my head right where it is on my shoulders, thank you." He shot me a pointed look. "But I've been keeping our team busy with the real Order work. Kyp has been chasing everything even remotely resembling a lead, so we started feeding him real ones, hoping he'd narrow them down for us."

"That's incredibly stupid," I said. "Especially because I'm the one who's taking Lavinia down."

"Yeah, yeah, you've mentioned that." He sighed. "Cass told Zane he was reckless. Says no matter how much he asks, we're not to give him any more leads. If he finds Liv, he'll die." Ray buried his head in his hands. "It has to be us from now on. At least that's the paraphrased version. Cass gave Zane a right bollocking."

"So you want to reach out to them? So we can do what? Undo the mess you made when you made a four-year-old boy who wasn't capable of forgetting swear his absolute, undying fealty to me? Feeling like maybe that wasn't such a good idea now?"

Ray's head whipped up. "I'm feeling like he needs me."

"He always has." Anger bubbled in my blood. "It didn't stop you from running before."

"To protect you, yes," Ray snapped back. "But now? I'm helping you hide."

"To protect me. Just like when you hid."

"No." His hands balled in his lap. "You want to kill Liv. Kyp wants to kill Liv. You're on the same page."

I couldn't do this. "Have you forgotten that Kyp made all your running to protect me unnecessary? That he brought me into a world that killed Mom and Gana and nearly killed me?"

"That's not why you don't want to face him." A muscle in Ray's cheek jumped. "Your mam used to say you were like me. She was wrong. You've got a stitch of her in you, like your undying need to make people admit they're an arse."

I missed Mom. Every single day I missed Mom, but especially during moments like this, where I had hard decisions to make.

Tears clouded my vision. I didn't even notice Ray leaning forward until he was pushing my dark hair out of my eyes.

"But your mam, she liked her monsters nice and obvious. Meanwhile, you think it's easier to blame Kyp. Sure, none of this would have happened if it weren't for him. But this isn't his fault. It's Lavinia's. And only Lavinia's. And all you can do in the face of a monster like her is band together."

"I can't go back to the estate." I could barely breathe as it was.

"They could come here. Plenty of room."

He was right. The brownstone had three floors, two of them filled with bedrooms. It was a possibility. So why was my heart jackhammering at the thought of it?

Because you left Kyp. You left him and you wouldn't talk to him again. And he missed you. Until he stopped missing you. And now he probably hates you.

"It's your call, Birdie," Ray said, and this time his voice was kinder. "But we're at a standstill. You want revenge we can't seem to get. He wants peace and can't move on. I want to end this, so you're both safe. The Guardians will go to the ends of the earth for us. But we'll never be able to protect them while Lavinia still lives. I want to protect you. I do. But I can't. Kyp can't. There's no protection from this world we live in. We have to stop grieving and beating around the actual problem. If we want to move forward? We have to fight for it."

My tears spilled over. "I'll think about it. That's all I can give you. For now, I'm going to sleep. I think I need to just turn my brain off for a while."

"Okay, Birdie."

I cracked a smile, swiping the tears from my face. "You only call me Birdie so often when you're tiptoeing around me and it makes me want to punch you in the face."

"You could try." He held out his arms like it was an actual challenge.

"Don't be stupid, old man. I'd never aim for your face if you told me to do it. I'd punch you in the stomach instead."

He sputtered a laugh. "There's the fire in your belly."

"I was born with it." It connected me with Mom. With Gana.

A wry smile, green eyes twinkling, dimples flashing. It was so rare. "Rest well, Jacklyn." He took a step toward the doorway. Hesitated. Turned and pressed a kiss to my forehead, then rushed for the door.

He'd tried to do that once a few months ago, and I'd hurled a dagger at him. I hadn't really meant to hit him. If I had, I wouldn't have missed. He hadn't tried it again until now.

This time, I didn't want to hurl something at him.

This time, it was kind of nice.

I laid back down and burrowed deep in my blankets. I could take a mental health day. I didn't have a job. I wasn't going to school. It meant I could afford to rest. Especially after where yesterday had taken me.

Yesterday.

Thinking about it made my stomach swim. My chest

suddenly felt achy and wrong. I'd forgotten something. There was something I was meant to remember. Something about yesterday that I urgently needed to take care of, but what?

There was the nagging feeling that I shouldn't remember it. That I wasn't ready to.

I let my eyes slip closed and relaxed my body, sliding into a meditative state. Breaths in and out, chest expanding and contracting, thoughts arriving and pushed aside. And then I heard a voice.

"I don't really believe in God." A boy. A teenage boy. "I've never seen any proof of him. Not here. Not with the needles and the pain. But I believe in you. And I pray, because Rennie says prayer is as much for you as it is for what you're praying to. So, I pray. To you. To Jacklyn and to Kyp. To my parents. I don't know what the hell I am, or if I'm even real. But I need you."

I gasped and jolted upward, clutching my shirt and struggling to make sense of whatever the hell had just gone through my head. What I remembered from the day before, though I couldn't pinpoint when I'd originally heard it.

But I knew. I knew it deep in my bones, like I'd never known anything before.

My child was alive. And we needed to find him. Fast.

THREE

KYP

"Okay." Kyp settled into a corner of the couch in the common room and turned to face the adorable kid who'd stormed into his life. Cass and Drew sat on the floor in front of them. "I'm going to need you to start at the very beginning. Mostly because I don't have a kid. Also... I'm not old enough for you to be mine."

Kyp was really trying not to harp on the fact that the child had traitorously referred to herself as Jaina.

The little girl glared at him, her chubby face showing nothing but absolute impatience. Instead of answering, she took another bite of one of the cookies she'd baked with Drew while he and Cass were gone.

"I'm not a kid. A kid is a young goat. I am a child. I'd assumed you'd be more intelligent." Her nose screwed up in disgust.

Drew stifled a laugh and pushed his glasses up his nose. "She's adorable and I already love her but she talks like a little professor."

"She talks exactly like a Mind Key child," Cass explained. "You know, like an old person."

Kyp glared at Cass. Drew pointed and elbowed Cass in her side. "He made the face she just made. Like the exact same face."

"Don't get used to her, Drew," Cass warned. "She's not staying."

"These cookies are delicious, Andrew." The kid—no, *child*—completely ignored Cass. "You were right about using this recipe."

Drew smiled, open and kind as he always was. "I may not be a super-genius like you, but I do know a few things." He turned to Cass. "Why wouldn't she be staying?"

"Because she's a trap," Cass argued. "She's not his child. What if this is Lavinia in some sort of disguise?"

Kyp snorted. "If she was Lavinia, we'd already be dead."

Jaina's eyes grew wide, her gaze flicking between Kyp and Drew, like Drew had sold her a bag of goods that wasn't as advertised.

"Guys, you're scaring her!" Drew snapped. "We've all gotten the Arvokian Ritual to protect our minds from that psycho. You did it to me before you'd even talk to me about anything to do with the Order. Remember my initiation?"

When Kyp had met Drew, he was using his Aegis to give himself an edge in competitive high school swimming. If he could control water, he would control it to his advantage. But he lost his college scholarship after he was accused of doping. As

Kyp searched for new Guardians, he was inspired by Jacklyn's impossible track race, the one that drew the Gorvhans' attention to her.

Drew took a steroid test. It came back negative. But it ruined his future career options. He had pushed the use of his Aegis too far for the regular world. A foster child living in a non-Aegis home, he'd taught himself what he could about his abilities. He'd lived his entire life without a full understanding of who he was, of what he could be.

Kyp and Cass had promised him answers but wouldn't provide any until he'd done the Ritual to protect his mind from Lavinia. It had only been three months after they'd lost everything that they found someone new who fit them. They'd been teaching him ever since.

It didn't take long for them to see Drew's heart of gold. But along with Drew's heart of gold came an iron will.

"I see a child. A child that kinda looks like Kyp. And while you guys were out doing" —he sneered— "what you were doing... I was hearing what she had to say. I suggest you trust me enough to listen."

Jaina offered him a polite nod. "Thank you, Andrew."

Drew snorted a laugh and shook his head in response.

As cute as she was, and she was cute, Kyp needed facts. Because he knew who this child reminded him of, and the thought made his pulse roar in his ears.

With every passing moment, it grew more and more true; she

was the image of the Jacklyn that had first left him, but with his sharper nose and more intense eyes. This child, this Jaina, was his daughter with Jacklyn. A beautiful impossibility.

"If you promise to stop looking at me like that, I will tell you everything I know." She frowned.

Kyp raised his eyebrows. "I think you'll be doing that either way. You didn't come here to sit and play coy with me. You came here to deliver a message, and I suggest you say it before I lose my patience."

The words were out of his mouth before he could stop them, and they shook something deep in his core.

Kyp, my child, I suggest you stop muttering and explain yourself, lest I lose my patience.

The blood left his head fast enough to make him dizzy.

"Are you okay?" the child asked, features pinched as she examined him.

"Are you talking yet?" he asked, but the previous venom was gone from his voice.

For a moment, they just glared at each other, locked in a stalemate.

Sighing, Jaina gave in. "I don't remember too much, but my brother told me what to say to you if I left the lab."

"There's another one of you?" Kyp's voice squeaked slightly.

Jaina's head bobbed. "His name is Jordan. He's the best. Sometimes, when I'm hungry, he sneaks me extra fruit. He and the other kids call me Jainey. He says it suits me."

Kyp agreed. He liked the name Jainey much better. "And he's your brother... because I'm his father too?"

"And our mother is Jacklyn Madison." She glanced around the room. "Where is she? I've been here for a long time and I haven't seen her yet."

Kyp's heart twisted. "She's... she doesn't live here."

Jainey's shoulders drooped. "Jeez. Is anything in my life going to be normal? Where does she live then?"

"That's not important right now, Jainey," Kyp struggled to control the conversation. "You said other kids. How many kids are there where you're from?" Kyp avoided the other question, screaming through his brain—how many of those kids were his?

"I don't know. About ten?" Kyp must've looked faint all over again, because she quickly followed up with, "They aren't all yours. I only have one brother and no sisters. Chill."

"Chill, says the impossible child," Cass grumbled. "She sounds like *her*."

Kyp swallowed around the lump in his throat.

Jainey looked down at her red sneakers. "I'm the youngest one there. Jordan and his friends are the only ones who talk to me. And that's only sometimes. They're usually too busy doing teenager stuff."

Drew looked at Kyp. "You and Jacklyn? How many..."

"Only the once." Heat rushed to his face.

"And yet, two children of different ages."

"Different, impossible ages," Cass confirmed. "Jacklyn left a year ago."

"And you're sure Jordan has the same parents as you?" Drew asked Jainey.

"We were both—" Kyp blurted, then he reached out and covered both of Jainey's ears. "We were virgins." His face felt ready to burn off.

Jainey angrily swatted his hands away. "What? What did you say?"

"Don't worry about it, honey." Drew took out a notebook from his back pocket and scribbled down some notes. "I'm working on a theory. You said you escaped from a lab. Is that where you lived? Or did you live somewhere else?"

"I don't know what to call it." She kicked her feet back and forth. "A school?"

Cass chewed her lip. "Well, what do you do every day?"

"Um... Wake up, have breakfast, testing, classes, practice, lunch, treatment, recovery time, training, dinner, and sleep." She shrugged.

"Recovery time." A chill slid along Kyp's spine. "Recovery from what?"

"From our treatment," Jainey said. "It hurts, so we need time to rest afterward."

He didn't even know this girl. They'd spoken for ten minutes and the mere mention of her pain had his hands clenching into fists. "Do you know who these people are?"

"There are doctors. And caretakers. Some are nice. Some

aren't. But there's one who really looks after us. He's the one who told us who our parents were and where to find you. Jordan says he named me."

"He does sound nice," Drew said, which was good, because Kyp was too busy grinding his teeth into dust. "What's his name?"

As Drew spoke, Cass tugged on her earlobe, the group's universal symbol, granting permission to Kyp to read their mind.

"Do not react like a psycho."

Is that what they thought of him? A crazy person who flew off the handle with minimal provocation?

"His name is Mr. Ross."

Ross. Ross Ebell. The traitor who turned his back on Kyp's rebellion.

Kyp jumped to his feet. "That mother—"

"Kyp!" Cass snapped, cutting him off. Properly scolded and a little annoyed by it, he settled back down on the couch.

"You don't like Mr. Ross." Her lips twitched, as if restraining a smile.

Good observation, kid. You deserve a medal.

"No, I do not. But if he was kind to you, I'm grateful."

"He's never hurt me, and sometimes when I'm not behaving, he keeps me from getting punished. He even tells Caleb to stop when he picks on me, and Caleb always whines like 'Dad!' but Mr. Ross tells him he has to be nice to the other kids, anyway."

"He calls him dad?" Cass said. "Caleb is Ross' son?"

Jainey nodded.

"Do all you Keys pop out kids who are fully formed?" Drew asked.

Kyp wasn't sure if his question was serious, but he answered anyway. "No, this isn't an average day in the Order of the Key. Something is up." He returned his attention to Jainey. "Please tell us more."

"He's Jordan's best friend. Well, he has two best friends, but Rennie doesn't count. He has a giant crush on her." She smiled, a wide, toothy grin that brought Kyp right back to his childhood with Jacklyn.

Another earlobe pull from Cass. Kyp used his Aegis to peek inside her thoughts.

"I want to say Ross could have lied, but... damn, she looks like you guys."

Kyp deeply, fiercely, wanted to peer into the child's mind, but he was worried he'd scare her. Instead, he opened his senses to search for the feeling of any Aegis flowing through her veins.

What he found was incredibly powerful. More powerful than any Aegis he'd ever felt. Familiar and unfamiliar all at once. The Skeleton Key.

Kyp's brain grasped for any topic besides Jacklyn and the growing apprehension as he realized he was going to have to see her again before this whole thing was through. "Did Ross tell you to come here?"

"No. He told us about our parents. Like you were fairy tales. Jordan sent me to go find you."

"Did he tell you why?"

"He said he didn't want me getting hurt anymore. Because the treatments... they hurt more on the younger kids, and—" Tears filled her eyes. "He really wanted to get out too, but he wanted me to get out of there more. So I walked as far as I could off-road and then hitchhiked here."

"That's dangerous, Jainey," Drew said, concern evident in the furrow of his brow. "You were very lucky to have found someone nice."

"They weren't all nice." She sobbed, a horrible sound, and Kyp was powerless against the need to scoop her into a hug. "But I made that car crash and ran away before he could hurt me."

Kyp, Drew, and Cass shared equally horrified looks.

"I'm scared," she cried into his shoulder. "I'm scared and I didn't want to come here by myself. Please don't make me go back. I don't like it there. I don't want to go back."

Kyp gave in to his earlier impulse, reaching into her mind just enough to feel true desperation and terror in her young heart. She was little more than a massive jumble of emotions, and many of them weren't good. Wading through her mind was like walking through a syrupy fog of confusion and fear.

"Okay, here's what we're going to do," Kyp said, rubbing the child's back gently. She looked up at him, her lower lip shaking. "You're gonna go upstairs and get some rest. Tomorrow morning, we'll get you some clothes, and we'll see if we can figure out where you were this whole time. Then..." He didn't even want to say the next part out loud. "Depending on what's going on..."

"We may have to call in help to get your brother and the other kids out of there," Cass finished for him.

"But we'll figure it out," Drew said, eyes locking on Kyp's as though asking. Kyp nodded, and Drew finished the thought. "We'll save your brother."

"You promise?" She gripped him a little tighter, her fingers wrapped in the fabric of his t-shirt.

He hesitated. He didn't want to promise her something he couldn't give. To protect her, he would need to leave her with Cass or Drew. Which meant he would have to go in with only one other person. Into a place filled with doctors who knew enough about their abilities to want to utilize them and who possibly had Aegis of their own. If he counted Ross, there was at least one Key-level Aegis. He couldn't go in half-cocked.

He'd have to plan. And he'd need help.

He'd need Jacklyn.

Shit.

"I promise."

Once Jainey was settled in Gana's old bedroom, Kyp collapsed on the couch and prepared himself to be skewered by his team.

"What the hell is wrong with you?" Drew asked, the warmth in his eyes from earlier now completely absent. "You could have gotten both yourself and Cass killed with that... that... that stunt!"

"It wasn't what you're thinking," Kyp said.

"No? Because I think you ran into danger and nearly got yourself killed chasing an enemy who nearly killed your ex-girlfriend. If a Body Key couldn't beat her, what makes you think you can?"

"I have to, Drew," Kyp insisted. "She's *my* problem. I shouldn't have focused on only removing her from leadership. I should have killed her."

Drew shook his head and crossed his arms over his chest.

Cass sighed. "So what do we think is going on with this Jainey kid?"

"Some kind of experiment?" Kyp suggested. "A clone combining my DNA with Jacklyn's?"

"Is that even possible?" Cass asked. "There isn't an Aegis capable of this kind of—"

"A world of scientific advances were made while I could only learn what the Order gave me access to," Kyp said. "I think it's time for some research into case studies and unproven theories. We're talking about a pack of kids getting painful treatments and not being allowed to leave. Also, Ross is involved."

"Does that mean Lavinia is involved, too?" Cass grit her teeth.

"Tangentially at least," Kyp answered. "There were others. People Mother was answering to. It seems she couldn't provide them a Skeleton Key, so they found a way around that."

Drew's azure eyes flitted toward the ceiling, the upper floor where Jainey was now sleeping. "Meaning she is a Skeleton Key."

"Or something like it," Kyp agreed.

"And so are at least some of the other children in that facility," Cass said. "Crap. This is exactly what we wanted to avoid."

"And we're sure Lavinia isn't the ringleader here?" Drew asked.

"There's no way to be certain," Kyp said, "but she wasn't a fan of Ross. I doubt she would choose him as a caretaker for these very important children."

"Who would she choose?" Cass laughed. "Kylie? The children would hate her."

"True," Kyp answered. Of the other two Keys they knew of, Ross, while caustic, had a thread of good in him, however small. Kylie was grating and wicked, and children could spot that kind of thing a mile away.

He imagined Kylie and Ross wouldn't help him free the kids from the facility. He'd have to find a way around them to get to Jordan.

His son. Two kids at twenty. Definitely not what Kyp had imagined for his life. But were they really his kids? He didn't even know them. They were just genes that were stolen from him.

"Okay, I think that's enough for today," Kyp said. "I'm beat, and I need to approach this with a clearer head if I'm going to take on the science of genetics and cloning. In the meantime..." He sighed deeply, already overwhelmed and exhausted by what he was about to suggest. "Cass, reach out to Zane."

"No," Cass said. "Absolutely not. I cursed her out a few hours ago for continuing to give you leads. There is no way in hell I'm getting back on the phone with her—"

She did what? His chest tightened, and he felt the same tension from when he destroyed the tree return.

"Then apologize," he snapped. "Once we've figured out what direction we're going with this, and what exactly is going on, we'll need to bring them in, anyway..." A thought took the wind right out of his lungs. "We'll need to bring Jacklyn in." And in a quieter tone, "They're her blood, too." He closed his eyes, his world spinning.

What had he just been thinking? They weren't genes. They were people. And even if they were just genes that were stolen from him, they were Jacklyn's genes, too. Didn't that mean something?

God, he didn't even know what that meant.

When he opened his eyes, he found Cass gazing at him with a look he'd seen a lot in the past year, like he was a broken doll she ached to fix. He wondered when she would understand he was beyond repair.

"You gonna be okay?" Drew's brows knitted in concern.

"I am the leader of the Order of the Key." Kyp shot him a winning grin. "I have to be okay."

"You look like you just hurt yourself." Drew never hesitated to tell him the absolute truth.

Kyp flashed him the finger. "I'm going to bed. We'll touch base in the morning and work out a plan."

He headed upstairs toward the bathroom nearest his bedroom.

How hadn't he scared Jainey? Hadn't she seen the dried blood partially hidden behind the hair flopping into his eyes? Maybe she was used to seeing blood-caked faces in the facility.

He set the water to maximum pressure and dunked his head under the faucet. Just a quick wash-up before bed. The full shower would come in a few hours, when he wasn't dead on his feet. He let the water seep into his hair and drip forward over his face, let the warmth soothe him and...

"I want you to understand," Mother drawled as she pushed the stopper into the sink drain.

Terror shot through Kyp's chest and his breath stuttered out in a panic. She yanked him by the hair, her long fingernails scraping against his scalp. A hiss of pain escaped his lips.

"I don't care what your feelings for Raymond or Jacklyn are. They are not here anymore. They no longer dictate your actions."

She pushed him over the sink, the hard porcelain digging into his stomach. His breath rushed out of him on impact, and she took that moment to shove his head down under the faucet and into the water.

No!

His hands gripped the edge of the sink, and he struggled against her as the water built along with his fear, until he was shaking with it.

"You will not make this difficult for me, darling," she growled in his ear, and he felt the pull on his thoughts as she stole his will from him. "You will not fight me. You earned this punishment."

And he wouldn't, because it was easier if he didn't. He would let her control him. He couldn't win even if he tried. He might as well let her make it easier.

He remained still as the water filled the sink, filled his nostrils, filled his mouth and...

He yanked his head out of the sink, gasping for breath, and cursing himself.

He couldn't be a father. He didn't even know how to be a son.

FOUR

JACKLYN

I half-ran, half-stumbled into the gym in our basement, startling my team midway through their training.

Austin and Ray froze where they were sparring, while Zane waited a beat so she could rest the weight she was bench pressing before she sat up. I launched into an explanation as soon as I was sure I had their attention.

"You realize what you're saying is impossible." Ray walked to the weapons case, picking up a set of throwing knives and moving toward the target he had set up earlier. Sparring would be too noisy for the conversation we were going to have. "Jacklyn." Again, the voice that meant he was treating me with kid gloves. "When you lost the baby... It was too early. It couldn't have survived."

Austin went for the weights. "Because we live totally normal lives. Where normal things happen and all the rules apply." He looked at me. "You okay there, sweetheart?"

"Not doing my best." I lightly swung an unwrapped fist at the punching bag hanging in the center of the room.

Zane leaned back to return to benching. "Okay. Let's work through this logically." The way she said 'logically' definitely sounded like she thought I was being illogical. "Jacks, the baby died."

I turned to Ray. "Were you in the room?"

"What?"

"Did you watch them take that baby out of me?"

"No."

"Do you know where they took the baby? What they did to treat me?"

Ray squirmed. "No."

"They had to knock me out pretty hard to get me to stay down long enough to perform the surgery." Another mechanical punch to the bag. "My body was protecting it." *Punch.* "They couldn't get it out any normal way." *Punch.* "The only people who know what they did with the baby are Dr. Livingston and his staff."

The thought that Livingston could have done anything with the baby while tenderly comforting me made my stomach churn.

"Jacks, let me wrap your knuckles," Ray tried.

I shrugged him off.

"And you think they... did what?" Zane asked between lifts.

"I don't know. I just..." Another brutal punch.

"For all you know, Lavinia is trying to get into your head and this is how she's doing it," Ray said.

"Why now?" Austin winced when I hit the bag again. The

chain it hung from creaked.

"Kyp pissed her off? He and Cass did just kill a known associate of hers," Ray said.

"You're assuming she has the power to get into her head from this far away," Austin said.

"You're assuming she's far away," Zane countered.

A chill went down my spine. She could be right outside the brownstone for all we knew.

"*You're* assuming what you heard was anything more than what you wish you could hear." Ray lightly tapped me on the head. "There's no reason to believe it, Birdie."

My knuckles were cracking and bleeding. "Austin gets it. You do, right?"

Austin shrugged. "What's more weirdness to add to the stack?"

"Right!" I jabbed a finger at him. "Look, maybe it's because you all grew up with this, so you know the natural limits of the weird. But my life has been the equivalent of a bizarre action fantasy movie for the past year, and nothing seems impossible to me now. This kid I heard believes Kyp and I are his parents."

Ray's shoulders slumped. "Even if the baby made it, he wouldn't be old enough to talk, Jacks."

"How smart was Kyp as a baby? At five? How smart is he now?" I pushed. "If Kyp and I had a child, it would be a Skeleton Key. Who knows what it can do?"

The rest of the group exchanged looks, all attempts at working out stalled.

"He'd *sound* like a child," Zane said.

She had a point. But it didn't matter. It couldn't. If that boy was really mine, I couldn't let it go. I'd already allowed enough of my family to die.

Another punch at the bag, followed by a neat roundhouse. "You know if you guys don't help me, I'm just going to look into this myself, don't you?"

Austin chuckled. "Probably how you should have started the conversation."

"If I went straight for the big guns, no one would ever take me seriously."

Austin pointed at me and addressed the rest of the group. "I'm not leaving her to figure it out on her own. But where do we start?"

"We start with Livingston," Ray said. "But that's dangerous. He helps our people when they get sick and hurt and they don't have a healer. With you and me on the team, we may not need a healer, but Kyp and his team do."

"Do they, though?" Austin had a problem with Kyp. Ray thought he was jealous, that Austin would never pressure me, but he secretly wished I would move on from Kyp so we could be more than friends. But we didn't see each other that way.

"They do." I rolled my eyes. I figured Austin was just protective of me, and Kyp had gotten me into a whole lot of danger.

"He could have stopped this whole thing before it even started," Austin grumbled.

An image came to my mind unbidden. The fear in Kyp's eyes whenever he spoke of repercussions, of Lavinia killing him and bringing him back over and over again. Kyp couldn't fight back. She had horribly abused him. Even though he'd always wanted to end his suffering, he couldn't seem to find the strength to do it on his own. He was waiting for his heroes to save him. First Ray, then me.

And neither of us had managed it.

"Let's say the child is who and what you think," Ray said. "That he's a Skeleton Key. If Liv has what she set out to create, she will use it to her advantage. We'll have to go to war to get him, and if the Arvokians are on her side, we may not walk out of that war."

"It doesn't matter." The words spilled from my lips. "He's *our* blood, Ray. We don't get to run from this one."

As a child, when I imagined a future where I would have children of my own, I swore I would be there where my father wasn't and my mother couldn't be, because she was too busy providing for Gana and me. Even now that I understood their motives, my idea of parenting remained the same.

Those old fantasies replayed in my head. In my imagination, when I'd discovered I was pregnant, I would call Mom to squeal excitedly about her grandchild, while a nameless, faceless man waited anxiously for his turn to call his own mother. After I fell for Kyp, I'd imagined the two of us huddled over a tiny plastic would-be fortune teller on the bathroom sink. When the test came out positive, Kyp would wrap me up in his arms, twirl me around as we laughed, overjoyed with our discovery. He would kiss me tenderly, then throw the bathroom door open and bellow the news up and down the hall for all members of the newly united Order of the Key to hear.

Both were childish, innocent, and perhaps naïve imaginings, and my heart ached with the loss of them. Instead, I got my father panicking as my Aegis grew wildly out of control, believing it to be grief until he noticed the extra heartbeat in the room. I got history lessons of what happened to any of the other potential Skeleton Keys, and the mothers carrying them. I got to sit in on a meeting where my friends considered the wisdom of me keeping the child. And I got to fall in love with this new life anyway, and lose it just like I lost everything else.

I would never get anything like what I had imagined. I wouldn't get to see my child take their first steps or learn their first words. Instead, I was considering chasing down a phantom voice in my head belonging to someone that was already nearly my age.

But that wouldn't change how much I already loved him.

"Okay. Then we'll do whatever we need to do." Ray looked to Austin, then to Zane, who nodded reluctantly.

"Do we start with Livingston?" Austin asked.

"No. We have to be cautious and double check the information. Look into anyone on Livingston's staff who might have gone rogue. We have to be sure before we take away a potential ally with this accusation," Zane said.

"Very few people even know about the baby," I said. "Most of them are in this room and none of them have a motive. Then there's Dr. Livingston."

"Wait, but go back further," Austin chimed in. "Livingston and his staff at Lifestone Pharmaceuticals are for-hire help for anyone who wants to stay off the grid. You hired them for your medical needs. Maybe someone hired them to get their hands on your child. Or something else equally awful."

I looked at Ray. "But we're the only ones who knew I was pregnant."

"There are others who could have suspected." Zane stretched her long legs out in front of her and swiped her bangs out of her eyes. "Or hoped for it once you and Kyp..."

"Watch it," Ray cut in.

"Lavinia," I said.

"Kylie and Ross knew as well," Ray pointed out. "As did Cass and, forgive me Birdie, Kyp."

I shot him a death glare. "Kylie and Ross don't have the brainpower. And Kyp—"

"Let's not rule anything out yet," Austin cut in. "I know you want to say he would never, but... the stories about him make him seem like he's not all there."

Ray let out a long, low whistle. "Even I can't deny that. He's been off lately."

"It's not Kyp," I said, even if I knew they wouldn't listen. I was biased where he was concerned. "Let's focus on the kid. What do we think he was talking about?"

"He said something about needles and pain," Zane said. "It sounds like he's in a medical facility. That really leans toward Lifestone."

"It can't be that easy," Austin said.

"It won't be," Zane said. "There's no way they would just keep a kid at their lab."

"Follow the money," Ray said. "It'll lead to his location."

"But why? What is there to gain?" Austin asked.

"The child of two Keys is a very powerful being. A Skeleton Key," I explained. "A regular Key can close rifts between our world and the Dusk dimension. A Skeleton Key can also open them."

"So we're thinking it's someone who wants to open a rift," Austin said. "Smells like Sirins to me."

"Everything smells like Sirins to you, kid," Zane said. "Stop going with your preconceived notions. It kills your deductive skills."

"He's not entirely wrong, though," Ray said. "They would have the motive and, given the black-market dealings we've been seeing, likely the means."

"Lavinia was communicating with someone outside the Order when she was trying to maneuver us toward creating a Skeleton Key," I said. "Maybe that was Livingston? And if Lavinia's involved, Kylie and Ross may be too. They're her only remaining boot lickers."

"That we know of." Ray squeezed my shoulder. "And if they have access to the Arvokians, they could have been stockpiling DNA for much longer. We all provide some to gain access to the Arvokian Temple."

"But Jacks didn't donate any DNA to the Arvokians until about a year ago," Austin said. "So, same problem. How is a fetus talking to Jacklyn in a big boy voice?"

"He'd have Kyp's Aegis. Or Jacklyn's. Or both," Zane said. "He could be able to reach out telepathically."

"How does he even exist?" Ray asked.

Everyone grew quiet.

Ray waited a beat before speaking again. "Guys, a moment alone with Jacklyn, please."

Austin and Zane headed for the door. Austin stopped to bump his shoulder into mine on the way out.

Once they had left, Ray swept me into a hug, squeezing me tightly against him, like he was trying to keep me from running away.

"Ugh, why hugs? No hugs. What are you doing?" My words were muffled by his shoulder.

I wrapped my arms around his waist anyway and allowed him to calm my heart.

"Yeah, yeah. No hugs." He kissed the top of my head, a hand stroking through my hair.

It was hard to keep the tears back, so I gave into them. I hugged him even tighter and cried into his shoulder and hated myself a little for it.

I was too strong to need this from him.

I didn't need this from him.

And yet, I couldn't pull back.

"I know." His voice barely lifted above a whisper. "I get it. You don't want me for a da. You don't need another person to lose, and you already lost me once. Why bother, right? But here you are. I'm still figuring out how to treat you like my daughter. My daughter was a preschooler who still said 'pasghetti,' not some badass rebel chick and she sure as hell hadn't almost given me a grandchild. It's been a shocker, and it's all my fault, yeah?" I nodded against his shoulder. "But I'm a liar if I say I don't love you just as much as I did when you were five. You know, when you were two, you went missing for an hour. When your mam told me, I practically shat my heart out. Every time something like this happens, every time you want to march into danger, my heart spills out all over again. I'm trying to protect you, Jacks. Please let me."

I didn't know if I could. "You're trying to protect *you*. From your fear of anything happening to me. And from a mission you think is a waste. But it's not. Not to me. You can't stop me."

His jade eyes flickered closed, but when they opened again, they were brighter. "I never can."

FIVE

KYP

Kyp spotted Karen Zane standing in front of a bar tastefully named "Drunk Joe's." She leaned against the brick exterior, her painted red lips pulling from a cigarette. She had a friend, a bulky guy closer to Kyp's age, who happened to be ridiculously tall and built like a wall.

Zane was a techie whose sense of loyalty was somewhat smudged, and, true to type, she liked her run-down bars and her dark alleys. Her wardrobe, consisting mostly of motorcycle jackets, leather pants, and boots, screamed... something. She was either a true badass, trying too hard, or she despised cows.

Jacklyn probably loved her.

"Hello, Kyp Franklin," Zane greeted him. "You brought a friend."

"Just evening things out." Drew extended a hand for her to shake. "Andrew Clayson. We spoke on the phone."

Zane tossed her long, straight hair out of her eyes. She had to be about Ray's age, of Japanese descent, with hair so black it was nearly blue. She'd be short if it weren't for the heels, but she was mostly legs. The name of the bar was cast across her zipped up, black leather jacket every time the neon sign flickered to life. She stubbed her cigarette out on the side of the building.

"He's trying to act like he knew you'd be here." She smirked at the bruiser.

His light eyes narrowed. "Thinks we're stupid." His low voice rumbled out with a twang. "Don't like people thinkin' I'm stupid."

Zane's face shone with amusement. "Me neither. But then, intelligence is my stock and trade. His too, in fact." Her eyes were iced over as she assessed Kyp.

The man smiled, but instead of softening his features, it made the scar on his jaw stand out more starkly. "My strengths are more physical." He cracked his knuckles.

So. That's how this was going to be.

"Bite me, Tex." He sounded smug, even to his own ears. "Let's get on with this."

Zane smirked. "We've made Prince Kyp impatient."

"Shame, really." The big guy shrugged. "Getting information takes patience."

This pair of "badasses" were so obviously playing roles they'd seen on a bad television show. Kyp could smell the stench of anxiety wafting off them, even the big one, who was dressed like a farm boy in jeans, a red flannel shirt, and work boots. His dusty blond, shaggy hair completed the look. Farm Boy Dolt Chic.

Which one was actually smarter? Tougher? Cooler? That was the point; they wanted to create confusion. It made them worthy allies. Zane had always been a mystery, playing both sides of the fence, helping anyone who paid for the information she gathered. But before, she'd been warmer.

Kyp wondered if Jacklyn had altered her view of him.

"Okay, Tech and Tex." He held his hands up. "Why don't we get a drink and talk about your services?"

Zane's lips twitched as she looked at Tex. "He makes me sound like a hooker, Austin. Should I be insulted?"

"Don't see why ya would." Another shrug from the mountain posing as a man, this one accompanied by a twist of his lips. "Wait one darn minute—is that what you meant when you said 'not even if ya paid me?' Because in that case I think I'm the one who should be insulted."

She laughed loudly, her facade cracking as a giant, gleaming smile appeared.

"Come on. Beer's on me." She waved. "Hope you brought your fake ID, Baby Franklin."

Kyp scoffed. Tex had to be younger than him.

The cleanest part of Joe's was the liquor shelf and the bartender's domain. Kyp found that reassuring because it meant the people working behind the counter cared about the rampant spread of bacteria inherent in the foodservice industry.

Kyp rarely ate in outside establishments. He suppressed the shiver journeying along his spine. No shows of weakness.

A peanut shell crunched beneath the sole of his boot. They were everywhere, littering the floor and most of the tables. Zane crunched her way to a back table and swiped the shells off.

God, when was this place last cleaned? It stunk of old liquor and sweat.

A rotund woman approached. The chain running from her belt loop to something in her pocket jangled as she walked. She watched them through narrowed eyes. "What can I get for you, Zane?"

"Four glasses of my usual lager." Zane smiled.

The woman's expression melted into boredom. She turned to Kyp and Drew. "ID?" She held her hand out expectantly. The word 'Believe' was tattooed on her wrist in curly script.

Kyp implanted the memory of seeing two valid IDs in her mind.

"Coming right up," she answered in a zombie-like drawl.

Zane laughed. "Currently feeling super proud of myself for trading information for an Arvokian Mind Block Ritual that one time." She winked. "Comes in handy for me and Muscles over here when dealing with the likes of you." She drummed her fingers on the table and waited for Kyp's response.

"Ray didn't give it to you?" Drew asked casually, like he and Ray were old buds.

Zane made a dismissive sound. "Like I wait for Ray to give me anything. I had that Ritual long before I settled into working with him." She turned her gaze to Kyp. "Long before I realized the threat your darling mother was to the entire frickin' world."

"It's better for all of us that you did." Kyp's posture remained rigid no matter how often he reminded himself to relax. "It saves you the trouble of having to wonder, and it saves me the trouble of you asking me if I'm controlling you."

Zane glanced at Tex, who gave a short nod, clearly accepting his answer and telling her to move along. "You're here to contact Jacklyn."

"I am. And with good reason."

"Which is?" Tex grumbled.

"Not your business. Last I remember, Jacklyn is fully capable of taking care of herself." She'd made that more than clear plenty of times.

"Supposedly, you can too, but here you are, with a Guardian." He leaned back in his chair, never taking his eyes off Kyp, whose blood heated.

Zane's eyes darted between the pair for a moment before looking at Drew. "Well, they're going to be locked in this dick measuring contest for a while, but mine's the biggest. Wanna be the reasonable ones?"

"I'm all for being reasonable," Drew said. Kyp could hear the smile in his voice, but he wasn't going to let Tex think he wasn't up to the stare down challenge.

"From what I'm gathering, Kyp called on us because he wants to meet with Jacklyn about something important," Zane said. "Funnily enough, we'd been just about ready to schedule our own meeting with him when we received your call. You see, we have a problem. We may need some backup on something. Something big."

Tex finally broke eye contact to look at Drew. "We might be about to stir up some trouble."

"Trouble?" Kyp asked. "With Lavinia?"

"We've stumbled into a mystery that may include her," Zane said. "We're looking into it."

Kyp looked at Drew. "We have... something similar."

"So this meeting is to, what, join forces? Because Jacks ain't goin' back to that house. No way." Tex's voice was a low growl.

Was he protecting his... friend? Girlfriend? Kyp ignored the empty feeling in his heart. He'd be damned if he was going to team up just to have Tex and Jacklyn throw their relationship in his face.

"We're sharing information. Nothing more. Not yet, anyway."

"Kyp," Drew warned.

"That's the plan," Kyp said, an edge in his tone.

"Sharing information about a mission you don't intend to tell us anything about?" Zane asked. "That's not gonna cut it."

Kyp sighed. "We've got reason to believe someone is participating in experiments involving Aegis abilities."

"Experiments..." Zane looked at her partner. "Like with... needles?"

They were working on the same damn mission. Maybe they didn't have the same lead, but they were on the same track.

"Yes," Drew said. "Like with needles."

Kyp didn't like the edge in his voice. He didn't like the way Drew leaned forward in his seat toward Zane and Tex.

"There's a kid."

"Drew!"

"No, dammit!" Drew's eyes flashed with something angry Kyp had never seen in them before. "I'm not gonna take the chance that a kid will suffer. Whether you believe her story or not, you don't get to make this call."

Drew was right. And Mother was right about Kyp. He wasn't fit to lead. His decisions led to people he loved dying.

"There's... a... a kid?" Tex glanced back at Zane. "What can you tell us about them?"

"She came to the estate looking for me and Jacklyn," Kyp muttered. "Said we were her... parents."

"A girl?" Zane asked.

"Yeah."

"Jacklyn had some kind of dream or something," Tex admitted, his accent softening somewhat as he lost some of the tension in his shoulders.

The waitress from earlier took that moment to show up with their drinks.

Kyp had been allowed the rare taste of wine during Order functions when the group had been much larger. But he was completely unprepared for the gulp of beer he took to hide his self-loathing.

"God, this is disgusting." He wished he could wipe the taste off his tongue with a squeegee.

Drew snorted and drank a healthy gulp of his beer.

"You actually drink this shit?" Kyp was honestly appalled.

Zane giggled. "Baby Franklin, like I said."

"Got to say, he is not what I expected." Tex chuckled. "Jacklyn made you sound much cooler."

Kyp's head jerked up. "She did?"

Drew facepalmed so hard, the smack reverberated through the bar.

"You said something about a dream," Kyp nearly snarled.

Zane tossed her head back and laughed, a loud jarring sound, and Kyp winced.

"A boy talked to her," Austin said. "Referred to you two as his parents. Exactly how many ridiculously old children did you father last year?"

Kyp's lips twisted at the absurdity of it all. "Apparently two? The girl looks five, the boy is even older."

"How?" Zane asked.

Drew yanked his phone from his pocket. Kyp hadn't even known he still had it. The wards interfered with cell phone coverage, so he assumed he wouldn't bother using it anymore.

Drew tapped at the screen a few times before presenting it to the others. Kyp craned his head so he could see. At some point, Drew had taken a picture of Jainey.

For a moment, Austin and Zane stared at the image, blinking.

"That is the cutest damn thing I've ever seen," Austin cooed. "It's like a tiny baby Jackie!"

"No doubt that's her DNA," Zane said.

"The child says there's some kind of testing," Kyp murmured. "And that it's painful."

"The boy in Jacklyn's dream said something about needles and pain." Austin frowned.

"Her brother," Drew breathed. "The girl said she was kept with other kids. Her older brother's name is Jordan."

Zane swallowed hard. "I think we need to touch base with Jacklyn. Something is wrong, and I think she'll agree that we need all hands on deck."

Kyp nodded, his heartbeat picking up at the idea of seeing Jacklyn again. Dread settled low in his belly like a lead weight. "We could come to you. So she doesn't have to... be there. Again."

"That," Austin said quietly, "would probably be best."

"Do you have anything else for us? Anything we could start looking into in the meantime?" Zane asked. "I've got itchy hacker fingers."

Technomancy. Zane had a way with computers: she could commune with them. The Aegis ability fell under the umbrella of the Energy Key. Mother had killed the last of the Keys of that line, much like she had killed the last of the Spirit Keys that gave Cass her ability to commune with the dead. But the Guardians of that line still remained.

"Hack away." Drew grinned. "Find out whatever you can

about Ross Ebell. He's a Dark Element Key, and he's up to his elbows in this. Jainey knows him well enough that she thinks he's the nice one in the facility."

"On it. I'll see what I can find, talk to Jacklyn, and we'll set something up," Zane said, chugging down the last of her beer before rising from the table.

They followed her out of the relative warmth of the bar and into the increasingly frigid cold of the winter breeze. Kyp stuffed his hands into the pockets of his leather jacket.

"So you'll look into it?" Drew said.

"Yes." Austin stopped while Zane continued to head for the car. He turned back to Drew. "I'll talk to Jacklyn, Zane will search for Ross, and I'll be in touch."

He winked. At Drew.

Kyp blinked. His head tilted slightly as he took in Austin's sly grin, and the way Drew's eyes widened and his face reddened. Kyp was instantly sure he'd missed something important while he was wallowing.

"Be seein' you." Austin gave a little salute before turning and catching up to Zane in three broad steps.

Worse, Drew watched him go. *Really* watched him.

Kyp cleared his throat. "Um...what?"

Drew shrugged. "I'm as surprised as you. Not arguing though." His hand swiped over his face, but it did little to hide the smile there.

"I'm not sure I like him. And I was a hundred percent sure he was into Jacks...”

"Not everyone is into Jacks." Drew turned and headed for their car.

"I know," Kyp pouted, following after him.

"Do you, though?" Drew snapped. "Because you nearly walked away from what you promised that little girl, because you thought Jacklyn might have a new boyfriend."

He gritted his teeth. "Yes, you more than made your opinion on that known."

"Was I wrong, though?" Drew said. They slowed to a stop in front of the car.

"You're always wrong to compromise a plan in the field, Drew."

"A child is not a mission, asshole."

Kyp glared at him over the top of the car and got in on the driver's side. He started the car and stabbed at the temperature controls as though it would accomplish something. Drew busied himself with buckling his seatbelt.

"In the Order, children are soldiers, Andrew," Kyp said, even as the words cut deep under his skin. "We have to worry about how she'll be used against us. And what her existence means."

Drew massaged the bridge of his nose, his eyes squeezed shut. "That's not what I signed up for. You met my foster parents. I was raised as a damn afterthought. Jainey's a fucking science experiment. And you?" He sighed heavily. "You'd think you'd know better."

"I do!" Kyp smacked his palm on the steering wheel, and the sting brought him back to himself.

"I do," he said again with a sigh. "I'm sorry. You're right. I've... I don't know what I was thinking. This feels like some kind of whacked out fever dream, and I never wanted to see Jacklyn again, but here we are."

"You're lying," Drew said. "You want nothing more."

Kyp made a face. "I'm not... I'm not the same around her. All I see when I think about her is all of my mistakes. And all the ways I can never make it up to her." The wind punched out of him, and he let his head drop against the steering wheel. "She lost so much. And I'm the one who led her sister to her death."

"Just drive, Kyp." Drew sighed again.

Kyp followed orders, something he always did well when someone reasonable was giving them. He hated making difficult decisions, but he didn't have the luxury of taking a back seat anymore.

Although, sometimes it was nice to have a co-pilot.

Drew turned on the radio. Fiddled with it. Switched stations until he'd come back around to the one he'd started with. Then he started the process again. Kyp was about to smack his hand away when Drew dropped back against the seat, giving up.

"Look, maybe this is for the best. I don't know Jacklyn. I'm sure she's great. But I don't think she's what has you so twisted. I think what happened to the Order did this. I'm sure it feels safer to shut down, but if you shut everyone else out, you're going to lose sight of what you're doing, like you did in there. And that will put us all in jeopardy. You'll be better off when you can get some closure and put this whole thing behind you."

"This whole thing?" Kyp's fingers tightened around the steering wheel, and he transferred the burden on his shoulders to his foot on the pedal. His voice sounded dead to his own ears. "An entire lifetime of feeling the closest connection anyone can feel with another? That whole thing?"

"Yes. That whole thing."

And suddenly, in the silence of the rest of the ride, Kyp realized exactly what he needed to do if he was going to survive with his heart and, more importantly, his logical brain intact.

He couldn't face her without a level head. And now he knew what he needed to regain it.

"Oh good! You're home!" Jainey shouted as soon as Kyp and Drew walked through the door.

She stood in front of the doorway.

"Hey, kiddo," Drew greeted. "I guess you missed us."

"You, yes," Jainey said. "Him, not particularly." She flashed an unimpressed look at Kyp.

Kyp shot her a baleful glare.

"Cass is acting... weird."

"How would you know?" Kyp asked. "You just met her."

"Not weird for *her*," Jainey answered, like the snotty little sass master she'd proved she was. "Weird for... a person."

Kyp and Drew shared a look of concern. "Where is she?" they said, nearly in unison.

Jainey tipped her head toward the kitchen, and the boys followed. Kyp placed a careful hand on Jainey's shoulder and moved her behind them, trepidation spreading through his limbs.

They approached with caution, and the closer they got, the more noise they heard streaming from the kitchen. Clanging pots, clashing dishes, rustling paper, sloshing liquid. Kyp readied his Aegis for whatever threat lay beyond the room's entrance.

Kyp held up a hand, counting down with his fingers. One. Two. Three.

They both pushed through the doorway.

The kitchen was a mess. Pots and pans were being heated on every oven burner. Cass sat on the only unused section of the kitchen counter, surrounded by a storm of open cartons, boxes, and containers. She was digging into an overfilled bowl of cereal, milk sloshing out of the bowl. Her cheeks were filled with food, and a considerable milk-moustache covered the space over her upper lip.

"You are home," Cass said, but her voice wasn't her own. Kyp wasn't sure what to make of it. It was as if four people were speaking at once, voices overlapping, assembling into one.

Kyp's earlier trepidation continued to build. "Cass?"

"Cass." Drew's laugh crackled with nerves. "How nice of you to make dinner."

"Do you have any idea how hungry I've been?" A voice that

sounded like Cass', but was still completely wrong, broke through the multi-voice din. "It's been years since I've eaten anything, and I'd forgotten how much I enjoyed Fruit Loops."

"You're not Cass," Kyp said.

"Cass would be so pleased you noticed." Her smile was more lopsided than Cass' usual confident grin. "We're really not that different. I see why she admires you so much."

Kyp wasn't about to be flattered when he didn't know what was wrong with his friend. "Who are you?"

"My name is Mariana," she said. "I'm Cassandra's sister."

The tension drained from Kyp's shoulders. Right. Cass could channel spirits. Her sister was dead. She must have come for a visit. It was strange, but not dangerous. "Hi, Mari. Cass has told us so much about you. I'm glad you came for a visit, although it might not be the best time."

"Ah, yes. The child." She wiped the milk from her face.

"Yes," Kyp said. "We'd love to have you back when things are a bit calmer."

The voice shifted. "The child is why we're here."

That voice.

Kyp knew that voice.

However good-natured the tone, hearing that voice again made his heart skip.

Not-Cass seemed to find his reaction humorous. "What's wrong, kid? It's like you've heard a ghost."

Jaina Madison. Jacklyn's mother.

"You've probably never heard of the Skeleton Key's Sentinel," another voice said. This time, Kyp's blood truly did run cold. "You need inside knowledge to know about that, and only I have that, now that I'm..." She ran a hand across her throat, then tipped her head back, tongue lolling out of her mouth.

"Gana..." he whispered. Jacklyn's sister. Losing her was his biggest regret.

"The Sentinel is a warrior spirit whose sole purpose is to protect a Skeleton Key until it's experienced enough to protect itself. This warrior was meant to be chosen by those close to both the Key and its nearby spirit channeler. This was decided long ago, when one nearly came to be," Mari explained.

"And we had a bit of a problem," Jaina said. "Because there are three Skeleton Keys and no spirit channeler nearby."

"So all we could do was wait until Jainey found her way to Cass," Gana explained. "To protect the Skeleton Keys, we must share Cass' body, manifesting whenever she needs us to protect Jainey. So... um... surprise."

"Astounding," Jainey whispered, having somehow pressed her way between Kyp and Drew in their shock. She looked up at Cass like she was a god.

"We are the Three," the voices spoke together. "Our sole mission is to guard the Skeleton Keys. We are here with the vessel at her call."

"And we missed food," Mari said. She smashed another handful of Fruit Loops into her mouth. "A lot."

Six

IMAGINARY WALLS

KYP

The activator dripped off the ceremonial dagger, and it stunk like skunk spray with a side of acid. Kyp felt like his nose hairs were burning. He pressed the dagger to his fingertip and pushed it into his skin. It would hurt, but it wouldn't hurt nearly as much as the constant pull of Jacklyn in the back of his mind.

She didn't want to see him again, and she didn't want to be with him. If he was going to see her, he'd make it as easy for himself as he could.

Consider this a divorce, my love.

He closed his eyes and launched into the Ritual. He'd barely made it through the first line of Arvokian text when a throbbing pain shot through the center of his skull, obliterating his focus. He knew that feeling, but he hadn't felt it in a long time.

Someone was trying to break through the wards.

Kyp stumbled to his feet, holding his head as he stepped over the remnants of his attempted Ritual. The alarm beat a steady throb behind his right eye, insisting he protect his home.

He rushed to Lavinia's old room, their designated armory since she had left. It was never a bad thing to move the weapons closer to where the team spent the most time, but he'd chosen her room purely for the symbolism.

Cass and Drew joined him just a moment after he'd pushed in through the door.

"Jainey?" Drew asked.

"Sleeping in her room," Cass said, blessedly sounding like her normal self. "The Three left for the afterlife until we need them. Not too happy about them not warning me they were coming, but…" She shrugged, as if to say, *What can you do?* like this was just a part of life she had to deal with.

"If you can, you may need to call them." Kyp opened the door, sweeping the room for his favorite axe and a few other handy weapons.

"Let me get my contacts in. Grab me something good while I'm gone." Drew rushed back to his nearby room as Kyp gathered items.

"Remind me to book you laser eye surgery," Kyp shouted after him. He snatched up a mace for Drew before storming back out, assuming Cass had followed.

There was no time for hesitation. Someone intended to attack his home and he wouldn't allow it.

Not again.

Drew raced to catch up. "Okay, they're in. And no, you're not having lasers aimed at my eyes."

Kyp passed him the mace as he continued forward, his footsteps thundering down the stairs. He was glad he'd never taken off his boots, never bothered to turn in for the night. As he moved through the house and toward the front door, memories of other bloodshed in his home bounced through his mind like an echo off the walls of an abandoned chamber.

Blood on the walls. Desiccated Gorvhan husks piled along the floors of the foyer. A crimson flood in the kitchen. *L-I-V-E.*

He wouldn't let it affect him. He had a job to do, and he wouldn't allow the ghosts of his past to add more ghosts to his future.

He threw the front door open, and there she was. The person he'd nearly killed himself searching for.

Kyp's stomach swooped low, his blood heating at the very sight of her. His fingers clenched around the axe handle as he hauled it up over his shoulder, walking through the door and out to where the estate ended and the rest of the world began. To the edge of the wards. Where she could not pass.

"Kyp, you can't…"

"Listen, I don't trust imaginary walls, man."

Cass and Drew yelled after him even as they followed. None of them were ready. And Kyp had absolutely no intention of crossing that barrier.

Unless it was to kill her.

"Mother." His hands shook. "I'm sorry to see karma hasn't caught up with you."

She smiled, but it didn't reach her shadowed eyes, and her usual confidence and poise were replaced by slumped shoulders. "I love you too, son."

He glanced behind her, assessing the small crowd of villains she'd amassed. There were Gorvhans, inky black and droopily shaped, wearing collars. Sirins stood guard over them. A curious sight. He wondered at that, but wouldn't allow it to steer him off course. Sprinkled among them were several humans, likely born with Aegis abilities, but none of them had ever seen fit to join the ranks of the Order. They were likely people with gifts who used them for selfish gain, or they wouldn't have joined her.

"I see you have managed to find support from the dregs of our society. Congratulations. You're living proof of the supposition 'like attracts like.'"

Her nose twitched, and Kyp rejoiced. The barb had cut, at least a little.

"So surly," she remarked. "And murderous, too. Did you think I wouldn't find out what happened to Mason?"

Cass's breath hitched.

Kyp's hand tightened around the axe. "I was actually hoping you would." A vicious smile crept across his face. "You're not an easy person to find."

"Believe me, I know you've been looking. I've found the hints you've been leaving me in the form of abused informants." She picked at her nails like she was bored. He knew she was anything but. "Quite a bloody trail you're leaving behind. You, the arbiter of peace. The person who thought there was a better way. Do you even believe that still? Or are you beyond that, now that Raymond took your girl and left?" She leaned forward, lowering her voice, like there was a secret between them.

He leaned forward to meet her, the buzz of the energy field between them sparking at his nose. He practically needed to nail his feet to the ground to keep from running across the barrier. They weren't ready for the fight that would create.

"Raymond and the girl have been going around sealing rifts. And yet you've managed to seal none, because you've been too busy with your desperate quest for vengeance. Do you know what that signifies?"

"I'm sure you'll tell me whether I care to hear it or not." He squeezed the axe handle again, a reminder to stay cool. To keep her from getting under his skin. To pretend he'd ever been capable of avoiding that.

"It makes you their designated guard dog." Her lips twisted into a smirk. "All of the fight, none of the glory."

"I've never minded that. All that's ever mattered to me was the mandate of the Order. Keeping the people of this dimension safe. If I'm backup, I'll be the best damn backup. Whatever gets us to that end. You trained me too well in beliefs you only pretended to share. This is your own fault, really."

"*Kyp, darling,*" Lavinia said. "*Have you forgotten how to listen to me when I speak?"*

"You don't mean listen. You mean obey. And I will never obey you again."

"Kyp?" Cass asked tightly. "Did you hear her say something?"

His brain caught up with his mouth in time to stop himself from asking what she meant. Lavinia hadn't said anything out loud that time.

She was in his head. Again.

He was a fool. After his last death, he hadn't repeated the Mind Block Ritual. He should have, but he'd lost track of it with everything that had happened since. Perhaps she was just hopeful. Perhaps she had known of his error. Either way, when she'd prodded, she'd found an entrance. Thankfully, Kyp had his own abilities he could use to combat hers. It wouldn't be easy, but he could manage.

Lavinia straightened, her smirk stretching into a grin. She fed off his strife.

"What do you think you're going to do, boy? You and your two Guardians? Where are all your self-righteous ideas now? Being lived out by someone else, while you hide behind your pathetic wards. You're a shadow of what you were. At least Jacklyn is still a capable Key."

She was goading him, and every vulnerability she touched widened the door into his mind, making it easier for her to push through. All while he fought against the ink spill of her presence within him.

It was invasive and wrong and it spread through his head, a miasma perverting the only part of him still worth anything—his sense of hope. Panic pounded along his ribs and he gripped his head with both hands as she buzzed around his brain.

"Get out. Get out!" His right eye twitched. An iron tang reached his lips, alerting him to the blood dripping from his nose.

"I tried to keep the Order running." She looked pleased, like she'd proven a point. "I was willing to do whatever it took. If it meant I had to sacrifice a few to save many, fine. But you destroyed the entire thing, didn't you? Wouldn't sacrifice a few humans to save many, couldn't sacrifice a few Order members to save the rest. Couldn't make the hard choices. You had to save them *all*. It sounds nice in theory, but that is a child's reasoning. It's impossible."

Then, in his head, "*Do you think she's safe? Just because I haven't found Jacklyn yet doesn't mean I've failed. Your hero rescued your princess, and they ran off without you. Now what is left for you? Nothing. You like to pretend you are strong, but you won't be able to do a damn thing when I find her and tear her to pieces right in front of you. When I burn him alive. The Madisons are a pox on everything the Order has ever truly been, and they have tainted my firstborn son, taken him as one of theirs and ruined the soldier I was working so hard to create. I will find them. I will never stop trying until I've eliminated them from this world. And you can do nothing about it.*"

She growled each sentence in unison, one out loud and one in his brain.

"When you try to save everyone, everyone dies."

"*And I will kill them all.*"

Kyp lost control.

With a cry that sounded more animal than human, he crashed his head up into her nose, the collision making his throbbing headache return. He ignored it, taking advantage of the moment her hands flew to her nose to throw himself forward. His hands wrapped around her neck as he toppled onto her. All he had to do was squeeze, squeeze, dammit, and she would go away.

All of his problems would go away.

His purpose narrowed to one thing as she clawed at his hands, as she tried to get away.

How many had she sacrificed when leading the Order? How many *would* she if she ever got control again?

She was just another monster. No. She was *the* monster. The only one that mattered. With her gone, the world would be safe. One death, and Kyp would save millions, maybe more. Just one more dead monster and it would be over.

He could have used the axe, but it wasn't enough. He wanted to feel the life leave her body.

Hands tugged at his shoulders, and he used his Aegis to shove them aside, to create a barrier surrounding their battle. Beneath him, Lavinia turned blue. Her eyes bulged and rolled back in her head.

She reared up, almost tossing him free, but he returned his

hands to her throat the second he regained his balance. A single-minded killing machine, just like Mama always wanted.

Lavinia bucked beneath him. Once. Twice. The third time came with a desperate telekinetic shove with the last remnants of her Aegis, and he spilled over her, his head striking the ground with a dizzying crack. The world broke apart and reformed before his eyes.

It was only then that he'd realized what he'd done.

He'd crossed the barrier and was no longer protected by the wards. And his team had followed, ready to protect him.

Cass and Drew tangled in battle with at least fifteen enemies. He'd trained them well. But Drew was fairly fresh in battle. And Cass wasn't moving like Cass. Her fighting was the same, but she moved much more aggressively. Angrily. Was this the Three? And what if it threw her off her game?

She would die. They all would. They'd leave that poor child alone, like he and Cass had been when they had returned home to find all their friends gone, just one short year ago.

"What child?"

Mother. Still in his mind.

No. *No!*

He'd be damned if he lost even another centimeter of ground to that beast of a woman that bore him.

He forced the child from his mind and shoved against Lavinia's control with his full, enraged strength. His eyes twitched. His legs shook, giving out on him, and he stumbled. When he opened his eyes, the world had grown darker.

Everything went black, then red, then the world returned, tilted sideways and wrong.

Drew swore. "Cass! We need to get him back behind the barrier where she can't touch us."

The sounds of a scuffle surrounded him, but he couldn't get his vision to clear enough to see what was happening.

Mother's cruel voice sounded beside his ear, and he wasn't sure if she was really next to him or within his mind. It wasn't the first time she'd spoken to him that way, and the memories of her past words, of all the times she'd punished him, sent chills down his spine.

"My darling boy. I do hope you haven't done any redecorating in my house yet."

She punched him in the throat. He gasped for breath, and his fingers moved to feel for any damage. His throat was slick with blood. His fingers slid along the wound until they hit metal. The handle of an ornate dagger was protruding from the side of his neck.

Not a punch then.

Shit.

I'd bet it's Jacklyn's.

His vision tunneled, and he toppled forward.

Seven

Jacklyn

I had no idea why I'd been ordered into this car. Zane had burst into the training room when I'd been working out and demanded I get suited up and get my ass on the road. Zane didn't panic, and she didn't overreact; I knew to take her seriously. And so, we were all here, wrapped in lightweight Kevlar and leather—superhero costumes of our very own.

It wasn't uncommon for us.

The thing about working for Ray that was different from working for Lavinia, aside from the corruption and that Ray wasn't a murderous bitch, was that Ray didn't always stop at fighting interdimensionals. Sometimes he'd catch wind of a very human crime, and the next thing we knew, we'd be headed out to stop the bad guys.

Zane barely waited for the rest of our team to buckle in before she gunned the engine and took off toward the Henry Hudson Parkway. It was a good thing it was after midnight on a weeknight.

There would be a lot less traffic to navigate around.

"Where are we headed, Zane?" Ray asked. He shot a nervous glance over his shoulder at me.

"I didn't want to say anything, so she wouldn't have time to back out," she answered, cleanly steering the car in and out of traffic.

"Me?" I asked. The immediate realization left me nauseated and shaky. "The estate?"

My blood froze, shivers erupting through my body, and I forced myself to be still.

"I was looking for Ross Ebell, and my search led to a conversation with someone I couldn't seem to get a handle on. The conversation was nothing to write home about. But it was about his work, so I figured it was worth tracking."

Work. My child was Ross' job. My guess was Kylie wasn't far behind.

I was too numb to be angry. Kylie and Ross were awful, but they were just as twisted as the rest of the Order. Like Kyp, they were raised in the mess, just on different sides of it. Could they have grown to be better people if Lavinia hadn't raised them?

Kyp wasn't a bad person, and Lavinia was his mother. Yet my earliest memories of Kylie and Ross involved Kylie being cruel, and Ross following her around like a puppy, eager to do her bidding.

They probably would have turned out shitty, anyway.

"The other participant in the conversation used a burner

phone. I searched for whatever I could get from that." She stopped talking for a moment to maneuver the car onto the right highway lane. "The other messages were much more concerning. One said they were reclaiming the estate. Now."

"And Kyp?" Ray asked. "What did he say when you told him?"

"He'd have to pick up the damn phone for me to tell him anything." Zane made a sharp lane change.

Austin winced. "Reclaiming the estate? What does that mean?"

Ray glanced back over his shoulder with wide eyes. He was checking to see if I knew what that meant. As if there was ever any doubt.

Lavinia.

"We can't get closer than this without pulling up to their driveway, Birdie."

We'd parked a mile away from the estate in a clearing. We needed to get closer and fast. We needed to protect them. I wanted to believe Kyp could do it. But I couldn't.

Cass was cool, and I was sure the new guy was great, too. But the girl. The little girl.

And Kyp.

I couldn't lose them the way I'd lost Mom. The way I'd lost Gana.

"It's too far," I whispered harshly. A frantic glance around made dread settle deep in my gut. When I'd dug myself free from the earth and run as fast and as far as I could, this was where I'd stopped.

The memory brought back the taste of dirt on my tongue and I gagged.

"Jacks?" Austin laid a large, gentle hand against my back.

"Yeah, I know," Ray said. "I remember."

I'd met my father there.

Whose fault was it I'd lost so much? Who had run my father away from me?

I swiped a hand across my face. "I *will* kill her."

Zane caught my elbow and shot me a disappointed glare before I could take off. "Let's not get arrogant. We need a plan."

I grunted.

"Then you can let your baser instincts fly. Promise." She held out an earpiece. "You need the best piece of tech I managed to acquire. Not to boast, but I've even messed with the settings for clearer sounds and—"

"Didn't you say something about arrogance, Z?" Austin snatched the earpiece from her and passed it to me.

"Cool," I said. I created a sound barrier so nobody would hear me as I got closer. And then I ran.

I should probably have been sorry for being such a bitch, but I needed my anger. If I lost my fire, I would lose my will.

The forest was familiar. It lived under my skin. Not just from the few months I'd spent there the year before. Five years of running through the forest behind the estate with Ray. With my dad. Before we all ran away from here. I remembered this path like I'd never moved away. Everything about this place was cemented in my mind.

The rich smell of earth drifted to my nose with every pound of my booted feet against the ground. My heart throbbed with every beat.

I wasn't far. I channeled my Aegis and leapt for the nearest tree. My legs burned with the warmth of power that flooded through them. I caught a low branch and yanked myself up, the knobs on the limb scratching at my fingers. It shook and threatened to crack, but I used the leverage to boost myself higher into the tree. My boot treads gripped the bark as I pushed higher, gripping limb after limb until I was high within the cover of a thick group of naked branches. I found a sturdy branch that wouldn't snap and kill me if I balanced on it and used it to leap to the next tree.

The remaining crunchy leaves and the less sturdy branches rained down as I moved forward. It wasn't the smartest method of travel, or the quietest, but up in the trees, I could be mistaken for a particularly noisy squirrel. Okay. Raccoon. Something massive.

There weren't gorillas in the forests of upstate New York, right?

Voices broke through my thoughts.

I moved slower, getting as close as I could to inspect the area. I couldn't run in there unprepared. I wasn't that girl anymore. I needed to know what I was stepping into. Trees rustled behind me, alerting me to Ray's approach.

I rested against a sound tree branch, repositioned the strength of my Aegis into my eyes and ears. At first, all I could see was the glow of the lights from the house. As I focused further, I got a clearer picture.

On one side of the divide, there was an army of people and interdimensionals, stretching out to the far ends of the clearing that served as the estate's yard. On the other side, Cass stood with the new guy. Andrew, if I remembered right. Dead center was a tall woman with straight dark hair. I couldn't see her features from my angle, but I knew it was Lavinia. My limbs shook with the truth of it.

Kyp stood facing her. His hair was pushed back from his forehead and no longer hung in his face. It made his features more prominent—the deep, calm brown eyes, the thin pointed nose, the chiseled cheekbones, the way his chin came to a point, the full lips drawn back into a snarl as he snapped at his mother.

It was hard not to stare, but there were much more important things to worry about right now.

"Take your time, Jacklyn," Austin's voice came through the earpiece. "We don't have anywhere to be or anything."

"What?" I hissed. "I'm doing a damage assessment."

Ray whispered, but I could hear him through the mic and the trees nearby. "What is there to assess? This is going to be difficult. Lavinia's allies stretch far past what I think Kyp's allies believe. It's a damn good thing she seems to be stuck behind the barrier."

"We should wait," Zane said. "They may leave if they can't get through."

"Hell no!" I snapped. Beneath my fingertips, the branch I was gripping creaked. "She's fifty feet away from me. I've been looking for her for a year. This ends tonight."

"No, Birdie," Ray sighed. "That's a terrible idea."

"She's just one person."

"One person with resources and no problem running through everything in her path like a bulldozer," he said. "She's dangerous, and she lives by playing games you haven't even been introduced to yet."

"I know how to—"

"If you did, she'd be dead already."

I didn't have an answer to that.

"We should wait," Zane repeated, quieter this time. "She can't get through the wards. This standoff can't last forever; they'll have to leave at some point."

Unless Kyp stepped over that line.

His eyes were narrowed, his chin jutted, jaw locked.

Even then, I loved him with a force that frightened me. But I did not love him so much that I couldn't recognize how damn stupid he could be.

Kyp stepped over the line.

"Shit!" I was out of the tree and using a branch to swing myself forward before I could think about it.

I bent my knees and rolled with the landing, using my

momentum to speed my run. Voices whisper-shouted in my ear to stop. Soon enough, they changed their tune, shifting to backup orders.

A scuffle was already breaking out beyond me, even as I ate up the distance between it and me. The fight was still on my side of the wards. The child wasn't there. That meant she was safe. As long as she stayed inside.

It wasn't her I worried about.

I slowed to a stop behind a Sirin and yanked the hunting knife from the sheath I'd strapped to my thigh. I'd barely stopped before sliding the blade across its throat. Using its back as a springboard, I pushed myself over the head of two other beings to get further into the scuffle.

An angry-looking man raced toward me, and I swung my elbow backward, connecting with his stomach. His fingers wrapped around my hair and he yanked me backward. I stomped down on the man's foot and threw my head back to collide with his nose. It gave a satisfying crunch, and he released my hair. I turned and kneed him hard in the groin. His hands curled over the injured area, and I shoved him aside with little effort.

My team had followed my lead. We'd been working together for months now, and I knew when they were united behind me. Knowing they had my back freed me up to look for Lavinia. But her goons had crowded around her, blocking her from my view. Instead, my eyes landed on the bloody lump on the floor, clutching its throat.

Gana!

Cass grabbed the figure under its arms, and the image in my mind shifted. No longer was it Gana lying there.

Kyp.

"Go," Ray shouted behind me, grunting with exertion. "Heal the boy. We need him."

It was a lie. We could handle this without him. But like Ray, I couldn't watch anyone suffer, Key or Guardian, when I could put a stop to it.

I rushed to help Cass before I could second guess myself.

"Move!" I shouted. In an ideal situation, I would first say hello to an old friend I hadn't seen in a year, but this was far from ideal.

"Jacks!" Cass said, but her voice sounded wrong. I didn't think about it. I couldn't. Not when Kyp was staring up at me, wide-eyed and pale, my old dagger sticking from his neck.

I reached for him, but Kyp flinched, pulling away from me half-heartedly, like a misbehaving child.

I leaned in to speak directly into his ear. "We don't have time for this. Do you want to take her down or not?"

He couldn't answer, but he stopped straining against me, so I took that for agreement. Cass and, surprisingly, Austin fell into place to clear the way as I yanked Kyp over the barrier.

I laid him on the ground and crouched beside him, hissing curses as I leaned closer to inspect the wound.

Cass crouched beside me, her head tilted curiously. "Damn, that's ugly. You look ugly right now, Kyp. Did I look that ugly?"

She turned her attention to me, and I had to fight back a gasp.

Gana. Gana in Cass' body.

"N-no, kiddo. You're always beautiful." I glanced at Kyp and whispered a hushed apology as I gripped the dagger, feeling the handle's familiar pattern pressing into my palm. I yanked it free, and blood spurted from the wound. Kyp let out a hoarse yelp.

"Gana, Cass, you're needed out there." I pressed my hand firmly to Kyp's wound, healing it in an old, familiar dance. "I'll get him back on his feet and we'll rejoin the battle."

With a determined nod, Cass, G—whoever the hell she was, rejoined the battle.

I fought to keep my head in the game. Below me, Kyp was fading fast. His eyes were unfocused, his skin pale and clammy. I grabbed his collar with my other hand and gave him a shake.

"I'm awake, I'm fine." He jolted upright.

"Stay still. I've got you."

"Jacklyn? What in the—" He struggled to stand, but I held him in place.

"What part of 'stay still' are you having trouble with?"

Our eyes locked, and it was like all my senses focused on him and nothing else. The way the iron tang of blood mixed with his natural woodsy scent, the familiarity of his face. It drowned out the rest of the battle.

Kyp's mouth opened and closed uselessly, and I returned my attention to healing him. He muttered something under his breath. I would have almost believed he'd said I was astounding if I didn't know he hated me.

A Gorvhan screech filled the air, and it was enough to send me crashing back into the real world.

I had to ignore him if I was going to get back into the fray. I zeroed in on the flow of my Aegis within me and channeled it through my palm, healing his throat. The injured tissue sealed layer by layer, sewing itself together. I wished it could sew my life together, make everything right again.

But there wasn't an Aegis for rewriting history.

I checked my work, swiping away the blood staining his skin. Once I was sure I had accomplished my goal, I jerked back because at some point in the process I'd brought my face way too close to his.

Kyp cleared his throat, and I felt more awkward than ever.

"Uh... hi. You good?"

"No." It was a mere whisper, but it was enough to remind me how he felt.

I glanced back over my shoulder to find the battle in full swing. Cass was in rare form, her attacks a graceful but violent dance. Austin was brute strength, stomping through enemies like bursts of thunder. Zane was whip-fast and strategic. Drew worked over his adversaries with flowing movements and clever combinations, while Ray was equal parts force and finesse.

And Lavinia? Lavinia was getting away.

"Son of a bitch!"

"Yeah, that's me," Kyp muttered.

I threw myself to my feet, grabbing the dagger and taking off after her, tripping as my brain propelled me forward without consulting my legs.

I was done playing.

I scanned the area as I ran. Three Gorvhans and two Sirins stood between me and my purpose. There was no way around it. I'd have to fight them.

I channeled my Aegis once again and prayed my year of experience would better prepare me for this encounter with Lavinia.

She wouldn't have beaten me before if she hadn't nullified my Aegis. And she hadn't done that this time. Which meant she wasn't expecting me.

I didn't have time to get cocky. I still had six more contestants. I couldn't think about the others. Let Kyp and Ray worry about them; they were the leaders. I was the enforcer.

Tackling a Sirin with all my force, I slammed it to the ground. I jammed the dagger between its ribs, once, twice, three times, then threw it at an approaching Sirin, driving it into the center of its skull.

Lavinia was getting away, almost to the forest, where she could have an escape route waiting.

I moved my hand to the holster on my hip.

"Go!" Kyp shouted from somewhere behind me. "I'll cover you."

I ran.

"*Your problem,*" Ray had told me a few days after we'd found each other again, "*is the same as every other Order member's. They taught you to rely on your Aegis. Yes, you learn how to fight, but your Aegis is treated as your main weapon.*"

And then he trained me to beat Lavinia without my abilities. That's what I'd do now.

I didn't bother channeling my Aegis. Instead, I channeled that girl from the Bronx—the one who'd been bullied and had to prove she was tough enough to survive. Instead of getting in front of Lavinia, or barreling into her with my strength, I reached forward and grabbed hold of her hood.

Her upper body jerked to a stop. Her legs kept moving until they slid out from under her. She didn't hit the ground completely— she was still a trained member of the Order. She twisted with the slide and got back on her feet in time to look down the barrel of my handgun.

Her Aegis pulled at my mind like an insect's feelers dancing along my brain. Death or time could make the Arvokian Mind Block Ritual wear off.

I reapplied it daily. It may have been a bit obsessive, but I certainly appreciated my attention to detail at that moment.

Lavinia wasn't getting in. She never would. Never again.

A small smile slithered across her lips. "My dear, guns? Really?"

The sound of gunfire echoed behind me as I stared her down, followed by the roars of wounded Gorvhans.

"Seems to be working pretty well for them." I shrugged, willing my hands not to shake. I wouldn't balk. I would savor this moment.

Her eyebrows raised, and my attention narrowed to her and her alone.

"You're going to shoot me? You're going to end this in such a hands-off manner?" She took a step closer.

My hand tightened. I swallowed. She was right. I didn't want that.

"You don't want to shoot me. You want to watch me suffer. You want vengeance. And that's why you won't kill me. Not yet. I'm worth too much to you."

"You aren't worth—" I tried to pull the trigger. I failed. The gun jerked backward.

Lavinia's other ability. She couldn't read my mind, but she could use her telekinesis.

I grasped the gun with both hands, channeling my Aegis' strength into my arms and forcing the gun back to face her.

"Okay, maybe you would do it." She smirked. "But not anymore."

"Jacks!" Kyp shouted behind me.

The gun fought against my grip as I struggled to hold it still.

"Wouldn't it be worth it to end the nightmares?"

"Stop."

A child's voice, stern but soft.

My head shifted toward the voice, but Lavinia made sure the

gun swung in the same direction. I was staring down the aiming line of my arm, gun trained on a little girl with an innocent tilt to her head and eyes like fire.

I gasped. I knew who this was.

Lavinia stepped forward. "Jainey, my dear—"

I whipped my other gun free from the holster pressed against my back and pointed it at Lavinia. "Stay back." I couldn't move the gun she'd moved toward the kid, but I could kill her before she made me pull the first gun's trigger.

Cold metal pressed to the back of my head.

"I wouldn't." The garbled voice of a Sirin.

"Marcelo," Kyp hissed. "This is bigger than you or your drug dens. This is far beyond anything you're involved in. You don't know—"

"That's just insulting. I know exactly." His tone was flippant and lacked remorse.

Lavinia made another pull at my trigger finger. The one aiming at the child. My child. Her face was like looking into a family photo album. But this time, I also felt something pulling back.

"Mother, you have to stop this." His tentative footsteps inched forward.

"I don't think you're in a position to make demands," she said lightly. Like forcing me to point a gun at a child—*my* child— wasn't a big damn deal to her.

"Stop this," the girl said, quieter this time, less demanding.

"I don't think you are either." Kyp's voice was even, but I

could detect the edge in it, the sharpness that meant he wasn't okay. That he was anything but okay.

The girl's eyes went wide, and she heaved a breath. "Stop."

"Mother, if you make her pull that trigger, she'll pull hers," Kyp said. "She won't hesitate anymore."

"Please stop." Another deep, shuddering breath.

"Kyp, something's wrong with the kid." He ignored me.

"So help me, Mother," he growled. "So help me, if you shoot that child, I will lock you up. I will use the nullification Ritual you used on Jacklyn. And then I don't care what tries to stop me. I will speak the Ritual of the Unburdening over you even if it's done through bullet holes and bites and bruises."

"Please, please." The kid's eyes were filling with tears now, her hands coming up to grip her head, fingers clawing at her hair. "Please stop."

My heart pounded even harder.

"I will stand through every attack, die and take you with me out of this world, I swear it," Kyp shouted.

"Stop it!" The kid screamed, an ear-piercing scream morphing into something else, like a spear lancing into my brain and whiting out my vision.

The guns both dropped from my hands, the metal shaking and then disassembling in my hands and spilling away.

"Get behind the barrier," Kyp shouted, his voice sounding frantic and panicked.

My knees hit the ground before I knew I was falling. I dropped forward onto my hands, my fingers gripping the cracked and cold earth.

Like when I was buried.

The ground shook beneath me and I pitched forward into darkness.

EIGHT

KYP

Kyp collapsed onto the floor just beyond the estate's doorway. Jainey spilled from his arms as he stumbled. He swiveled as his knee hit the ground, moving to shout a command behind him, but it was like Drew already knew what he was going to say. He slammed the door and locked it.

As if a lock could keep them truly safe.

Drew's eyes latched onto his, then flicked around the room at the others before returning to his with a glare. The message was clear—the only thing protecting Kyp from the lecture of a lifetime was their guests, which was a blessing because his brain felt like a flattened piece of roadkill.

Not that he wouldn't deserve the lecture. He had stepped over the barrier and started this whole mess. He'd nearly gotten the child killed.

His child.

She lay on the floor before him, blood dribbling from her

nose, over her cheek and into her hair.

He swore, pressing his hand to her cheek. "Jainey? Kid? You okay?"

Her eyelashes fluttered, and she grumbled something he couldn't make out and turned her head away.

"Jainey?" He gave her a little shake.

Jacklyn dropped to the floor beside him with a thump. When he'd last looked, Ray had been carrying her. Her eyes were half-lidded and unfocused, and like him, she was coated in her own blood and covered in wounds, along with splotches of green interdimensional blood. Her hair was a messy cloud of tangles surrounding her head.

It was shorter than it had been a year ago.

"Try again," she said, voice graveled and thick. She bent forward, leaning toward the kid, using a shaky hand as leverage.

"Jainey, baby, I need you to open your eyes for me, okay, sweetheart?" The words tumbled out of him, and suddenly he felt like a dad, a confused dad whose baby was bleeding on the floor and he didn't know why. His heart twisted painfully in his chest. How had he become so attached to her so soon? How was it so easy to love the little adorable brat so quickly? He felt guilty for even thinking of her as a brat in that moment.

He'd almost lost her. The idea was unthinkable.

Jainey muttered again.

His fingertips pressed into the hardwood flooring.

"She said 'too soon for a treatment.'" Jacklyn's eyes locked on his, and he wanted to revel in it, wanted to shout at her and tell her not to dare look at him, but they didn't have time for any of that. "She said something about Ross the first time, but I'm still—" She waved her hands around her head in some gesture he supposed meant 'messed up.' "I couldn't hear her too well."

He grunted in response, his teeth grinding together. He was going to have a word with Ross. Very soon.

Jacklyn gave a full body shiver. "Is she gonna be okay?"

"Yes," Kyp said confidently. His shoulders drooped. "I think so." A sigh. "I have no idea."

"Is it something I can heal?" she asked. "I would try, but it's a surefire way to knock me out cold, and I'm not sure if anyone else needs healing. If it would help her, I would, but if not..."

He wiped blood from Jainey's dainty nose. "I don't think it would help. This isn't physical. It's related to her Aegis."

She sat back on her haunches. "What the hell happened out there?"

"She wants answers now?" Cass. "As though she's owed them. As though she doesn't have anything to answer for herself."

"Gonna start a fight with Jacklyn now?" Austin. "Feelin' adventurous?"

Kyp had forgotten anybody else was in the room with their trio. Father. Mother. Daughter. However unbelievable that was.

Jacklyn stood, and Kyp followed, lifting Jainey into his arms. She was light, but limp. A dead weight. It shook something within him, his stomach twisting.

If he wasn't careful, this could be permanent. Like Gana.

"Cass. Hello. It's good to see you. Why the hell were you using my dead sister's voice earlier?" Jacklyn snapped, and the sound echoed off the walls. Was it a new Aegis trick? Or was she that damn angry?

It wasn't enough to rouse Jainey.

When nobody answered, she lowered her voice. "I believe we all have oodles to speak about. And gobs to answer for." A deep breath. "We should wait. We need four people to do a perimeter check, make sure nobody found a way through the wards. We're all a mess. If I remember correctly, Kyp will apologize if he bleeds on anybody, so better clean up first." She smirked. "This conversation will take a while."

Kyp glared at her, his heart rate climbing with every sentence out of her mouth.

"Right," she said. "No jokes. Anyway, we should start with Jainey."

"Are you suddenly in charge here?" Kyp asked. "I am the leader here."

"A failed one." Austin stepped in between them. "There are problems you ain't been handling. That we've been taking care of."

"Enough outta the lot of ya." Ray.

It had been a long time since Kyp had heard Ray's voice in anything but memories. He'd missed him.

"Tradition says the oldest Key is in charge and that's me...

unless the little lady has more surprises up her sleeve than we realized."

Well, Kyp *had* missed him before he'd opened his mouth.

"Cassandra, I'm assuming you get along well enough with the girl?" Ray asked.

"Why? Because I'm a woman?" Cass folded her arms across her chest.

"No, you git, because the girl needs to be cleaned up and I wasn't about to assign one of the boys to do it," Ray said with a groan. "You know her, and Zane and Jacklyn don't know her a bit, so I figured you were the safer bet."

"So, it *is* because you're a woman." Drew elbowed Cass. "But not for the reason you thought."

"Cassandra, I get the concern, but there'll be none of that bullshit here," Ray said. "I'm not the type. I'm protective of Jacks because she's my daughter. And anyone who knows her would know that's a joke and a half, anyway. But other 'en that, I'll send you to the front of a line of soldiers and expect you to destroy as many enemies as any of the boys here. And if you don't, I'll be a mite disappointed. Bet your arse on that."

A smile flickered across Cass' face. "Fine. I'll take the kid." She headed toward Kyp, but stopped in front of Jacklyn first. "I'll explain later, Jacks." The pair locked gazes for a moment before she lifted Jainey from Kyp's arms.

He felt oddly light without her there. It wasn't relieving, like a weight being lifted. It was dizzying, like with one wrong move, he'd untether from his body.

A hand on his shoulder kept him anchored to the ground.

Ray looked different, as people did over time. Kyp needed to remind himself of that often. With his perfect memory, he found himself discomfited when time changed people. "Remembering it like it was yesterday" was real for him. And so, he could see every difference in Ray's face when he compared him to the man in his memories.

He looked healthy, his complexion ruddy, eyes dancing with mischief, the way they hadn't since Kyp was young. Could the joy on Ray's face be because of him?

"It's damn good to see you, boy." He wrapped his arms around him, and Kyp stared over his shoulder at Jacklyn, almost helplessly. He remembered Ray hugging him like this, but it hadn't been since he'd had to kneel down to do it, and Kyp didn't know how to react to this change.

Jacklyn glanced away at the floor, a smile playing at her lips, and it was almost like permission. Like she was saying it was okay for Kyp to love her father like he was his own.

Kyp hugged him back fiercely and buried his face in his shoulder. He smelled like worn leather and Old Spice, like he always did, and Kyp had to struggle for a moment to keep himself together. "Likewise, old man."

"You've grown well." Ray jabbed at his stomach and Kyp sidestepped the move. "Spry, you are. Alert too. Still stoic as heck, I see."

"I am who I am." Kyp shrugged.

They shared a smile. Then Ray jerked his head back toward the door. "I'm gonna go spend time out front playing sentry. Gotta make sure nobody made it through the barrier. Drew, Austin, come on."

Drew looked to Kyp for approval before rushing off after Ray.

Kyp tried to be nonchalant. But really, he wanted to grab Ray's arm and beg him not to go.

Please stay. Please take charge. I can't be responsible for this anymore, because when I am, people die. Can I just run off somewhere and be happy? Can we find someone with the ability to erase memories, someone who isn't my mother, who isn't me, and can we remove these thoughts from my mind so I don't know about interdimensionals? Then I can live in peace and never have to fight or lose again. Can I feel safe? Can you help me?

But that wasn't behavior becoming a leader in the Order. And Ray had abandoned his pledge toward the organization. His team worked outside of their world. It was Kyp's job to ensure they behaved according to the laws of the Order.

Whatever those meant anymore.

Kyp hated himself for his reaction. He was a warrior. A leader. A simpering loser in the face of his ex-girlfriend's father.

"I'm going to clean up." Jacklyn shoved her hands in her pockets. "I'll go..." She trailed off, looking down the hall in the direction of the ground floor bathroom. Her eyes went glassy as her gaze slowed in front of the kitchen.

"Shit," Zane muttered. "Jacks, focus. No walking down memory lane."

Kyp knew what was causing that look.

"I'll take this bathroom," he said. "I was gonna get some coffee started and bring it up to the sitting room. Use the third-floor bathroom."

She sighed and nodded her approval, and Kyp left her there, hoping Zane would help her.

Kyp placed a pot of coffee on the table in the center of the sitting room, along with the entire box of sugar and a box of varying tea selections. It had been a while since the Order had hosted this many warriors, and he didn't have the energy to dig out the supplies for such a gathering. Cass brought spoons and a whole gallon of milk, while Drew followed with a pot of hot water and a stack of mugs expertly balanced on a tray.

"Thank goodness for that part-time job at Denny's." Drew laughed as he lowered the tray onto the table without a single clink. "Really prepared me for fighting interdimensionals, or whatever this job is."

Jacklyn's hazel eyes lit up. "This job is rarely what we expect." She snagged a cup from the tray and got to work preparing her drink. "How are you liking it so far?"

Zane grunted. "Less talk, more coffee."

"It's okay," Drew said, ignoring Zane's grumbling. "I have two new besties, so that's a plus. But also, the world sucks and everything is horrible."

"I'll drink to that," Austin chimed in. "I can't imagine you've got anything harder than coffee, right, Baby Franklin?"

This crap again. "No— I—"

"Remember how he reacted to the beer?" Zane laughed.

Kyp didn't have the energy to be annoyed. "Zane, you and Ray are the only people here who are legally allowed to drink. And have been. For decades."

Austin snorted. "At what age are you legally allowed to kill interdimensionals?"

An image rose in his head, unbidden. The blood that splashed Kylie's blonde hair, like the red on a gold-edged marigold petal.

"Kyp?" Cass brought him back to the surface now as she had then. Her hand landed on his shoulder. "Grab a seat. We have a long talk ahead of us." There was that broken doll look from her again. There was no fixing him. He wished she'd stop trying.

"Where should we begin?" Jacklyn asked once everyone was seated and sipping at their own mug of coffee.

"Why don't we start with any information you may have on how you two have kids?" Drew's voice was light, but his eyes were dead serious.

She sighed. Sank into the chair. Closed her eyes. "I was pregnant when I left here."

"What?" Kyp heard the question, but it took him a moment to realize it had come from him.

She winced. "I know. I know." She leaned forward, resting her face in her hands. "I'm sorry, Kyp."

"You were pregnant. And you didn't tell me. You didn't call me. You didn't come back."

He'd been angry before. Now he was numb. Detached.

"I was going to. I was waiting to see how things went," Jacklyn continued. Her eyes met his, pleading. "The pregnancy was complicated from the beginning. I was sick. My Aegis went completely out of control."

"I took her to Dr. Livingston," Ray said. "It was risky, what with people looking for a Skeleton Key, but I didn't know what else to do. I'd just been reunited with her. I didn't want to lose her again."

"Dr. Livingston," Kyp whispered.

"He tried to help me," Jacklyn said. "But he couldn't. My body fought the baby at every turn. And eventually..." Her voice cracked.

"She lost the baby," Ray said. "She wasn't pregnant for more than a couple of months."

"I'm sorry," Cass said. "I don't want to seem insensitive, but..."

"How would that lead to this?" Drew asked. He winced. "Sorry."

"I'm not sure," Jacklyn said, "but that doctor has to be the starting point. His office is the only place to have any access to an actual blending of our genes."

"Maybe they used what they had to grow one of their own.

Same genetic makeup, grown outside the womb," Austin said. "Or they somehow kept it alive outside the womb long enough to get it on some kind of life support… or…"

Everyone turned to look at him.

"What? I watch more 'en enough sci-fi to put that together. There's a reason Jacks and I get along."

Drew snickered. "More than a pretty face, huh?"

Austin's face lit up, a bright splotchy red.

Jacklyn's head tilted as she observed the exchange.

"Anyway," Kyp said. "We think someone took a spontaneously aborted fetus and… grew their own babies."

"And in record time!" Drew said.

"One of the kids in the complex Jainey's told us about calls Ross his dad," Cass said.

"There are children in a facility that require our help," Ray said. "Interdimensional business or not, this sounds like our mandate."

"If Ross knows where they are, then we go to Ross for help." Cass sighed. "Can't throw him nearly far enough to trust him. But he has our answers."

"If I can get an internet connection that's worth a damn, I can start searching for some way to track him," Zane said. "I'll probably need some help sifting through the data."

"I can do that!" Drew bounced in his seat, hand raised like a schoolkid. It was kind of adorable.

"Perfect." She smiled and leaned back in her seat. "That's all

I need."

"She needs a better internet connection than the crap you've got here," Jacklyn said. "We should head back home, Zane."

"No way. You're not taking Drew from us now," Kyp argued. "I need my team here with me."

"Then Austin will take his place." She shrugged him off, making Kyp's blood boil. "Or you can all come back with us. But my team's not staying here."

"You're making excuses," Cass snapped, finger stabbing in the air at Jacklyn.

"Can't imagine why I wouldn't want to hang around in the place where my sister died," Jacklyn raked her fingers through her hair and leaned forward to drop her head into her hands.

"Jacklyn's right, anyway. The wards can't be trusted, and at least nobody will know where we are if we leave. If we hide our energy signatures, we should be able to fly under the radar," Ray explained.

Jacklyn's leg started bouncing in place, her hands flexing where they grasped hanks of her hair.

Ray continued speaking, slower this time, his eyes narrowing as he watched his daughter. "They never found me at our location, and I'm not exactly their favorite person."

As if she burst, Jacklyn's leg abruptly stopped bouncing, and she launched herself to her feet. "Why did you sound like Gana out there?" She jabbed her finger in Cass' direction. Her voice was ragged now and her energy signature spiked high.

Kyp didn't know what was happening, but it didn't look or feel good. When he opened his mind to feel her emotions, a dark, jittering miasma surrounded her.

Cass' glance flicked to Kyp, then back to Jacklyn, and she launched into the explanation Mari had given them earlier.

As she spoke, the color drained from Jacklyn's face. "Mom, too?"

Cass nodded. "I can channel Jaina for you. Or Gana. If you think it would help."

Jacklyn's back went ramrod straight. "I need to leave."

"Jacks." Ray lurched forward.

"No. Not now." Austin swore, scrubbing his hands over his face.

"I can't be here." Shoving Ray aside, she bolted out of the sitting room and down the hall, slowing to a stop in front of the wrap-around banister that overlooked the foyer.

Kyp followed.

Her blank gaze made her look unhinged. Her hand ran across the cherry wood of the banister, a meandering movement that made something in Kyp's stomach twist. "She cornered us up here." She looked over the edge, pulling herself up onto her tip-toes. "She threw Gana over the edge. But she held on. She made it. She saved me."

Her breathing was ragged, her voice harsh and grainy. She headed for the stairs, her movements abrupt and rigid, and Kyp followed her, Ray behind him, while the others continued watching from above.

"She saved me." A gasp, and tears spilled as she took her last step on the staircase. Another hiccupping gasp as she moved toward the kitchen. She dropped to her knees outside the kitchen. Where Kyp had found Gana.

"L-I-V-E." She traced where the letters had once been, written in her sister's blood. "L-I-V-E."

Kyp lowered himself to sit beside her, his heart aching.

She remembered the exact spot. His Aegis made his memory perfect. But her perfect memory of this moment was seared into her brain, cut into its folds by trauma like jagged graffiti. Kyp often believed his perfect memory was a burden. But at least his memory retained the good times as well as the bad.

He felt another twist, deeper in his soul, where he'd once felt their connection. God, was it back? Now, of all times? So he could feel her pain?

"I lived," she breathed, her arms wrapping around her knees. "You're still here, Jacks. You're still here. You lived. You did it. You lived. She didn't get you."

The words were barely whispers. Breaths. Huffs. Each stung, every word driving a dagger further into his chest.

She buried her face in her knees and Ray joined them on the floor.

With every breath she pulled in, she shuddered and rocked in place, all the while whispering her mantra, reminding herself she'd made it. Her energy spiked, her breathing out of control, her sorrow leaving her in waves Kyp could feel without trying.

"I'm a survivor. I did what you asked. I'm here."

"Yeah, you are, love." Ray brushed her hair from her eyes, the affectionate gesture one he'd used with her since childhood.

"Ray, please." A sharp gasp accompanied each word.

"I've got you, Birdie." He pressed a hand to her forehead.

It took just a moment, and then she slumped forward into his arms. Asleep.

"Drained her energy," Ray explained. "It needed to be done. If she doesn't control her Aegis when she's like that... She died that way once. Gave herself a damn heart attack. Her power levels have been off since the pregnancy. Never quite made it all the way back to normal."

Kyp swore. He was torn. He wanted to comfort her. He wanted her to leave. He missed the days when his heart didn't betray him. Missed the days when he knew exactly what he wanted, no matter how twisted those desires may be.

"Drew." He looked up. "Could you dig the old computer out of storage and get Zane started on her search? Cass, please assist Austin in preparing the rooms for our guests."

With a nod and a hand motion, Drew led Zane upstairs without a word.

"Come on, big guy." Cass smiled at Austin. "Linen closet's this way." Austin responded with a grunt and followed her.

Ray lifted Jacklyn, cradling her in his arms. "Where's her room?"

"Are you sure?" Kyp answered. "I don't want her to wake up in there and—"

"I'll sleep in there too. Make sure she isn't afraid when she wakes."

Kyp smiled, but he wasn't sure he meant it. "You two sure have gotten close. A year back together and she's already forgotten you abandoned her."

"Hmmm. You don't forget that easily."

As always, Ray knew what the real problem was.

"I don't understand how everything is supposed to go back to normal."

Ray hoisted Jacklyn higher in his arms, getting a bit more comfortable. "Kid, there isn't a thing about this that's normal. You aren't supposed to act like everything's normal. You keep rolling with it, like we all do."

"'Normal' is all I've ever wanted," he said, but he had to agree. "Her room is on the third floor. Fourth door from the right."

"Still next door to yours." There was a knowing twinkle in his eyes. "You and I are going to have a long talk about my daughter. You know that, right?"

"Good night, Ray."

Ray chuckled. "Yeah, good night, kid."

It was only when Kyp heard Ray close the door behind him that Kyp remembered he hadn't moved a thing in Jacklyn's room since she left.

He really hoped Ray didn't judge him for that.

NINE

JACKLYN

I jerked awake, gasping at the sound of gunfire that may have been real, or may have been from my dream. My gaze whipped around the darkness, my Aegis slow to respond when I tried kick-starting it.

Severely low on energy. *Damn*. It had happened again.

When my eyes grew more accustomed to the dark, I spotted Ray. He was asleep, slumped in a nearby chair. I smiled. Sometimes he was an asshole, but sometimes he could be a pretty good dad.

I gave in to the nostalgic urge I'd been struggling with since I first saw Kyp. I knocked a pattern on the wall, hoping he would press his palm to his side of the wall in answer, the way he once had.

Nothing.

I needed air. As quietly as I could, I rose from my bed.

It was still etched into my mind—the darkness of this place at night, the absence of city lights filtering through the curtains, the roughness of the carpet beneath my feet. Surprisingly, Kyp hadn't destroyed it. Destruction was the balm for all ills. Or maybe that was just me. Not then, but now.

I inched toward the window, pushing the curtain aside. I wanted to go to the forest again. It probably wasn't wise, but before I knew it, I was opening the window. I grabbed the gun and dagger from my bedside table where Ray had wisely left them and slid my feet into my boots.

I was just in my t-shirt and jeans. Ray must have removed the tactical jacket and holsters. I tucked my gun into the waist of my jeans. The cold air bit at my arms, but I climbed out anyway, making my way down the trellis and onto the cracking earth.

Nobody was there. Nobody to follow me, nobody to fight me.

I headed for the forest, twigs and leaves cracking beneath my feet. I made my way through the more wooded areas cautiously, ducking under tree branches and stepping over undergrowth until I found myself in a familiar clearing. I followed the route, exhausted and barely bothering to consider what led me there.

I turned the corner, following the path I'd taken so many times before—to the majesty of my beautiful willow tree.

Our willow tree.

My heart missed a beat, and I pressed a hand to my chest as if I could keep it from growing wings and flying away.

The tree Kyp and I had visited since childhood was torn up by its roots. It lay, decaying, across the exact spot where we'd shared our first kiss, where we'd...

"I destroyed it."

Kyp. I nearly jumped out of my skin. I may have been a soldier who'd been taught to pay attention to my surroundings, but my shock must have blocked out the sound of approaching footsteps.

Though his voice was in my ear, and his warmth was just over my shoulder, I couldn't bring myself to look away. "Why would you do this?" But as soon as the question left my mouth, I knew the answer. I wasn't around to hurt, so he hurt our memories.

He had that arrogant, haughty tone to his voice, and I was glad I couldn't bring myself to look at him. "I was a bit angry."

"You were selfish."

"I didn't think you'd ever come back to see it. I didn't think it mattered." A pause. "It's cold. Come back to the house. I'll make you some chamomile tea. We can... talk."

I didn't have to look to know he was inclining his head, speaking like Data from Trek, the way he always did when he finally got his emotions in check and decided they wouldn't be making any more appearances.

"I didn't intend to wake you." There was only the slightest edge to my voice, and yet, compared to his level of calm, I sounded downright belligerent.

"When one does not intend to wake anybody, one should probably not clomp through the forest like a blinded bull."

"No way you heard that from your room." I whirled to face him. "You were patrolling, weren't you? Making sure Lavinia hadn't found a way in. That's just obsessive enough to be a Kyp thing to do."

His hair was slicked away from his face. A slight smirk played on the edges of his lips and his eyes sparkled. "You say obsessive, I say protective." He reached to place a hand on my shoulder, but halted the move halfway, his hand lingering awkwardly before returning to his side. "You're cold. We should go inside."

"And get some tea? That's Ray's go to, but I've gotta tell you, it never calms me down when he makes it either." I shot him a mistrustful glare.

"Maybe it won't. Maybe you could just have tea."

"What is it with you and the damn tea?" I snapped. "Sure, Kyp! I'll come back to the house with you and sip tea. And maybe, if we keep the lights off, I won't see the shadow of my sister's body on the damn kitchen floor."

He flinched. "You—you're right. You're right. I— Never mind." He turned and started heading back to the house. "If you have any energy left, you should use your Aegis to warm you."

I stormed after him. "It's why I left. You know that, right?"

"We don't have to do this." He sped up, but it was useless. I was faster than him, even without engaging my Aegis.

Once upon a time, I'd raced other high school kids. I thought that would be my future—a track scholarship. Not this.

I never could have imagined this.

"Wait. Kyp!" I grabbed for his arm.

He stopped, but didn't turn.

"I didn't leave because I blamed you." My throat tightened

and my lungs burned. "I left because I wished I had never met you."

"Wow, Jacks."

"Can you blame me?" I winced at how shrill it came out. "Meeting you, coming here, it was the beginning of the end for my family. It wasn't about you."

Nothing.

"I couldn't be here. I couldn't be here, and I couldn't be with you. Not until I was steadier."

His shoulders slumped and he turned to face me. "It was my responsibility." He swiped at his eyes. "I should have found another way to protect you without happily dragging you into my mess." He took my elbows in his hands and stepped closer. "For whatever it's worth, I do regret bringing you here."

The sorrow in his voice drew me to look him in the eyes, to find the same emotion reflected there.

"You can't change the past." I didn't know if I was trying to comfort him or stating a fact.

He leaned forward, his hands rubbing up and down my upper arms, soothing the goosebumps forming there. "Can you use your Aegis to warm you?"

"Can't. I'm tapped. Yesterday..." I trailed off.

"About that..."

"It started after the, um, the pregnancy. It made my Aegis go nuts. I now understand why there haven't been any Skeleton Keys in recorded history."

"And about that... you were *pregnant*." His hands tightened on my arms, and he gave me a little shake to accentuate the insanity of that statement.

"I know you're probably angry at me for not telling you." I stepped back, breaking his hold on me. "Come on, let's head back and I'll explain."

He nodded. "You're cold. I'll make tea."

I glared at him to get a smile. It was slight, but it was there.

I headed for the house and he fell into step beside me. "When I first realized what was happening, Ray and I talked about going to you. But I realized I didn't want you to live through whatever the baby may do to me. And what might happen to it. I didn't want you to be stuck with those memories forever."

"It wasn't your decision to make," Kyp said, his tone even.

I hated when he was right.

I hated when anybody was right, if it meant I was wrong.

"Maybe not. I may not need to protect you, but I wanted to." It was what he'd said to me a year ago. It made me kiss him for the first time.

We walked for a minute or two in silence. I fought the urge to reach for his hand the way I would have before. But we weren't there yet. We might never be there again. I didn't even know if I wanted to be.

"It couldn't have been easy for you. Dealing with that."

"Just another reason I didn't want to come back here," I said.

"We'll go to your headquarters tomorrow. I told Ray earlier."

"Thank you. You have no idea how helpful that is."

"I haven't been unaffected by... all of it." He slowed to a stop. "I'm sorry I didn't tell you about Ray sooner."

I stopped short. "That came out of nowhere."

"I have a list in my brain of things I need to apologize for."

"And things you expect me to apologize for, too, I'm sure." My eyes narrowed.

He laughed, his usual hoarse chuckle, and I knew it was true. "I *am* sorry."

"It's fine." It wasn't. But what more was there to say? It couldn't be changed. And I knew it was what Ray had asked for.

He nodded and started walking again. "For the longest time, my loyalty was to Ray and only Ray. I wanted you to still be... I wanted to believe I could trust you, but I wasn't sure how you'd react once you were told about the Order. And I'd already violated Ray's trust by bringing you back into all of this. So I told his lie. And I kept telling it. And by the time I'd decided where my allegiance belonged, only to you, I thought I'd lose you if I told you the truth." He took a deep breath. "I'm sorry. I never should have kept his secret."

I sighed. "Look, I get it. You're allowed to mess up, Kyp. Ray was the better choice if it was between him and Lavinia. But neither is the right choice."

"I..." He hesitated.

He pulled me to a stop and turned to face me again. This time, the lights from the estate windows were close enough to illuminate his tired eyes. "I don't understand. What do you mean?"

I took a deep breath and steeled myself. "Lavinia is a monster. Absolutely, one thousand percent. You know I'm not going to disagree with you there."

"Of course not."

"But Ray?" I said. "He's my father, and I've started to get to know him again this past year. I care about him. I really do. But he's not the good guy either. He led the Order into a civil war that decimated a large portion of his own side and Lavinia's and made them all vulnerable to interdimensional attack."

"Decisions are made in war," Kyp argued. "We can't always foresee what could happen."

"There was probably a better way to do it."

"You weren't there. You have no idea."

I'd touched a nerve. "That loyalty issue's gonna be hard to break, huh?"

"I didn't—I mean. Damn it, Jacklyn!" He turned bright red, fists clenching at his sides. It was adorable, but a little annoying.

"Both of them were disastrous to the Order. Ray just had his heart in the right place." It was something I'd been considering ever since Kyp told me the truth about the rebellion. "So disastrous that there's almost nothing left of the Order. If we don't start getting these rifts closed, there will be no Order left to do it. Then our real enemy wins."

"Don't you think I know that?" We were back to yelling. "When was I supposed to do that? You could. You *did*. You ran off and found a new crew. Suddenly you're all reckless. Ain't you fixin' for a good ol' fashioned shootin'?" He said that last little burst in a mock Texan accent that froze my blood.

I swallowed hard, cracking my knuckles one by one as I spoke through gritted teeth. "You have a problem with Austin?"

"I have a problem with you changing everything about who you are because your new team told you to. We're not in the Wild West, Jacks."

"The guns," I huffed. "That's the problem with you!"

"Does it matter if I want to know your opinion?" He loomed over me. "I don't think a

freight train could stop you."

"You play by the rules. The bad guys? They don't! We use swords and sais because of the Order's favorite line. 'It's how it's always been done.' Except they grab our swords from us. Sometimes they come into battle with weapons of their own. But things escalate. A damn Sirin held a gun to my head during our last battle, or have you forgotten that? If someone wants you dead, they're not going to hold back. If you want to beat darkness, you have to wallow in the muck yourself."

"Guns are different. It's too easy to harm a bystander or someone on your own side," he said.

"The first time I died, it was because someone used my own sword to kill me. You're too attached to the Order's antiquated traditions to change with the times."

Our eyes locked, our anger dancing around us, electricity in the air. Mere inches from each other. Our emotions toward each other were as intense as ever, but tinged with a different flavor.

My fists loosened. He leaned forward the slightest bit.

He turned back toward the house, slamming his hands into his pockets like he was restraining himself.

I followed his gaze to find most of the windows lit. I took a deep breath to calm myself. "Doesn't look like too many people are actually sleeping up there, does it?"

"Our lives dictate that sleep will not come easy for any of us. But it's not the number of people that are keeping me awake. It's actually easier when this place is full. It makes me less prone to sit up all night and play count the ghosts."

I smiled weakly. "You play that game too?"

"Maybe it's time for us to just give up and admit we're on the road to destruction." The look he sent my way was tinged with mischief.

"Not bloody likely." I grinned.

"One: you sound like Ray, and two: that's the Jacklyn I remember." He scowled at me, but his eyes smiled, and the return to camaraderie lifted my spirits.

"I get that we have different views as far as how our teams operate, but we'll find a middle ground," I said as we continued walking. "For right now, we'll worry about protecting these kids. And once we figure that out, we can decide where we go from there."

He nodded, opening the screen door for me. My breath

hitched the moment the white kitchen tiles came into view, my vision tunneling and energy spiking.

Kyp's fingers tangled with mine. I jumped at the contact and he clamped down on my hand. "You survived. You're safe. You're here."

He ushered me through the kitchen, his Aegis pulling the energy from mine.

"I gotta tell you," I said, my voice shakier than I liked. "I really wish I wasn't."

"In this house, or here at all?"

My throat seized up. "I... don't..."

We made it through the kitchen and out of the hall. Up the stairs. He never let go of my hand. He walked me all the way up to my bedroom door.

"You need to figure out the answer to that question, you know." His hand slipped from mine, and he turned toward his door.

He wasn't wrong. I didn't think I truly wanted to... not be there. But I wasn't the same as I had been. I didn't have hopes or plans for the future. No good ones, anyway. All I had planned was vengeance. But after that?

Was there anything after that?

"Kyp?" I called before he locked himself away from me for the rest of the night.

He barely cracked the door open enough that I could see him watching me with expectant eyes.

I fidgeted with the hem of my t-shirt. "For whatever it's

worth... and I'm sure it doesn't mean much..." I exhaled my next words in a rush of air. "I've missed you. I've missed just... just talking to you."

He smiled then, the kind that lit up his whole face, made his eyes shine, and was rarely bestowed upon anyone. "It's worth a lot. I've missed you too. Good night, Jacklyn."

"Good night, Kyp."

I closed my door behind me and climbed into my bed as quietly as I could, so as not to wake Ray. And if I pressed my hand against the wall, and if, maybe, I felt a little of Kyp's energy on the other side? Nobody needed to know that but us.

TEN

KYP

Kyp waited until his new team had made it through breakfast peacefully, albeit in various stages of wakefulness, before announcing his plan for the morning. The group was crowded into the dining area, a room that hadn't been used in a year. There hadn't been a point. When it had only been the three of them, they had eaten at the kitchen table.

"Today we will be splitting up into three groups," Kyp said when the general chatter in the room had died down.

"Guys, shhhh," Jacklyn said. "Boss man's talking." She rolled her eyes.

Kyp flashed her the finger, but ruined it with a smirk. "Yes, boss man *is* talking."

"Let me be the judge of that, yeah?" Ray said. "What's the plan?"

Jainey looked up from her plate eagerly. Though it had once been piled high with pancakes, it was completely clean now, aside from a small puddle of syrup. Her adorable button nose bore the evidence of her voracious appetite.

"Jainey, you've got syrup." He pointed at his nose.

She screwed her nose up as though she intended to lick it off before giving up and swiping it off with a chubby finger. She then, indelicately, shoved the digit into her mouth.

"You're cute, kiddo," Jacklyn proclaimed.

Jainey glanced around. "Wha—oh. Thanks, Mama."

Jacklyn's eyes went wide. Everyone at the table shared an uneasy glance, one that Jainey remained blissfully unaware of. She was too busy sticking her finger into the remaining syrup on her plate.

"Who made this?" Jainey asked.

"Um... I did, sweetheart," Ray said.

He'd woken up, woke Zane to stay with Jacklyn, cooked them all a fine meal, then switched with Zane so he could wake Jainey. Kyp had finally roused himself from his fleeting sleep about midway through the process.

"I've never eaten this before," Jainey said. "It's really good. Thanks."

"You are very welcome." Ray watched her with a bemused smile.

"Okay, back on track." Kyp smiled. "I got distracted by syrup-face."

Jainey continued mopping up her leftover syrup with her fingertips. "Well, focus is essential. If you lose your focus, how will your Aegis stay under control? You could hurt someone or yourself if you don't stop it from going off."

She didn't notice the group staring at her.

"Jainey, do you have to keep your Aegis under control at all times?" Kyp asked. He had started the meeting standing at the head of the table, but now he lowered himself into a chair.

"I just said that." Another finger-full of syrup.

"Like, you don't have to try hard to channel your Aegis?" Jacklyn asked. "Most times I run fast because I trained. But if I want to run *really* fast? I have to channel my Aegis."

Jainey stopped and looked up at her with a thoughtful hum. "Nope. That's what happened yesterday. I lost control and my Aegis got too loud."

Jacklyn looked at Kyp. He had no answers.

"Good to know." He didn't want to worry Jainey. "Anyway, here's our three groups. Zane, Drew, and Jainey, I want you guys working on tracking down any leads to the compound where Jordan and the other kids are being held. Jainey, they're gonna have a lot of questions for you, so do your best to answer what you can. It's all so we can find your brother. Understand?"

"Okay." She nodded, disheveled brown curls bouncing around her head.

"Cass and Austin, I need you to start packing up. Any important texts and weapons, load them in our truck or Ray's car. We'll need them when we move into Ray's place."

Cass and Austin agreed, although it was with thinned lips and averted gazes. Neither of them seemed to like the idea.

"And that leaves us." Kyp sat back in his seat. "Ray, Jacklyn. We need to pay a visit to Cxarana."

"No," Austin said. "Absolutely not."

"Excuse me?" This wasn't the time for insolence.

"Kyp, can it," Jacklyn said. "We talked about this. I get that it helps you to plan things when everything's going bonkers, which is the only reason I haven't said anything sooner, but you're not in charge here. We are a team. I told you my view of the Order long ago, and it was never about Keys leading Guardians. We're all supposed to be equal."

"Birdie, I told you—" Ray started.

"—it's always been done that way," she cut him off. "I know. But that way was crap. We're creating something different here. Or we're not doing this at all."

She was right. Kyp hated when she was right.

"It's in our training," Cass said, somewhat helplessly. "It's how we were born to—"

"Bullshit. And you know it," Jacklyn challenged. "You were taught to be subordinate, but you're not. If every non-Key person with an Aegis were born to be subordinate to Keys, then the gang in this room are examples of the world's worst anomalies. You guys are opinionated nightmares. And that's good. It's because none of us see you as subordinates." She glanced at Drew. "Though I don't know you yet. So I could be wrong about you."

"Nope. I'm definitely a nightmare." He grinned.

Kyp had to hand it to Drew. He knew how to make people love him. Even Kyp couldn't help but smile.

"Austin doesn't think we should go," Jacklyn said. "And since we're all trying to get along here, and we all have what's best for these kids at heart, you should listen to him."

Austin smiled wickedly at Kyp. "I'm her favorite."

Jacklyn kicked him hard enough under the table that the dishes jumped. Jainey looked up at her and scowled.

Zane reached around Austin to Cass. "Hey, you gonna eat that roll?"

Cass sighed deeply. "I guess not." She handed her the roll.

"Austin, state your opinion without being a total arse," Ray said.

Kyp hadn't expected Ray to defend him.

"I already did, but your boy ain't listening." Austin leaned back in his chair and folded his arms over his chest. "Y'all shouldn't go visit an Arvokian after what Jacklyn's told me about 'em."

Kyp's brow creased. "Which is?"

"That they sold you guys out the first time."

"Lavinia bought our play, at first," Jacklyn explained. "But before she called us in for that meeting in the morning, she'd received a visit from a member of the Arvokian Council."

The very idea nauseated Kyp. "No."

"Someone told her that we reported her."

"Not Cxarana." She was a batty old witch, but they had an understanding. He couldn't believe it could have been her.

"I don't know," she admitted. "All I know is she knew. She said she was blocking the Council, but she lied."

"Or" —Kyp thought about it for a moment— "she thought she was blocking them. But they lied to her."

"Also possible," Cass chimed in. "So how do we know which is true?"

Kyp didn't have an answer. He believed Cxarana wouldn't betray them, but he had no idea how to prove it.

"Exactly," Austin said. "We don't have any way to know. You could walk in there and expose us."

"What don't you want them to know?" Jainey asked, twirling a curl around her finger with the utmost concentration.

"Where we're going," Jacklyn said. "We don't want the lady from yesterday, Lavinia, or any of the people where you're from to know where Ray and I have been staying, so we can keep you safe there."

"And why do you have to see Zigzagarina?" She looked at Kyp.

He snorted a laugh. "Cxarana. I would like to see if she knows anything about you or your brother and if she can offer any leads on where we can find the other kids, so we can get them out of there."

"How do you know you can trust what she tells you?" she batted back.

"We don't," Austin said. "That's why we shouldn't go."

"But there's no harm in it, is there?" Jainey asked. "If I'm comprehending the facts, as long as you're not communicating any information about where we're going, a simple risk assessment would imply there is minimal chance of exposure."

"Holy crap." Zane shot an alarmed look between the two of them. "She's a mini you, Baby Franklin."

He ignored Zane. "There are risks that can be viewed as outliers. Cxarana has some abilities we don't quite understand. If we walk in knowing information she doesn't know, she could find out anyway."

"Then whoever goes shouldn't know where we're going." Jainey shrugged. "Maybe I should go."

"You're not going by yourself," Kyp said. "You don't have a clue how to handle Cxarana."

"But you could go, too. You don't know where we're going, Kyp," Drew said. "Do you?"

He blinked. "No."

"You don't?" Jacklyn said. "I thought... you just didn't... go there."

What the hell? Had she wanted him to come for her? Ray had told him she couldn't see him. He'd thought that was true. But he hadn't asked her himself, had he? He'd trusted Ray at his word. And maybe that was his problem. Always trusting Ray at his word.

"That true?" Austin asked. He scratched at a healing wound on his arm. "How'd you get Ray to come here and help Jacks?"

Zane leaned forward in her chair. "He had Cass get in touch

with me. I told her. We took steps to keep Lavinia from figuring out how to contact Raymond."

"Are you sure you don't know?" Ray asked. "I know I didn't tell you, kiddo, but if you have even an inkling, you need to tell us."

Kyp straightened. He needed to project confidence, even if the truth was a bit humiliating. "I never managed to figure it out. I know you're in New York City. That's as targeted as I got."

"Let's make a deal." Jainey held out a hand for him to shake, standing up and half climbing onto the table so she could reach his hand from where she sat beside Drew. "Mama and Grandpa Ray can help him" —she pointed at Austin— "and Cass pack up. They're both strong. They can probably carry a lot."

"And?" Kyp asked.

Her mouth screwed up.

"You said it was a deal. What's the other part?" he asked.

"Oh, yeah." She nodded sharply. "I'll let you pull whatever answers I can give you about the facility from my brain." She shrugged, the collar of the enormous t-shirt she'd borrowed from Cass sliding off her shoulder.

"I did that when you first came," Kyp said.

"Nope." Another shrug. "You only saw what I wanted you to see."

"Sure, Jainey." Kyp rolled his eyes. "You weren't locking me out of anything. I would have been able to tell. It would have taken effort that would have been easy for me to sense."

"Not for me." She slid back off the table and picked up her plate. "Cass, may I take your plate? It looks like you're done."

Cass nodded, but she looked as unnerved as Kyp felt. The plates clanged as Jainey piled them together, then walked into the kitchen to place them in the sink. Once she was out of range, Jacklyn turned her head slowly toward Kyp. She mouthed an over-emphasized "Wooooow."

Ray shook his head with a snort. He pushed back his chair, the wood creaking. "This is why I long ago decided the Madisons and Franklins shouldn't breed together." He collected the rest of the dishes. "Thanks for reversing that decision for us."

Kyp and Jacklyn shot him a perverse hand gesture in unison.

Ray joined Jainey in the kitchen. The rest of them waited until the water started to run before anybody dared speak.

"So," Drew said. "We're going with her plan, yes?"

Ray chanted in Arvokian to begin the Ritual to open the entrance to the temple.

Jacklyn volunteered to mash the violet Shula leaves with a mortar and pestle because, as she said, "destruction is more my thing." She wrinkled her nose as she poured in the Ropslankin tincture. It smelled awful.

"Gross," Jainey complained from beside Kyp.

Kyp snorted. "Wait 'till she sets it on fire."

As if on cue, Jacklyn lit the mixture on fire, and Jainey grabbed her nose.

Kyp knelt in front of her in an attempt to pull her attention back to him.

"Remember, you have to stay one step ahead of Cxarana. That's true normally, but especially when we're trying to keep a secret from her. Be careful," Kyp said.

Jacklyn piped up from where the entryway now stood. The grass that was once in their backyard rolled back like a carpet to reveal a pit. "If she doesn't want to listen, you can always threaten her with the old slice and dice."

"Or pelt her with rocks," Ray added. "There's a lot of them down there."

"That isn't funny," Kyp scolded. "She needs to know how to properly—"

Jacklyn knelt in front of the girl, hands on her shoulders. "Be cool. Take no crap. Give nothing away. You've got this." She maneuvered her toward the opening in the ground before turning to Kyp. "You're driving *me* crazy and I'm not the one going in there. Chiiiiiiilll."

"Yes," Kyp said. "Let's be lax about watching our every move. That's worked so well in the past."

The look Jacklyn flashed him was glacial.

Kyp walked past her and headed for the pit, standing beside Jainey. "Ready?"

"Yes." She looked up at him with big, round eyes. "We've got this."

Her hopeful gaze doused the acid in his stomach. "You're

right. I just worry too much. Promise." He lowered himself down into the pit, his foot catching on the first rung. "Follow me."

Together, they made their way down the ladder and into the cold, fire-lit cavern of the Arvokian Temple. Their steps echoed as they walked, and they'd only taken a couple before Jainey reached for his hand, jamming hers into his without so much as a questioning glance. Her dark eyes were zeroed in on the end of the long, narrow hallway with its walls of craggy rocks.

"Mr. Franklin." Cxarana's wispy voice floated disembodied, as it always did when they first entered the cave. Sometimes he wondered if it was a deterrent to avoid an Order member walking in on an Arvokian with their feet up, watching TV and eating a pizza. Couldn't have them barging in and ruining the illusion of indifference.

"Hello, Cxarana," Kyp greeted.

"What have you brought for me today?" Her voice fluttered Jainey's curls, and the child slapped her hand down onto them, glaring at the empty space beside her. "A Guardian to be?"

Cxarana appeared before them, almost elven in appearance with her tall, slender physique, long limbs, and bruise-colored skin. Her eggshell white hair was braided across the top of her head, shorter hairs waving in the ever-present breeze of the cavern. Her night-black, fishlike eyes glittered in the firelight.

"She's a bit young for a Guardian pledge, is she not?" she rasped, eyes on Jainey.

Jainey stiffened, looking like she was one hiccup away from

bolting.

"Recruiting children was never below the Order," Kyp said. "I was taught to fight at a young age and was never shielded from the evils of war."

Cxarana made a high-pitched humming noise. "You knew better than that."

Kyp snorted a laugh. "Better than what, exactly? I'm not even certain which side you're on."

Another hum. "She favors your paramour."

"Jacklyn is *not* my paramour," Kyp said firmly. "And that isn't the point."

"Fair skin, dark curly hair, rounded cheeks... She has your eyes though, Mr. Franklin."

"Cxarana," Kyp growled.

Jainey released an overly exaggerated yawn. "This is boring. Yes, Jacklyn and Kyp are my parents. That's why we're here."

Cxarana's lips twitched. "How shocking. Sarcasm from Jacklyn Madison's child."

"You should be shocked," Kyp said. "Any child of ours shouldn't even be old enough to walk yet."

Cxarana turned on her heel and waved a hand in their direction. "And yet, she can walk just fine. Follow me."

Kyp placed a hand on Jainey's back and motioned her forward.

They stepped deeper into the cave to the place where Keys were sworn in. A large marble table stood in the center of the space, a gold dagger and bowl resting atop it.

"You've come to learn how she came to be?" Cxarana asked.

"Yes."

"I would need a blood sample."

"She will provide it."

Jainey frowned. "I'm right here."

"We are aware, child." Cxarana bent to take a closer look at her face, one long, spindly finger running across her jaw. "She was grown from natural roots." Cxarana sauntered around the table, hips swaying. She lifted the ceremonial gold dagger and approached her, point forward. "But something different was added. An ingredient I cannot recognize on sight alone."

"Um, Papa?" Jainey backed into Kyp. "D-did nobody ever teach her knife safety?"

Cxarana made an odd stuttering sound that may have been a laugh. "I will not harm you, but I do need a blood sample." She took Jainey's small hand between her long, pointy fingers. "I'm going to poke you with the dagger, only enough to make you bleed a drop."

Jainey looked up at Kyp. "She's gonna make me bleed, but she's not going to hurt me?"

"It will be a tiny finger prick. Promise."

Jainey's hand shook within Cxarana's. She hissed as the dagger punctured the tip of her finger. A tiny bubble of blood appeared and Cxarana's snake-like tongue licked it up.

"Ew!" Jainey yanked her hand back and glared at Cxarana. Her head pushed against Kyp's chest like she was trying to move right through him.

"Senefestrian," hissed from between Cxarana's lips.

Like a computer, Kyp accessed any memories connected with that word. "A species of interdimensional that doesn't journey here. Mostly because they're far too large to fit through rifts." He glanced at the child. "She's a little small to be a Senefestrian. And a little too human. I've never seen them before, though I know they don't shapeshift." Kyp flipped through his memories, looking for anything about humanoid Senefestrians and found nothing. But there were other important facts. "Their blood has healing properties. The Order used to go to the Dusk to harvest their blood whenever they found and killed one to use for teams that didn't have a healer."

"You realize this is much less fun when you rattle facts off in that dead cadence," Cxarana teased gently. "The child is not Senefestrian, of course. The child is the Skeleton Key."

"Not *the* Skeleton Key. *A* Skeleton Key. There's more than one," Kyp said.

Jainey looked back at him, confused. "What does that mean?"

"You're the child of two Keys," he explained. "It's extremely rare."

"Extremely," Cxarana agreed. "It's only happened once in history. It isn't spoken of because of the identity of the mother." She leaned forward, like she was telling a campfire tale. "She was a half-breed. The product of an Arvokian and a human Key. They also don't talk about how she survived labor. Her Arvokian half needed to be within our pocket dimension to survive. We Arvokians are not so strong outside of it."

Kyp thoughtlessly cracked his knuckles as his mind worked through the information. "She wasn't born naturally. A lab intervened without our consent. They're creating them."

Cxarana nodded. "And they're using Senefestrian blood to aid in their creation."

"I don't understand," Kyp said. "Are they using Senefestrian blood to help the child develop enough to be able to live outside of the womb?"

"No." Cxarana shook her head. "The reason a Key cannot bear a Skeleton Key is because of a power imbalance. The woman is expected to bear an Aegis that is native to her but has double the power. That same woman is often also expected to bear an unfamiliar Aegis, that of the child's father, within her. It is too much for the woman's body to handle, and as the child's power grows, it overshadows the mother's. The mother's Aegis is lost to the child's, or the mother is overwhelmed by that which grows within her."

Jainey perked up beside him. "Would that power issue continue after childbirth? Like would the mother and the child still feel... I dunno... *off*, power wise?"

Cxarana produced a rag from behind the stone bowl's stand and cleaned the dagger. "I imagine it would, in full-blooded humans. It's hard to say."

"Jordan," Jainey breathed. "He has power bursts. He goes into overload."

"Like you did yesterday," Kyp confirmed. "With that dog whistle thing you did in everyone's minds."

And Jacklyn. She was still affected. It was probably what caused the power surges that accompanied her anxiety attacks.

Jainey nodded, chewing the inside of her cheek.

Cxarana stepped further into her cavern, stopping at a small herb garden. Arvokian herbs didn't need light to grow because there was no light in the Dusk, their natural home.

"Senefestrian blood can do two things, depending on how it is treated after harvest," Cxarana explained as she began to tend to her plants. "In its raw form, it can do untold damage to the cells of a Key. Damage that no Ritual could reverse."

Kyp nearly gasped. "It could kill a Key?"

"Depending on how much enters the bloodstream, yes," Cxarana said. "It is the only thing stronger than the Ritual of the Unburdening."

The only thing that could disconnect a Key permanently from the cycle of its life without its consent.

"Why didn't I know this?" he asked.

"Please do not ask me to explain your shortcomings," she said. "I imagine you would find this information in your books, if you researched deeper."

Kyp doubted that. Highly. He wasn't sure if Cxarana was lying to him or if Cxarana had been played as soundly as he had.

"The blood requires treatment by some of our herbs to take

on its healing qualities. It breaks down the" —her head tipped— "cellular structure, I believe is the phrase. I do not have to speak of complex science in your English often. It can break it down or, if treated, accelerate its growth. In her, I'd imagine it is singularly responsible for her advanced age."

"Is the Senefestrian blood all you" —Kyp searched his words for a minute— "came up with from her sample?"

"Aside from the obvious, yes," Cxarana said. "Though she was created through unnatural means, she is undoubtedly real." She smiled at Jainey. "Welcome to the Order of the Key, young one. It will be interesting to see what you bring to our world."

Jainey beamed. It was good that she was happy, but Cxarana's pronouncement made Kyp nervous for another reason.

"No reading? No poetic sendoff?"

"Unfortunately, I cannot read her," Cxarana said. "Perhaps the synthetic nature of her birth is interfering. However, if you wish for a poetic sendoff, I shall provide one." She leaned forward, pressing one hand to each of their foreheads. "I have cared for your father since he was a child, my dear new Key. His course is the course I follow. His course is that which I believe in. The Order of the Key will be mighty, and it will be your legacy." She straightened. "And that is no deception." She met Kyp's eyes with her own, the golden rimmed blackness shimmering wetly. "Child. Please head for the ladder. Your father will be with you shortly."

Jainey glanced between the two of them, her eyes wide and frightened. Kyp nodded his approval, and she ran for the ladder, likely grateful for the exit.

Once she was out of sight, Cxarana stepped closer, her cheek pressing to Kyp's, the sensation like tissue paper against his skin.

"You are my friend," she whispered, voice crisp as the dried leaves Jainey crunched through before they'd come here. "I believe you know that. My people have indeed betrayed you, but I will not. I have allowed myself to care too deeply for this generation of humans. It is a choice that has not been well met by the Arvokian Council." She pulled back, taking his hand in hers. "Be well, Mr. Franklin."

His heart sank with fear for Cxarana, for what her pronouncement could mean about the Arvokian Council and her own safety. He wanted to bring her with him, to protect her. He didn't know how he could.

Instead, he pressed a gentle hand to her cheek and smiled. "Be well, Cxarana."

He dreaded what he would discover the next time he visited.

ELEVEN

KYP

Kyp didn't know why he'd walked out this way, or why he'd asked Ray to join him. It wasn't a smart idea to discuss anything weighty before a mission, especially one where he was the star of the show, the man entering the battlefield. But the rest of the team had decided to take a walk on the beach. It was cold, but also exciting. None of them got the chance to see the ocean often.

For a moment, when everyone had piled out of the car, it had just been him and Jacklyn. She had turned to him and said, "When this is over, you should come travel with us. We closed rifts in Tanzania, Italy, Taiwan… even one on a little island off the Honduran coast." She smiled at him, and it lit him up despite everything. "The world is beautiful."

He'd sighed. "But I bet the evil is all the same." End of conversation.

He found a rickety bench and settled on it, kicking his feet through the sand, watching the grains drop from the grips in the soles of his boots.

"So you figured it out," Ray muttered, stepping up behind Kyp. "Had memories you needed to hash out?"

Kyp knew this place, but in his mind, it was different. In his memories, there were flashing lights, and the sand was almost painfully hot on the soles of his feet. But some things were the same, even in the winter. The somewhat unsteady wood of the boardwalk, the roar of the surf, the rotting benches, the smell of the salt water. This was where Ray had taken Kyp and Jacklyn on the day he had told them he had to leave.

Ray walked around the bench to stand in front of Kyp, hands jammed into the pockets of khaki-colored cargo pants. He almost looked the same. Though his face was slightly lined and his dark curls were now threaded with silver, he was still the same man that had left Kyp crying on this exact bench when he was only five years old.

Kyp's knees shook. He almost didn't have the strength to say what he'd come here to say. "What happened to you? You've changed. You're... darker than I remember."

Ray propped himself against the bench. When he answered, his voice was laced with disbelief. "Tragedy after tragedy, Kyp. Did you think revolution was easy?"

Kyp's throat was a bottlenecked tunnel entrance. "Why didn't you tell me about the baby?"

He tipped his head back, teeth gritted. "Come on, Jacklyn

already explained this to you."

"I'm not asking Jacklyn," Kyp said sharply. "I'm asking you."

"This. This goddamned beach! You remember everything about what happened here. I couldn't hurt you like that again. Give you the hope of a child, only to let you remember losing it in vividly colored detail every day."

Kyp stood. "I could have helped her."

"And how would you have done that?"

"I don't know. By being there?"

"She didn't want you there," Ray said. "You think you can fix it with her, but every time you just muck it all up. It was time for you to stay where you were. Let her help herself."

"And that worked?" Kyp asked. Because if it had, maybe he wouldn't feel like he'd failed so horribly. His throat hurt as if he'd swallowed lit matches.

Ray sighed. "Not all the way. She's broken up, but less 'an she was. Her mood is pitch black. She emphatically does not give a shit. That's who she is now."

"I find I'm not much better," Kyp said. "But we care about the children."

"Shame about them, really," Ray said, kicking at a rock sticking up from the sand. "Created just to be pawns in this damned war. It'd be better if things had stayed as they were."

Kyp blinked. "The way they were?"

"The children weren't meant to survive," Ray clarified. "Would that not be better than being forced to be part of a war they can't win?"

Kyp didn't lose control. He just swung. He didn't even think about it, though he didn't regret it. Ray's eyes widened in shock and it was all the fuel he needed to follow through. The feeling of his knuckles meeting Ray's jaw was satisfying. So was his stumble backwards.

"How fucking dare you? You'd rather they were dead than forced to be pawns in somebody else's war? You made Jacklyn a pawn! You made me a pawn!" Kyp's voice was acid, burning through his throat, splashing Ray with his pain.

This time, when Kyp hit him, Ray spilled backwards onto his ass in the sand, his face a bloodless mask of shock. A cut formed on his cheek and healed nearly as quickly as it appeared.

The pained look in Ray's eyes told Kyp he didn't even disagree.

"I've been blaming myself for Jaina and Gana's deaths and everything that's happened to Jacklyn. It was easier to blame myself, but it isn't on me, is it? It's on you," he growled, grabbing Ray by his chin and forcing him to look him dead in the eye. "You left me with a monster, left Jacks with no idea of who she was or what was in store. And you called us your children!"

"I love you both." His voice was flat and emotionless.

"I'm not sure you know how to love anybody." Kyp released his face and turned his back to him, looking over his shoulder. "I've been wanting to shout at you for a long time. I don't think I knew why until this moment. You made a mess of us. I hope you're prepared to stick around long enough to fix it this time."

Kyp prayed he hadn't just wasted his breath trying to make Ray a better parent.

Most of the team watched from the boardwalk, except Zane, who rushed forward to help Ray. Kyp's eyes flicked to Jacklyn. She had an arm out, holding Austin back. He didn't know if Jacklyn agreed with what he'd done, but she hadn't stopped him, either. That had to mean something.

They stood in front of a rickety blue house, braving the cutting winds of the shore as they blew inland. It made sense that Ross bought a house near this beach. The families in the Order used to come out here often in better days. Ross would find himself at home here.

Kyp glanced at Drew and wished Cass was there. It may have been insensitive, but she'd been his right hand for so long, and he always felt a little less prepared without her. However, she was now Jainey's protector, and Jainey needed her more than he did.

The house was quaint, painted with a nautical theme; white siding was offset by navy blue awnings above each window. The porch was also bright white, and an American flag had been whipped around so hard in the wind it had completely curled around itself, more of a staff painted in the country's colors than a symbol of freedom and patriotism. A picture window gave way to the view of a red chaise lounge chair that beckoned for him to take a load off, sit down and read, take in the sunlight. He imagined, in the summer, it was quite the slice of Americana. It was a shame he wouldn't return after today.

Kyp wasn't afraid. He had backup. He just didn't know what to expect.

He and Drew walked up the paved drive leading to the house. Before his feet had even touched the stairs, the door inched open.

"Don't climb another step, Kyp Franklin, or I swear I will shoot you dead."

He froze. Kylie aimed a shotgun through the gap in the door.

"Ugh, it figures," Jacklyn hissed into the earpiece she had forced on him before they'd separated. She was stationed close by, waiting to intervene if necessary.

"Kylie, you can put the gun away."

"Why should I?" she asked, face shrouded in shadow. "After what you did to me? I should shoot you for target practice."

She was probably right. "Sorry, Kylie. I didn't bring flowers, but I do need to speak to you. We may have the same interests at heart this time around."

"I have nothing in common with you." Her voice was high and reedy.

"I was fighting for my life and Cass' life. I was fighting to get back to Jacklyn. We both did what we had to do. But things are different now. Lavinia is no longer breathing down our necks. We can make our own choices. Why don't you let me in and we can sit down and talk?"

"I'm not having a little tête-à-tête with the man who destroyed my face."

That piqued Kyp's curiosity. He didn't think he was guilty of whatever she thought he was guilty of.

"What are you afraid of, exactly?" Kyp asked. He glanced at Drew, who remained silent and focused on the barrel of the gun. "If you don't want to come out, you could send Ross to come talk to us. That's who I really want to speak with, anyway."

"Oh, I'm not important enough for you now?" Kylie asked. "After using me to shut your mother up for years?"

"You used me just as much." He shrugged. "I already tried to talk to you. You have nothing to be afraid of. It's you and Ross and a shotgun versus me and my new associate here, Drew."

"So the gun makes you outnumbered? Do you think I'm stupid?" Her voice was shrill as ever, but frayed at the ends.

Kyp resolved to give her a chance to take him down, so she'd feel a little more at home. And to do that, he had to be the one thing he was really good at being.

"I don't think you're stupid. Just not as smart as me."

A jackass.

He almost expected a gunshot to the chest. Drew even flinched beside him. But, as he'd hoped, a trace of his trademark arrogance reminded her of the somewhat thin track record they shared as allies. She lowered the gun.

"Fine. Come in. What do I have to lose?" She stepped out of their way.

Kyp and Drew walked up the rest of the creaking wooden

stairs leading up to the house. The closer Kyp got, the more of Kylie he saw and the clearer her meaning from earlier became. A jagged pink scar stretched from her forehead to the tip of her chin. Her other cheek was littered with pock marks. Bite marks. Gorvhan bites.

Sometimes, fate made your outsides match your insides. One side of him could brush it off as that. The side of him that sounded less like Mother made him want to cry, knowing the damage had been his doing.

"He's in," Jacklyn reported into the headset to where Ray, Austin, and Zane waited in the car. "I will wait one full minute and then we'll start working our way in."

Because they weren't going to trust Kylie Robertson at her word.

The inside of the house was summery and warm. The floors were hardwood, the furniture appearing staged, unlived in, and quite possibly unused since 1980. They must have bought the place furnished, because this was not Kylie's style. The giant white couch, peppered with blue flowers, accompanied by a matching recliner, stood out starkly. Kylie probably despised it.

"I love your couch." He made himself at home, settling down on it and kicking his feet up on the glass-topped coffee table just to watch her seethe.

"Would you like something to drink?" she sneered. "I'm sure I have some poison I can slip you."

"He'll decline," Drew said from where he was stationed by

the door.

"I wasn't speaking to the help," Kylie snipped.

"Rephrase that?" Kyp asked.

"No." Kylie didn't miss a beat. "You hate me. Enough to make Gorvhans eat my face. But you obviously need me enough to break bread with me. I don't think niceties are necessary here."

A whispered swear echoed in his earpiece. Kyp couldn't make out who had said it, but he felt the judgment deep in his soul.

"I hadn't intended... I didn't mean for them to do permanent damage to you. When I took control of them, I only had them attack you. I needed them to hold you off long enough for me to keep Cass safe and get the hell back to Jacklyn and Gana." It was an inadequate apology, but what kind of flowers do you send someone when you've left them for dead?

"Ah, yes. It all comes back to Jacklyn. You know the funny thing?" Kylie said. "I would have chosen your side."

Something twisted low in his gut. "What?"

"I hate Lavinia. I would have had your back, had you bothered to clue me in on anything that was happening." She rested the shotgun against the wall and paced closer, slowly. "You lost your shot when you sold me out."

"I haven't lost my shot yet." He nearly winced at his own arrogance. "You didn't slam the door in my face."

She sat on the edge of the coffee table. "I'm hoping whatever it is you have to say will benefit me somehow."

"For what it's worth, I truly believed you would either be able to hold them off, or they would kill you and you'd come back. I did not expect this."

It was hard to look at her. It looked painful, what they had done to her. And he had been responsible. Once a wound was a scar, it was with a Key forever.

"Go to hell, Kyp. Just tell me what you want."

"Don't you want to call Ross down first?" He gestured toward the pale wood staircase that curved around to the upper floor.

"He's at work," she said.

"That's my cue," Jacklyn said through the earpiece. "I'm going in."

"Work?" Kyp huffed a laugh, playing his role. "Ross has a job now?"

"Yes, people need money to live, rich boy," Kylie said. "You may have the entire Order's wallet at your fingertips, but most people have to work."

"True." Kyp nodded. "Or they could just use a dead Order member's financial information." He smiled. "It's how we found the house."

She swore. "Of course it is." She sighed. "What do you want?"

"I want to know where Ross works."

"I don't know," she groaned. "And I don't want to know. He goes somewhere in upstate New York for two weeks, then he's home for a week. I told him that was all I wanted to know when he mentioned something about Key genes. I'm done with all of this. I don't want a duty or a destiny."

The idea was familiar. Kyp had always wanted to live a normal life. But there were steps to be taken. "So what? You pretend it doesn't exist, and it goes away? You know that's not how this works."

"You don't want to stop the Gorvhans?" Drew asked. He'd been silent the whole time, letting Kyp lead the conversation. "If they'd done that to me, I would want to hurt them."

"Not the point," Kylie said. "You're new here, so you clearly don't get there's always more to it than that. The Order comes with its own set of manipulations and indoctrinations. One day, you think you're going to help save the world and the next day, you're following orders to kill people. It's not just what happened to my face making me want to get away from this."

Her voice shook as she spoke, and Kyp found himself riveted. And also, a little afraid.

"What if I told you I want to end it too?"

"What are you doing? This is way too far off-book," Jacklyn snapped.

"What are you talking about?" Kylie asked.

"I wanted control of the Order so I could end it," Kyp said. "That's why Mother didn't want me in charge. Because I wanted to seal the rifts and end this. And she wanted her Aegis more than she wanted a normal life."

"Are you trying to bring her in? Have you lost your mind?" Jacklyn said in the earpiece. "Her allegiances are too messy. Don't let her guilt trip you into giving a damn."

Kylie leaned forward and put her head in her hands. She let out a deep sigh. "Oh, my dear boy toy, I would love to help, but I don't think I currently have much fight in me."

He hated himself for having to push. He knew this feeling. It was why he hadn't closed a rift, even without Lavinia holding him back. His heart hadn't really been in it. All he'd wanted was to end his mother's reign of terror. And now, all he wanted was to help the children. If he could close rifts and give kids like Jainey a safer life, then he'd do it. But it wasn't his mission the way it once was.

Mother had destroyed all that.

"Then don't fight," he said. "You don't have to lift a finger. Just help us. Tell us what you know about Ross' job. Please."

"And what?" Kylie sneered. "You'll protect me from Lavinia? Like you protected the Madisons?"

He tensed. "I didn't see you rushing to help them."

"Who would have protected me if I had?" she asked. "I know very little. Like I said, I didn't want to get involved. All he told me is that science can do more for us than any Arvokian Ritual ever could."

"Science cannot duplicate what we are capable of," Kyp countered.

"Yet," Kylie said. "There are studies and Ross is assisting. He's helping so we have a chance. A future."

Kyp's eyes narrowed. A future. The only kind of future these people seemed to be interested in was… oh. "A child. You want a child? With Ross?"

She blinked. Twice. "I regularly perform a Mind Block Ritual."

"I didn't read your mind, Kylie." He leaned back in his chair. He was so damn exhausted. "I seem to have acquired a daughter. That daughter was created at a facility. A man named Ross works there. That coupled with you discussing the future? You want a child."

"Not... like... now. Eventually." She flushed.

"With Ross," Kyp said again. "I thought he was just convenient for you."

She glanced away, swallowing hard. "He was, at first. Then he still looked at me like I was me. Even scarred. And I realized he was more than convenient."

It was like a punch in the stomach. He didn't want to care about Kylie, but he did. He'd known her all his life. Their relationship was strained, but there was something almost familial there, the twisted interplay between members of the same brutally dysfunctional family.

She frowned. "Look, all I know is this is bigger than Lavinia. Bigger than all of us. So please don't ask me to help you anymore. There is nothing else I can give you that won't take more away from me. And I think you've taken enough already."

"Please. You can't be okay with letting secretive activities involving Key blood happen. I grew up with you. I know you're better than that." She'd said she would have sided with him. Maybe there was still a chance. Maybe she and Ross could be saved.

Maybe he was too much of an idealist for his own good.

"You always expect the best in people," she muttered as she rose to her feet. "No. I will not be helping you any further. Whatever you've taken from this conversation is all you're getting. In the meantime, while you're playing lead interrogator, you better hope the child you mentioned is somewhere very safe. She'll either end up as a tool or she'll end up just like that flighty whore Jaina, that big-mouthed fool Jacklyn, or that uptight bitch Gana." She blew the door open behind them. "Dead on your watch."

Kyp gritted his teeth. He was surprised to find he was disappointed in her.

"Kyp, report," Jacklyn said into the earpiece. "I'm out. I got what we needed but... Kyp, report!"

"Look at you." Kylie's head tipped sideways in pity. "You look so sad." She placed a hand on Kyp's arm. A cool breeze picked up in the living room, blowing the curtains. "Kyp, you really have to stop believing in people. It'll keep you alive longer."

Drew stepped between them, breaking the connection. "Girl, you need to keep your hands to yourself."

"Kyp, report!" Jacklyn shout-whispered in his ear. "Report NOW."

Kylie smiled and looked around him at Kyp. The breeze got stronger, lifting a takeout menu that had been sitting on the coffee table, whipping it toward the door. The next burst of air was a gale force, and it ripped Drew away from him and through the exit.

"Do yourself a favor and never let me see your face again."

Kyp was running for the door before he heard the collision. His feet were still moving when another gust of air forced him to grasp the door frame to stop himself, his body halfway through the exit. Austin, because of course Austin, had caught Drew and crashed to the ground, both of them winded and battered for it.

Jacklyn stood beside them, chin raised defiantly. "Kyp. Out of the house."

Kylie used her control over the wind to shove him forward, his feet struggling to keep up, so he made it down the stairs without tripping all the way down.

She stepped out of the doorway, a smirk twisting her face. "Well, Jacklyn. Here you are, alive."

Jacklyn returned the smirk, but her eyes were black and empty. "No thanks to you."

Kyp stepped aside, though he knew he shouldn't. He knew Jacklyn had heard everything Kylie said through their earpieces.

With merely a snap of her fingers, the front of the house went up in flames.

"Jacks! No!" Kyp shouted and reached out instinctively, but Jacklyn batted his hand aside as if swatting a bug.

Kylie shrieked when her sweatpants caught fire. It took a moment before she seemed to remember she was a Light Element Key and channeled her water Aegis. Drew rushed to add his water to hers.

"What the hell is he doing?" Jacklyn yelled as Austin silently looked at her for guidance. She whirled on Kyp. "She doesn't need our help. She controls water and air. She can put that fire out in no time."

"Kylie!" Kyp turned his back on Jacklyn and took a step toward the blaze, which had now caught on the wooden beams of the house and was spreading. "Smother the fire!"

"Are you frickin' kidding?" Jacklyn shoved him hard, and if he hadn't been prepared, he would have toppled over.

Kylie and Drew were getting the fire under control, but Jacklyn wasn't finished. Her face was red, her eyes like a flickering candle. She leaned into Kyp's space and he stepped back. He couldn't gauge what she would do next.

"Get your arses to the car!" Ray shouted into their earpieces.

"Is this what your word means?" Kylie asked Kyp. "Is this what it means to trust you and your team?"

"You didn't trust us much in return," he answered. "And Jacklyn is... an unstable element."

Jacklyn whirled to face Kylie. "You held them back so she could kill my sister. You don't deserve to live, and the only damn thing keeping you alive right now is Kyp." She glared at him. "So you better cherish it, because I've imagined twisting you up in a knot and tossing you out in the garbage since the day I laid eyes on you, so he's doing you a helluva favor."

"This has gotten out of control," Ray said again. "I want you all back here, now."

"My deal still stands," Kyp said. "I will protect you from

Lavinia."

"And who's gonna protect me from her?" Kylie asked. She shook her head. "No matter. Come at me again, Jacklyn, and I'll remind you all about our last fight and why you lost."

Jacklyn snarled, and Kyp caught her by the elbow.

"Ray is calling," he whispered.

Jacklyn glared at him.

She looked from him back to Kylie, her muscles tensed, her entire body leaning toward Kylie.

"Jacks," he whispered.

"Fine!" She turned on her heel and stormed toward the car, her anger on the verge of bursting free at the slightest provocation.

Kyp closed his eyes and prayed Kylie would keep her mouth shut until they were gone.

Drew and Austin followed, the awkward silence extending to them. Kyp kept an eye on Kylie until he'd closed the car door behind him.

"What the fuck was that?" Ray shouted, speeding the car out of its parking spot.

"Don't start," Jacklyn snapped.

"What happened was we were working on a ceasefire, until Jacklyn stormed in and ruined it," Drew said.

"Kylie blasted you out the front door!" Austin argued.

Kyp stared openly at Jacklyn. He wasn't even sure who he was seeing anymore. "You weren't protecting Drew," Kyp muttered. "You enjoyed every damn minute of that. When did you start enjoying the bloodshed?"

"I don't know," she fired back. "When did you start feeding people to Gorvhans?"

Kyp turned away from her, arms crossed. He knew he looked like a petulant child.

"I don't enjoy it. But if death's going to be hanging around so much, we might as well get better acquainted."

Kyp focused his attention out the window. He couldn't bear to look at her.

"I can't be your good influence, Kyp. These days I'm in need of a good influence of my own."

He knew. He'd seen it in her eyes when she'd set Kylie's house on fire.

He wasn't sure he could be her good influence, either.

Twelve

Jacklyn

My son was being held at a facility off Boardman Creek in Ithaca, New York. A four-hour drive upstate. We'd figured it out based on the information I'd stolen from Ross' house. He had created a Google account under a fake name, and the maps app had directed him to that address repeatedly.

My boy was four hours away. I was going to rescue him.

Kyp sat beside me on the car ride, observing me. I ran a cleaning cloth over my Glock 45 and checked the parts to make sure they were properly lubricated. I examined it closely as I reassembled it, making sure everything was correctly placed.

I didn't allow my gaze to drift to his until I was finished. His eyebrows pulled together, but his shoulders leaned back and away, as if he wasn't sure if he wanted to learn more about the gun or cower from it.

I sighed. "Do you know why I carry it?"

He frowned. "Because it's easier? If you don't have to use

martial arts or fight training, you don't have to expend your Aegis."

I hadn't expected him to understand, but I still found myself disappointed. "So close, but not quite." I picked the gun up, letting my finger slide against the metal. "Most times that's true. For certain shots, I still need to use my Aegis to aim."

"Austin and Zane don't." He tipped his head toward where Austin sat up front with Ray.

"If you have a tool at your disposal that guarantees the bullet hits the bullseye, you use it. And I often fight and use my Aegis in the same battles I use my guns in."

"Then why do you carry it?"

"Because it doesn't falter. I can't rely on my Aegis, so I found something I *could* rely on. I will never be powerless again."

He looked away, staring out the window like he couldn't bear to look at the gun *or* me. I tried not to get angry. Plenty of people were uncomfortable with guns. Hell, I used to be one of those people.

Strange how trauma could change you. I thought my life had been hard before. I'd had no idea.

"For what it's worth, I'm sorry," I said. "For ruining whatever you were trying to do with Kylie."

He nodded, but remained silent. He hadn't spoken to me much since the car ride back to the brownstone last night.

"You okay, kiddo?" Kyp asked Jainey. She was strapped into a car seat, and hating every minute of it.

"I'm fine," she dismissed. "Please remember what we talked

about?"

All morning, she'd made a point of telling us how nice Ross had been to her during her captivity. She wasn't sure if it was Jordan or Ross that had left the note that told her where to find us.

That meant we might owe Ross for her appearance in our lives.

Didn't mean we were going to take it easy on him.

We'd spent the night before examining the blueprints to the main building, an old research lab that had been defunded by the nearby college.

I'd wanted to just show up. Kyp argued against it. Zane had noted the presence of proximity alarms set up around the main building that would alert everyone to our presence and put the building in lockdown. If we barged in, we ran the risk of alerting them before we were ready.

We chose to break into a storage shed on the property where supply deliveries were housed. It wasn't protected by the proximity alarms, which made it the best spot to wait for an entrance into the facility. The actual breaking in would be simple enough. Jainey didn't even have to break a sweat to make the guards take a nap. It was as simple as breathing for her.

It didn't make me feel better about bringing her along, but she was right about one thing. If Ross had been trying to protect her, and if I had made the situation with him worse by attacking Kylie, having her with us might be the only thing that convinced him to help us.

Zane's technomancy made beating the security system easy-peasy, and before we knew it, we were rooming with two unconscious security officers and a structure filled with metal shelves packed to the ceiling. Unfortunately, there were supposed to be four guards, which limited our options.

The door closed behind us, sealing us in.

"Wonderful day for people to call out," Cass grumbled.

"Okay, great, perfect," I said, grabbing an unconscious security officer's hat and placing it on my head.

"No, wait," Drew said. "You can't go in there. You'll be recognized."

"I need to," I said. "He's my son."

"Yes, but you're a familiar face to them. If you're spotted, you tip everyone off."

He was right, but there was no way I'd hang out in the storage shed and wait for someone to find Jordan and the others.

"I said what I said."

Kyp stepped between us. "Okay, okay, let's think about this. Who needs to go in there? I have to stay here to keep these two knocked out."

Cass' eyes lit up with the green glow that signified the presence of the Three. This time, it was Mari. "The child requires my protection. If she is to enter the facility, I must follow." She swiped the hat from my hand, and just like that, she was Gana. "Sorry, big sis."

Hearing Gana's voice come from Cass was a sword through

the spine. I would know.

"Hey Cass, could you get your personalities under control so I can focus on my job?" I snapped. I couldn't talk to Gana. Not after the way I'd failed her. Not when I could still see her blood when I closed my eyes.

Disapproving stares leaned heavily on my shoulders, but I'd long since run out of fucks to give. They didn't have to agree with my outburst. They needed me at my best and having Mom and Gana around would only distract me.

"Sorry, Jacks," Cass said, but it didn't hold the bite she'd normally dole out when I got snippy with her. A glance at her revealed her eyes darting around like she was reading something on the far wall. Her face flickered between emotions.

"I should be here watching Kyp's back," Ray said. "Brains over brawn is all well and good, and Kyp could probably kick the ass of anyone who wanders in here, but he shouldn't be distracted from his task. He needs a powerhouse in his corner."

Kyp nodded. "And if one powerhouse stays, one should go. Although, Jacklyn, I would advise against you wearing a guard's uniform and waltzing in. Assuming the person in charge is Dr. Livingston, you'll be recognized."

"I'll bring Zane with me," I said. "And don't worry. I've got a plan."

"Whatever it is, I'm sure I disagree." Kyp argued.

He agreed. I wasn't sure that was a good thing.

To sneak in, I'd hidden in a heavy-duty shipping crate, and poured plastic-wrapped single use medical supplies on top of myself. The plastic stuck to my sweaty skin. Every time I pushed my Aegis harder in an attempt to see anything through the slightly cracked opening, it also enhanced the odor of the plastic. If I kept that up, my cover wouldn't be blown by my lack of awareness, but by the sounds of my retching.

This was your idea, Jacklyn.

It wasn't a *bad* idea, although it was uncomfortable. The shipping crates were large and required a dolly operator to push them inside, which worked, because that's where we needed to be. Zane could operate any security computers we ran into along the way, and Jainey and I would use them to get to Ross. I'd rather have had Austin with me, but since Cass had gone and gotten herself appointed as the protector of my offspring, she would have to come along for the ride.

I hoped Jainey wasn't mentally cursing my existence too much. I focused on that so my mind wouldn't linger.

I was buried. In a small space.

Plastic wrapped hypodermic needles, goggles, blood collection tubes. Not rocks and leaves and dirt.

There were slats in the crate, air in my lungs.

No soil.

I forced air into my nose and out through my mouth.

I'm fine. I'm alive. Except for when I'm not.

Zane pushed my crate while Cass pushed Jainey's. We'd used

the tablets the delivery guys held to track down Ross' office, so the trip there was seamless.

Which meant it was bound to go completely off the rails.

The crates had been filled with medical supplies shipped from Lifestone Pharmaceuticals. That pretty much clinched it. The man whose kind eyes and sorrowful expression had become etched into every memory of my pregnancy had been responsible for this.

We couldn't save the baby.

I'm so sorry.

R.D. Livingston had played me.

I was well past the point where I allowed people to survive for that slight.

As Zane slowed the cart to a stop, I mentally lined up my priorities.

1) Deal with Ross.

2) Deal with Livingston.

3) Get my son back.

4) Free the other children.

Lists were good. Lists gave me focus when things were spiraling. They kept me from getting too caught up in my emotional reactions.

Lists were good.

Yeah.

"Excuse me," a voice sounded, breaking through my thoughts. "Can I help you with those?"

That wasn't Ross.

"No sir," Cass said smoothly. "We're just taking these down the hall. A delivery for a Ross... Ehble?"

"Identification, please."

My heart plummeted. Cass and Zane had fake IDs we'd created last night for this mission—every one of us did, in case we were discovered—but what if there was a way to tell they were fake? Maybe Jainey could pull a Jedi mind trick? But could she do it from inside a box? And what were the chances that people who worked here wouldn't be sufficiently mind blocked?

"Hey! Are those my packages?" Ross.

Shit. One look at Cass and he'd blow this whole thing wide open. Damn her and her insistence on wheeling the kid around.

"Are you Mr. Ebell?" Zane asked. The top of the storage crate creaked as she leaned her slight weight on it.

The warmth of my Aegis traveled through my body, crackling like a live wire.

"That's me," Ross answered, all cheer.

My fingers tightened around the grip of my handgun.

"Perfect," Zane said. "Sign here?"

Come on, Zane. Move it along.

"Actually, can you wheel them into my office?" Ross asked. "Last time they screwed up my delivery, and I didn't realize it until I'd unpacked everything. I don't want the hassle of calling you back."

"Sure, where would you like them?" Zane again. Cass's complete silence rang all the alarms my brain had built for a mission that was on the edge of going completely sideways.

The door clicked open, and we were rolling again. A piece of plastic tipped forward and covered my nostrils. I jerked my head to the side to avoid it.

This was my plan. My plan. My idea.

I couldn't run away from my demons. Not now.

Shuffling. The click of a door closing. Muffled, but present, thanks to my Aegis.

"Cass?"

I slowly slid my gun free from its holster.

"Ross." Cass answered without hesitation. "What in the hell have you gotten yourself mixed up in?"

"I'm sorry?"

I pushed the crate's lid up and over, gun trained on Ross as I rose. "She wants to know what mess you've found yourself in."

I met his wide, panicked eyes. His face hadn't changed much. Same blonde hair, same jock aesthetic, same pinched, just-sucked-a-lemon expression.

"We all do, actually," Zane said, her gun joining mine.

Ross smirked. "Well, would you look at that? They sent the chick squad after me."

I pushed the gun closer to his face.

"Yeah, yeah, you're a badass." Ross held his hands up. "Just tell me if she's okay."

"Why do you care?" I snapped. "You helped hold her here."

He stepped in closer, glancing around for a minute before

speaking lower. "You think I really have a choice? Keep that gun on me. There are cameras in here."

"Don't worry about that," Zane said. "I found my way in. I'm looping the footage, so it's all you working from earlier. You're just a glorified stock boy, huh?"

"Inventory," he corrected, jaw clenched. "I don't want them to know I'm helping you. I can't help you if I'm not here."

"You're not helping, anyway." I looked at his stupid face, and I didn't see whatever he was trying to make me see. I only saw the guy who kept my daughter away from me.

"I *am*." He gritted his teeth. "You have no idea what I've given up. And I'll keep helping you with whatever you're planning right now if you just tell me she's all right." He glanced away, unable to meet my eyes, and I realized he meant it. Like when he had slipped up and admitted he had feelings for Kylie, he was showing his vulnerability. Only this time...

I reached over to the crate beside mine and ripped it open. It was an impatient gesture, most gestures I made these days were, but Jainey went with it, leaping free from the medical supplies with gusto.

She smoothed her hair until her eyes lit on Ross. "Hi, Ross!" A small wave. "It's good to see you."

Ross grabbed Jainey's pudgy, little hand. "Jeez kid, I'm so glad you're okay."

"She could have been even better if you'd gotten in your car and driven her to the estate yourself, but you had to go be stupid on my time," I snapped.

"Mama," Jainey hissed, the tiny hand that wasn't in Ross' slapping me on the arm. "I thought you actually wanted him to help?"

"It's okay, Jainey," Ross said calmly. He stepped forward, letting her hand slip from his. "Jacks, I get it. You're not a fan. You shouldn't be. I made the wrong decision. And I kept making the wrong decisions. So, I don't blame you." He inhaled deeply, steadying himself in a way I understood. I needed cleansing breaths myself. "I did the right thing this time. If I'd left, I wouldn't be able to help the other kids. They need me."

"All of them?" I asked. "Or just Caleb?"

Ross' eyes slid to Jainey.

"Don't look at her! Look at me!"

"Jacks," Cass hissed. "Keep it down."

As though I hadn't had a sound block up around me before I even got out of the crate.

"Tell me what you're playing at here, Ross, or I swear to God, I will make your next death excruciating—"

"*Last* death," Ross cut me off. "Final. You kill me here and it's over for me. Got it?"

His words rang through me. "That's... but you're a Key."

"Not anymore." His laugh was bitter. "Not until they accomplish their plans. Don't you see what this place is, Jacklyn? This is what they do. They play with people's Aegis. They want to see what turns the genetic markers on, and what turns them off.

And they've mostly figured that out. Mapped the Key genome. And the Guardian one too."

Zane gulped beside me.

Ross huffed. "God, do you even know what I'm talking about?" He threw his arms in the air. "I wish you'd brought Kyp."

"Don't worry, Ross." Jainey smiled. "I'll explain it to them later."

I glared at the kid, but I couldn't really argue. My face heated, less because Jainey understood better than I did, and more because *Ross* did. I didn't get it, and as I always did around a Franklin, I felt like an idiot.

She was so much like him. So much like me, in so many ways. I hadn't even had time to process it, didn't have time to feel, just act. But then things like this would happen, and I'd think—we made her. But we didn't. And I didn't know what to make of that. So I stuck with what I did know.

I pushed the barrel of the gun beneath his chin. "Why don't *you* explain why I shouldn't paint your brains on the walls? Break it down into little words for me."

His eyes hardened and his jaw tightened. "I. Will. Die. And I won't come back. Livingston and his team found a way to take my Aegis away from me."

My throat went dry. "What, like, a nullification Ritual?"

"No," Ross explained. "Like it's gone. And they won't graft it back on until I finish helping them with their plan."

"Can they even put it back?" Cass asked, her hand flying to

her mouth.

"Who knows?" Ross grumbled. "We're looking at the cross street of science and magic. I don't expect that shit to make sense. And you shouldn't either."

"If it worked, it has to make sense to somebody." Jainey shrugged. Her voice was soft and small, her eyebrows knitted.

"Well, that somebody's not me," Ross answered. "But trust me. They want me on their side, and if I can find a way to get my Aegis back, I'll take it. But I definitely don't want to hold a bunch of kids hostage to do it. Which is where you come in. If I break them out, I don't get my Aegis back. But if you storm in here and free them for me, I might hold on to being on their good side."

"And we get to do the dirty work for you," I said. "You haven't changed much in the past year, have you, Ross?"

His eyes hardened as they bore into mine. "You really think that? I made myself into a babysitter for your kids and protected them. And trust me, I *did* have to protect them. They both inherited your big mouth."

"Hey!" Jainey argued. "That was one time!"

Ross smiled, and I wanted to punch him in the kidney. If I'd gotten anything from this whole parenting thing so far, it was an instinct to protect that was nearly stronger than I could control.

"Can you tell us where to find the children?" Zane asked. "We'll free all of them except for your kid and—"

"—no!" Ross cut in. "I want you to take Caleb with you. He's safer with you, for now."

I frowned. "And I suppose you'll want to know where to find us?"

"Leave him with Cxarana. I'll check later with her." He leaned forward. "I really don't want him left behind. Especially if Jordan gets out. Everything will fall on his shoulders."

"Where can we find them?" Cass said. "How can you help us get through security so we have a better chance?"

"I have an idea." He glared at me with suspicion. "But you're gonna have to knock me out."

I grinned, shoving my gun into its holster and cracking my knuckles through my fingerless gloves. "I'm not gonna complain."

DISTRACTION

KYP

"Did punching me right things for you?" Ray asked, settling down on a shipping crate beside Kyp.

Kyp scowled. "Don't ask me that."

"I'm serious. Did it help?" He placed a hand on his shoulder.

Kyp shook it free and let his eyes slip closed so he could focus on his connections to the others. His impression of Jacklyn wasn't as strong as it had once been, but he could feel her, and she didn't seem panicked or wrong in any way—there was just the general sense of sorrow that always spilled from her since they had reunited.

That should be wrong, but it wasn't.

"Oi! Did you fall asleep over there?"

"Ray, shut up!"

"What are you doing?" he pestered.

"Mr. Madison," Drew piped up from behind them where he and Austin worked their way through stacks of shipping crates, searching for evidence to confirm what they already knew. "Did it occur to you that he's trying not to punch you again?"

Austin snorted a laugh, but continued sifting through crates and creating a photo-inventory of everything he found. From where Kyp sat in front of the unconscious guards, it mostly appeared to be various blood drawing paraphernalia.

"That's Clayson's answer, but it ain't yours," Ray argued. He glanced over his shoulder. "And this isn't a laughing matter, Austin."

Austin shrugged. "Way I see it, you've had that coming for a long time. The kid isn't wrong."

"I'm older than you." Kyp cringed at how petulant he sounded.

"Barely." Austin raked his fingers through his blond hair.

For a moment, everyone was quiet, and Kyp tightened his hold on the guards.

"I'm sorry," Ray broke the silence. "I stayed behind hoping we could talk."

Austin groaned. "Will you stop?"

"Did you put a sound block around this place?" Drew asked, his voice pitched high in a way Kyp knew meant he was on the verge of throwing things. "Did you even think before you decided on this heart to heart?"

Austin held a finger up. "They're in with Ross." He was listening to his earpiece. Only Kyp had chosen to go without one to avoid distraction.

A lot of good that did him.

"Okay, great," Ray said. "I'm not worried about that right now. Jacks and Zane have got this. And I assume Cass has a few tricks up her sleeves as well, what with the whole spirit channeling thing." He tipped his head up, eyes rolling to the ceiling. "At the very least, I know what Jaina's capable of, and it's mighty."

"And what *are* you worried about?" Kyp drawled.

"I'm worried about this family. I'm worried about us."

"You're worried about *you*. That's all you're ever worried about." Kyp turned back to the guards.

Ray settled into a crouch before him, doing a first-rate job of proving everything Kyp had said while trying to prove him wrong.

Kyp tuned the others out, first their hushed whispers, then their movements, then Ray's voice. He stared out into the middle distance and allowed his vision to blur as he focused on the minds of the two unconscious men.

Who were they? How had they found themselves mixed up in this mess? Did they have any idea what went on here? What if they were simply innocent victims in this ongoing war, like so many before them?

"... could be like regular kids... warriors..."

The words bled through his thoughts, tumbling from Ray's lips. Ray who wouldn't let it go. Ray, who kept pushing for forgiveness. Ray, who never cared about these things. Who prioritized the mission above all things, even his own children.

Child. He only had one child.

Kyp needed to listen to him. No, he needed to stay aware

of the guards, make sure he could still feel the swirling vortex of their minds and the way they clung to the dreams Jainey had triggered within them.

It was an advanced Key skill, one she shouldn't have at her age, but that was par for the course with her.

Shit. Stupid. He needed to return to the men. He couldn't think about Jainey or Ray.

He threw himself into their thoughts, watching as their concerns spun around. Strange nightmares he didn't understand, but he didn't need to.

Not until he saw Jainey's face swim into their vision. She danced in a field of daisies, the white dress she wore pulling away from her as she spun. He joined her there, pacing around her, trying to catch her expression as she moved.

Red dots fell upon the flowers. They started out tiny, but they grew with each step forward until he made it to her, and bent to pick one, the sun heating his back.

Blood. The flowers were soaked with it.

He looked at her, a question in his gaze, but she wasn't looking at him. Her eyes rolled backward into her head, and she reached out to the guards, pudgy hands thrusting forward. They grasped at their throats, their eyes wide, their bodies going rigid.

The child showed no compassion. She made no move to stop.

No, Jainey! No!

The men snapped awake, and Kyp flew from their subconscious like a punted football. His arms flailed backward, and he grabbed onto the back of the crate he sat on, just barely keeping himself from stumbling.

"Kyp! Are you okay?" Ray gripped him by the shoulders, shaking him.

Kyp's mind reeled, his control over his Aegis shattered. He didn't have time to re-establish it. Instead, he pushed past Ray and dove for the men on the floor. His hands wrapped around one of the man's wrists and he yanked him backward, away from the door, before throwing himself forward for the next one.

He knew it would be too late before he'd even grabbed for the man's wrist.

A light flashed before Kyp's eyes like a strobe.

"Ya'll seein' that?" Austin rushed over to them, Drew following closely behind. "We were going through the inventory and—" A horn sounded, adding to the lights. "What in the blue hell happened up here?"

Kyp had screwed up, and now they were all in danger.

JACKLYN

"I said," I enunciated, to be sure he could fully hear me over the blaring alarm, "tell me who you signaled!" I shoved him against the wall, my forearm jammed against his throat.

"We don't have time for this!" Cass yanked her sai from underneath her uniform shirt. "We need to get out of here."

"We're not going anywhere without my brother!" Jainey stomped her way in front of the door, right into Zane's path.

"What she said." My eyes didn't leave Ross.

"I didn't alert anybody," Ross gasped. "Knock me out and get to the basement. There's a tunnel system that leads to a building about a mile away. It's a small housing complex. The kids are kept there. There's five of them. The other caretakers are probably already gathering them and packing up."

"They taught us an evacuation procedure," Jainey confirmed. "We need to get to that complex. It moves fast once it starts."

"Take my key card." Ross shoved it into my hand before I could argue. His eyes were wild, his teeth clenched. "Get out of here. I—I'm sorry. I never should have... Just *go*."

I released him, reared back, and slugged him in the jaw. My knuckles cried out, that enhanced pain response that came with my Aegis, making my eyes sting with tears.

Ross fell to the floor with a thump.

I shook my hand out, hoping to expel the pain. "Zane?"

She yanked her sleeve up, looking at the wrist computer she wore. "Nothing in the schematics show anything about tunnels constructed under the building."

Panic zinged through my veins. "There's got to be a way to get down there. Find me a route. Cass, reopen the line to Kyp's team and find out what the hell is happening. Jainey, can you do something to cover us?"

"Yep," Jainey confirmed.

I moved to the door and listened for footsteps. "They're moving away from us."

"Out toward the shed," Cass said. "They're heading for the boys. One of the delivery guys who wasn't there must've shown up and tripped an alarm."

"I've got a route!" Zane said.

I turned my earpiece back on. "Kyp, get out of there."

"Working on it!" The sound on the other end was distorted. They were on the move.

"Last thing they knew, we weren't working together. Let's try to make this look like it was your team. They may not know we're inside." I said. "Let them keep believing we aren't. Get out of here."

"I agree." He sounded breathless. "One condition. Cass takes Jainey and comes with me. I'll send you your team back."

"Absolutely not," I snapped. "We don't have time for an exchange."

"Actually, we do," Kyp grumbled. "If you're ready to split the team up because you think we'll be discovered, I'm not risking her getting captured. I take off with her and mind control whoever is following to lose us on the road, and she's safe. So either you send her out to me, or you all get out of there and we try this another way. But I'm not losing her while failing to save Jordan."

"God, why are you like this?" I groaned. "Fine. I'll send them out. Have Ray and Austin look for a building within a mile of this facility. They'll have to figure out where it is. There's a tunnel entrance from here. It should be large enough to house six children."

"Jacks. Please leave," Kyp said. "You're going to get yourself killed."

"No. I'm going to save our son." I disconnected and turned to Zane. "Can I please burn this place to the ground?"

"No. Innocents or whatever." She shrugged.

"Kyp's being Kyp, so Cass and Jainey, we're going to have to get you out through the front door. Then—" I turned to Zane. "You and I are tunnel-bound."

"Awesome," Cass said with a sigh. "How?"

"But I want to find Jordan," Jainey argued. "I *have* to be there. He's not going to trust you otherwise. He won't know who you are."

Her words stabbed at something deep in my core, but there was no time to curl up on the ground and cry for my losses. I pushed aside all my emotions. I pushed aside everything. I had to find Jordan.

"You may have had to figure things out before, but you don't have to anymore. This is what we were trained to do. You're brilliant, but you don't have our battlefield experience. So, for now? Just listen to your mother." My voice cracked. I was trying so hard to be cool, but my throat was tight and I felt like I was being torn in half by the need to protect her and the need to get to Jordan. I scooped Jainey up in a tight hug, so quickly she barely had time to squeeze back.

It nearly comforted the ache in my chest. I dropped her into Cass's arms. "Get her out of here. I don't care how you do it. Bring her to Kyp."

She was going with Kyp. Kyp was her father. He would die to protect her, too.

Cass's eyes glowed green. Mari answered, "I will."

Jainey looked too stunned to argue, and I took that as a sign to plunge forward. "Don't give her any trouble. I *will* bring Jordan home. I promise you that."

It was impossible to tell what made her listen, but she nodded.

"Please."

"You got it, kiddo." I pressed my ear to the door. "The hallway is almost empty. Gunshots will only draw more attention." I channeled my Aegis through my fingers until flames licked along their edges. I glanced at Jainey's Guardian. "Ready your firepower?"

It was Gana's knife-edged grin that flitted across Cass' lips. "Together on three?"

I nodded, despite the way my heartbeat fluttered. "On three. But you all, Cass, and me are going to have to have a conversation when this is all over."

"That's ominous," Cass said.

"It's not," I said. "I miss my friend." I took a deep breath to refocus myself. "One."

"Two," Cass added.

"Three!" I threw the door open and Cass let loose an inferno, aimed ahead at any potential guards.

Cass lowered Jainey until her feet touched the floor, then stepped forward, hands held out, holding the fire at bay. "Stay behind me."

The curtain of fire flickered, revealing a few guards heading toward the entrance. One of the guards bolted for the other side of the room, straight for a button on the wall, his hand radio a melted puddle of plastic on the floor.

"No more surprise alarm buttons!" Kyp's face was hidden in the smoke, but there was no mistaking it. The guard flew face first into the wall with a crack and slumped to the floor.

Nice work, Kyp.

"I've got them," he said. "Go!"

"Jacks!" Zane called. I whirled to find her in the smoke.

"Let's go!" She jerked her head in the other direction, away from the mess.

I followed her around a corner to an elevator. Footsteps were getting closer. We weren't going to make it. I had to think fast.

"We can't let them see where we're going." Zane pressed her hand to the panel on the wall.

I fingered my earpiece. "Cass, you out?"

No answer.

"Cass?"

More silence. I pulled out my Glock. This was going to get ugly fast, and if it was a choice between saving Jordan and taking a few people off this earth, I knew what I'd choose, and I wouldn't hesitate. Not anymore.

Smoke wafted around the corner, and I choked while I called out again. "Gana, Mom, Mari, anybody?"

I stood on the tips of my toes, ready to spring forward and rescue Jainey, even if it meant this mission failed.

"Almost there," Zane whispered. "Overriding security protocols."

"I've got them," Kyp yelled through my earpiece.

Two guards made their way around the corner just as the elevator dinged.

I fired four times. One for each knee. It took all my internal control not to fire at their heads.

I reached behind me while the men were still screaming and held the elevator door. "Zane, their earpieces."

Zane jumped forward once I had the doors open and reached for the flailing men's earpieces, shorting them out. The elevator doors dinged a closing warning, and I leaned my back against them, holding them open.

The doors pushed against my back, and my boots slipped precariously on the floor as I fought their stubborn attempts to close. Zane slid in as I began to lose too much ground, and I ducked in behind her as they slammed shut. The jolt as they sealed was rough. I winced, glad to be out of their way.

Zane yanked open the elevator panel and got to work.

Nobody came to stop us, but the elevator was clearly angered by our hostile takeover. It jerked repetitively, reluctant to take off, starting and stopping as Zane tried to force its cooperation.

"Z?"

"Security is trying to override my override, which means they know we're here. I'm communicating directly with the data output of the elevator to keep it moving, which means I'm currently having two conversations at once." She shot a pointed glance my way, and I took the hint and shut up.

Watching her work was a marvel. It made me question what that Aegis had been capable of before technology was so prevalent. One day I'd have to ask her—if she even knew.

I channeled my Aegis so I could listen for whoever waited outside the elevator door. A crash sounded from downstairs and I winced. It had to be guards slamming through a door. I should have realized guards would be there to greet us, but all I could think about was getting to Jordan. Anything I ran into along the way, I would barrel through.

There was no way we were getting out of this unscathed, unless I thought of an ingenious plan in the next minute.

"Zane, we're gonna have to prepare if we want to get out of this alive."

"I can't do much. The security system is pretty damn good here. Keeps overriding my overrides. I have to keep working." Her eyes flickered and flashed an electric blue as she leaned forward to get a closer look. "You're gonna have to cover me."

"I'll do my best."

"Sub-basement in two floors," Zane announced.

I stepped forward, angling myself so I blocked Zane. At least that way I'd have a fighting chance of defending her.

The elevator binged.

One floor.

I reloaded my gun.

Another bing.

"Zane?" I glanced back at her, hoping to see she had defeated the security system.

She hadn't, but she kept one hand on the circuitry of the control panel, the other resting on the grip of her gun.

"Let's do something illegal." I smirked, refocusing my attention and whatever was about to come through that door.

"Literally everything we've done today has been illegal." I could hear the smile in her voice.

"Semantics."

A click from Zane's direction and the door popped open.

My gun went up and my finger pressed against the trigger, waiting. Nobody rushed the elevator, but the floor was littered with disarmed and unconscious guards.

I tensed and peeked out from the elevator.

"Don't shoot." Ray grinned, surrounded by bodies. Austin stood beside him, wiping sweat from his brow.

"What the hell? I told you to meet me at the end of the tunnel!"

"I thought that was advice." Austin shrugged. "Brave and all, but it seemed smarter to help from the inside."

With a sigh and a shake of my head, I headed into the darkened tunnel that stretched out before me while Zane disabled the elevator. My footsteps echoed on the tiled floor. I thought back to my training with Kyp, which was much more ninja and much less brawler than my Ray training.

"I think Kyp is keeping a distance but following along." Ray fell into step beside me while Austin and Zane brought up the rear. "He wants to keep Jainey out of their hands, but he also wanted to stay close in case things went sideways."

My blood boiled. "Things have *already* gone sideways."

"He swore he'd honor his promise and not put himself in a

position to be seen with us," Ray said. "But this place hired loads of mercenaries to fight and die on Livingston's behalf."

The litany of curses I mumbled under my breath was the last purposeful sound any of us made for a while.

The tunnel walls were painted a foreboding gray and pipes ran across them with abandon. Fluorescent lights hung from the ceiling, but they flickered on and off, an ominous buzz filling the air.

The place brought back memories of a time before I'd had any idea that a Key could do more than open a door. Right before I'd learned about my Key heritage, I'd been exploring prospective colleges, and one of them had a series of tunnels that connected the various buildings on campus. The tunnels had been the best part about it for me. I could see adventure around every corner. But Gana had been excited about everything it had to offer. She couldn't wait to be old enough for college.

"I think we're almost there," Zane said.

I'd been floating outside my body and she'd yanked me back. I returned with a jolt, and a flood of yearning and grief weighed my soul. Gana had never gotten to go to college. Mom had never gotten to see me graduate.

As I readied my Aegis to be used however it would be most needed, as we slowed our steps to prepare for an attack, a vow deeper than any I'd ever uttered filled me.

Jordan and Jainey would get to live a real life. They would have their chance. We'd find a way if I had to kill every living being we encountered with my teeth. I'd give them the life that had been taken from me, from Gana. I'd give them the chance to dream about a future that didn't involve threats nobody but a precious few even knew existed.

I needed to bring this nightmare to an end.

Finally, we reached what appeared to be the end of the dimly lit, barren tunnel. Only about thirty feet away, the narrow space opened out into an actual room. An elevator waited, open, as if beckoning us.

Austin motioned to it, smirking. "Yeah, right."

"With the way Jacks conducted herself at the beginning of this mission, I half expected her to run for the elevator," Ray groused.

I shot him the finger.

"Seconding Jacks here," Austin whispered. "Since you were the one who distracted Kyp enough to completely bungle our side of the mission."

I tried to combine admonishment and questioning into one look. Ray glanced away.

Idiot. What had he done?

"Zane, you and Ray confirm the coast is clear. Look for a staircase." Without a word of argument, Zane switched spots with me. I barely needed to look at Austin for him to lean down and whisper what I'd missed into my ear.

I couldn't imagine what Ray was thinking. Lavinia had understood Ray far better than we'd realized. He didn't deserve what had happened to him. He wasn't the monster she made him out to be, but there was something fundamentally wrong with his thought process. Once something got into his head, he seemed unable to consider the consequences. Zane balanced him in a way I knew my mother never could have.

I tried not to acknowledge whatever they had chosen to be to each other, mostly because they didn't seem to want it acknowledged. Zane could be as mercurial and boisterous as he could, but she also knew the limits, and it usually only took a gentling hand from her on his shoulder to stay an outburst.

I remembered loving his wildness as a child. I remembered Mom struggling to contain him, fighting against the forest with fire. Zane didn't fight him. She tamed him enough to slide him into polite company without destroying the beauty of who he was.

I realized I shouldn't allow them to separate on future missions. She could balance him during missions. And as much as I enjoyed Zane's company, her relationship with Ray built an awkwardness between us that grew the longer it went unaddressed. Austin and I formed a much smoother alliance.

Up ahead, Zane beckoned for us to follow. We moved forward cautiously, but there was no reason for caution. There was nobody there.

"We got a laundry room and a staircase," Austin said. "I think I know where we're going."

We took off up the stairs, striking a balance between speed and stealth.

Two stories up, I turned the corner and nearly trampled over a girl. I pulled my gun and held it up before I'd even processed anything about her.

The girl leapt to her feet with a gasp, her hands going up. She had tight, curly brown hair and deep brown skin. She had to be about Gana's age.

"I'm sorry!" she cried. "When the lockdown went into effect, all the hallway doors locked and we couldn't get back in. Jordan went upstairs to check for one that might be open. We were just waiting for someone to come looking for us."

Her fear broke my heart. Her mention of Jordan made my spirits soar.

I lowered my gun, slowly, watching her. I held my hand back, gesturing at the others to stop. I couldn't risk scaring her any more than I already had.

She lowered her arms once my gun went down, her hands moving to clasp a pendant of a silver feather that hung from her neck. "I'm sorry."

"It's okay. I didn't mean to scare you." I stepped out onto the landing, moving toward her. "I'm not one of the guards. I don't work here."

"Then who are you?"

"She's my mother, Rennie." A deep voice echoed from above and my heart clenched. The voice was a little higher in pitch, but it was nearly Kyp's voice. It had to be Jordan. His footsteps followed.

Rennie made a face. "She looks too young to be your—"

"Long story," Jordan cut in as he appeared around the corner. His black hair was shorter, and his eyes were mine, but his face...

"Jainey's you, but the boy? Kyp, for certain," Ray said from over my shoulder.

"Jainey must have found you." Jordan swallowed hard. "I need your help. I'm in over my head. And I still don't understand why you left me here, but I think you made a mistake. I think you—"

"Left you?" I cut him off. "You were *taken*."

"I'm not stupid, *Mother*," he spat.

"Oh, I don't doubt it, *kid*. I know whose genes you have and it would be literally impossible for you to not be a genius. But you're wrong."

"You're lying," Jordan hissed. "I used to believe it, but last week, I finally got to meet Grandma Liv. She's gonna break me out as soon as it's safe. She said you kept me from my dad and left me here. *So don't lie to me*."

My gut clenched. I turned to Austin, mouthing "Grandma Liv" in complete disbelief.

"Yeah, well, I'm Grandpa Ray, and your granny has slung a handful of right bullshit yer way." Ray stepped up. "Jacklyn's not the liar here."

"It's true," Zane said. "She was searching for you before Jainey even came looking for us."

"I don't understand." His voice was breathy, and his hand fluttered to his chest.

I was about to ask if he was okay, but Rennie beat me to it, laying a gentle hand on his shoulder. He flinched.

"Jordan, you can't let yourself get too overwhelmed," she whispered.

"What happens if he does?" Ray asked, eyes narrowed.

"Stop, none of that is important." I stepped between my team and Jordan. "Look, I don't care what you believe. I'd rather you believe me, but Lavinia clearly got to you first. In the end, it doesn't matter. You called out for me because you needed help. You want to get out of here and get back to your sister, don't you?"

Rennie leaned against Jordan's arm, and he glanced over his shoulder at her, his breathing somewhat calmer but not yet back to normal.

Not that I knew what normal was for my son. Not that I knew anything about him.

"I do want to get out of here," Jordan said. "But if I go, she comes with me."

"If you go, I prefer all the kids come with you," I said. "I'm here to put this place out of business."

Rennie and Jordan shared a look. "I'm not sure what your chances are," she said. "The other kids have probably already been evacuated. The lockdown started when we were in the hallway—"

"—hiding. We were hiding," Jordan cut her off, nodding like a bobblehead. "We were hiding because I..."

"... didn't want to get his treatment." Rennie grimaced. "He hates those."

Austin snorted and elbowed me in the side. "They were making out."

"What?" Rennie gasped.

"No way," Jordan answered. "Like. Never." A long pause. "Ew."

"Ew?" Rennie glared at him.

Ew was right. I wondered if she had any idea how young Jordan really was. I cleared my throat. "As adorable and traumatizing as this is, I need to know the post-lockdown procedure. Now."

"We're supposed to wait in our rooms," Rennie said.

"But we couldn't get back to them because... well, anyway, I tried to find a way out of this hallway because we didn't know what triggered the lockdown."

"*You* sent for me to come get you. It didn't occur to you that—"

"It could have just as easily been interdimensionals," Jordan said. "It wouldn't be the first time."

"It wouldn't even be the second time." Rennie grinned.

Looking at her smile brought a smile to Jordan's face. He turned his gaze to me. "I kicked their asses."

"Not bad," I said. "So, when they don't find you in your rooms?"

"If they're evacuating?" Rennie said. "They would have sent everyone they found on their way. Then, they'd send a strike force to get us out."

"The strike force is already here," Jordan said. "They're

searching room by room first, starting on the bottom floor. B staircase goes up, A staircase goes down. We're in A. We can't head back down until they're on the far side of the facility, or they'll find us. If you really want to get us out of here, we've got about another minute before we head back out of here and sneak back to where you came from."

"The tunnel again," Ray said.

"How do you know where the strike force is?" I asked.

"My brain is fitted with a map of this place, and I can hear the movements of everyone in it." He pulled at the frayed wrists of his gray sweatshirt, gaze averted.

Mind and Body. Me and Kyp.

My throat went dry, and it took a moment for me to force my words out. "All right then. Say when."

I listened for whatever he was hearing. As much as I wanted to believe Jordan had chosen us, the Grandma Liv thing dug hooks under my skin. How did I know he wouldn't lead us into an ambush?

"Okay." Jordan smiled. It was a wide, charming smile, the kind Kyp's face rarely managed. "Wanna see the outside world, Renita?" He held out his arm for her to take.

"It's been a while." She looped her arm through his.

"I'll lead the way," Ray announced. "Austin, bring up the rear, yeah?"

"On it."

Zane stepped to Ray's side. I gestured for the kids to go next and took the space between them and Austin.

We headed down the stairs at a cautious pace, stopping to listen for guards every few steps, and continued back through the tunnel to the other side.

Jordan shoved a hand through his hair and it stuck up everywhere. "If you were lying about leaving me here, can you tell me now?" He jammed his hands into the pockets of his sweatshirt. "I don't want to feel stupid when I find out you lied to me and I was naïve enough to believe it. Rennie says I'm naïve sometimes. She doesn't say it to be insulting. She only tells me because she's looking out for me."

My heart twisted. "I'm not lying."

"Good. In that case, I'd like in on the whole 'take this place down' thing, if I could." He squeezed Rennie's hand. "If that's cool with you."

Another stabbing pain somewhere deep. When I saw these kids trotting out into battle, it was like watching the ghost of Gana swirling through Cass.

"We'll see," I muttered.

From that point, we walked in silence until the tunnel widened. We closed ranks. This was the most likely place for the bad guys to find us.

We exited the tunnel to silence and spread out, filling the room as we glanced around warily, prepared for the fight we feared would come.

But it didn't.

"Mom," Jordan said, his voice hushed. "Can I call you Mom?"

It was weird. It was weird when Jainey did it, but it was even weirder when Jordan did. Parent or not, I sort of expected our arrangement to be more like Bruce Wayne and Dick Grayson, better known as Robin. Batman and his first Robin were years apart in age, but not enough to be father and son. They behaved more like partners, despite Batman taking him in as his ward. Even in the comics where they did behave like Batman was Robin's father, Dick called Batman Bruce. But that was because Dick already had a father, one that he'd lost.

And despite our age difference, Jordan had never had anything resembling a mom.

"Yeah. You can. It may take a little getting used to though."

"Sure, yeah, of course."

"Not seeing anyone," Austin said. "Looks safe."

"Someone is here," Rennie said. "And they're angry."

How did she know that? I wasn't sure I wanted to know.

"Hello horror movie dialogue," Zane said.

"No, but seriously, she's right," Ray said. "There are people overhead. They're probably heading for the staircase to come down."

Crap. I hadn't been paying attention like I should have. Jordan's comment had been enough to throw my focus.

"Can we take the elevator, Z?" Austin asked.

"The timing could be off, and we could end up fighting the whole group," Zane said. "The system's fighting to keep me out."

"It's our way out. Get it working." I turned my attention to the kids. "You guys stay against that wall. We'll take whoever makes it down here first."

Jordan looked reluctant, but Rennie pushed him behind her with a sly grin.

I was probably going to like her.

We prepared for security to enter through the staircase. Which was why we weren't ready for the explosion behind us.

FIFTEEN

A GOOD SHOT

JACKLYN

My ears rang and my face ached from where it had smacked the floor. Blood dripped from my nose and a cut on my forehead. I squinted, my eyes darting around before latching onto Austin's silhouette through the smokey air. He scrambled to his feet. Ray followed.

I pushed myself up, my feet gaining purchase beneath me. Soot and dust rained from the sky. Flames traveled across the floor, and I quelled them with my Aegis.

Zane was sprawled in front of the elevator, burns and cuts littering her face and the skin exposed by tears in her clothing. Ray fled to her, pressing his hands to her wounds. Healing her.

I understood.

On the far side of the space, Rennie and Jordan cowered against the wall. Two Gorvhans on leashes strained toward them. Sirins held the leashes, taunting the kids.

I blinked the smoke from my eyes, but yes, that was still what

I saw. Gorvhans being walked like dogs. But what I'd missed was the way Jordan was barely holding himself up against the wall. He was gasping for air, struggling, as Rennie pled with the Sirins.

Austin's eyes darted between Ray and Zane, the kids, and me. He was looking for direction and I had no idea what orders to give him.

Jordan gripped his head tightly between his hands. My brain stuttered, grasping for what it could mean and where I'd seen it before. My eyes locked with Rennie's horrified eyes.

I swore and dove for Austin. Whatever had gone off in that elevator was not the only thing set to explode.

Austin tipped over, and we crashed onto the floor. Power erupted from Jordan in shafts of blue light that tore through both of the Sirin and Gorvhan pairs in an instant. I buried my face in Austin's side, where I'd landed when we'd hit the floor. The brightness was unbearable.

"Jacks," Austin gasped. "Trouble."

My ears were still ringing, and I barely heard him. My stupid Aegis had been opened wide, letting all the sound in when the bomb blew.

Shielding my eyes from the glow, I followed Austin's line of sight. Jordan backed away from the wall, his body maneuvering, so the light that blasted from him didn't shine on any of us.

I was grateful, since it had reduced those interdimensionals to atoms. Rennie followed, nearby but tentative, and far enough away that she wouldn't be a burden.

"Jacks!" Ray sounded like he was whispering, though I knew he had to be yelling. I turned to where he was healing Zane. "Drain him!"

Drain him. Just like Ray did for me when my power overloaded.

Jordan's Aegis was strong, and it was getting stronger. If it kept building, that power could take down the whole room, and us along with it.

I hadn't done the maneuver since the day the estate had been attacked by interdimensionals. I'd vowed never to do it again. It seemed I couldn't even keep my promises to myself.

I focused my Aegis on reversing my output, pulling energy back into me from another source. I had to be cautious. Last time, I'd left the Gorvhans dried up husks.

"Rennie, out of the way. Jordan, see if you can push in the direction I'm pulling."

Jordan dropped to his knees.

I couldn't wait for him to get on board with the plan. My energy latched onto his like it was a rope and I yanked back as hard as I could, pulling his excess into me, feeling the power fill my veins and feed back into the pull. It wasn't the same as the sick feeling of the interdimensionals' energy filling me. This was familiar. Warm. My Aegis and Kyp's. But it was so much.

Too much. I was stronger from the mix of energy, but it made me feel twitchy and wrong.

It could have been seconds, minutes, hours, but finally, Jordan broke away, falling onto the floor, gasping in relief. Rennie rushed forward to help him.

The door to the stairway, the door right behind them, swung open. I leapt to my feet. No way that could be good. No way.

Two Sirins stood in the doorway. One had a gun cocked and aimed at the back of Jordan's head.

What was it with assholes aiming guns at my children?

I reached for my holster. My gun was gone.

"Thank you." The Sirin with the gun yanked Jordan to his feet by his hair. "I never could have controlled him without your help. Not while he was overloading."

My throat went dry. I did this. I drained his power. Made him unable to defend himself.

There was movement out of the corner of my eye.

"Don't you dare move. The kid's replaceable." He yanked at Jordan's hair again, and Jordan winced.

"Bastard," Ray growled.

"Don't." I held out both of my hands pleadingly.

He cocked the gun. "I know what your hands are capable of."

Damn it. My heart slammed in my chest. Everything within me shook.

"Rennie?" the other henchman summoned.

"Yes?" Her teeth ground together, her hands clenched at her sides.

"You'll be coming with me now."

I had to do something. I had to save these kids.

"Crelius, please," Jordan whispered. He knew this Sirin well enough to know him by name. "Please. I'll go with you, but does Rennie need to? She can't help the doctor with what he needs."

"We've got orders. She comes too."

The doctor had to be Dr. Livingston. What could he need? Livingston was known to be on the cutting edge of fringe medical advancements, the kind of doctor who made his entire living being above board by day and hiding in questionable laboratories by night. His clinic was well-established in our community, criminal communities, and immigrant communities who couldn't afford to invite any unwanted attention. Many of our people had no problem contributing tissue for testing if it took a little off the bill.

Not everyone with an Aegis lived off the Franklin family's healthy income.

"Don't move a muscle until we're gone," Crelius commanded. "If you do, he's dead. The doctor has more cloned cells where these came from. He'd mean a lot more to you than he does to us, since the doc took him directly from you. I'm sure that makes him special to someone."

Bile rose in my throat. That didn't matter. Jainey wasn't the first, and I'd still protect her with my life. I didn't have a choice.

"*Mom?*" His voice was clear in my mind.

I projected back to him, hoping he could hear me. "*Save your energy. I'm coming after you. Be ready.*"

"You have your win," I said. "Just go."

Crelius sneered. "You're lucky the boss wants you alive. Stay here for ten minutes. I see you before then, the girl dies."

The look Jordan shot at the Sirin was downright murderous. *Atta boy.*

I nodded. Rennie threw one last terrified look over her shoulder and they disappeared from my sight.

I dropped to my knees.

"Why not just kill us?" Austin asked.

"The Sirin said Livingston wants us alive," I said.

"They didn't say Livingston," Austin said. "They said the boss. They were calling Livingston the doc. This has to be someone else."

"It's probably because they need us if they're going to find Jainey," Ray said. He looked down at Zane, who still looked rough. "She needs to be healed. I'm running out of time."

"Do what you can," I said. "Austin, guard them."

I started toward the exit, but Austin grabbed my arm.

"Ten minutes."

"Nah." I shook his arm off.

"Don't you 'nah' me, girl," he shouted. "They'll kill them!"

"Only if they see me," I hissed. "Now get off me. Jordan's important or they would have just shot him and the rest of us. They're bluffing and we're out of time. There's a whole tree line along the highway outside. They won't see me if I go through the trees."

"Jacks!" Ray shouted.

I couldn't wait. If I was going to catch up, I'd have to move fast.

If there was an A and B staircase in the facility they'd kept the kids in, there could be dual staircases in this one. I dropped to Zane's side.

"Sorry, girl." I grabbed her handgun from her holster to replace my own and booted up her wrist computer for a quick look at the schematics. Just before the tunnel entrance, there was a door to the right.

"What are you doing?" Ray asked.

"Whatever it takes to protect my children." I let the acid I felt toward him leak through. "As any parent should. Heal your girlfriend. Then follow me out."

Ignoring Ray's protests, I took off for the staircase. I was faster than ever. Absorbing Jordan's power had given my Aegis a temporary boost.

When I got to the first floor, I flattened myself against a wall to avoid detection. Following the wall toward the entrance, I worked my way past Ross's office, focused my Aegis on my eyes, and peered around the corner.

A Sirin stood at the entrance, back facing me. Instincts said to shoot him now while I had a clear shot. To deal a blow to them the way they'd dealt so many blows to me. I'd worry about the consequences later—the ache in my heart, the one that still flared up like an illness every time I was responsible for ending someone's, anyone's, life.

But it wasn't smart. I couldn't risk being detected. Not with

Jordan's life on the line.

I allowed my eyes to return to normal and moved my focus to my ears. A series of beeps. Like a code. A security system? What was the point of that?

We were their biggest threat of infiltration. So why set...

Near my head, a box beeped. Beeps sounded up and down the hall. I cringed.

I was wrong. It wasn't an alarm. It was a timer.

I doubled back around the corner and put a little distance between me and the Sirin, tapping my earpiece to activate it. "Austin, come in."

A burst of static. "Here. What's cookin'?"

"You're about to be. Get everyone out now. This place is set to self-destruct. You've got a minute. I'll be right in front of you."

"Jacks—"

"Get them *out*."

"On it. Jacks—"

"I know." He was worried. I was too. But I trusted Austin with my life, and I knew he would get them out alive. In the meantime, I had to move.

I rushed back to the corner and peered around it. The Sirin was gone. I ran for the door and ducked to the side so I couldn't be spotted through the medical facility's glass doors.

They were already driving away. I'd missed my shot.

Shot.

I glanced at my gun.

I didn't miss shots. Not anymore.

I burst through the door and hit the ground running for the tree line on the side of the building.

Austin, get them out. It ran through my mind like a chant, a prayer as I leapt for the lowest tree limb I could find.

I moved from one tree to another, using my Aegis to keep me going at the speed I needed to reach them. To reach him.

What was I thinking? I'd sworn I could handle this, that I could save him. But it was a moving car, building speed before it took a turn onto the highway. What if I—

The tree limb I stood on cracked beneath me.

I flailed for something to grab hold of, another tree branch, a piece of bark, anything to stop my fall.

I hit the ground with a crash and a blast of pain that cut through my senses. I'd been moving so fast. I'd gotten so far, but I'd killed my lead. I pushed myself up, but my right leg buckled underneath me with the grind of bone against bone, and pain lanced through my leg. Vomit surged out of my mouth.

Ignoring it, I dragged myself to the road. It was a straightaway from where I stood, but the car was maybe thirty seconds away from veering onto the highway entrance. If they made it to that highway, I lost Jordan. Maybe forever.

I dropped to my belly with a groan and took aim just as the car was turning the corner.

One shot in the front tire and another in the back in quick succession. The car was still turning for a moment before the balance shifted from the exploded tires and the car skidded off the road and onto the highway's grassy sidelines. It lurched forward, then dipped as the front end descended into the ditch ahead of it and it flipped once, twice, down the ditch before it crashed into the nearest tree.

Horror rose through me with the sting of acid. That wasn't how I thought that shot would go.

I struggled to my feet and cried out. I'd forgotten about the leg.

Who gave a shit about the leg?

I killed my son.

And then, as if my universe needed another barrel roll, an explosion split the air.

No, the car!

But it wasn't the car. It was the lab. The lab I'd abandoned my team in.

I couldn't breathe.

I shoved my hands in my hair and gasped. It could have been a minute. It could have been an hour.

"Jacks!" Austin. He was shouting. I looked around me, but he wasn't there.

Right. The earpiece.

"Austin?" My voice shook. He was alive.

"Where are you, girl?" he shouted. "I've been shouting at you for a full minute!"

"They crashed and my leg is broken. I can't get to Jordan." I cringed at the way the words exited, robotic and stilted.

Another voice in my ear swore loudly. "We're on our way." Kyp.

"Did" —I had to swallow, clear my throat— "did you get them out?"

Austin's answer came with huffed breaths and I could envision him. His tall frame, eating up the distance between us as he ran. I may have even been able to see him if I could take my eyes away from where the car had skidded off the road. "I got them out."

Thank goodness. My father. Zane. They weren't gone.

My Aegis picked that moment to zoom in on the skid marks, the destroyed brush from where the car had plowed through.

I was responsible for that.

I rubbed my eyes with my fists, pressing them in as though the image would disappear.

It didn't.

I felt Austin's arrival before I saw him. I recognized the rhythm of his boots pounding the ground as he booked it toward me. I wanted to turn to face him, but I couldn't.

He was in front of me now, brown leather gloves brushing my cheeks, blue eyes latched onto mine. "C'mon, sweetheart. You in there?"

I blinked once. Twice.

"I shot out their tires. They crashed into the ditch. I killed them. I thought I'd stop them but I killed them." My lip wobbled.

"You seen the bodies?" He cupped my face in his hands and

pressed a kiss to my forehead.

"What? No."

"Then they aren't dead yet." Austin looked me up and down. "I'm gonna lift you and run you over there. Remember what Ray and I worked on with you?"

I nodded. "Pain can't kill you. Pain is a distraction. You will heal. Fight through it."

"That's right, girlie. On three."

I counted with him, preparing myself to breathe through what my body was about to throw at me. As promised, he hoisted me up on three, and I grunted, nearly biting down on my tongue to silence the cry trying to escape.

Pain can't kill you. Not you.

I focused on the slice of raised flesh just under Austin's right eye. The only scar on a man born with the ability to heal. It had been a close call, one where he'd used his entire Aegis healing a much more mortal wound.

Pain is a distraction.

My fingers dug into his jacket, nails denting the leather as he took off at a run toward the wreck. A thick cloud of smoke formed in the air.

Austin swore. "Can we not have a third explosion today?"

If my body wasn't in so much pain, if my spirit wasn't so numb, I might have laughed. It had been more than a year of this and I still wanted to cry for the days I didn't have an explosion counter in my head.

We descended into the ditch, Austin taking careful steps over the rocky, uneven terrain.

You will heal.

The misty gray car was more of a hunk of twisted steel than a recognizable vehicle. It was upside down and half wrapped around a tree.

Fight through it.

"Lower me to the ground next to the car," I said, shaking free from my stupor. I did this. I'd be damned if I wouldn't at least make a good effort of fixing it.

Glitter-painted fingernails. A hand hanging free from the backseat window. I channeled my Aegis, but it was getting shaky. I was wearing thin.

Pain won't kill me.

I diverted every ounce of Aegis I had left into my hands, my arms, and away from my leg, where it was working to heal, where it was working to smother the pain. I had work to do.

Pain is a distraction.

I wrenched the car door open, pulling hard enough to further bend the steel. "Austin, pull her out."

A peek into the car revealed both teens in the back, faces pallid, breathing heavy.

"You. Came," Jordan uttered, eyes wide and locked on me.

"I made a bit of a mess of the rescue, kiddo."

I wouldn't cry. There was no time for that.

Fight through it.

"Rennie?" Austin said, voice rough and tight. "That's your name, right?"

"Jordan," Rennie said, wincing. "Get him out first."

"No damn way," Jordan said. "Her or I don't go anywhere with you."

That look was so damn familiar. That fierce protectiveness.

Pain is a distraction.

"Rennie," Austin said again, ducking into the window of the car. "What's that short for?"

She took a deep breath. "Renita."

"That's pretty. Do you know what it means?" He backed out and yanked off his jacket, then crawled further in. "Hold that thought for after. First, I'm gonna—"

"Look out!" Rennie and Jordan shouted with more force than they'd looked capable of just moments ago.

I couldn't see from my angle, but I dragged myself forward. Austin shouted.

Pain.

Pain couldn't kill us.

The Sirin from the facility leaned over from the passenger seat and latched onto Austin, needle-sharp teeth digging into his shoulder.

I lunged forward, landing a punch square in the thing's nose. It didn't let go, clenching tighter instead. Austin visibly fought back the pain as he turned to the side and gripped the creature's jaws, trying to pry it free.

I felt for the gun in my holster, but it wasn't on me. I must've left it behind. Zane wouldn't be happy. I pulled myself farther in and swung at it again, my fist crashing into it but not doing much damage.

The window behind the Sirin exploded. A booted heel crashed through it, followed immediately by one of Cass's sai. The sai jammed through the Sirin, at the base of its brain. It clamped down harder on Austin's shoulder, blood oozing from the wound, then slumped forward, dropping its weight onto him.

I whipped my head around. Cass and Kyp stood near the front of the car. Cass pulled her sai free from the Sirin.

It was damn good to see them, looking like true heroes, standing triumphant over their enemies. The way they looked when I'd first met them.

I looked around them. "Where's Drew? Jainey?"

Cass reached forward and pried the Sirin's jaw free from Austin's shoulder. Blood oozed from his wounds.

"I sent Drew home with Jainey, Ray, and Zane," Cass said. She shook out her hands, like wringing an ache free. "Felt like the right thing to do."

Austin pulled himself free from the car, swearing up a storm.

"What about the Three?" I asked, looking at the kids in the car and offering them a reassuring thumbs up. It didn't seem to help.

"They were torn between protecting Jainey and Jordan. Kyp decided he was going to help with Jordan." She offered a soft smile. "I won this time. But we'll have to talk, later."

It was touching that her lifetime spent as Kyp's Guardian created a devotion that could break through the strength of three powerful spirits. The numbness from before slightly abated in the face of their potent bond.

"Later," I agreed. "First, how are we getting these kids out?"

"We're not until I've looked at the car," Kyp said. "They're pinned inside?"

"And upside down," I confirmed, like that needed confirming.

His eyes narrowed, but he stepped forward, his hand brushing over my hair so quickly I could have dismissed it as an accident. It felt more like comfort. He knelt beside me before I could react.

"Hello." His voice cracked halfway through the word. I supposed he'd just seen Jordan. "I'm Kyp. I'm going to use my Aegis to move the metal pinning you while I check your wounds."

"I—I don't think I'm wounded," Jordan said.

"That could be shock. What about you?" He glanced at Rennie.

Rennie struggled to breathe. "Definitely injured."

Jordan's eyes ticked to hers. "What?"

"Okay." Kyp swallowed. "Okay." I recognized this look. He was panicking, but he wasn't going to show it. "This may hurt. The car is crushed and a large portion is pinning you to your seats. I won't push the metal up and off of you too quickly." He looked behind him. "Can you guys help brace it?"

"With my other shoulder, I guess." Austin rushed to brace the car on Jordan's side.

Cass stepped to the other side.

Guilt flared up within me. Kyp didn't ask me for help. He knew whose fault this was.

The car moved and Rennie cried out. It was a terrible sound. Beside her, Jordan whimpered.

What good were superpowers if we couldn't save these kids?

"Okay, I've seen enough. Lower it slowly on three." He leaned into the car. "Sorry about that. You all right?"

"No. No. No," Rennie said.

"You have to help her," Jordan cried.

"We will," Kyp said. "I promise. I'm going to speak to the others for a moment and make a plan. Once we do, we're going to have to work quickly. But we'll get you out of this, I promise."

"I don't even know what happened." Jordan sniffled. "The car just..."

"Jordan," Kyp said, and I could hear the fake reassuring smile on his face without seeing it. "Hi. Do you know who I am?"

"Yes. Grandma Liv... was wrong, wasn't she?"

Kyp practically hissed his response. "She usually is. We'll be right back."

He knelt back down across from me, and Austin and Cass joined us.

"Sorry to intrude. I don't want them to hear," Kyp spoke within our minds. *"I'll be blunt, because frankly, we're running out of time. We're going to need a hell of a lot of healing to get them out of there. If I lift the crumpled metal free, which will take a considerable amount of Aegis to manage, maybe more than I*

have, they are going to start bleeding. Profusely. We don't heal them in time and... I don't know if we have enough in us." He turned to me. *"Jacks? Your Aegis?"*

"Weak, but I'll do my best."

"Shit. I should've brought Ray."

"He was wasted out," Cass said. *"He couldn't have helped much."*

Kyp swallowed hard. "He will come back. If we don't have enough energy, we prioritize Rennie. Jordan will come back."

The numbness I had been struggling with this entire time disappeared, replaced by a horror rivaled only by one other moment in my mind.

A thin line of blood spreading across Gana's throat.

If we did what Kyp was suggesting, I would have killed Jordan for the first time.

"Jacks, it was an accident. You can't see it that way," Austin said.

"We don't have time for this," Kyp said. *"I'm sorry, but this is the most logical course of action."* He said it with conviction, but his face crumpled, like he was sickened by his own thoughts.

No. No, it wasn't.

"Hey Kyp," I said, out loud this time, my eyes meeting his, both shielded by the film of tears in our eyes. "How would you like to make a miracle again?"

"A miracle?" Austin asked.

Kyp stared at me, dumbstruck. I held out my hand to him.

"We're stronger together, remember?" My jaw clenched.

"We can't," he choked out.

"What? You toddler married me. Did you divorce me without asking first?" It was an attempt at a joke, but it came out flat and emotionless.

"No." Through our mental connection, *"But I thought about it."*

"Then we can do this. Besides, I got a power boost earlier. I'll explain later." It was the first bit of hope I'd had in a long time.

"Stronger together." Kyp nodded.

The words were as real, as tangible as if he had already threaded his fingers between mine, as if the words themselves held all of our power, our connection.

"How can we help?" Cass asked.

"I'll peel up the piece of the car that's cutting into them. Once I remove that, it will get real bloody real fast. You and Austin have to pull them out of the car. Lay them before us and we will heal them as much as we can. Then you'll have to figure out how to get us home. We'll probably be unconscious." His lips twitched, but it was a dark smile.

"Okay. Go team." I shuffled closer to the car.

Rennie gripped the silver feather pendant around her neck again. "Guys, I'm not feeling too good."

"I'm sure," Austin said. "Listen, kiddos. We're gonna pull up what's pinning you down, and it's gonna hurt. But then we'll yank y'all out of the car and heal you up, best we can."

"Jordan can heal," Rennie said, but her voice sounded distant, her eyes staring off into the middle distance. "It's cold. It's cold, right?"

"Hell yes it is. It's damn near Thanksgiving," Austin said. "Gonna make you guys a turkey and everything."

"Get her out first," Jordan said.

"That was the plan," Kyp said.

Warmth and bitterness flooded me, like a gulp of hard liquor.

Jordan settled after that. Had he died before? He was far more terrified for her than he was for himself. But then, that was love, wasn't it?

Love is sacrifice.

Kyp had told me that once. It was the first time he'd felt he truly understood love.

It hadn't helped us. But it had protected me.

"Get in position. One. Two. Three. Go." Kyp pulled back the piece of metal with relative ease.

This would have all been much easier if we hadn't already had a battle for our lives today.

Austin and Cass moved with efficiency, pulling Rennie and then Jordan free from the wreck.

Rennie, as it turned out, swore like a sailor. "You owe me turkey and a whole fucking lot of soda."

I tried not to look at the blood staining her lovely green blouse, right across her midsection. I laid my hand on her and got to work stitching together everything torn asunder. The wound was deep, and as soon as Jordan was laid out beside her, I reached for Kyp, flailing aimlessly for his hand.

God, I couldn't do this by myself. I may not even be able to do this with him. This was practically bringing someone back from the dead. That piece of metal had cut right through to her spine.

Kyp's hand clamped around mine. *I got you.* He knelt beside me, pushing more energy into me. He pressed his other hand down on Jordan's legs, where they had been caught under the metal, sliced into just as deeply as Rennie's torso.

My energy started to wane, my eyes flagging. I almost had her healed. Almost.

"Here, can you drain me?" Austin asked. He reached over Jordan, ready to add his hand to ours. He stopped midway. "Kyp, did you see that?"

I whirled around, but I missed whatever happened, and the movement only served to make my head spin.

"What in the..." Kyp answered, his eyes going wide, even as he continued to feed into our connection.

And then Austin did something crazy. He grabbed a dagger from his boot and he sliced it across his hand.

Black pressed in on the edges of my vision. Almost there. I just had to hang on for a minute longer.

Austin pressed his hand to the wound on Jordan's leg, and it appeared to... it appeared to heal.

But that wasn't what Austin's Aegis did. He was a Guardian with a power like Wolverine in X-Men. He could heal himself.

But not others. How was he healing someone else?

"Are you guys okay?" Rennie asked, sitting up. "Jordan!"

She moved out of the way, quickly and without pain, and the grass she'd been lying in, coated heartily in blood, rushed up at my face.

Kyp yanked me up by our clasped hands, turning me so my head rested in his lap while he used the last of my energy, together with Austin, to heal our son.

My eyes closed on the image of my love and my best friend, working together to save our kid. I slipped out of consciousness with a prayer on my lips that they would be able to save him.

SIXTEEN

KYP

A ball of warmth shoved itself into Kyp's lower back with force, and Kyp grumbled, sleep-addled and frustrated, ready to growl at whatever was trying to push him off his own bed.

Reality hit him in waves. This wasn't his bed. The sheets were a cheaper thread count than he was used to, scratchier than what Franklin money regularly bought. Sunlight streamed through the large windows, so dazzling he could barely make out the figure who'd somehow appeared on the other side of his mattress.

Turning, he discovered the cause of the pushing. A tiny foot digging into his spine. He smiled and brushed a bundle of dark curls from Jainey's chubby little face. Her eyes were clenched shut, but her mouth hung open, a light snore filling the air with her every breath.

Adorable little bean.

Flashes of what he'd seen in the heads of the security guards at the facility ran through his head.

Adorable but very scary little bean.

Why had she done that? Had she lost control of her abilities? He'd have to work with her on that and they'd definitely need to speak about it. She needed to control the darkness they all had within them. He'd thought it was just his family, but there was something about being a Key that did this to them. He'd known Ross and Kylie were tainted. He'd known he and his mother were as capable of being heroic as they were blights on the world. But to him, Jacklyn and Raymond had always been forces for true good in the world.

The flaw in his thinking was obvious. Though he still loved both Body Keys, to quite an annoying degree, there was something wrong there as well. Something deep in their psyche that pushed them to darkness the way it did all the others.

Austin's sudden ability to heal others hadn't helped the doubt building within him. He hadn't had the chance to question him about it since he had passed out just after seeing it.

Just in time to watch the kids' wounds heal.

He sat up slowly, careful not to rock the bed too much, so Jainey would get what was likely much needed rest.

"She had a nightmare." Cass stood in the doorway, leaning against the doorframe and looking more like herself than she had in weeks. Gone was the constant training apparel that had come with the Three. Now she wore a cream-colored sweater, a light red scarf draped artfully around her neck. She smiled warmly. "She wouldn't sleep until I brought her here."

He tilted his head so he could see Jainey again, his heart squeezing when he considered he could bring her a feeling of safety. "As weird as it is, Jordan and Jainey are really our kids, aren't they?"

She snorted and walked to the bed, settling across from him. "Don't look now, but Rennie has adopted Austin as a big brother."

He made a face. "No accounting for taste." But there was no real heat behind it. Austin wasn't his favorite person in the world, but when it came down to it, they worked together to save those kids, like a team, like a family. "I want to thank you. For yesterday and for everything before. I never could have made it through any of this without you."

She smirked and shook her head, hoop earrings bouncing. "We're best friends. This is what we do. And even if we've adopted Drew, and then the others, we're the O.G. members of the resistance. Nothing will ever change that."

They exchanged smiles. Cass knew him. She knew how uncomfortable emotional displays could be for him. It was what had thrown him so out of sorts with Jacklyn the first time she'd come back. That discomfort coupled with the overwhelming relief of having her by his side again set something ablaze within him. He'd damned their team because the force of his love overrode his common sense. He wouldn't let that happen again.

Cass cleared her throat and boosted herself a little further up onto the bed, her argyle socked feet kicked up onto his thigh.

"How are you feeling today?" Kyp dropped his hand on her feet, then pushed them off his lap teasingly. "Better than yesterday?"

"Yesterday?" she scoffed. "You've been knocked out for two days. Jacklyn too. Scared the crap out of the kids."

"You know what I meant." Though that didn't mean he wasn't concerned about what could have happened in the couple of days he'd been dead to the world. "Are you okay? What happened out there?"

Cass dropped her gaze to where her hands rested in her lap. "I didn't choose this—it comes with my Aegis."

"You could speak with spirits, but this? This is something else. I didn't have time to question it before, with the kids in danger, but..."

"There are still children in danger," Cass said. "Jordan's friend Caleb and two others."

"Yes, and we will help them soon. But we can wait until we're all recovered from this complete disaster of a mission first."

"I don't know what changed, Kyp," she admitted. "But I'm your Guardian. I needed to choose you this time."

"I thought we both agreed that none of the Guardians belong to the Keys."

She narrowed her eyes. "You know I became a Guardian to protect you."

"But now you're the bearer of 'the Three,'" he said, air quotes and all. "What does that mean for you and what you want?"

"Nobody really asked me that." She shrugged. "Mari did the big sister thing and barged her way into my brain. It was for a good cause, but still not cool. And from there, all three of them were fighting over me. Mari wanted to lead me around so she could do some good again. Jaina wanted to correct her mistakes, and Gana wanted to tell Jacks her death wasn't her fault. She's come to the surface a few times trying, but Jacks won't look at me when I speak as her."

"It's hard for her." If his voice came out a little more gruff than he intended, he hoped Cass wouldn't notice.

"And it's effortless for you." She shoved his shoulder.

She got an eye roll for an answer. "You got the Three under control. Are they going to fight back again?"

"I don't know," Cass said. "They've calmed somewhat. They're three spirits, sent to protect three different Skeleton Keys. If there were any other Spirit-centric Guardians, or a Spirit Key, they'd be able to handle this. Instead, they're all warring within me."

"You seem pretty nonchalant about all this," Kyp said.

"Yeah, well, you adapt," Cass said. "Whoever's in charge of the dead Keys and Guardians gave me the spirits they did because they knew I'd accept them. Mari is apparently assigned to Caleb, so she's the most frustrated right now since we lost our shot at saving him."

"You can tell her I haven't forgotten about him." He pondered what she'd said for a moment. "So, there are only three Keys. The rest are Guardians?"

"Bingo." She smiled. "You know, Kyp, I'm really happy to see you invested in something again." She fiddled with the chocolate brown blanket, twisting a loose thread around steady fingers. "It was hard. Seeing you suffer the way you did. It's been easier since Drew, but even with your" —she paused— "precarious position with the Madisons, it's almost like you're yourself again."

Kyp swallowed back the lump in his throat. "I'm trying. There's a lot here, and it's scary. But it's different. Like we're moving into a future where we can really make a difference."

"Yeah." She flashed him a beaming smile. "Are you gonna wake the kid, or leave her here?"

"Give us a minute?" Kyp asked.

"Sure." She squeezed his shoulder as she headed for the door.

He waited for her to close the door behind her before taking a deep breath. They were safe for now. Which meant it was time to recover. He turned over to where his cherubic angel slept beside him.

He wasn't ready for this. He wasn't even really old enough to be her father. But when had anything in his life been normal? If he had a kid—no, *kids*—he was going to do his best to do right by them. To be a real father.

They may have the abilities of a Mind Key, making them uniquely able to cope with the truth, but they were less than a year old. He was their father, and what kind of father would he be if he pushed his children away because they looked and acted differently than he'd expected?

He flopped down onto the bed so he was facing Jainey. "Jainey baby, it's time to wake up." He nudged her shoulder, just the slightest bit, and her eyes blinked open sluggishly, the hazel catching the sunlight, highlighting the green flecks in her irises.

All at once, her eyes lit up, and she threw her arms around his neck. "Papa! You scared me!" She pulled back and slugged him in the arm. She had her mother's right hook.

He smiled, charmed. "Sorry. I'll try not to do it again."

"Can we stay here for a little while?" Jainey said, her voice strained as she nuzzled against his chest. "I've had a really hard week."

Yeah. He could do that.

Jacklyn was still in bed when Kyp paid her a visit. She was awake, but resting. Austin had kicked his feet up on the bed, right next to her head, and was leaning back in a chair, speaking to her in an animated voice, hands flailing to punctuate his words.

"I mean, I can do this, right?" Austin said. "He's just so... well, you know. And I'm... well, you know. And I don't even know how? Am I ready? When will I be ready?"

"You're ridiculous," Jacklyn said, her voice weak, but her smile spoke volumes about her amusement. "I thought you guys were already... well, you know."

"For whatever it's worth, Drew too," Kyp jumped into the conversation.

"Drew too, what?" Austin asked, dropping his chair onto all four legs and whirling toward Kyp. "What did I say? Did I say something? I said everything, didn't I?"

Jacklyn met Kyp's gaze. She was still slightly pale from their ordeal, but her eyes were sharp. "You. Be nice or I'll pop your eyeballs."

Kyp fought a smile. "You'll try." He took a few steps into the room. "All I'm saying is that you should be having this conversation with Drew, not Jacklyn. He'd probably be a much greater help."

Austin frowned. "Are you trying to get rid of me so you can talk to her?"

"No, actually. It was you I came to see."

"Weird. Why?"

Kyp gestured toward the foot of the bed. "May I?"

"Be my guest," Jacklyn said. "This better not be you being a snot."

"This is a mission-related conversation."

"Ohhhh." She leaned slightly toward Austin. "He's less of a snot when it's a mission-related conversation."

A dramatic sigh brought their attention back to him. "The healing thing, Austin."

"Yeah." Austin sat up straight. "Sorry, boss man, I haven't the slightest. One day, I have one ability, like any other Guardian. If that Sirin hadn't bit me, if I hadn't dripped blood on Jordan's wounds, I never would have known."

The facts swirled through Kyp's head. He was missing something. *Puzzle, puzzle.* But it wasn't the same kind of puzzle. That game was there to make him capable of seeing gaps in his otherwise perfect memory. This wasn't anything he already knew. It was something missing in a series of clues. The connecting piece to make things make sense.

"Mystery number three," he muttered.

"What are one and two?" Jacklyn asked. "You know, in the interest of full disclosure?"

Perhaps talking through it would help. "Mystery one: I get why they need Skeleton Keys. Same reason Moth—" —a fierce shake of his head— "Lavinia wanted one. She wants her Aegis to stay active. We know that we lose our Aegis if the rifts close. But do we know why? Or if that's even true? And why are they making Guardians instead of recruiting them?"

"Basic corporate greed?" Ray stepped in behind them.

"Hey!" Jacklyn smiled at him. "How's Zane?"

"Right as rain. It drained me a bit, but she's all healed up now."

"I'm glad," Kyp added.

"I just got back from training the boy. He's clever and energetic."

"Training?" Kyp asked.

"I know," Ray said, holding his hands up plaintively. "I'm not training him because I'm trying to make him into a soldier. I heard you loud and clear on that front. I'm training him because I want him to learn discipline and how to control his Aegis. And I want him to be able to fight, to defend himself."

Kyp took a moment to gather himself.

"I get it, kids. I made a mess of things. Seeing as I'm their grandfather, and Zane and I are the closest things to actual adult parents they're going to have—"

"We're their parents," Jacklyn cut him off. She looked at Kyp.

"Yes. We're their parents. However, we understand why we'd need help." Then, more pointedly, "But *we* make the decisions. You should've spoken to us first before taking liberties. I don't care if we were unconscious."

Jacklyn nodded, arms crossed over her chest. It might have been the closest they'd been to being on the same page in a long time. Maybe ever.

Ray nodded once, sharply. "Got it. I won't make that mistake again." He laid a hand on Kyp's shoulder. "Continue talking. I want to hear the rest of your mysteries."

Sure, he was angry at Ray, but there was something about his hand resting on his shoulder that immediately encouraged him. Ray had heard him. Kyp wasn't sure if he understood, but progress had been made. Ray knew he'd screwed up with him. And he was still there, encouraging him...

Maybe Kyp was starved for parental kindness. Hector and Lavinia had deliberately tortured him. Ray had abandoned him, but he had always been kind when he'd been with him, and Kyp didn't know how to keep hating him. He could chalk it up to another mystery, but maybe it was something more ephemeral, like love—something he would never solve or understand.

Kyp shot a smile over his shoulder. That was all Ray would get from him.

He recapped what Cass had told him earlier. "Why would she be chosen to do this, when she doesn't have that ability?"

"Maybe she did," Austin said, "and she didn't know it yet. Like me with the healing."

"So maybe our second and third mystery are the same," Jacklyn said.

"Maybe they are. I'd ask Cxarana if I thought I could speak to her again without the Council finding out," Kyp said. "I don't want them to know what we're figuring out."

"Probably for the best," Jacklyn said.

Drew barged into the room, gripping the door frame. "Something's wrong with Jordan."

They rushed after Drew, following him down the two flights of stairs leading to the first floor living room. When they hit the landing, Jacklyn's legs buckled. Kyp noticed. He always noticed her.

He caught her elbow to steady her. "You okay?"

She frowned. "Still working on okay. Just exhausted."

Kyp nodded and released her. They turned in towards one of the once unoccupied bedrooms and discovered Jordan kneeling in the center of the floor, clutching his head in his hands.

"Jordan?" Jacklyn approached tentatively.

"My head," he gasped. "It hurts. There's so much. There's too much."

"Too much what?" She stroked a gentling hand over his hair, only to be answered with a groan. He tightened his fingers in his hair and yanked.

Jacklyn looked at Rennie.

"Too much power?" Rennie shrugged. "I don't know. He doesn't like talking about it." She looked away.

"Kyp?" Jacks reached back, blindly grasping his wrist. "Can you help? Maybe you can see what's going on?"

"I can try. But only if it's okay with Jordan."

"It is *not* okay with Jordan," Jordan gasped, rocking in place.

Rennie rubbed his back, leaning into him and whispering kind words into his ear.

"It doesn't matter if it's okay with him," Jainey's voice cut in.

Jordan let out something akin to a whimper. "No, Jainey, you have to go."

"Nah," Jainey said. "This is why we're a team. You're the powerful one. I'm the practical one." It was a weird statement coming from such a petite person. Like there was a thirty-five-year-old trapped in there. She turned her hazel eyes on Kyp. "Papa, he's used to me in his head, but he knows I won't open doors he doesn't want you in. I'll take you there."

Kyp wanted to ask what doors he couldn't go through and why. This, plus Jainey's use of her abilities in the facility, concerned him deeply. But there wasn't time for that.

Kyp knelt beside them both on the floor. He wanted to suggest Jainey run the show, but Kyp had seen how dark things got when her control lacked. He wouldn't risk hurting either of them. "Whatever makes it more comfortable for him."

The boy in question smacked the floor, as though it would relieve whatever was in his head. One, two, three times, before an odd crackle and a pop emitted from him.

"Crap," Rennie swore. "Don't look now, he's going radioactive."

"As in actually nuclear?" Kyp asked.

Jacklyn didn't wait for anyone to answer. "If you aren't immediate family, you all need to leave."

"But—" Rennie started, but Jacklyn grabbed her by the arm. "Not you."

"Thanks." She sighed. "You remember what happened at the facility. If he blows…"

"He disintegrated four interdimensionals," Jacklyn said. "Like... poof."

"Jacklyn, maybe you can pull his energy from him? Like you did the last time?" Rennie asked.

"Yes." She reached for him.

"I'd agree with you, but then we'd both be wrong," Kyp said. "You're still too weak. Jainey, can you do it?"

"I already have too much power," Jainey said. "We'd just transfer the problem to me."

"We... could... call Ray back?" Kyp offered.

"Like I said," Jacklyn said. "I'm gonna do it."

"Ugh… deal," Kyp agreed. "Ready, Jainey?"

"Ready." She sounded tentative, but Jordan's breathing was speeding up.

"Jordan," Jacklyn said. "Ready?"

"Please," he cried. "I'm getting really frickin' sick of being rescued."

Kyp could relate. He was sure Jacklyn could, too. He grabbed Jainey's hand and touched a hand to Jordan's forehead, brushing his hair aside.

"Kyp, come on!" Jacklyn grumbled.

"Give me a sec, dammit. Jordan, look at me. Eye contact."

He raised his eyes to meet Kyp's. The same eyes he marveled at on Jainey. Their mother's eyes. Jacklyn's mother's eyes.

He counted down for Jordan, so he wasn't surprised. And then on one, he threw his consciousness into Jordan's mind, Jainey following along with him.

Visions and voices whirled around him. Rennie sitting at a desk. Jainey laughing and blowing bubbles at him. A boy with dusty blonde hair holding a hand out for Jordan to help him up. The sound of Jacklyn singing a gentle lullaby. When had he heard that? The few months she'd been pregnant with him? And then, surprisingly, Kyp himself, leaning into the car with an awkward wave, looking uncomfortable but fond, ready to help.

"What are we looking for?" Jainey asked.

"A catalyst, and, hopefully, a way to help him manage it."

Jainey gave the mental equivalent of a terse nod. He went with it, scouring Jordan's surface thoughts, looking for signs of recent anxiety that he could help assuage. He wouldn't go deeper without Jainey's consent.

After a few suspicious glimpses Jainey warned him away from, something they would definitely be talking about later, Kyp spotted a sparking, throbbing mass. Jainey coaxed him forward. He'd found it. He pressed against the barrier within the mindscape, and became the proverbial fly on the wall, watching Ray chat with Jordan in the kitchen while Jordan grabbed an orange.

"So, you spent time training with throwing knives," Ray said. "Any idea why?"

"They never told me," Jordan admitted. He didn't want to talk about it. About why he was created. He only had suspicions anyway. "All they said was that they wanted us to be able to protect ourselves in case someone tried to take us away from them. They said we were meant to replace the Keys and Guardians that already existed. We were meant to be better, stronger. The world needed us."

Jordan had his doubts. More likely, they were pawns in a game, and on the wrong side of the board.

"That why your knuckles are bruised up?" Ray asked.

"Punching bag." Jordan shrugged.

Ray fiddled with the pack of gum in his hand. "D'ya like bubble gum?"

"Sure."

"Play a little game with me, and you can have the whole pack." He shot him a crooked grin.

The memory jumped forward. They were in the training room.

Ray draped a blindfold around Jordan's eyes. Jordan didn't like it. It felt like a lifeline was stolen from him.

His breath caught.

"You're fine, kid. It's just your eyes. You've got plenty of other senses, and they're stronger than the average person's. You're better equipped than you realize." A pause. "Besides, no harm's gonna come to you here."

Jordan wasn't so sure. After all, ever since these people arrived in his life, he'd had a gun held to his head, been attacked by Gorvhans and Sirins, and been in a car accident that nearly killed him.

Sure, the facility was sometimes worse, but this had come on so quickly.

Kyp would definitely not be repeating that to Jacklyn. She'd blame herself for all of it.

Jordan pushed his hands through his hair and took a steadying breath, but his chest remained uncomfortably tight. He didn't know what would happen if he made these people angry. Rennie had told him horrible stories about how her foster mother had punished her, stories that made his blood boil and his skin tighten. Stories that made him want to destroy.

Ray pressed something into his hands. Smooth handles... knives. He'd been asking about throwing knives. He wanted him to throw knives blindfolded. Crap.

"Listen to the sound of my voice," Ray said. "Follow it. I'm standing beside the target, just to the left. I want you to throw the knife to the right of my voice."

Jordan scratched his face under the blindfold. "What? Have you been binge watching Daredevil*?"*

"Jacklyn didn't get her geekiness from nowhere. I didn't know they let you watch Netflix at the facility."

Jordan shifted. "We couldn't do anything personal, like social media, but TV was fine." He flipped one of the knives in his hand and impressed himself when he caught it on the right end. And then, based on the sound of Ray's voice, he threw the knife just to the right, where Ray'd said the target would be.

A crash and a bang. A loud choking swear. Jordan yanked the blindfold from his eyes in horror.

Ray doubled over laughing. The shelving unit beside him was turned over, but the knife was sticking out of the target. "I... I knocked it over. I wanted to see your, ha, I wanted to see your face! You thought you got me! Oh my God." He grabbed his sides.

Jordan didn't laugh. His breath caught again.

"Oh crap, son. I was just goofing with you." He stepped in closer. "How 'bout we cut this training junk and I get you some hot cocoa, and you can punch the shit out of me once you're not having a heart attack, yeah?"

The memory moved forward again. They were back in the kitchen, sipping hot cocoa, and Ray was telling him about the wars. All the wars. He told him about the war against the interdimensionals and the civil war that had split the Order down the middle, and he told him why Lavinia couldn't be trusted. As Kyp listened to Ray speak with Jordan so freely, a roiling mix of anger and envy churned within him.

Would he ever feel this comfortable speaking to Jordan? A kid was one thing, but a younger teenager? And why was Jordan getting Ray's version of the story before he got his or Jacklyn's?

"But you won?" Jordan said.

"That's the thing about war," Ray said. "Nobody wins. You survive. Eventually, you accomplish a goal, and it ends. But nobody really wins when you lose as much as you do. War is like a dirty alley that way."

"I have no clue what that means. I've never been to a dirty alley." Jordan groaned in frustration. "You can't screw up if you don't try. Trying has to count for something, doesn't it?"

"Sure, it does," Ray said. But there was something dark in his eyes, unspoken words that chilled Jordan to the bone. He felt it. This war had taken and taken from Ray, and it would likely keep taking.

Kyp understood. Jordan's fear flowed into Kyp, and Kyp replaced it with a warm reassurance that he would do whatever it took to keep them safe, everything he could to find the other kids.

When Kyp returned to his own head, he stared down at the hideous mustard-colored sweater someone had given Jordan. Kyp guessed it had been Drew. His fashion sense could be interesting.

Jordan collapsed into his arms, exhausted, and buried his face into his shoulder. Kyp ran a soothing hand up and down the boy's back. Jainey leaned on Rennie, who mouthed a thank you at him.

Kyp lifted Jordan and carried him to his bed, while Rennie gave Jainey over to Jacklyn. Taking one more look to be sure the kid was none the worse for wear, Kyp settled down on the floor beside Jacklyn, back propped against the wall, while Rennie took up position looking over Jordan. Jainey had already fallen asleep on her mother.

Kyp placed a hand on Jacklyn's shoulder. "You okay?"

Her eyes sparked with energy. "Yeah. Topped me off with Aegis energy. Wish the circumstances were better."

Kyp nodded. "He remembers you. I don't know how. Clips from before you lost him? Or the same kind of mental link that told you he was still alive? I have no idea, but he can remember you singing to him. He remembers your voice."

Jacklyn choked on a gasp. "I loved him before he was really even a person. I'm sorry I took that chance away from you."

"I think I understand," Kyp said. "If we'd lost him in that car accident, it would have hurt to lose him, and I didn't even know him yet. And how do I do that? How do I get to know him? I don't know how to talk to him."

She laughed. "You don't really know how to talk to anybody." She turned her hand, threading her fingers with Kyp's, a hint that she was just messing with him. "Don't worry about it so much. Ask how he feels about the weather."

Kyp smiled. "That's stupid."

"You know what I mean. He's going through complete upheaval right now. You felt perfectly comfy rooting around in his head to help him get in control, but you don't feel comfortable asking him 'how 'bout them Mets?'"

"I'm partial to the Yankees myself."

"You would be," she scoffed. "You get my point though, right?"

"I do."

"Just talk to him. Like he's a person. The rest will come in time." She leaned her head on his shoulder. After a few moments, her breathing evened out, taking on a gentle rhythm that calmed the fear tripping its way through Kyp's heart.

Before he knew it, his eyelids were drooping. It wasn't the most comfortable place to catch a nap, but the company made it better.

SEVENTEEN

JACKLYN

I woke with Kyp's head propped on mine. My head was on his shoulder. And we were sitting against the wall with a five-year-old using our legs as pillows. I refused to move.

Jordan groaned, and Kyp snapped awake with a snort.

"Jacks?" he asked, looking at me with clouded eyes.

I squeezed his hand. We hadn't let go. It had been hours, it had gotten dark, and we hadn't let go.

"Jordan's waking up," I whispered. Jainey stirred.

"Jordy?" she asked sleepily.

"Jainey." Jordan shot up in bed, then groaned, hands covering his face.

Jainey scuttled from our laps and threw herself into the bed. "Don't do that. You need rest." She threw her arms around him and tackled him back down on the bed.

Kyp snatched his hand from mine, absently wiping it on his jeans. Like holding my hand disgusted him.

I balled my hand into a fist and shook it out, like I could shake away the ache in my heart. "He's awake. Maybe this is your chance?"

Kyp didn't look terribly positive about the prospect.

"You've got this." I sighed and pushed myself to my feet. This was an opportunity I had to take advantage of. "Okay, little nugget! You're coming with me."

"No, it's okay." Jordan cuddled her closer and dropped a kiss on top of her head.

"I know, but I need one-on-one Jainey time." I wrapped an arm around her waist and lifted her into my arms. "I've got a plan for an astounding day. One night of zero Order work before we start looking for the rest of your friends. Want to help?"

She looked dubious.

I leaned forward and whispered in her ear. "We're gonna throw a party."

"Really?" she half-shrieked.

"Dude, super hearing!" I headed out the door.

"But why can't they come with us?" Jainey pouted, glancing back at Kyp as he settled on Jordan's bed.

"I want to let him have time with his son." Kyp was scared of talking to Jordan. The sooner he got it over with, the better he'd feel. "And you and I should get to have some time together, too!"

Her face screwed up.

She didn't believe me? Where had I messed this up?

"Are you at least psyched about the party idea?" I offered her a tentative smile. Maybe a day out would do wonders for both of us.

"Yes! Let's do it!"

"There's my girl!"

Going to the mall was so weird. Every time I'd been to one in the last year, I'd spent the entire time feeling like I'd stepped into some kind of surreal world, where the most crucial thing was a sale, and monsters only existed in the form of Karens shouting at customer service reps.

We brought Cass and Austin along for the ride, because we were Keys. We weren't allowed to go out for an actual mommy daughter day with just the two of us.

Though I cringed at the crush of people, the scents from snack stations and perfumes and the sheer normalcy of families out for a regular day of shopping were wonderful reminders of everything we fought for every day. We hurt so these people could survive. That was worth something.

We barely bought anything for my impromptu party, spending our time instead introducing Jainey to the beauty of real life, and letting her raid the stores. A wonderful afternoon that continued through our return home and the preparation of our backyard for the party.

When we were done, I stood back, gazing at our efforts with pride. This was the best idea I'd ever had.

Fairy lights lined the fences, highlighting the ivy vines crawling up and around the stone wall of the building next door.

There was outdoor seating in bursts along every wall—wood benches and chairs, wicker sets with sofa-style cushioning. The matching tables were covered with finger-foods, chips and dip, soft drinks and beer. We probably shouldn't have picked up beer, as most of us were nineteen or twenty, but I decided we could take a pass on that law since we were usually saving the world. An iPhone speaker on a table waited for someone to blast music from their phone through it.

In the center was a lit fire pit. There were chocolate bars, graham crackers, and marshmallows at the ready.

Ray wrapped an arm around me after dropping off a case of soda at the nearest table. "You know, this was what I wanted this space to be used for. That's why I bought all the furniture."

I huffed a laugh. "I wondered about that."

"The estate had such a beautiful backyard. When I found this place, I imagined I'd create a new Order here, and I hoped to give people the same experience. Back when I was young, the estate was a huge family home. We did more than train. We did things like this. We didn't all like each other, but there were family groups and close friends, and when we took a break, the gatherings were lovely. I wanted something like that again. I wanted to create a home for those who came here. But when everything shook out, and the dust cleared? It was hard to find anyone who wouldn't either run to Lavinia or refuse to sign up. Not quite my own Order of the Key."

"Not then, but you've got a full house now."

"A full house, yes," he said. "But this Order is of yours and Kyp's making. I had nothing to do with it."

I leaned my head back on his shoulder. "Maybe one day we'll leave it to you. Run away to be normal people and let you take care of all the hard stuff."

Ray snorted. "Like I don't know you both. You're seeing this through to the end. Then maybe you'll run away. For a vacation or something."

"We're not together, you know." It sounded like he needed a reminder.

"Pfffft." He waved dismissively, as if offended. "I never suggested anything of the sort."

Jerk.

The backyard door swung open and Drew and Zane marched through.

"Pizza's here," Drew announced.

No kidding. The stack was piled over his line of sight.

"I'm helping." Zane snickered. Her version of helping was maneuvering Drew without bothering to take any of the boxes.

"Hey, Zane!" I greeted. "Damn good to see you back on your feet."

"Table is in front of you. You can lower them," she instructed Drew. Then she turned a smile my way. "Thanks! I've been up and about for a bit, but you've been mostly knocked out."

"Like ships passing in the night," I teased.

"I ordered two plain, two chicken and broccoli, two mushroom, and two pepperoni. You think that's enough?" Drew asked.

"It should be. Jeez," I said.

"I don't know about you, but I could eat an entire pie by myself." He rubbed his belly.

"And then it disappears." Zane rolled her eyes. "Drew's real super power is his absurd ability to burn fat."

One by one, the crew meandered outside, Jainey dutifully performing her assigned task to drag everyone out. Nobody could say no to Jainey. Not even our resident grump, apparently. Jainey pulled Kyp while Jordan pushed him along with both hands on his shoulders.

Good for him. His time with Jordan must have gone very well if they were goofing around.

"Wow!" Kyp's eyes darted around the yard. "Whose idea was this?"

I sauntered over. "Mine, but Jainey decorated."

We'd only bought one decoration on our trip to the mall: fairy lights.

Jainey scampered up onto a bench. "Do you like the lights, Papa?"

"She's so freaking cute," Kyp muttered, like he was frustrated at his own powerlessness in the face of Jainey's special brand of adorable. "Absolutely, sweetie! A brilliant touch!"

I grinned at him. He sighed and headed straight for the beer.

I sighed just as hard.

Behind me, Austin said, "That should be fun. Kid doesn't

drink. Whaddya think he's like when he drowns his sorrows?"

"I have no idea," Drew said. "I feel like I should stop him before I find out."

"This is phenomenal!" Rennie cheered. "What better way for us all to get to know each other than a party. I love this."

I hoped this idea was as good as I thought it would be, but I was starting to feel concerned. Maybe chicken and broccoli pizza would alleviate my worries. Medicating my worries with food sounded like a terrible idea. Still, I dashed to the pizza table.

The gathering went on as planned. We ate pizza, drank soda and beer, told stories and laughed. We danced to music. Or rather, most of us did, and Kyp stood on the sidelines, tipping a beer to his lips and evaluating everyone through snotty-looking asides to Cass.

Could it be because Austin and I were dancing? Or was I imagining that? Wishful thinking and all.

"What made you decide to do this?" Austin asked, twirling me out and back in again.

I laughed, because the dance move didn't fit the hard rock beat in the slightest. "I really needed it. I feel like it's been a lifetime since I've celebrated anything. But the kids are here. I have no idea what to do about them, but we won. One strike against the bad guy. And it made me feel like I could breathe again."

"Good timing, too," Austin reasoned. "A bit more of a temperature drop and we'd be wearing more than sweaters out here."

I leaned closer. "Well, if we came out in our fur-lined tactical gear, the neighbors would notice."

"You know," Austin said. "It's okay to be uncertain."

He pulled me closer when the music slowed, his hands resting on my waist. I threw my arms around his neck. "Is there wisdom to be had?"

"You're nervous about taking this time to breathe. You're nervous about what Ray was sayin' earlier, too. About a new Order created by you and Kyp." He looked at me expectantly.

I dropped my head forward. "Ideally? We retrieve the kids. Find out where they came from. Return them to any parents we can find. See if there's anybody we can recruit to help us. Continue closing rifts. Have a real team that destroys the interference. It's a nice idea."

"Ah, but you're not an idealist." He bumped his forehead against mine. "You're a realist. It's the realists that hold things together. And they're the ones that stay sane." He patted me on the head. "Try to hold on to the whole realist thing, Jacks. I can't live with another idealist. They're always disappointed."

His eyes darted off in Kyp's direction before returning to mine.

"Pretty sure I know when the idealist in me died."

He turned me around, and the movement revealed Kyp, whose eyes were burning a hole into the back of Austin's shoulder.

Austin whispered in my ear, "He's so damn mad right now."

I giggled. I hadn't giggled in a long time. Was this what healing felt like?

But I was no idealist.

"I love you, kiddo." He pressed a kiss to my forehead. "But I think this is where our dance ends."

It was like my chest emptied. My heart stopped. "What do you mean?"

"Shit." He squeezed me a little. "I'm not going anywhere. I'm sorry. I'm saying... you know we flirt."

"I—"

He cut me off. "We do. It's cool. I don't know if you realized that it was kinda real to me. Sometimes. I don't know. I was hopeful."

I guess I did know. I just couldn't imagine it. I was always so hung up on the past.

"We would've been good."

"Yeah, but you already found your guy," Austin said. "And now I did, too. So it's okay. But I'm not gonna be able to move ahead with him until I close this door."

"Okay." I took a deep breath. "So, this is the last dance. But you're still my best friend."

"That, darlin', will never change. I just told you, I love you."

I laughed. "God, why? I'm a mess."

He planted a rough kiss on my temple and flicked me on the cheek. "Nah, that's expected. You're just getting back on your feet. What you've been through, it's no small stuff." He released me from his hold and took my hand. "C'mon."

He marched me over to the table Kyp and Cass had parked

at. Once we arrived, he loudly announced, "Here. You sit with the wallflowers. I've got a man to chat up."

"Really?" Kyp laughed, and it came out a little too loosely. The table was littered with bottles, and I was relatively certain very few of them belonged to Cass. No wonder his laugh sounded so lubricated.

"Yes, really," Austin said. "Thought you already knew where my interests lay."

"Didn't seem like it a minute ago," Kyp grumped.

Austin nodded, then snatched the beers Kyp had lined up unopened on the table. "You're runnin' your mouth today. You shouldn't have these 'cause you've had enough of 'em. I'm gonna walk these over to Drew. I'm sure he'll appreciate it."

Kyp looked more offended about Austin stealing the beer than he had about him dancing with me. "Those are mine."

Austin rolled his eyes. "You're a fool. You never had to worry about Jacklyn. Not because I didn't want her, but because she chose you. She'll always choose you. And now I'm choosing Drew." He winked at me and strolled away.

I was going to kill him.

"Well," Cass said. "That was uncomfortable."

"For real." I pushed my hands through my hair and yanked at it in frustration.

"I like your hair," Kyp blurted.

My head snapped up so hard I yanked a muscle. "What?"

"Your hair." He motioned toward my head, like I didn't know

what the word meant.

"You cut it." Cass glanced between me and Kyp, gesturing toward my chin-length cut.

"So did you." I pointed out her close-cropped curls. "You have the perfect face for short hair. It really suits you." She did, but I had no idea why we were talking about it.

Kyp's smile was halfway between actual amusement and blind terror. His lips were pulled back tight, teeth bared, but his eyes sparkled. "You look... you look very nice. Lovely. And, um, words are failing me at the moment."

I should have probably just accepted the compliment. "Cass, is he okay?"

"From what I can gather?" Cass said. "Nope. Drinking alcohol has seemingly removed some..."

Kyp twisted one of my curls around his finger. "They're bouncier when they're shorter."

"...No, *every* brain to mouth barrier he has." Cass scrunched her nose. "I took him away from the group the minute I realized."

"You're a good friend," I said.

"The best." Kyp leaned a head on her shoulder, starry-eyed.

I didn't want to giggle outright, and I didn't want to torture him with my presence. "I'm gonna go bother the kids."

"Bye!" Kyp said, and for the briefest moment, I could hear his little boy voice from my memories. "See you later."

I grinned. "Later!"

I only took two steps away before Cass called her thanks to

me. I waved a thumbs up over my head and headed for Jainey.

Surrounded by all of her protectors, Jainey lay on a huge pillow she'd bought just because she liked it. It was her size and what she'd proclaimed to be her favorite color, a pale, airy blue. She sprawled across it on her stomach, her feet kicked up behind her, enthralled by the flames cracking in the firepit as they caught on the kindling Ray had recently added.

I knelt down beside her. "Hey, booger. You enjoying yourself?"

Jainey glanced away from the fire, a brief acknowledgement of my presence, before her eyes returned to its splendor. "I am. I like it here. It's still dangerous, but everyone... seems to care? Like, at the facility, Ross and the other kids cared, but the adults just wanted to teach us. Or test us. They said that's what the Order of the Key was like and that I, *we*, should get used to it." She turned onto her side. "Is that true?"

My heart stuttered in my chest. "Ray says it was like it is here, now, when he was younger. Then Lavinia took over. And it became more like it was at the facility."

"You're not gonna let her make it all scary and mean again, are you?" Jainey asked.

It wasn't a question, really. More of a statement. She knew the answer already.

"Never." I placed a comforting hand on her back and rubbed. I wasn't sure who was comforting who, but it felt good to just be.

We sat there for a while in silence, her watching the fire, and me watching the flickering reflection of the flames dancing across her face as the sun went down and the moon rose in the sky.

Mom would have adored her.

Eventually, Jainey drifted off to sleep. Even with the noise of the party surrounding her, she felt safe enough, comfortable enough, that she could rest, and my spirit soared. We'd missed many moments just like this, moments Livingston stole from us. But at least we had this. At least we had now.

I'd been trying so hard not to think about how much we'd missed. Sure, it had been a year, but Jainey and Jordan were whole people who had formed when we weren't looking. We missed first steps, first words, and, in Jordan's case, first crushes. But we were together now. And now they would get to grow up surrounded by family and love, not experiments and pain.

I hadn't been able to give them much yet. Just my genetics and their freedom. But I was just getting started. I would give them everything they wanted in the world if they let me.

Across from where we sat, at the far end of the backyard, Austin and Drew sat shoulder to shoulder, speaking quietly. Exchanging tender looks, they swayed toward each other as they spoke, like the pull between them was unavoidable.

Cass knelt beside me. "Ray and Zane headed in, and I think Kyp's thinking about doing the same. I figured I'd take this munch upstairs, if you're not ready to head in yet."

"Yeah, okay," I said. "She probably shouldn't stay out here too long. The fire's beginning to die down and I don't want her to freeze."

"Got it." Cass lifted Jainey. "See you inside."

I waved goodbye, then headed to one of the empty benches. I kicked my feet up and laid back on the cushioned seat, clasping my hands behind my head and shoving everything else from my mind. This whole day had been about turning around my way of thinking. I needed to find my way through the pain of everything I'd been through. If I didn't, someone else could die.

The bench creaked. Someone had plopped onto the edge. I cracked my eyelids open. "Who dares disturb my slumber?"

Rennie snorted. "This isn't *Aladdin*."

"You watched that at the facility?" I peered at her through half-closed eyes. She sat beside my head with a comb and bottle of conditioner in her hands.

"Nah," she said. "I watched it when I lived with my mama. Before I knew what any of this crap even was. Anyway, I was trying to get Jordan to braid my hair, but then Kyp brought his drunk behind over there and started to chat it up with my boy—"

I smiled at her, begging her to continue.

"—that is a friend. Which I also wanted to talk to you about, actually. If you have a minute."

That piqued my interest. "Okay, take a seat." I straddled the bench and gestured for her to do the same. When she was settled in with her back to me, I waved my fingers at her. "Conditioner."

She handed it over to me. "Okay, so first? Can we talk about Jordan?"

"Okay." I squeezed out a healthy amount of the pink

conditioner into my hands and worked it through her thick hair. "You know him better than I do, so I'm not sure how I can help unless it's Order business or something."

"No," she said, and I regretted that I couldn't see her eyes when she spoke. She sounded weird. Uncomfortable. "I figure you're his mom, and will be the most defensive of him, so if I'm a mess, you'll tell me."

My hands stilled in her hair. "Did you do something to hurt him?"

"Not intentionally," she said. "Okay, I'll just spit it out. I found out about the whole clone thing on the day I met you. I didn't know. Not when I met him, and certainly not when I started...you know, feeling things. For him. But he's like...one? Can I still like him? That's super creepy, right? Like Bella and Edward creepy. Worse. It's like Jacob and Renesmee creepy."

I sighed and continued working through her hair. "I knew I liked you for a reason."

"You do?"

"Yeah. You make pop culture references, which are totally my thing." I held out my hand. "Comb. And you obviously care about Jordan. So, here's my advice to you." I considered my next words carefully. "When you had no idea how old he was, you connected with Jordan. And there are two truths I'll impart to you that may help. One, Mind Keys are never the age they seem. They are fully grown before they should be. Have you ever talked to Jainey? She's like a slightly childish adult."

"True, true."

"Okay, so they've given Jordan a cocktail of something to make him develop like an actual teenager. Meaning he's gotta have a teenager's hormones and crap, which I totally don't want to think about because ew, yuck, that's my flesh and blood. He's got the mind of an adult, a mind that's probably smarter than mine, because he's at least fifty percent Mind Key. Then there's point number two."

Rennie braced herself, and I tried not to tug too hard as I combed through her hair.

"This life? Being a Key or a Guardian? It's a short one. We die far too young and far too often, and I want you guys to get the opportunity to be happy while you can. I mean, I'd love to avoid thinking bad thoughts like that at all, but a good friend of mine just told me how much he valued what a realist I am, and I value his opinion."

"Austin?"

"He's a clever guy," I said. "Not the same kind of smart as Kyp, but an equally important kind of smart."

"True that." She leaned into the pull of the comb in her hair. "So you're saying it's okay if I date him?"

"I'm saying that I'm hardly a mom." My heart twisted at the thought. "No matter how I'd like to have been, circumstances stole that from us. But whatever we are, which is still damn well family, I trust you with him. Just remember, he's emotionally vulnerable. So if there is even the slightest chance that you won't do right by him, you've gotta back out now. Because if you hurt him for something you could've seen coming, I'll shoot out your tires on purpose."

"Why is that somehow reassuring?" She laughed.

"For exactly the reason I'm not killing this whole idea right now," I said. "I believe you'll protect his heart."

"With my life," she vowed in a breathless whisper.

Her hair was difficult to get the comb through, although the conditioner helped considerably. I focused on it until the blur in my eyes subsided. "Gana used to detangle my hair." My voice was too thick, and I hadn't meant for the words to come out, so I let them hang between us as the comb hit snag after snag. I shoved up the sleeves of my black turtleneck before diving in again.

Rennie managed to wait a full minute before asking, "Your sister, right? Do you still miss her?"

"Every day. Mom, too." I held her hair in a bunch closer to her scalp so I could get the comb through without pulling so much.

Rennie nodded, and the comb bounced where it was still locked into a tangle. "I miss my mom, too. She gave me this." She held her feather necklace out for me to see. "It's been a long time, but it never goes away."

I separated her hair in three sections, which I began to weave together, distracting myself from the sadness. "It probably shouldn't."

She jerked her head to where Kyp and Jordan sat. "He wants you two to get back together, you know."

"Stay still, would ya?" I guided her head back into position. "Did he tell you that?"

"He didn't have to."

I threw up all my mental walls, despite knowing it wouldn't matter. "You can't use your Aegis on people without their permission."

Rennie let out an agitated sigh. "It doesn't work that way. And we really haven't had time to discuss who or what I am. But I don't have a normal Aegis. Caleb, Jainey, and Jordan are the only living clone kids. The rest of us? We've all been given Guardian-style powers in a manufactured Aegis. We have the abilities, but not the control. I can't turn it off. I don't have a choice. I just know what people are feeling."

I grunted in understanding as my hands continued weaving the braid. "Useful."

"Sure, until I start feeling whatever everyone else is feeling. That's the sucky part. At least it helps me to tell when I'm screwing up with him. Jordan is really naïve. I just thought it was a sweet trait before, but now that I think about it, what young kid doesn't want their parents to get back together? I mean, so I've heard, anyway. I never wanted my parents to get together."

I was a couple of seconds from asking why that was when it finally dawned on me. "You meant Jordan wanted us back together."

Rennie giggled. "Oh, you thought I meant Kyp? He doesn't have any idea what he wants. Pick a day and it's the opposite of what he wanted yesterday."

I didn't pull her hair on purpose. It was a byproduct of the braiding process. I swear.

Drew and Austin walked past us, hand in hand. Drew switched off the music and nabbed his cell phone from the speaker dock before heading inside, with Austin following behind.

"I'm really glad that one seems to have worked itself out," Rennie said.

"They're happy and quiet," I teased. "Kyp and I are too loud to be easy." I tied off the bottom of her braid with an elastic band and she turned to face me. "Jordan wants a normal family."

She shrugged. "He doesn't get that there is nothing about any of us that could ever be normal."

"He takes after his father in that way," I said. "Always wanting something normal."

Rennie nodded. "Maybe, if we work hard enough and care deeply enough, we can find a way to give that to them?"

"Maybe." I laughed, swatting her playfully on the arm. "Please never repeat that to Kyp."

"Heads up," she said. "If you want to keep it quiet, now would be the time to zip it."

I looked up to see Jordan approaching. "Mom, can I steal Ren for a while? I want to spend a little time with her before lights out."

My eyes widened. "Only if it's in a populated room."

"Naturally," Rennie said before Jordan could respond. He

shot her a bemused look, and I realized he didn't fully grasp what I was getting at.

"Go on, get out of here. Don't do anything I wouldn't do."

"You got pregnant at eighteen," Rennie pointed out.

That little shit. "On second thought, don't do anything I would do. I'm truly a terrible influence. Now, get out of here."

Rennie and Jordan were all the way to the back door before Rennie glanced over her shoulder with a smile. "Mom didn't pull my hair as much. Work on that?"

My grinchy heart grew another size. These damn kids were gonna kill me. "Will do."

Jordan smiled warmly at me as they disappeared into the house.

Kyp slid onto the bench behind me, straddling it like I was. I tensed. We were completely alone now, and I had somehow missed that.

"Relax, it's me."

That was exactly why I could not relax. "Oh! I thought you were a Gorvhan, but this is far worse."

"Hilarious."

"You thought it was very funny. You can't hide it from me."

"Frankly, I can't hide from anyone right now." He sputtered a laugh. "Franklin-y."

I shot him a blank look.

"Shut up." He slid closer, his chest pressed against my back.

"What are you doing?" My voice shook.

He huffed a laugh. "I have no idea." His fingers played in my hair, combing through it. "We should do this 'Break Day' thing more often. It lifted everyone's spirits pretty effectively. Everyone's getting along. It felt like the old days at the estate. Before... everything."

I tried not to loll my head back against him. Nope, I was a strong woman. It would take more than playing with my hair to reduce me to dust. Probably. With him, it was hard to tell. "Required quite a few drinks for you though, didn't it?"

He was close enough for me to feel his head shake. "I promise, next time I will not drink like that... um... like this. It was dumb. I lost track. Everything blurred, and it was… liberating. But maybe I was a little too free with my thoughts. Particularly with Austin."

I glanced at him over my shoulder. Unfocused eyes, timid smile. He was heartbreaking.

"Why drink like that? Zane told me about the bar and how you couldn't handle a sip of beer. I mean, Drunk Joe's fare is awful even to Austin and Zane, but why?"

His eyes dropped to my lips before coming back up to meet mine. "It was stupid. I don't know how to do this kind of thing. And I don't know how to be around you anymore. I thought it would help. So I wouldn't be so uncomfortable."

"And instead you just got more uncomfortable because you couldn't keep your mouth shut."

With deliberate movements, as if careful not to spook me, he looped an arm around my waist. "Probably a bad side effect for most people. But maybe this wasn't so awful. Maybe I needed to run my mouth."

I relaxed against him, relishing his warmth as the evening air descended into a chill. He rested his chin on my shoulder.

"I've missed you," he admitted. "Talking to you. Trusting you. Being with you. I miss my best friend. I miss my girlfriend. I miss my partner. And I wish I could forget why you were gone."

I turned, so I was facing him, and my eyes locked onto his darker ones, which suddenly weren't so unfocused.

He leaned forward, his fingers ghosting along my hip, and my eyes fluttered closed. I was as drawn to him as I ever was. I wanted this so badly.

I almost couldn't see clearly enough to stop it.

I turned my head, and his lips brushed my cheek. He pressed the kiss there instead, but when he pulled back, he looked torn, hurt. But he didn't say a word.

I leaned forward again, this time pressing my forehead to his. "If I'd let you go through with that, you'd hate me when you sobered up. I'd hate myself too."

"Hmmm." His eyes were still locked onto mine. "Can you explain how I can feel like this one minute and absolutely hate you the next?"

"If we hated each other, this would be easier." It was the only thing I was confident about these days. "We frustrate the hell out of each other and I'm not who I used to be, always eager for your approval. You've gotta figure out if it's me you want to kiss, or that girl on the pedestal you built."

Kyp's eyes widened, a small crooked smile forming on his lips. "You looked for my approval?" His fingers threaded through mine, gripping tightly.

"I didn't want to live without you, but I could. And I needed to prove that to myself. I needed to know that if Lavinia won, I could survive. That sounds cruel, I know. But I was in survival mode. I'm sorry I hurt you."

"And I'm sorry I failed you." It was an honest admission, raw and painful, and I nearly kissed him despite my earlier, wiser decision. But I held on.

"We both made mistakes," I said. "Maybe we leave this here and see how things look in the harsh light of day?"

"Or maybe I try to cut the memory of you out of my brain." He laughed, but it was mirthless and hollow.

"Why don't we stop trying to see each other as we were and start figuring out if we work as who we are?"

Kyp blinked, and I felt like I could almost hear him whirring like a computer fan that had been working too hard. "That's… a plan." He slid off the bench, almost smoothly enough to convince me he wasn't drunk, but not quite.

"Goodnight, Jacklyn. I'll see you in the morning?"

"Goodnight, Kyp."

He walked away, and I was all alone. I laid back down on the bench and let the thoughts cycle through my brain. It wasn't like I slept anymore, anyway.

EIGHTEEN

LIFE HANGOVER

KYP

Kyp walked through a thick fog. He was missing something.

Puzzle, puzzle, what was the puzzle?

Jordan, Jainey, Rennie. Caleb and the other children. Ross, Kylie. Livingston. Lavinia, Marcelo. The Arvokian Council. They all fit together. He just couldn't figure out how. A puzzle box filled only with corner pieces.

He drifted through the mist.

"This isn't over." Jacklyn's voice, ever-present in his mind.

Lavinia's voice was always his worst thoughts spoken aloud. The personification of everything he despised and feared about himself. Jacklyn's was always righteous fury, fierce and almost playful in its sharp edges.

"We're never safe," Jacklyn said. "But we could be safer."

How could Kyp keep them safe?

Pieces of his conversation with Jordan sped through his head.

"Why make two of you?" Kyp had asked.

Jordan had shied away. "They said there was something wrong with me."

Something wrong with Jordan. And there was, wasn't there? What Jainey had done once out of self-defense, Jordan had done twice in the short time they'd had him, and only once had been a reaction to an actual threat.

Lavinia had wanted a Key to open rifts as she saw fit.

"Shouldn't we be moving before they find us?" Jacklyn again, from his mind, not his memory. "Before they take them again?"

He'd marveled at his ability to speak to children who had only recently been born. Their status as Mind Keys made that possible. But Caleb was Ross's.

How were Caleb and Jordan best friends?

"Good for you, Kyp. You've had children. So have I." Mother. "Does that make you a father? Does that make you anything?"

Arvokians would want to keep their power as much as Lavinia. Marcelo and the interdimensionals would want to keep access to their favorite drug. Why Livingston? What did he gain?

And what had spooked Ross enough to shoot himself in the foot?

Mother emerged from the fog before him. "You'll never put it together," she sneered. "You don't have all the pieces you need."

"Puzzle, puzzle." Ray. "You've got a puzzle to solve."

Mother reached her hands forward and the floor beneath his feet shifted and spun. Alarmed, Kyp dropped to his knees, struggling to keep his balance, to keep the world from tumbling out from under him.

"We need to protect them," Cass said, an otherworldly green glowing in her eyes.

"Aren't you supposed to be some big leader?" Drew.

"You need to take a risk." Zane.

"This is why you're angry at me, but at least I did something. At least I protected her, even for a little while, even if I couldn't protect you." Ray.

"Look what happened the last time you took a risk." Gana.

"Playing with the lives of my children didn't work out that well for you, did it?" Jaina.

"Get your head in the game, man." Austin.

"Help us."

"Help us."

"Help us."

The world spun around him. Around and around and around.

Kyp leapt out of bed, snagged his foot on the blanket, and promptly puked on the floor.

"Fuuuuuuuuuck."

He wasn't going to get up. He would lie here, beside his vomit, with his face pressed to the floor, the hardwood soaking up the slight chill in the air. He slumped against the floor and surrendered to the pounding in his brain.

Some leader.

Whoever came into his room didn't bother to knock. They just walked in, booted feet stopping right in his eyeline.

"Good morning." Jacklyn, because he hadn't heard enough from her already today. "What have we learned?"

"Beer is no," Kyp said, ever wise.

"One beer is okay. Even two or three. An entire case is not."

"I didn't drink an entire case. Cass had some."

Jacklyn laughed, but to her credit, it wasn't her full-bodied guffaw. She held it back for the sake of Kyp's head.

Kyp dragged his gaze off the floor to Jacklyn's beige ankle boots, up her bare legs, over her knee-length dress. Wrapped in the gauzy emerald fabric, she was quite a vision.

"You're dressy. What are we celebrating?"

She squatted down in front of him. "We're just trying to be happy. Can you let us have that?"

Her voice was bright, musical, like the Jacklyn of his childhood. He definitely would not object to a little bit of happiness. "Yes, please."

A chuckle, and her hands wrapped around his arms and yanked him into a standing position. "Go to the bathroom. Take a shower and freshen up. I'll take care of the mess."

"No, I—"

"Kyp," she said. "Just shut up and do it."

Ah, yes. It was peculiar how the words made his heart sing. Telling each other to shut up with affection was a hallmark of their interactions.

He did as she instructed and as the steam of the shower filled the bathroom, as the hot water streamed over him, the seed of a plan began to take root in his brain. He was pretty sure it needed more than beer to grow, so he headed downstairs for nourishment as soon as he was dressed.

The sun pushed through the blinds in the kitchen, where Jacklyn worked at the stove.

"Everyone already ate breakfast, but I'm making you something extra special to feed that hangover." She didn't turn around as she addressed him.

He grumbled, sliding onto a stool. "I'm a model leader."

"You're human," she said.

Whatever she was making smelled divine.

"It's a grilled cheese sandwich." She peeked back at him. "Stop sniffing the air like a cartoon dog."

He muttered a curse under his breath, but only under his breath, because she was taking care of him and he needed it.

"Where are the others?"

"Living room." She tossed him a bottled water. "Drink that. All of it. And take the headache meds on the napkin."

"Medicine?" It wasn't a whine. "Can't you just heal me?"

She turned, hand on her hip, looking gorgeous with amusement in her eyes. "The man went a year without a healer and wants to use one to heal his aching pride."

"You're mean."

"I am." She rolled her eyes, reached behind her and switched the stove off. She slid the sandwich onto a plate and walked around the kitchen island where he'd parked himself.

She placed the plate in front of him, leaning in close. His breath caught in his chest when her perfume, lavender and vanilla, drifted on the air to him. Her lips brushed his forehead, warmth from her Aegis soothing the pain in his head. Her hand brushed through his hair, smoothing it.

His heart beat out of control, jerking around like an old rusty car engine. He lifted his head, eyes meeting hers, and God, he wanted to kiss her, but his brain raged against the idea. He couldn't forget how he'd felt when she left. If he let himself hope again, he'd never recover. She'd said he should wait to see what the harsh light of day showed them. The harsh light of day made his mistakes so much clearer.

And yet, he leaned up, just slightly.

The doorbell rang, and they jumped apart, gasping for breath. They hadn't even done anything, but the closeness had rattled them. He turned to the table, grabbing the pills and gulping them down dry.

"I'm gonna go see what's up." Her voice trembled.

He mumbled a thank you before diving into the food and water. He gobbled down everything and polished off two more water bottles, because damn it, his throat was parched and he didn't know if it was the alcohol dehydrating him or the near-kiss.

Drew appeared in the doorway, face ashen. "Sorry to interrupt your recovery, but you need to join us."

He knew that doorbell was trouble. Kyp strode off toward the front door as fast as he could manage without dizziness striking. "Who was it?"

"Kylie and Ross."

Kyp stopped short. "That's not funny, Drew."

Drew glared out over his glasses, which had slid onto his nose. "I'm not laughing."

Kyp pushed the glasses back up Drew's nose. "Wonderful. Why did I drink last night?"

"Because you're stupid."

"Very helpful."

The entire team was gathered in the first floor living room, gawking so much at their two guests that they barely noticed Kyp entering the room. Kylie, however, did.

"Hey there, ex-boyfriend," she called out over Jordan, who was excitedly recounting his escape from the facility to *Ross*, of all people.

"Kylie, how and why are you here?" Kyp asked.

Ross placed a hand on Jordan's shoulder to quiet him. "In all the confusion, I stuck behind to track you and managed to get between another car that tried to follow Ray and the rest home while you went on your hero mission to save the others. If I'd known Caleb wasn't with you, I would have been less jazzed about helping."

"We wanted to get Caleb out, but things went sideways," Jacklyn explained. "We only managed to find Rennie and Jordan because they weren't where they were supposed to be during the lockdown."

Kyp stepped into the center of the room, finally commanding the attention of everyone present, as he was accustomed. Ross wrapped a protective arm around Kylie. She scowled in response.

"No talking around this. Why. Are. You. Here?"

Kylie met his glare. "We need to find Caleb and we need safety. There's nobody else out there that can help. I don't think the others will ever let us go without a fight. At least this way, we come by it honestly."

Jacklyn snorted. "Have you ever been able to say that before?"

"Screw you," Kylie said. "We don't have to like each other, but don't antagonize me. We're in this part together."

Something from his dream jumped into focus in Kyp's mind. "Jordan, is Caleb like you? A clone aged at an accelerated rate?"

"Yes, but he's a little younger. I'm the only one left of my trial set. The other one got sick. I don't know what happened to him." Jordan's eyes dropped to the floor, and he swallowed hard.

"Ross? Please explain."

"Can't have an interrogation without snacks." Austin bumped Drew with his hip. "Catch me up, babe."

Drew rubbed the back of his neck. "Will do."

"Everyone, have a seat," Jacklyn said. "I imagine Ross has a lot to say."

Kyp settled onto a gray tufted ottoman that matched the couch. "Ross, I'm trying to be patient, but I need to know everything you know."

"That shouldn't take long," Jacklyn grumbled.

"Enough!" Kyp shouted. "This is important. Stop messing with them. You play at being inviting, but you're trying to push them out the door with both hands. Do you want to rescue the other children or not?"

Jacklyn sat back, arms crossed, looking properly chastised, and only then did Kyp realize he had just returned himself to the doghouse.

Ross lowered himself to the arm of the couch, glancing between Jacklyn and Kyp. Kylie sat on the spot nearest him. They both settled at the very edge of their seats, clearly unnerved about being there.

"The truth is, I don't know much," Ross admitted. "Jacklyn may have been mocking me, but they didn't let me in on much."

"You may know more than you realize. Or at least more than us," Kyp reasoned. "Tell me what you can."

Ross sighed. "They assigned me as the children's caretaker until I objected to... something. Then they made me a test subject. They expected me to stay in line after that."

"Who are *they*?" Ray asked.

"Livingston, of course, and this Sirin guy named Marcelo. Dresses in a trench and a freaking fedora."

"Funny, because I would have totally pegged Ross for owning a fedora before I ever would have believed a Sirin would," Cass stage-whispered to Jacklyn.

Kylie looked like she'd hiss at her if she wouldn't get thrown out for doing it.

"Liv, because of freakin' course," Ross continued as if they hadn't said a word. "And… I don't know. There's someone else I don't know. But I think they're Arvokian. They look like Cxarana, but it's definitely not her."

"Kylie, have you ever seen this person?" Zane asked.

"No. I wasn't lying when Kyp came for his little visit. Ross kept me completely out of it, especially after he was punished."

Austin walked in with a tray of beverages and a plate of cookies, one of which he slid to Jainey when he thought nobody was looking.

Dammit. Kyp was starting to like the lunkhead.

"What did you protest against?" Jacklyn asked.

Ross looked away. "I'd rather not discuss that."

Jacklyn rose from her chair with grace. She was only average height, but the way she held herself when in warrior mode intimidated even Kyp. "You're asking for protection, and where I'm from that doesn't come for nothing. I expect information, and you're starting to stress me out. You know what I do when I'm stressed out?" She leaned forward. "I set things on fire. It relaxes me."

Cass's eyes glowed green, and she snapped her fingers, twin flames dancing on her pointer and middle fingers. "Yeah," she spoke in Jaina and Gana's voices simultaneously, and Kyp's skin crawled. "Nothing's more relaxing than setting things on fire."

Ray snorted a laugh. He'd told Kyp once that he'd met Jaina

after she'd started a fire in a gas station large enough to cause a significant amount of trouble, though not without somewhat good reason. He went to investigate and met his future wife.

When Cass spoke again, Gana's voice came through much clearer. "From what I hear, you both contributed to my death. And you can't exactly control fire anymore, can you, Ross? Isn't that what they punished you with?"

Kylie paled. Ross opened his mouth, but nothing came out. He cleared his throat and tried again. "When the hell did you start doing that?"

"Secret weapon." Gana grinned wickedly. "Turns out the afterlife decided these kids need a little extra protection. So they gave Cass a new trick."

Ross blinked. "You're right. They took my Aegis. I wasn't purposely keeping anything from you to cause trouble. It's personal, and it's painful."

"And irrelevant to you," Kylie chimed in.

"Any puzzle pieces added to the board will help me get a better picture," Kyp said.

Kylie's jaw tensed, and for a moment Kyp almost felt bad. But Cass was right. He couldn't forget who he was dealing with.

"The child Jordan remembers from the first trial was ours," Ross explained. "Kylie and I... we... it didn't work. At first, it was fine. They figured out their way around the power drain issue. They found people with an Aegis who didn't want one. They volunteered to allow them to drain off the Aegis energy into an artificial womb. It worked for everyone involved. Jordan and our baby grew, and all the people who hated their Aegis got to be normal. Everyone was happy. Hell, even if you wanted to be angry about Livingston taking Jordan, it meant he got to live. He never would have survived without Livingston's intervention."

"And those people who donated their Aegis found yet another way to give everything in service of the all-powerful and venerated Keys," Jacklyn spat.

"Are you still on about that?" Kylie snarled. "It was a choice, and no harm came to them. It likely *saved* them. It's just like being a Guardian is a choice. Don't think I haven't noticed you're still protected by plenty of Guardians who have volunteered their services."

She had a point.

"Yes, I'm still on about that," Jacklyn said. "Something about my family dying offended me. Call me crazy."

If Kyp turned around and walked right back upstairs to go to sleep, would he be judged?

"None of that is the point." Ross stomped. "The child was fine until they introduced the age-accelerant treatments. Its mind didn't age with the body. It was stuck." Tears filled his eyes, sudden and abrupt. "They said it was a mercy."

Jordan sucked in a burst of air. Rennie grabbed for his hand.

"They figured out the problem." Kylie pursed her lips, eyes hardening. "It was no problem to clone a Key. But to have a Key that you could rapidly age and its mind would keep up? You needed a Mind Key."

Kyp's stomach flipped. "Then Caleb—"

"—is not yours," Ross said. "Or mine, even though I stepped up and treated him like my own. Caleb is fifty percent Kylie's DNA and fifty percent Lavinia's. Which makes Caleb—"

"—my brother." Kyp cut in. He squeezed his eyes shut. *A brother.*

"So, Caleb is our uncle?" Jainey's face soured.

"Trippy," Rennie said.

"After that, it was all about improving upon the original. Jordan had been given too much Key energy. More than he could handle," Ross explained. "Caleb, too little. And guess who the third little bear was?"

"Jainey was just right," Drew breathed. He looked at the child in question, his eyebrows knitting together. "What about the age thing? Will they just keep rapidly aging?"

"Not if they don't get the age-accelerant treatments. It's why I wanted to get them out of there. It took a while to find an opening," Ross said. "I spoke up after the first child. And again after the others in Caleb's age group. And I pissed people off. Lavinia believed I would run to you. Said I was weak. Too pure. So they held my Aegis over my head. When I fought, they performed surgery." He tugged his burgundy sweater up. There was evidence of an incision scar on his side. "They removed a gland from me and implanted it into Livingston. Apparently, it's the root of our Aegis. The one big difference they found between those with an

Aegis and those without. Livingston decided he deserved it more than I did. Then they started transplanting abilities from one Guardian to another."

Rennie stood and pulled her shirt up. She had the same incision. It was how she had received her Guardian Aegis.

"They're playing God." Ray booted the throw pillow he sat beside halfway across the room. "When will they stop?"

"They won't," Kylie said. "Ross was scared of them. And he should be. I was the one who demanded we come here. As much as I hate to admit it, we need to be on each other's sides. If we can't work together, we'll lose."

Kyp rolled it around in his head, still missing a huge piece in his puzzle. "To what end?"

"To stop them?" Kylie narrowed her eyes at him, crossing her arms over her chest.

"Why are you staring at me like that?"

"Because what kind of stupid question is that? Do you think we came over to plan dinner with the enemy?" Kylie still had the most grating voice. Even if she had discovered her conscience.

He held his hand up to stop her. "Maybe." He smiled. "Maybe that's exactly what we should do."

"I don't understand," Jacklyn said.

"I do." Drew jumped to his feet. "Jacklyn and her team were at the facility, but Kyp wiped the memories of the only people that saw him. Which means Kyp, Cass, and I have no connection to breaking Jordan and Rennie out."

"But Lavinia and Marcelo definitely saw Jainey with us," Austin reminded him.

"They know Jainey was with us then," Drew said. "But what if Jacklyn went crazy after? She tried to break all the kids out of the lab. That's just insane, isn't it? And when we tried to confront her about it, convince her she was only endangering the children further, she took Jainey and took off. We've been looking for her ever since."

"So we go to Livingston," Kyp said. "We ask to meet. Explain that Jacklyn's team has gone off the rails and that we're fighting against them. Then we ask for his help. We'll get Jacklyn and her team out of their hair and we can keep the children we have and call it even, including Jainey, once we get her back from Jacklyn."

"You're never going to sell that." Jacklyn's eyes widened.

"Well, you shot out the tires of the car my son was in," Kyp said. "You nearly killed him. And his companion. And you won't let me see my daughter."

Jainey giggled, and it made Jacklyn stop looking at him like she was about to kill him.

"What do you hope to gain from that?" Zane asked. "I've already hacked every facility we know about and found zilch."

"We demand to meet at his home. Just Drew and me. Drew's power is easily neutralized by Livingston's fire. And he absolutely has an Arvokian Mind Block. He'd be relatively safe, as would we. We go in under the guise of a ceasefire, while you, Jacks, Ray and Austin, find a way into his personal files. He *has* to have paper files. The facility would be a more difficult target, but we start here. If he has any idea what Lavinia can be like, he's keeping those files as close to him as possible."

"And this plan won't go wonderfully wrong?" Cass asked.

"Of course it will." Kyp laughed. "But when *do* our plans go right?"

"We're accepting chaos now?" Kylie asked. "How the mighty have fallen."

"Yes, we're accepting chaos. My plans tend to... not go well."

Jacklyn laughed. "I mean, he's not wrong."

"And where do we go?" Jordan asked. "Are we supposed to sit here and wait?" Beside him, Rennie chewed at a cuticle.

Jainey gripped a turquoise bear with teardrop shaped eyes she'd scored at the mall under one arm. It was the first toy she'd ever had that was just hers. With her other hand, she doodled on the pad Drew had given her after they'd had her sketch the facility's layout. "We probably should. Unless you want more treatments." She didn't even look up.

"Smarty pants has a point," Zane said.

That caught Jainey's attention, and she turned to look up at her, a brilliant smile on her face.

How was it possible for Kyp to love her this strongly in such a short time?

"Okay. Cass, Ray, Ross, and Kylie will stay with the kids while we try to pull this mess of a plan off," Jacklyn said.

"And where would I be through this whole debacle? I mean,

what will Livingston think? Lavinia knows I exist." Cass asked.

"True. Maybe you got hurt fighting Jacklyn for Jainey." Drew said, "Or we let Livingston believe she's scouting. We'd be stupid not to have a scout. And he probably will, too."

"This is a mess. It will never work," Ray said. "He won't go for it."

"You're missing something," Rennie said. "You would definitely want to keep hold of Jainey and Jordan, so they can't be bargained with. But you would happily hand over the bonus test subject you took out of obligation. And it will be one he wants." She made a face, her eyes dropping to the floor.

"I doubt that would be enough," Kyp said.

Rennie took a step forward. "Oh, I think I can sweeten the pot. Because I'm not just any kid. I'm Dr. R.D. Livingston's daughter."

Well, crap. That might be just what they needed.

But what would it cost them?

Nineteen

Jacklyn

Livingston had been surprisingly receptive to Kyp's call, though Kyp had been convincing. He could act cold as liquid nitrogen when he wanted. A meeting was set for a week from then.

But as I strolled down Second Avenue, and the last of the fall leaves rained down, dancing on the wind before they drifted to the ground, that wasn't what filled my thoughts. There was a rising tension in our home. I didn't like Ross and Kylie staying there, nor that we had allowed them to find us. I didn't trust them and I didn't like feeling bad for them. I didn't like how close Ross was to the kids, nor that he and Kylie were wiggling their way into Kyp's brain, too.

A new conversation had begun floating around the brownstone. What happened when we freed the children? Once we stomped out this rogue alliance, what then? Ray and I had traveled to rifts to close them before all this. Working with a larger team, one that could split up to cover more ground, would make it so much easier to complete our mission. And when we did, how would we keep the children safe from all the things that weren't as simple or as complicated as interdimensionals?

A familiar conversation, the kind of rhetoric that made Lavinia join up with the interdimensionals in the first place. But with this new spin on it, I found myself indecisive. Lavinia had always had a point. How hard would it be to return to normal, to being vulnerable?

Being capable of sympathizing with Lavinia's perspective chilled my blood.

A few more steps toward my favorite place in Central Park to sit and relax, and I found my bench was already taken.

Zane rested her head on Ray's shoulder. It was the kind of outward sign of affection they never displayed in front of me. I thought Ray was uncomfortable with PDA, but here he was, in the middle of the most populated park in NYC, stroking a hand through Zane's straight dark tresses like it was second nature.

I slowed my footsteps, using my Aegis to block the sound of my approach.

Zane leaned up toward Ray, kissing him sweetly. "I understand, but consider this—Jacks didn't even know you and Jaina as a couple. Maybe she won't mind as much as you think?"

"It's not just her," Ray said.

"You forget I was there for the whole debacle. Lavinia, Jaina. Both ill-fated, but they brought you the two people you love the most. Lavinia and Jaina moved on. Why can't you?"

I doubted Mom would have ever wanted to be lumped in with Lavinia that way. But it couldn't be denied, could it? The three great loves of Raymond Madison: Lavinia Franklin, Jaina Doswell, and Karen Zane. Lavinia once said Body Keys were fickle. I didn't think I fit that bill, but if she was basing her opinion on my father...

Ray chuckled. "It's funny. I was never cautious enough when they were children. And now, I may be too cautious. But I worry. There's so much right now. Adding this too?"

"Drew and Austin were a new development." She spoke with her matter-of-fact voice. The one that said what her eyes likely weren't. She was mocking him.

A passing ambulance siren cut off my ability to hear, and I continued my approach. I was nearly there.

"I can't afford to screw things up with Jacklyn. *Or* Kyp, for that matter."

"Your devotion is sweet, but a little late," I said, tired of hearing him dig himself deeper into the ground with every word.

Ray jumped. "How long were you standing there?"

"Probably a lot longer than you'd like." I walked around the bench and flopped down beside Zane. "For what it's worth, I figured it out a long time ago and I really don't care. Have you asked Cass? Is Mom okay with the whole thing?"

"I... no, I didn't. Should I?" Ray scrambled.

"No," Zane said, but it was more of an order than an answer.

She turned to me. "You don't actually expect him to do that, do you?"

"Not at all." I smiled. "I said that to point out how ridiculous he was being."

Ray groaned. "Why do you do things like this to me?"

I laughed. "Because you're the literal worst. Zane, are you sure you want to get with all this?"

Zane sighed. "I've already tied myself to 'all this.'" She yanked a chain out from under the collar of her sweater. Hanging from the chain was a gorgeous silver ring, shining with sapphires.

"That's quite a gift," I said. "Does it mean what I think it does?"

"It does," Ray said.

It was like a knot in my chest unraveled, like the slightest bit of my hope for humanity was restored. "Congratulations! That's incredible news. Why don't you guys spend the day outside? Go do something nice together? I'll tell the others."

They agreed, both appearing grateful. And while I was ecstatic about their engagement, I realized there was something I had to do. It didn't have anything to do with them, just my earlier teasing question. Of course, Ray hadn't spoken to my mother. But why hadn't I?

I had avoided it. I couldn't visit Mom without visiting Gana. And visiting Gana meant facing everything I'd lost and every mistake I'd made. I owed it to them both, but I couldn't afford to break down.

For the first time since they'd returned through Cass, for the first time since I'd had the option, the mission was on hold.

For the first time, I could do it. So, I would.

It was time to raise the dead.

On my way into the brownstone, I spotted Austin and told him the good news with a smile that hopefully hid the panic I felt within. I told him to spread the word so I could cut out the need to speak to everyone before I did what I needed to do. Everything within me churned. Forcing my way through it, I jogged up the stairs and headed for Cass' room.

I knocked on her door while bouncing on my heels. My nerves sparked and frizzed. I wanted this, and I didn't.

Cass opened the door, and I didn't wait. I was too antsy. Too jazzed. Too absolutely terrified.

"I want to speak to Mom and Gana. I'm ready."

Cass blinked. "Oh. Um. Now?"

"The sooner the better," I said. "I don't know when I'll feel ready again."

Cass looked over her shoulder. "Um, okay." She opened her door further. "Come in."

"I want to hear what they think about the kids, about what I've done since they left."

Kyp sat on her bed, knees pulled up, back up against the headboard. "Hey. Everything okay?"

"I'm fine. Dad asked Zane to marry him."

Kyp's eyes widened. "That's surprising."

"I'm so happy for them, but it made me realize I need to talk to Mom and Gana. I've been putting it off. But I'm more nervous than I thought I'd be!"

Kyp stood and took my hands. "Breathe. We've got you."

"I should have come looking for you first."

He wrapped his arms around me, and it was the last stop on the emotional roller coaster I'd been riding. I fell apart, leaning on Kyp, sobbing into his shoulder, my tears staining his shirt.

"Shh, it's okay," he whispered. "I get it. You're happy. It's weird. I've been there."

And that was it, really. I *was* happy. The kids were safe. I was starting to figure out where I stood with them, to feel like I was their mother. Things were less weird between me and Kyp. My dad and his best friend were getting married. My favorite people were all here with me. Hell, I could speak to Mom and Gana. It wasn't perfect, but it was better. Better than I'd been for a year.

That glimmer of hope broke me. We still had so much more to do, and I knew how these things worked. Nothing ever went the way we needed it to. We were going to lose someone. What would we do then?

When the tears finally slowed, Kyp pressed a kiss to my temple before pulling back. "Better?"

I was still a bit overwhelmed. "Better. Thanks."

He nodded, the tiniest quirk of a smile on his lips.

"Okay, Cass." My eyes never left Kyp. "I'm ready."

She sighed. "Are you sure about this? What if it gets too emotional again?"

Kyp took my hand. "I've got you." He lowered himself to where he'd been sitting before, on the bed against the headboard, only this time he sat with one leg underneath him, the other dangling onto the floor. He angled himself so I could sit in front of him on the bed where he'd be within arm's reach.

I sat in the spot he'd left for me and steeled myself. "I'm ready. Really."

Cass mirrored us when she also settled onto the bed.

"Wait," Kyp said. "Are you okay with this, Cass?"

Yeah, I probably should have made sure it was a good time for her. Bad friend.

"What?" She shook her head. "Yeah, I'm okay. It mostly feels like I'm sitting in the room, hanging out. I don't lose control anymore." With a cheerful smile, she added, "Your sister negotiated a power agreement with the other try-hards. I have the control now. I call upon them when I need them. They don't just take over. Gana assured them that if they didn't, she would direct Kyp to perform the Arvokian Ritual to oust them completely."

That girl. Gana. The only person who could surprise me, even from the grave.

He laughed, but there was a sadness to it. "Nice bluff. She always was so freaking good at this."

"So, Jacks, who first?"

"Mom."

Cass closed her eyes, and I did the same. I didn't want to see Cass's face eerily mimicking Mom's expressions. I wanted to hear Mom's voice and pretend, for just a moment, she was in the room with me.

"Hey there, Birdie. I was wondering how long it would take you to come for a visit."

Mom. I hiccupped a sob. Kyp's hand found mine, a source of unerring support.

"Hey, Mom." I squeezed my eyes closed even tighter, like that would help me process this. "I don't know what to say."

Now that her voice was a melody in my ears, all my words danced away.

"It's okay, honey. Take your time. And if you're not ready yet, you can always call me back." There was a smirk hiding in that tone.

I grinned through my tears. "True, I guess."

"I know you probably won't, though. You're stubborn about that. Your self-reliance." She sighed. "I guess I built that, didn't I?"

I didn't answer. I wasn't here to argue with her about her choices. I'd done that enough in my last few months with her.

"Hi, Kyp," she said. "How's that arrogance working out for you?"

Never once had I considered that Kyp staying for this had the potential to wound him, too, but I should have. I knew what he'd lost that day. I squeezed his hand, hoping he felt the mix of gratefulness and remorse I sent him.

"Effectively squashed," Kyp said. "If it helps, I now have no confidence in my plans and assume they'll all end in disaster."

"And yet, you keep making them. Jacklyn, the visit with Livingston is bound for failure."

This was not why I called her. "We need access to his files. And we need him distracted while we search for them. We all approved it. The way it always should have been. Keys and Guardians agreeing to work together."

Mom grumbled. "You kids always think you know better."

"It's called progress, Mom. And it's not even close to why I called you here."

"Why *did* you call me here, Jacks? So you could wallow in guilt?"

Kyp squeezed my hand fiercely, as though he was trying to distract me from the slicing burn in my chest.

"I called you here because I missed you. And I wanted to tell you I love you. Since I didn't get the chance to tell you before you died."

Fingers ran through my hair. "I like the new cut." A sigh. "Maybe I should have sugarcoated it for you. I don't know. I'm atrocious with that, and so are you. So is your father, for that matter. Might be one of the few things we had in common."

I smiled through the tears. "Speaking of Dad..."

"I'm happy for them. There was always chemistry between him and Zane. I met her the day after I met him, you know. She's good for him, kid. Don't sweat it. Tell him I said congratulations."

"I will, but he'll be awkward about it."

She snorted a laugh. "Don't I know it. You don't have to worry about me. I died doing my duty. I believed in what we were doing. I still do. It was an honor to go down in battle fighting an interdimensional to protect all of humanity. Gana would agree. If she had to go down, she was honored it was while she was protecting you."

"No." Tears choked me. "Don't treat that like it was an honor. He stole her life from her."

A light squeeze of my hand felt like a question in my mind. One I didn't have time to answer.

"Maybe you should talk to Gana about that," Mom said. "Are you ready to speak with her now?"

"Maybe?"

"Isn't it amazing that you get to?" Mom laughed. "I mean, if we couldn't be together... okay. One bit of parting advice?"

I nodded.

"Don't be afraid. You're a mother now. You always understood how to be a parent better than Ray and I did. You knew what Gana needed. You'll know what to do with them, too. I love you."

"I love you too, Mom." I took a deep breath and swiped at my eyes to clear the tears. "Cass. I'm ready. Are you okay to do this?"

"I'm ready. Just give me a second."

A beat.

"Well, well, well. Look who it is. She doesn't call, she doesn't write."

Where Mom's voice had brought sobs, Gana's brought a smile to my face. It was good to hear her sound exactly like I remembered her best. Snarky.

"Little sis! I've missed you."

"Yeah, I've heard." I could practically hear her rolling her eyes. It was a balm for my soul.

"Why you gotta make it sound like that?" Even as I joked, I felt the burn of her disapproval. She could be critical, my baby sister; the quintessential smart ass and sometimes I missed her like I'd miss breathing. She'd always been able to make me laugh or cry with barely a sentence.

"You've developed quite a knack for sulking lately," Gana said. "If you don't remember, I scoff at sulking."

"You scoff at everything," I said. "Gana, I'm so sor—"

"Don't say it!" She cut me off. "I already know. God, Jacks. I know. I knew it while I was still alive. It's why I wrote the message to you, but you don't seem to have gotten it."

I played with the sleeve of my navy-blue sweater, picking at the edges. I would unravel the whole thing if I thought it would calm my nerves.

"Jacks."

"I'm listening." My voice shook.

"You've grieved," she said. "I know it hurt losing what you did. I was only part of that."

"You're wrong, Gana. You were everything. You were my

best friend and my sister and you died protecting me and I barely knew what was happening, and then you were gone. And if you hadn't told me to live for you, I would have died right there. I would have let her kill me."

"And then I would have died for nothing!"

I flinched.

"Damn it, Jacks. I died so you could live. *You.* Not whatever facsimile of a person you've been living as for the last year."

My breath came harder as I tried to stop the oncoming flood of tears. I'd been holding it together, a tear or two sliding down, but that? That killed me.

"I *am* me."

"No, I think you died when you killed Hector and enjoyed it. You got careless. What you pulled at the facility? You didn't know Jordan had been before the Arvokian Council, and you didn't know you could have healed Rennie. You nearly killed them both. You stopped valuing life that day. I just... ugh!" She swatted me upside the head. "For fuck's sake, Jacks. Get it together."

I flinched and clenched my eyes shut even tighter. My instinct was to give her the big sister Jacklyn look, but I couldn't bear to see Cass in Gana's place when I opened my eyes. It wasn't like I would mean it, anyway. She was right. I was making a mess of things. But I wasn't about to admit it.

"You're just doing this because Jordan's your Key," I argued. "You don't like the risk I took because then you wouldn't have done your job." And maybe it was spiteful, but that was Gana.

Nothing if not a girl on a mission.

She made a buzzer noise. "Nope. Wrong. The risk you took wasn't *worth it*. Not just for Jordan, but for you. Or did you forget it was also my job to keep *you* alive? Livingston and his people kept them alive that long. You could have saved them another way. Kyp was terrified. The crown prince has more sense than you lately, and he's barely got any! I don't need a hardened killer. I need my sister. I need Jacks to help me protect her son. He's a mission, yes, but when did I ever participate in a mission when I didn't want to? The only reason I didn't protest being a Guardian was because protecting you was a given! He's my nephew! I got a chance to help him. Why do you think I got the first Skeleton Key in line?"

I'd never thought about that.

"You were never weak, Jacks. You were always a fighter. You didn't need your Aegis then, and you don't need your guns now. All you need is you. Your tenacity. You're my hero. You always have been. All of those things, they're tools. Use them wisely, because they will either make you or break you. And if they break you?" She sighed, long and weary. "Then this all falls apart."

I took a big gulp of air, and Kyp wrapped an arm around my waist, and rested his chin on my shoulder.

"You've got this," he whispered, his fingertips tracing random patterns against my side. "You're not alone. We've got you."

"Okay, Gana. I hear you." I struggled to push the words free past the blockage in my chest, the tightness of my throat.

"Thanks, big sis. Live. For real. You won't regret it. You're already getting started. I'm sorry I can't be there with you in body, but I am there in spirit."

I could not believe she just said that. The laugh burst out of me. Her and her dark as hell sense of humor.

"I knew I'd get one out of you." A laugh, a genuine Gana laugh. "Anyway, Cass is beat. I should be quiet for a while. But I'm here whenever you need me. The perks of having a Cass."

"I'm sure Cass would love to hear that."

"I love you," she said.

"I love you too, kiddo. So much."

For a moment, there was silence, and then Kyp broke it.

"Ah, that Gana. She's always so charismatic." He gripped me even tighter, his head leaning against mine. It felt normal, like something I'd been missing for a long time.

"Unlike you, who has all the charisma of a brick," Cass said. Her voice returned to her own, as expected, but it still hurt to know they weren't there anymore. That I couldn't have them with me forever.

I forced my eyes open to reality. Cass grabbed my other hand. "You okay?"

"I don't know."

I truly didn't.

TWENTY

KYP

Kyp woke up with Jainey in his bed again. He wasn't surprised. She was nervous about his meeting with Livingston later that day. If he was being honest with himself, so was he. If he was not being honest with himself, he was ready to take on the world, despite the risks.

Dropping a kiss on her forehead, he moved carefully, so as not to wake the adorable child.

As he took a shower, he pushed thoughts of the mission from his mind and replaced them with thoughts of Jacklyn and her conversations with Jaina and Gana. He hadn't asked before, because it would have been impertinent, but he had wondered what had happened at the estate the night Gana had died.

It probably shouldn't have been a surprise that Jacklyn had killed Hector. It wasn't like Kyp had a loving relationship with his biological father, but the man had tried to protect him. Jacklyn killing him meant Hector had failed in his battle against Lavinia's control.

Jacklyn would not have killed him unless he'd killed Gana. And then his mother had come along and tried to kill Jacklyn.

It was a wonder Jacklyn could even look at him.

Yeah, maybe thinking about the meeting with Livingston was a better plan.

He dressed in an immaculate navy blue suit with a white shirt and a crimson tie. A jar of Drew's gel had materialized in the bathroom. Kyp could take a hint, so he combed his hair back and away from his face and gelled it in place.

Drew would relish the opportunity to see him actually taking care of himself. Kyp had barely been sleeping, eating, or showering when he met Drew. He was remembering who he was. It wasn't the way things were healing between him and Jacklyn, or that he was starting to understand how to be a dad to Jainey and Jordan, although that was all wonderful. Rather, it was the way this mission reminded him of his purpose and made him feel like, maybe, he hadn't destroyed everything.

He could pull a life free from this mess. No. He *would* pull a life from this.

"You look handsome, Papa," Jainey said, voice softened by sleep. She rubbed her eyes and sat up in the bed. "You're uncomfortable."

He laughed. "An astute observation. The day will be arduous, but I will survive."

"Hopefully," she grumbled.

"You understood that? I purposely threw in vocabulary words."

"I read a dictionary at the facility." She bounced out of the bed. "It was boring there."

Another laugh. He didn't think he'd laughed nearly as much in his life as he had since this kid had arrived. "Go get dressed. I'll see you in a little bit."

"'Kay." She threw her arms around his waist and dug her face into his stomach. "Love you, Papa."

He hugged her back, stunned. "Love you too, little bean."

She raced out of his room, completely unaware that she'd gifted Kyp with some of her trademark buoyancy.

He jogged down the stairs until he reached the finished basement. The hall split off in two directions. On one side, grunts, cheers, and the slap of bodies hitting the mat spoke of sparring matches. The noises distracted him from his goal, leading him toward the training room instead of the server room.

He'd barely made it through the door before Rennie rolled across the floor and landed flat on her back in front of him. Her gray t-shirt was dark with sweat, but her smile was beatific as she looked up at him.

"Hello Rennie," he greeted. "I'm glad to see you're having a good time."

"I am," she cheered. "Cass is kicking my ass."

Cass laughed, drawing Kyp's focus to the rest of the room. She stood across from where Rennie had landed. Ray was working with Austin, and Jacklyn was explaining a complicated maneuver to Jordan.

"I wish someone had told me we were having a sparring session." Kyp walked across the mats.

Jacklyn turned to him, grinning. "We couldn't. You had to get spiffy for us." She tugged on his tie a little, then smoothed it. "Schmancy."

He stared after her, bemused. As had been the case since she'd returned, war erupted in his mind. One side wanted to implore her to behave professionally. They were teammates and nothing more. The other side remembered how it felt to kiss her and wanted to do it again. Every encounter threw him further out of balance.

He shook off the desire to grab her wrist and pull her back to him before she'd gotten too far.

"Do I clean up okay?" leaked from his throat.

Idiot. Gibberish would have been a better choice. Behind her, Jordan mimed vomiting.

She smirked. "You do all right." She winked before returning her attention to Jordan.

"Well, good luck guys. I was just stopping in to see what you were up to before I left." He wished he could run away and hide his burning face.

"Or to see Jacklyn," Rennie sing-songed.

"Goodbye!" He marched back out, refusing to look at anyone as he made his escape.

He was relieved when he made it across the hall to the server room where Zane worked her technomancy magic and Drew's brain did the rest of the work.

Walking inside was like stepping into a freezer. The low temperature was intentional, an effort to keep the tech from overheating, but Kyp's face was already overheated, so it felt particularly nippy to him.

He passed the various surveillance set-ups, server towers, and wiring as he weaved through the room, finally scouting out the space that contained the central units, where he would find his pair of computer wizards.

Zane was perched in her corner of their shared desk, skimming through various computer files with dizzying speed. As she worked, she drummed the silver rings she wore on her slim fingers against the desk, the musical clacks blending with the clicks of Drew's fingers against his keyboard.

Drew noticed Kyp's entrance and spun in a full circle in his swivel chair. "Kyp! You're looking spiffy." He spun the chair again and it let out an unholy screech. "I see you found the gel I left you."

Zane reached out and planted her hand on the armrest, wrestling his chair to stillness without looking away from the computer. "Andrew, could you not?"

He looked to Kyp. "She calls me Andrew."

"I'm gonna start calling you Andy if you keep it up," she hissed.

"She's stressed." Kyp shrugged.

"It wouldn't kill me to relax, but it might kill you," Zane warned.

"In her defense, it *is* a *huge* deal," Drew said. "She's searching through employee files she found in the facility's systems."

"What?" Kyp asked. "When?"

"Austin snatched the phones off the Sirins who were driving the car Jacks crashed. I used some of the information to hack into their servers." She turned around long enough to grin, then returned to her screen. "There's a lot of unimportant junk in here, but I'm indexing it. If this mission doesn't get us where we need to be, we can start personally visiting employees and... persuading them."

Kyp was hoping this would be easier than that, but he also knew how his plans usually worked out.

Zane looked ready for a break-in. Black hoodie, black jeans, black sneakers. Drew, like Kyp, was dressed for a business dinner in a tight-cut brown business suit with a mint green shirt and a brown and green bowtie.

Kyp took in his look and grinned. "Been to see Austin yet?"

"Oh, yes." Drew graced him with a thousand-megawatt smile. "Been to see Jacks?"

His face heated up again. Damn, sometimes he hated that blushing was a tell he couldn't control.

"I'll take that as a yes."

"I know I slept in late," Kyp said. "But we've still some time. Is there anything I need to know to guarantee this plan works?"

"Our job is relatively easy," Drew said. "We keep Livingston talking long enough for Jacklyn and her team to get in and out."

"Why do I have a feeling we're walking right into a trap?" Kyp said.

"We probably are. We just have to make sure our trap is a better one," Drew said.

Kyp grunted. It wasn't the safest plan. But at this point, they'd tried two levels of safe. They'd been overly cautious and trouble had come for them. They'd tried an intricate plan and had only accomplished a portion of it. They couldn't keep invading labs and secure locations. This was reckless, but it wasn't betting the entire farm.

Which was good. An all-out war wasn't on his appointment calendar. Maybe next year.

"If all else fails," Zane said, leaning back in her chair, "I have complete and total faith in you just stabbing everyone dead."

"And mess up my nice suit?" Kyp asked. "No, thanks."

Kyp was definitely going to have to mess up his nice suit.

It wasn't the first time he'd met Dr. R.D. Livingston. He'd worked with him several times in the past. Livingston was the person who taught him field medicine during their first stint without a healer. But knowing what he knew now, what he'd done, put a negative spin on his memories of him. Kyp had once believed he was harmless.

What had once struck Kyp as the appearance of a kind man

now looked like just another element of the ruse. His manner of dress was somewhat slouchy, despite his clothes being obviously finely made. Mostly bald, the hair at his temples was silver, threaded through with some black strands that remained from his younger days. He was a broad, smiling man, with a forehead creased with age, warmth in his eyes and a roundness in his belly. A thin black mustache stretched across his face like a particularly furry worm.

Livingston was wealthy, and his home was comparable to the estate. And while Zane would be able to root out whatever technology was there, he wasn't sure they could remain undetected. If Livingston and his team believed Jacklyn was after them, they likely knew Zane was with her, which may be why Zane was having such a hard time getting much from their system.

Whatever records existed had to be paper files, and those would be harder to find.

In the meantime, Livingston played games with them.

"I would like to begin by thanking you for your... contribution to my scientific research." He walked them through his home.

Had he meant that as a taunt? Either way, Livingston was an undeniable asshole. Kyp allowed an inelegant snort and attempted to maintain a pleasant demeanor despite what he said next. "It wasn't as if I had any other option, Dr. Livingston."

Unlike the estate, which came from old money and was decorated with antique furniture and art, the doctor's home was all pristine white surfaces with high-tech devices built into every room.

Kyp bet *he* had a dishwasher.

As they walked, Kyp noted every hall, every doorway. The estate possessed an old, somewhat musty odor, but this place smelled like furniture polish and lemon disinfectant. Kyp frowned and pushed down his homesickness. Even when this was over, he wouldn't be able to return home. Jacklyn couldn't walk down a single hall there without a bad memory.

And here he was, assuming Jacklyn would want him around when this was all said and done. Being co-parents didn't require them to be a couple, and he was letting their bonding over their children pull him back into thinking about a relationship with her.

Focus, Kyp, and keep him talking.

Sometimes, all the memories and thoughts in his head got the better of him. He cleared his throat. "I hope you don't mind Mr. Clayson's presence."

Drew walked behind him, doing his own reconnaissance.

"No, not at all, Mr. Franklin. I've been working with the Order of the Key for decades. I'm well aware of the hierarchy as well as the purpose of Mr. Clayson's presence here." He led them into the dining room. "I have arranged a buffet dinner for us." Livingston flashed them a toothy smile. "I've heard that Mr. Franklin's paranoia is unparalleled, so in the event there was a fear of poisoning, I wanted to allay those fears."

"Dr. Livingston, I assure you, I am not afraid of you," Kyp said. "If I was, I would not be here."

"Security system disabled," Zane crowed through the mental connection they had established beforehand. "We're in."

"Wonderful," Livingston said. "I hope the food appeals to your sensibilities."

"Definitely glad you met up with him," Austin said. "I would have yanked the stick out of his ass already." A pause. "Come to think of it, Kyp was the perfect person to meet with him."

"In the interest of full disclosure," Livingston said as all three men prepared their plates, "I didn't bring you here to negotiate with you."

"I'm not asking for a negotiation." Kyp used the provided serving spoons to procure lemon chicken, sauteed mushrooms, and green beans. "I'm asking for cooperation."

"And if I don't wish to cooperate?"

"Then we're going to have trouble getting along." Kyp smiled, sharp-edged and threatening.

Livington sighed. "So brutish. I had wished for a more civilized solution from a man of your level of intelligence, but you were born and bred a Key. I suppose I shouldn't have expected more."

"Rumor is, you've been working with my mother for quite some time, so I'm certain you do not expect me to react gently. Mother is a stone-cold sadist. You must have caught on to that by now."

Through the connection, Jacklyn murmured a curse. "There is a lot of paperwork here, boys. I'm not sure how much of it we're going to be able to go through."

Kyp shot a message back through their link. *"Narrow it down as much as you can and take what you can't with you. I don't care if he figures out what we did once we've put distance between us."*

"Roger that."

When they were done fixing their plates, the men took their seats at the dining table. Drew slid in beside Kyp while Livingston sat across from them.

"I have many powerful allies," Livingston said, draping a napkin over his clothing. "It would be wonderful to add you to that list. But you must understand, I have my own qualifications for accepting your assistance."

"First mine," Kyp said. "No harm will come to the children."

Livingston chuckled, his eyes tightening at the corners. "I'm sorry, Mr. Franklin. That's impossible. A pipe dream. I hope you understand that when I look at you, I see a child. If you expect me to treat you as an adult, you must negotiate like one."

Kyp pursed his lips. He really wanted to punch this man. He spoke affably, with a warm smile and encouraging eyes, yet every word was chosen with cruelty.

"I will be the one dictating the terms of this agreement." Livingston cut into a piece of skirt steak, prim even as he sunk his teeth into the juicy piece with carnivorous vigor. "The children are my asset."

"Jordan and Jainey consist of stolen genetic material." Drew speared a potato with his fork. "You took it from their mother under false pretenses."

"If we hadn't taken the child, they both would have died."

"So you claim," Drew said. "However, we have no proof of that. If your interests were to save the parent and the child, surely you would have informed the parent that the removal was for their own survival. Instead, you told her the child was dead."

"What he said." Kyp grinned wickedly. "While we may not agree with the way Jacklyn is reacting, she isn't wrong to feel... slighted."

"Perhaps not," Livingston allowed. "But we will not give up our test subjects. We will find Jacklyn, and we will take them back from her. What I'd like to know is why you're not with her right now?"

Kyp felt the first pang of concern for how this was going. He was used to high-level negotiations with Lavinia, attempts to out-speak each other without overstepping any boundaries, all the while believing they were trying to work toward a common interest, when really neither of them would ever bend to the other.

Livingston's question was unsettling. It meant he saw holes in their story.

"I've got something. I think I know what they're planning," Jacklyn said into the earpiece. "Keep the piece of crap talking."

Kyp did as directed. "As I explained on the phone, my initial instinct was to assist Jacklyn on her misguided quest. But she went too far when she broke into your lab to get Jordan and took your daughter. She risked endangering all of the children with her stunt. I never agreed to that. Clearly, Jacklyn is firmly under her father's influence, and I'm sure Mother explained the way his flights of fancy are frequently at odds with reality. He will do literally anything to thwart her, and while I'm not always opposed to that spirit, he isn't beyond burning down the entire house to kill a roach. Case in point: the original Order, which he brought into a civil war."

Livingston chewed through more meat as he chewed through his thoughts. And then, finally, after a slight exhale, "In return for the children, I am willing to give you access to Jordan and only Jordan. You can have him, keep him as your son." Livingston took another bite of his steak, gesturing with a wave of his hand. "I have since perfected the process. Jordan is an old model, an obsolete failure."

Kyp's hands tightened into fists.

"Jainey, however, is mine."

"*Stay cool,*" Zane cautioned.

Kyp barely fought down a growl. "And your daughter?"

Livingston was surprisingly serene when he responded. "I suppose it would be nice to have Rennie back, but the truth is, she's a stranger. She grew up with her mother, who didn't make me aware of her existence. I only discovered her after her mother died. She was eager to come to me, but grew rather ungrateful. So, yes. I would like her returned, but I also believe she will fight me and make my life difficult in the wake of Jordan's departure."

Classy. Had to love a man who would gladly give away

his daughter to a potential adversary because she may become *difficult*.

"Did it occur to you that she may have become ungrateful, as you say, because you decided to experiment on her?" Drew asked.

Kyp understood, but Drew was veering off course. He held out a hand to stop him without taking his gaze off Livingston. "As compelling an offer as that is, I need a full accounting of your terms before I agree to anything."

"The terms are simple." A slight smile played on his lips. "You raid the camp of Jacklyn's team, ensure they will no longer be a thorn in our side, and procure Jainey. In return, I will allow you to have Jordan and will not cross paths with yourself, Mr. Clayson, or Ms. Noble in the future."

"*Drew! Kyp!*" Austin. "*We've been played. Get out of there. I repeat. We were set up.*"

Damn it. He'd seen this coming.

"You brought us here to kill us, didn't you?" Kyp said calmly as he slid a switchblade free from his sleeve.

"Honestly." Livingston bared his teeth. "I'm unsure why you'd have expected anything else."

Kyp leapt to his feet, the chair tipping to the floor with a clatter. Livingston was already hurtling a fireball toward him, and his hands flew up to protect himself. Drew pulled the water from a pitcher on the table and launched it toward the fireball in an eruption of steam.

Kyp channeled his telekinesis and upended the table in

Livingston's direction. Grabbing Drew's arm, Kyp led him backward, ducking into another hallway.

"You got this?" Drew asked. "You fight, I'll try to find out what's going on downstairs."

Kyp nodded and rushed back into the fray, cursing his pinchy dress shoes all the way. Except there wasn't a fray to rush into. Livingston wasn't in the dining room. At least not anywhere visible.

Kyp strolled along the perimeter of the room, checking every darkened corner. "Awww, where did you go? I thought we were finally being honest with each other." He grimaced. Jacklyn and her team were rubbing off on him.

"*We've got a new player here!*" Austin shouted through their connection.

Livingston's voice floated in from the doorway on the far side of the dining area. The kitchen, most likely.

Wonderful. Where the kitchen knives lived.

"Sadly, I would have honored our deal had you agreed. But I suspected that was impossible."

Kyp walked closer, switchblade at the ready.

"You couldn't resist."

He leaned against the door, letting his enemy finish his monologue, giving him time to prepare his attack.

"Your mother suspected as much."

He burst through the door.

"Which is why I planned to take what I wanted for myself."

Take it for himself? How would he...

Anger and frustration at his own damn stupidity bubbled up within him.

This was exactly what Lavinia had done to him the night Gana died. She sent him on a mission while she went after Gana and Jacklyn.

Livingston tackled him, landing one punch to the stomach, another to his jaw, and another stiff punch to his eye. He stumbled, crashing back into the dining room. The collision drove the air from his lungs.

Whatever. He needed the time to send his message through.

"Let me deal with Livingston. Get out of here. They're at the brownstone."

"Kylie and Ross! We never should have trusted them!" Jacklyn shrieked back through to him.

Kyp didn't think Ross or Kylie were lying, but he didn't have time to piece together an alternative.

Livingston dropped onto him, pinning him in place. For an older guy—definitely older than Ray, and without the added health and vigor of a Body Key Aegis—the man packed quite a punch. His eye and jaw throbbed enough to prove it. But Kyp was done delaying the inevitable. With a twist of his hips, he dislodged Livingston, sending him tumbling into the nearby wall.

He channeled all that frustration and anger he felt at letting himself be fooled yet again with his Aegis, and poured it all into his fists as he pounded them into Livingston's smug face.

His heart played and replayed Jainey's sweet smile and her hugs and her voice when she called him Papa.

He plunged the switchblade into Livingston's belly, watched the smile melt off the man's face. "She's a child, you son of a bitch." He drew the switchblade back and launched him into the wall. He would not give him time to recuperate. "If anything happens to her, I will tear you apart atom by atom, I swear it."

Livingston dropped to a crouch on the floor, lighting the carpet between them on fire. "Do you think this is a one-on-one fight? This is a movement. And we are not alone."

Kyp lunged forward, ready to walk through flames to destroy this pariah, but arms caught him from behind, wrapping around his chest. Kyp shoved backwards, fighting his way free, before whirling on the culprit.

A boy—he couldn't have been more than fourteen. Blond hair, short and spiky, and pale skin, with freckles dusting his nose. He had a light bone structure that appeared frail, but he was surprisingly strong despite it. It made him think of a girl he once knew. And the dejected woman she had grown to become.

"You must be Caleb." His brother. He had a brother. It still didn't feel real.

Two other kids stood on either side of the boy. A wiry girl with wavy red hair eyed him warily. A boy with brown skin, hair in braids and a reluctant, frightened and concerned look on his face, even as he took a step closer to Caleb.

Kyp held his hands up. "I'm not going to hurt you. But you're backing the wrong side. If you leave with me, I'll keep you safe. No more treatments, no more pain, and your own destiny. You don't have to do this."

"*Kyp! Jacklyn stayed behind to stop the new player and we can't get to her,*" Drew shouted within his mind.

One problem too many. How was he going to get them out of this mess?

"What *does* he want you for?" Kyp asked the kids. "Do any of you even know?"

They glanced between each other before Caleb turned back toward him, eyes hard. "We wouldn't even be here if it weren't for him."

Kyp whirled around. The rug burned beneath his feet, the air growing thicker as the smoke started to cloud his vision and his eyes began to burn. The acrid scent of burning fibers filled the air between them. Livingston was gone.

"No!" The exclamation tore from Kyp's throat. He couldn't run after him. The flames were burning too steadily, and there wasn't anything he could telekinetically move, unless he lifted the whole carpet, which was weighed down by the table and a grand mahogany hutch containing wine glasses and expensive china. It would take far too much of his remaining Aegis strength.

Kyp looked back at the kids. The unnamed boy's eyes were lowered, watching the carpet burn. The others watched Kyp with tensed muscles, clenched fists, and determination burning in their eyes.

"Look, you can come with me or not. But you need to get out of here. I won't be able to stop this fire," Kyp said.

The girl narrowed her eyes at him, as if considering his offer. The boy looked at Caleb as if waiting for him to make the decision.

Caleb's fists clenched. "We are not coming with you. The Order will die. And we will replace the corrupt empire you've built."

For a moment, Kyp almost wished Kylie was there. Maybe she could talk some sense into the boy.

Flames leapt and grew, eventually reaching the wooden hutch. It crackled and spit, and he was done waiting for an answer.

He used his Aegis to hold them back with his mind as he left, turning his back on these children he was supposed to save because they weren't cooperating. He ignored the angered cries behind him. For now, his own children mattered more.

He rushed away from the scene, heart racing with worry for Jacklyn, his head aching from the punches he'd taken, his throat sore, his eyes stinging from the thick smoke clouding the air.

Did he make the right choice? He couldn't fight three children who didn't want to come with him when there was potentially a worse threat waiting for him below.

Let the others judge him. He was saving his girl.

"*Jacks!*" He reached out with his mind, anxiety tearing through him as he made a turn down the nearest staircase, drawing upon the blueprints Zane had found for him.

Jacklyn didn't answer.

Hideous memories spun through his mind as he pounded his way down the stairs. Jacklyn's broken body lying in the grass, blood crusted on her swollen face, surrounded by burning Arvokian herbs that signaled a permanent death. The overturned dirt he'd discovered, the torn-out hair he'd found from her escape from her own grave, signifying her death hadn't been nearly as permanent as he'd believed. The horrifying wound in her chest when she died her first death, as she cried in fear, and he begged her to come back as the Jacklyn he loved.

He wasn't convinced she ever had. She wasn't evil, but she was never the same afterwards.

A spiral staircase led to a floor of well-furnished rooms Kyp raced through in a blur. Later, he'd be able to recreate every choice of decor in the hallway, rewind and play it back frame by frame like a movie, as fast or as slow as he needed. Later, he'd be able to sift through what he was feeling and whether his choices had been the right ones. But now, none of that registered. Because Jacklyn was alone in that room, alone with a new player.

She wasn't answering him. But Jacks was protected against Lavinia. And she could handle Marcelo.

Either this was a completely new individual, which would be scary enough, or Jacklyn was trapped by the Arvokian Ross had mentioned.

Not good. Not good at all.

Twenty One

Jacklyn

In the year since I'd joined the Order of the Key, I'd been in a lot of chaotic situations and seen a lot of weird things. Even more so in the time I'd been running with Ray. But this I'd never seen.

An Arvokian towered over me, lanky and wrapped in a long cloak embroidered in gold. They held themself with poise and grace, straightening the robes, as if to make sure I saw the jewel encrusted weapon belted to their side. Nothing Cxarana wore had ever looked so rich. Their off-white hair hung long, their bruise-colored skin slick, and they stared down their nose at me in a regal fashion. They weren't just any Arvokian, they were *important*. Or they were a legend in their own mind.

Judging by the way they'd built a wall between me and my team, brick by brick in seconds, their ego was probably exactly as big as it should be. There were about fifteen feet between me and the Arvokian, and the wall was about ten feet behind me. Not much room to fight, if it came to that.

"Jacklyn Katherine Madison," they said in a deeper version of Cxarana's rasp. "Greetings."

They were taller than Cxarana, limbs longer, but their shoulders were broader. Their eyes, however, were very similar to hers, and that made me wonder if they were related. Did the slickness of their skin, the difference between this Arvokian and Cxarana, mean this one was a male in his species, or did gender not matter to them?

"Kind of you to question. I am, indeed, a male of my species. I am Zelnick," he said.

Damn it. I forgot they could peek into minds.

"Have you heard of me?" he continued.

"No," I said. "Are you, like, important or something?"

"Yes, I am. I've heard a lot about you and your humor," he said. "I am not here to entertain you. In fact, you're here to entertain me."

I clenched my teeth. "I don't understand. Why don't you spell it out for me?"

"It's simple. I'll tell you what I'm not here for first. I'm certainly not here to quibble about to whom our creations belong. There would not be Keys and Guardians at all had it not been for us."

"Are Arvokians incapable of straightforward answers?" I brushed plaster off my clothing from the battle with the Sirins that had heralded my new friend's arrival.

"That, my new friend, is specist."

"Well, damn, you're right. Sorry. That wasn't cool." I mean, I wasn't a complete asshole. Only a little bit of an asshole.

Zelnick bowed slightly. "Apology accepted. Given the others you've met from the Dusk, it's understandable you'd hold a grudge."

"It's not the rest of the interdimensionals I'm holding a grudge against. If you're working with Lavinia, you're probably the one that told her I put her under investigation. If you were looking to extend an olive branch, I'm looking to snap that branch in half. There would not be rifts if it weren't for your people. I don't blame the Arvokians for running from a horrible existence. But your escape brought your enemies here. And then you decide to team up with them?"

"Is that what you were taught?" Zelnick's thin white lips twisted into a smirk.

"That's what we were all taught," I said. "Are you saying the Order of the Key, *gasp,* lied to us? Kyp will be *so* disappointed."

"I'm saying no group is homogenous. You do not all have the same traits, nor do I expect you to." Zelnick paced forward. "For example, I do not expect the Order to help us. But you. Despite Lavinia's loathing for you, I wouldn't mind having you on our side. You have a certain determination. And a certain darkness. I have been watching you over the last year. The mission where you and your associate were beaten and held captive by Sirins, and you timed their security rounds? Killed yourself to skip waiting to heal? And your friend, so shortsighted! He didn't appreciate your hard work. Your brilliant insight. But it freed you both, didn't it? That's the kind of cutthroat work we need here."

The case I had wrapped before this all began.

"You intrigue me," Zelnick said. "Think of all we could do if you joined me."

I snorted a laugh. "I'm not going to help you destroy humanity no matter how many cookies you bribe me with."

"I was not thinking of your dimension's desserts. I was thinking more of that lovely idiom 'just desserts.' Would you like a little justice, child?"

A chill raced down my spine. I did not like where this was going.

"I could give you Lavinia. She would be yours to kill."

It was tempting to say yes just to get at her, then walk away. "That's not very sportsman-like."

"Was what she did to you very sportsman-like?"

"No, but do you know the difference between me and her?" I'd asked myself this question more times than I could count. "I prefer to win fairly."

"Since your first race, I assume." His fish-eyes were trained on me as I paced the floor in front of him, looking for a way to strike out, to take him down.

"I get it. You've been watching me. You know who I am. But whatever it is you're trying to sell me, nothing, *nothing*, will ever matter more to me than protecting humanity from the interdimensionals that threaten them."

Zelnick frowned. "We would have made a wonderful team."

The wall behind me shook, dust raining down. Was Zelnick going to pull the wall down on me?

But a glance at the Arvokian told me he wasn't the one responsible.

"We'll never find out."

Taking the distraction I'd been granted, I pitched forward, looking to run at my new friend. With one hand extended, Zelnick threw me back against the wall. I crashed against the bricks, my head aching, feet scrambling to gain purchase on the floor.

A brick worked itself loose, and a crack formed in the wall. The warmth of Kyp's Aegis blew through the gap.

Before that moment, I hadn't allowed myself to accept that I was afraid. I was separated from my friends, and alone with a being with abilities I couldn't begin to comprehend. I hadn't had time to worry. I could only stay observant enough to try to find a way out of the mess, or a way to beat Zelnick. But feeling Kyp brought an overwhelming relief that nearly blindsided me. I needed to douse the swell of it and remain focused.

"In the end," Zelnick said, "you will either join, or you will die." Not spoken as a threat, but a fact.

"Is that it?" I asked. "I was expecting some kind of long, evil monologue with a ton of threats. And 'join or die' is all I get?"

"Oh, Ms. Madison." He smiled, a creepy needle-toothed grin. "Gods do not speak to their worshippers. You're simply a plaything, albeit an intriguing one." A twist of his fingers sucked the air from my lungs.

I heard a brick fall to the ground behind me.

"Jacks!"

Kyp worked his way through the wall. His hand brushed mine, and I grabbed hold. Warmth rushed up my arm and into my center. I focused a blast of fire on the would-be god.

He swiped my fire aside with ease. *Dammit.* My kingdom for my gun. I hadn't brought it after the last mission.

It probably wouldn't have killed him, anyway.

Dust exploded through the air and I covered my face with my free hand as Kyp sent the entire brick wall between us flying past me, aiming for Zelnick. I squinted through the cloud before me, trying to spot the Arvokian, but I couldn't find him in the aftermath.

"Some god," Kyp scoffed. "Gods are infallible. You, clearly, aren't."

Air flew back into my lungs as Zelnick lost his hold over me. I sucked in greedy gulps of air, then choked on dust and soot. I hacked and gagged, my lungs searching for clean air.

Beside me, Kyp fell to his knees. I barely kept myself standing on shaky legs. Fighting against an Arvokian's power was no easy task, even with the force of our combined Aegis.

When the dust cleared, a boy with ash-blond hair stood where Zelnick had once been. And he held a shotgun in his hands, ready to fire.

"Caleb!" Kyp shouted. "No!"

Kyp yanked me back by my hand. My boots slipped along the dust on the floor and I scrambled to keep my footing.

Caleb wouldn't shoot me, right?

An explosive blast hit my chest with such force I rocketed back into Kyp.

My ears rang and my chest ached, and one look at Kyp's face told me I'd guessed wrong. Caleb had fired at me, and Kyp had tried to yank me away, but it didn't work. My chest…

I coughed up blood until I had nothing left.

My eyes fluttered open. With a gasp, I jolted forward, only to be yanked back. I couldn't move. I lashed out, ready to take on Zelnick, Caleb, whoever was restraining me.

"Welcome back." Kyp. Right beside me.

Had we both been captured?

A wrenching shiver rose within me, and I convulsed with it. I gave myself a second or two to breathe before I grabbed for the thing holding me back. A strap from my shoulder to my hip.

A seat belt. I was in a car.

And Kyp was in the driver's seat. So, not being held captive.

"Here, let me get that," he said, leaning over and unbuckling the seat belt. "Give yourself a minute to recover." He flicked the overhead light on. "I need one as well. My Aegis bottomed out. I'm running on nothing more than adrenaline right now."

I glanced out of my window. We were parked on a city street, not far from home. I could see a high-rise building outside. That told me nothing. A glance through Kyp's window revealed the border of Central Park. In the street, horse-drawn carriages moved along with traffic, surrounded by cars and buses. I'd always longed to go on one of those carriage rides.

Kyp stared resolutely at the steering wheel he held in an iron grip. His suit jacket was gone, and his tie hung loosely around his neck. I took in the blood crusted on his knuckles. His swollen eye. The bruise welling on his jaw.

"Hi." My voice was gruff and strained, the word barely audible. Not exactly my usual vivacious self. I stretched, massaging the kinks from my neck. "What *happened*? Last thing I remember, I was dealing with an Arvokian, and you were on the other side of a brick wall."

Kyp's brow furrowed and his lips pursed. "Well, for starters, you died." He motioned toward my chest and I found a nasty dark stain, covered in stringy wet strips from the remains of... well, so much for my awesome Metallica t-shirt.

I reached out to crank up the heat, but it was already maxed. "Damn it! Who brings a gun to an interdimensional fight?"

"You. Every time." Kyp cracked a wan smile and turned toward me, draping an arm over the steering wheel. "Livingston and the Arvokian ran. And my darling newfound little brother shot you. Then I had to carry you, and steal a car... It was a process. Be grateful we got here alive." He was trying to be funny, but the stress in his voice shone through.

I tried to keep the attempt at humor going as I warmed my hands over the vent. "You stole a car? Wow Kyp, I never knew you had it in you!"

"Hector taught me how to hot-wire once for a mission." He acted like it was no big deal that he'd just used a skill his father had taught him. I knew differently. "You know me—once it's in, it never comes back out."

"Right, perfect memory." I smiled.

"I can still remember what the dirt I buried you in smelled like." The words tumbled from his mouth and my stomach swooped. With wide eyes, he turned back to the steering wheel, his mouth moving as though he was trying to pull the words back in. He took a deep breath, then turned to look at me again. A crooked smile inched across his face. "I drove top speed all the way here. Well, as fast as I could in traffic. I nearly got pulled over once."

The story did its job, turning my attention away from his horrible admission.

"With a dead body in the passenger seat? That would have been fun!" The image in my head was hilarious: Kyp playing *Weekend at Bernie's*, trying to explain the girl with the gaping chest wound in the passenger seat who could wake up any minute.

He chuckled, some of the life returning to his eyes as he swiped his hand in front of him like a Jedi. "This is not the dead body you're looking for." He offered me that soft smile again, and the cold from my recent resurrection melted away.

I stopped second guessing myself and threw my arms around

his neck. He gave in easily, leaning over the car's center console, wrapping his arms around me, resting his head on my shoulder.

"When you were behind that wall and I couldn't get to you was the longest twenty minutes of my life." He pulled me closer until I rested in his lap.

It felt good. Good to have his arms around me. Good to feel the familiarity of his presence, to hear the beat of his pulse, smell the scent of the outdoors mixed with something undeniably him. Good to be able to close my eyes and sink against him, knowing we could keep each other safe, protect each other from anything that could harm us.

I allowed myself a moment to feel better, to revel in another step taken. But just for a moment. Because up until then, I'd been so wrapped up in coming back from the dead and all the complex emotions and terrible feelings that came with dying, I'd temporarily lost sight of the fact that the others left us there to protect the kids at the brownstone.

Meaning the kids were in danger, and I was here sharing an emotional hug with my not-boyfriend.

What the hell was wrong with me? With him?

I pulled back. "Kyp, why are we waiting out here? Did you already go inside?"

Kyp eyed me. "Do you want the selfless version or the selfish one?"

"Oh, both of course."

"Selfless—I wanted to make sure your strength was up to

dealing with what we're going to find in there. I've been watching the door. Nobody has gone in or out since we got here. Whatever happened is already done. If I went in there to find out before you were back, I'd be leaving you alone and defenseless out here."

"And the selfish version?"

"I'm terrified, Jacks. Nobody is answering my calls. My Aegis is shaky. I can't go in alone. I have no idea what to expect."

Cold dread spread through me. I tried to mentally prepare myself, but I couldn't.

I threw the door open and jumped out of the car faster than I should have. Kyp was behind me to catch me before my wobbling legs gave out.

"Okay. *Okay.*" He steeled himself, but his hands shook.

I was still recovering, and he was running on fumes.

I took his hand in mine. "We've gotta do this. We need to know the bad news. Until we do, we can't figure out how to deal with it."

He turned to me, eyes alight with tears. "What if we can't deal with it?"

"With what we've been through? We can deal with anything, as long as we do it together."

"You don't even believe that," Kyp murmured.

"I didn't before. I do now. Let's face this."

On unsteady legs, we walked the block and a half to the brownstone. The security system had been bypassed and hadn't been reset. We walked right through the doors without a single security check.

"Shit. They have a technomancer." My stomach twisted.

Kyp grunted. "This could be a trap. Stay close."

I nodded.

The inside of our home was a disaster. Broken glass, cracked wood, and twisted metal littered the floor. We were pretty minimalist as far as decorating went, but anything we did have was shattered to pieces on the floor of our foyer. Even the balusters of the staircase were splintered.

A whimper bubbled up in my throat. "I'm going to tear every one of them to pieces."

Kyp closed his eyes, jaw clenching.

"Jacks? Kyp?" Drew called to us from the first floor sitting room. His voice was thick with emotion.

Whatever miniscule amount of hope I was hanging on to melted away.

I rushed through the door, dragging Kyp along with me.

Austin sat on a chair in the center of the room, staring out into space while he stroked Zane's hair where her head lay against his knee. She was sprawled on the floor, eyes red with tears. Austin's other hand gripped Drew's fiercely as Drew struggled not to cry, all but holding Cass up. Cass looked defeated. Lost. Behind them, Rennie held Jordan in her arms as he sobbed into her shoulder.

And then there was the elephant in the absolutely destroyed room. Kylie. She knelt in the middle of it all, with Ross lying broken and bloodied in her arms. She rocked him gently, skin ashen, her expression more broken than I'd ever seen.

I dove to the floor beside her, summoning what I could of my Aegis. I pressed my warmed hands to his chest. There had to be something I could do. There had to be.

"You're too late, Jacklyn." Kylie's voice was flat. "They killed him before they did anything else. Liv took his defection personally."

I lifted my hands from Ross. I didn't know what we were to each other. Friends? No. That family member you don't really like, but sometimes he's funny, and you're often stuck sharing air with? Yes. It still left me feeling empty, and my chest tightened.

"Will he come back?" I asked.

"I think that disappeared when he lost his Aegis," she said.

"For safety's sake, we should avoid... burying him. Until we're certain. Or..."

"No. We're not doing the Ritual to drag him back. We're not using Lavinia's method of torture to see if he's alive," Kylie said. "The last time he went through it, he told me he'd rather stay dead. If he can come back to me, he will."

Kyp laid a hand on Kylie's shoulder and squeezed. "I'm sorry, Kylie."

She let out one angry, ragged sob. "We'll kill them. All of them. We're going to take them down."

Nobody would look me in the eye. "Yes. We need to work on a plan. Where's Ray? And Jainey? They're sure to have input."

Kylie scoffed, but it was a sad, broken sound. "Silly girl. Do you think Lavinia broke in here and left without what she came for?"

My eyes met hers and I knew.

"She took Jainey," I said, my voice strangled.

"She took both of them."

Twenty Two

Kyp

Jainey and Ray.

His ears rang.

What had he expected? He'd known it would be bad.

"Crap! Lover boy! Get it together!" Kylie.

Kyp snapped free from his spiraling thoughts thanks to Kylie, of all people.

"You back now? Something's wrong with Jacklyn."

Jacklyn had fallen forward beside Ross' body. *Ross was dead*, and she was struggling.

"She's doing what Jordan does," Rennie observed, her voice nasally from all the tears.

"What the hell, slacker!" Kylie snapped. "You love her, go fix her." She stood, stepping away from her vigil and yanking Kyp by the sleeve. "You still can!" She shoved him onto the floor beside Jacklyn, though he went willingly.

He stared into her beautiful hazel eyes as she shook apart in front of him. Everything he couldn't express was reflected in those eyes, but he couldn't fall apart. Falling apart had been beaten out of him, so he was stuck in this limbo state where he wanted to collapse, but he couldn't. He just couldn't. He pushed himself up on trembling hands and started to control the few things still in his grasp.

Did he have the temerity to believe he could still hold his life together? Even as option after option was destroyed, as the floor beneath his feet was obliterated tile by tile?

Jacklyn wheezed and huffed, and he knew she wouldn't die, but this terrified him. He'd love her in happiness or misery, near or far. It didn't matter. But he wanted to spare her any pain.

"Jordan. I need your help, if you can."

"I'll try." Jordan walked around the others, a journey impaired by the limp his body hadn't yet healed. The battle must've taken a lot out of him. Would he even be able to do what they needed to help Jacklyn?

He glanced back at Jacklyn. She was lost in her mind somewhere.

"Can you drain her?" Kyp asked. "Just to take the edge off. It's her power levels."

"It happened to her when she was pregnant with me, didn't it?" Jordan looked downright waterlogged, and Kyp could hardly look at him.

He threw his arms around the kid. "I'm so sorry. We'll protect you. We'll get them back. I swear."

Jordan clung to him. "I don't know if I can help. I don't think I have anything left."

Kyp frowned. The kid could barely keep his head up. He pressed a kiss into his hair. "Don't try. I don't want you knocking yourself out. You need to recover."

Jordan nodded and pulled away, and Kyp reached out and brushed the hair from Jacklyn's face.

She flinched. "Get away from me! Don't touch me!" She swung out at him and Kyp dodged, catching her before she hit the floor. She screamed and crab walked away from him.

Jacklyn was broken.

She'd come back wrong. They all did. Every time they came back. They were breaking. Rebirth by rebirth.

The others murmured around them. Worried sounds. Confused sounds. It was all a blur. None of it mattered.

"Austin!" Kyp called.

"Yeah." His voice sounded small.

"Carry her to her room. We need a minute and I need to do this alone."

Austin wrapped his arms around Jacklyn, who sobbed breathlessly on the floor, her eyes red and swollen. His hold was meant to restrain, and she fought it, kicking and flexing.

Kyp rose, and she lashed out at him too, trying to headbutt him the minute he was close enough.

"What the hell is wrong with her?" Kylie asked. Was she actually concerned?

"Been happening for a while now," Austin said. "It's worse this time though."

"I hope so."

"Austin, please take her up and keep her there," Kyp said. "I'll be right behind you."

He did as Kyp asked, Jacklyn shrieking all the way.

Kyp turned to the others. "I'm not even going to pretend I have any idea how we could have done this better. We had each group well-powered and well-prepared. It was a dangerous play, but it was supposed to be dangerous for my team and Jacklyn's. Not for the base. The other team had more surprises than we anticipated. Next time, we will be better prepared."

"Next time," Rennie said.

"Yes. We'll regroup. We will read through the information from the enemy, we'll construct a new plan and we will thwart whatever they have planned for Ray and Jainey. Sleep. Recover."

"Kyp," Zane started.

"We'll get them back," Kyp promised. He would not allow any more of their family to perish. He would not.

"Zane, do me a favor. Spend a few minutes on the security system. Get it back up in working order. If you can block their technomancer, go for it. If not... they aren't coming back tonight. They got what they were after."

"And Ross?" Kylie asked.

"I'll talk to Austin. We'll take care of him, the best we can."

She nodded and swallowed hard, glancing away.

"Rennie, take care of Jordan?" Kyp asked.

"Of course." Fresh tear tracks still cut through the dried blood and bruises they all sported.

"Rest well. Tomorrow we plan."

He took the stairs to Jacklyn's room. Austin had lowered Jacklyn onto the bed, and she sat on the edge, her head buried in her hands, shuddering and gasping.

"She gave herself a bloody nose. Clocked it right into my head," Austin said.

"Grab me a wet towel and the desk chair from my room, please?"

He nodded and silently disappeared down the hall.

"I don't want your help," Jacklyn choked out.

"Yeah? And why is that?" She didn't answer. If Kyp had to guess… "You blame me."

"They were your orders."

"They always are. I don't want to be in charge anymore. I'd give anything for a new leader. But this isn't about today."

Austin returned with the wet towel and the chair.

"Thank you," Kyp said. "I need one more favor."

Another nod from the usually talkative Austin. All this time, Kyp had wanted Tex to shut up, and now that he had, it was another reminder of how far they'd fallen.

"Work with Drew? Find a way to put Ross on ice until we're sure…"

"Got it." It was nearly a whisper. "You'll take care of her?"

"Yeah."

"I don't want his help," Jacklyn hissed.

Austin rolled his eyes. "You'd rather suffer?"

"You're both dicks." She sagged forward.

"Atta girl. Keep fighting." He turned to Kyp. "Holler if you need more help. We'll be up and about for a while, I'm sure."

"Thanks, Tex." Kyp smiled, but he could tell it came out wobbly and wrong.

Then Austin was gone, and it was just Kyp and Jacklyn.

"That wasn't very nice." A stupid thing for him to say.

"*I'm* not very nice." Her breathing was returning to normal, but she was still shaking and there was a terrible darkness emanating from her through their connection.

"Jacklyn." He took her hand in his. She didn't fight him. Just snarled in response. He brushed his fingers through her soft curls, tipping her head back a bit so he could see the injury she'd given herself fighting Austin.

Gently, he pressed his fingers to the bridge of her nose, using her Aegis mixed with his to heal it. He wiped the towel gently over her nose and chin, washing away the blood.

She stared at him, an eerily blank stare. At least she'd stopped trying to get away.

"I'm sorry." He rested his hands on her shoulders, but it wasn't enough to distract her from whatever was roiling in her brain. "I'm going to dive in and find you."

She was going to be so pissed when she realized what he'd

done, but she wasn't getting better and there was a desperation in her that frightened him. He let his consciousness seep into hers, careful not to startle her. He'd expected to find a shattered mindscape, something disorganized and frantic. Instead, he found Jacklyn.

Just Jacklyn.

Dark curls tumbled over her shoulders the way they had when she'd returned to the estate. She wore a Voltron t-shirt, loose sweatpants, and sneakers, and sat criss-cross-applesauce in a clearing of green grass in front of a willow tree. Their tree.

"They're gone," she said.

"We'll get them back, Jacks."

"I've lost so many..."

"Shhhh, Jacks, I know." Emotion clogged his throat.

"Lost because I let them go when they upended their whole lives for my safety, lost because I dragged them into a war they wanted no part in, lost because I didn't properly protect them as I gallivanted off on some mission, lost because I took someone's lies at face value, lost because I didn't ask more questions, lost because I couldn't shut my damn mouth, lost because I can't stop running. I can never stop running. He ran, so I run, and I can't stop. I can't."

"You have," Kyp said, and the minute the words were out of his mouth, he knew they were true. She'd run from him. She had. But she'd come back. Maybe she'd never really meant to leave for as long as she had. Maybe she'd mourned his loss as much as he'd mourned hers.

They were back in his kitchen. Gana's blood soaked into the knees of her jeans, her sister's last message painted on the floor in front of her.

Maybe she really couldn't come back.

God, he'd been a fool.

She gasped again, and she grabbed at her throat, her eyes widening. She said nothing, but her words echoed around her mindscape.

I couldn't breathe. My God, I couldn't breathe. I shouldn't breathe.

We'll lose everyone. And God, had I wished for this? To be somebody special?

I am death and destruction. I bring it to everyone around me. I should have died in that alley before I could cause any more pain. You never should have saved me.

"Stop, Jacklyn. Just stop it. You don't mean that. You can't."

He could spend hours contemplating her words and how often they had spun through his own mind. The guilt of surviving longer than those he loved and was supposed to protect. The guilt of making decisions that put others at risk.

These thoughts would come and go. Some days, he was able to find peace with his friends. With her. Some days, it even felt like happiness.

And then something like this would happen and he drowned in the dark.

He knew how she felt, but it couldn't continue. That kind of thinking had brought him to that Sirin drug den without an ounce of protection. It led to him being reckless enough to die several times in the year they'd been separated.

"Enough!" Kyp bellowed, cutting through the noise in her head. Finally, it was silent.

He dove in front of her, pressing his forehead to hers. "Breathe, Jacklyn." He took her hand in his and pressed it to his chest. "Match your breathing to mine." He took measured breaths, in and out, in and out. "Breathe, Jacklyn. Please. Just breathe."

He pressed a kiss to her forehead, determined to pull her free from this and show her everything she still had. He peeled her anxiety and pain away from her, layer by layer. There was so much to fight for. To live for.

"Jacks, you need to be here. We need you."

"I couldn't save them and I can't save you," she said. "What do you even see when you look at me?"

He answered by projecting images into her brain. Jacklyn bumping shoulders with Austin. Jokingly competing with Zane over who could take apart and reassemble their guns the fastest. Laughing over cookies with Cass. Spinning in an office chair until she got dizzy at Drew's coaxing. Jogging with Ray. Braiding Rennie's hair. Sitting with Jainey in front of the fire. Taking the time to train Jordan without freaking him out. And sitting on Kyp's lap, healing his wounds with her tender touches, her words, the beauty of her soul.

"They still need you. *I* still need you."

She opened her beautiful hazel eyes and stared into his, and they were back in her room. She'd pushed him out of her mind and brought herself out with him. He half-expected her to push him away, but she didn't.

Instead, she climbed into his lap, her arms wrapped firmly around him, her forehead pressing hard enough against his to leave a bruise. Her body heat warmed his panic-chilled skin and the power of their connection hummed around them. Tears streamed down both of their faces.

"Jacks?"

She sniffled. "I'm here. I'm sorry. You're scared and you love them, too. I shouldn't have fallen apart like that."

"No." He pulled her impossibly closer, tucking her head against his shoulder. "If you hadn't, I would have. Believe it or not, I think helping you held me together."

She scoffed. "I tried to make myself strong so Lavinia couldn't touch me. And here I am, falling apart."

"Anyone would fall apart over what you've been through, Jacks." He shook his head, pulling back and cupping her face in his hands. "It doesn't make you weak. To love the way you do? After losing the two people you loved most? That's strength."

She nodded, sniffling. "Facing my fears." The slightest smile graced her lips, and it was like the world had begun to right itself.

"We both are."

"We are?" She tipped her head.

He nodded, returning her smile, and pressed a kiss to her cheek. "You should probably get some rest. I told the others they need rest too. We can't help Jainey until we have time to regroup. We have time. Whatever they have planned, it will take them time to get it underway. We will find them before they can hurt her. But only if we're at full strength."

He wouldn't mention Ray. He knew Ray would fight to protect Jainey. And that he might die for it. But they couldn't do anything yet. They were all too wounded to fight and too low in Aegis to bring themselves back to fighting form.

"And you're gonna get some rest, too?" She climbed off his lap shakily.

"In theory." He stood.

He didn't want to let her go. He wanted to kiss her, to take solace in her, to keep her close, to keep her from slipping away from him again. But he knew she was vulnerable. They'd done that last time, took comfort in each other when they were both vulnerable and not thinking as clearly as they should have been. It hadn't been a mistake. They'd loved each other. And it had brought them Jordan, which would have been a challenge for any teenage couple, but they were cursed with the maturity of warriors and blessed with the Franklin money. Still, they could have been smarter.

"They won't kill her." His throat tightened. "Doesn't mean they won't harm her."

"Safer isn't safe, I know. But when are we ever safe? We'll

never be able to help her if we don't heal." She recited the words like she was reading them from a book. Like she knew what she *should* say.

He stepped closer to her again. "Goodnight, Jacks." He pressed a kiss to her cheek.

"Goodnight, Kyp."

If he didn't walk away now, he'd never let himself.

Twenty Three

Jacklyn

Four thirty in the morning. The bright red numbers on my alarm clock had been taunting me for hours and every single time I closed my eyes, all I could see was what I imagined could be happening to Ray. To *Jainey*.

Sweat dripped along my body as I tossed and turned, struggling to get comfortable, propping my pillow in various positions. My head hurt, my eyes burned, and my chest ached from all my earlier gasping. With a growl of frustration, I hurled myself out of bed and threw open the door to my room.

The hardwood floors were cold against my bare feet as I padded down the hall and the stairs.

I made it as far as the base of the hall stairs when stepping downward sent a slicing pain through my foot. With a hiss of air between my teeth, I fell gracelessly onto my ass on the stair above.

I lifted my foot onto the opposite knee and was greeted by a huge, jagged piece of glass jutting from my heel. With a sigh, I prepared to tug the shard from my foot.

"Sorry." Kyp appeared on the far side of the room. "I started cleaning up over here. Didn't get to that side yet."

I glanced up at him and grinned, despite the throbbing in my foot. He wore track pants, a t-shirt and sneakers, looking for all the world like he was about to go for a jog, a broom and dustpan in hand. It was endearing.

"Now that is a fabulous sight." I winked. "Hey there, tough guy."

"You're pretty laugh-inducing yourself," he countered with a crooked grin.

I glanced at my white and pink tank top with a smiling strawberry across the front and my matching berry-dotted short shorts. "I don't get it."

Kyp barked a laugh.

I looked back down at the nasty shard of glass in my foot, tugging it free with a wince and a groan. "I swear, if I didn't have healing powers, I'd be dead by now."

Kyp gaped at me, the ghost of a smile still on his face. "Obvious statement from the girl who had a hole blown through her today."

"Hmmm… that was yesterday," I corrected.

"Not if you didn't sleep, it wasn't."

I rolled my eyes, setting to work healing my foot. "Whatever. I meant death by my own clumsiness, not death by asshole."

Kyp returned his attention to sweeping up more glass and

debris.

"Jeez. This place is a mess. I only barely noticed last night."

Kyp shrugged. "You were anxious about the others. I was similarly preoccupied." He held up a bandaged hand. "I grabbed a knife off the counter by the blade while tidying up. Who knows how I managed to avoid the minefield of glass."

I patted the space next to me on the stair. "Let me take a look."

He continued sweeping. "It's bandaged. You don't need to waste your energy on it."

Did he know how not to be difficult? "Get over here and sit. Nothing is ever wasted healing you."

His shoulders slumped. "Fine." He trudged toward the stairs and threw himself down beside me.

I took his calloused hand in mine and unwrapped the bandage. "We spoke about how I was feeling about everything. Now it's your turn."

"You really want to do part two?"

"If I don't ask, will you ever tell me why you can't sleep?" I channeled my Aegis through my hand and into his.

"No." He sighed. "You're right. The walls need to come down. No more fronts."

"Yep." I tried for cheerfulness, but it fell flat. There wasn't much to be cheerful about.

"I tried to sleep," he admitted. "Did you know Jainey has been sneaking into my room at night? I couldn't sleep without her tiny feet digging into my back."

"Oh, Kyp." My throat tightened, and tears filled my eyes. I let my head drop onto his shoulder.

"There's also the anger. Like a fireball in my gut. She still thinks I'm an idiot, and I keep proving her right."

"She who?"

He looked away.

"Wait, Lavinia?" I winced at the way her name shrieked out of me. "I don't understand." I tried to soften my voice so he wouldn't feel judged, but I couldn't believe the absurdity. I squeezed his hand even tighter, despite the healing wound in his palm. "You're doing your best. We all are. You're intelligent, strong, an excellent leader, a fine tactician." I slid my fingertips across his stubbled chin, turning him to face me. "She is a ruthless, heartless, murderous monster who doesn't care about destroying her son or killing innocents, if that is what it takes to keep her power. Believe me, if a person like that isn't proud of you, that's a good thing. You want her to be ashamed of you."

"She thinks I'm weak," he said, his tone clipped.

"Then she'll underestimate you. She mistakes kindness and a sense of decency for weakness. And that will be her downfall."

"Her downfall," he repeated hollowly.

"This is Lavinia we're talking about here, or need I remind you?" I said firmly. "I know she's your mother, but you can't hesitate when you come against her. Their lives are at stake."

He stared straight ahead, his eyes getting that blank look again.

"And in the meantime, I swear if you ever measure yourself according to what Lavinia thinks of you again, I'll kill you and sing the ritual with the proportional jolliness of a caroler on Christmas."

His lips twitched. "What would it be like to have normal parents? Can you imagine how the kids must feel?"

"Are you implying we're not normal?" I laid my head on his shoulder.

"No way! Most kids have parents that are only a little bit older than them and fight interdimensional monsters for a living, right?" He barely cracked a smile.

"At least we're the good guys." I laughed. "We may not be quite ready, and Ray is trying to be all of our parents, and he's a cluster himself..."

"You're excellent at this pep talk thing."

"Right?" He wouldn't deter me. "What I'm trying to say is, at least we're all on the same page."

"We are," Kyp agreed.

"I don't care if Livingston and that Arvokian dude say they created her. She's ours. And we're bringing home what's ours."

"Both of them," he said, voice hoarse.

I reveled in having him warm and close to me. He, at least, was safe. I lifted my head from his shoulder. "I'm gonna make us tea."

"Tea?" His eyebrows raised.

"Yes, *tea*. Go downstairs. Work off some energy in the training room. I'll finish sweeping up the glass and bring you tea to help relax you even more."

"You're turning the tea thing on me?" He looked at me like I'd just introduced a foreign element into his life, or like I told him I sometimes sprouted an extra arm to help me with chores.

"I know I used to be a 'coffee only' type, but Ray is far too hyper to handle caffeine. So, herbal tea is a thing. Austin too. If Austin drinks a cup of coffee, it's not a pretty sight."

"Really? Like he bounces off the walls?" Kyp seemed a little too eager to gain some information that might make Austin look bad.

Why not indulge him? "And then he crashes in a mess rife with sleep-drool."

Kyp chuckled. "You are so kind to me."

"I try. Now, go."

He agreed, but he looked back at me a few times as he walked away.

I removed anything dangerous left in the main hall by the time the teakettle whistled. Balancing two piping hot tea cups and one of those adorable honey bottles shaped like a bear on a tray, I headed downstairs.

Kyp seemed skeptical when I suggested it, but I was determined to help him rest, even if he ended up sleeping until noon. Our team could go through the research we found while he did. We were about to face our greatest challenge, and even though we had more than enough reasons to wallow in our depression, we'd never win unless we pulled ourselves out of the doldrums. Though our emotions made us capable of draining the deepest of our Aegis abilities, loss wasn't the right emotion for it. Determination would be better.

I'd had trouble with that earlier, but Kyp had helped me shake it. I needed to do the same for him.

It wasn't entirely selfless. I felt better when Kyp did.

Ugh. Sometimes I nauseated myself.

I hoped he'd worn himself out. I barely had the strength to navigate the stairs to the training room without losing my balance. The slap of fists hitting the punching bag and the shrieking of the chain as it swung greeted me.

Kyp had messily yanked his hair into a ponytail, although it was already coming undone. He may need a haircut, but I wasn't complaining. It wasn't a bad look for him.

His dark gaze was fixed on the bag, mouth twisted into a scowl. His taped hands clenched tightly, even when he took a break to catch his breath and steady the bag. A sharp turn, and he executed a perfect roundhouse kick to the bag. He stopped there, and I thought he was going to come sit with me and drink the tea, but he swiped the sweat from his brow with his t-shirt before continuing another sequence of hard punches, feints, and kicks.

Release. I felt it flowing from him with every collision. This was how he was getting it all out. While some of us could laugh and joke, talk about it or even cry about it, Kyp had never allowed himself such an option. He fancied himself the King of Control, though he cracked more often than he believed. Lavinia had created that rigid version of him, trained him not to allow anyone to peek behind the curtain.

He was shedding that, slowly, but it wasn't easy for him.

My knees shook with exhaustion. I lowered myself to the stairs and doctored my tea. I'd drink mine while watching him, and I'd be there when he was ready to drink his.

The frustration and anger were coming off him in waves, beating against the shore of my mind over and over again, just like he was beating against the bag, giving it everything he had, pouring out the emotions he struggled to express. It felt good to watch him get it out, to finally unwind that coil that was wrapped so tightly, ready to pop.

I wasn't sure what it said about me, but the feeling was mirrored within me, and my eyelids drooped, lulled by a symphony of punches to the heavy bag and grunts of exertion. I didn't remember falling asleep, or even putting down my tea, but when my eyes next blinked open, I was being lowered to my bed.

Kyp stood over me. He must've carried me to my room. Now he seemed to stall, rocking in place, as if I'd caught him when I opened my eyes, and he didn't know what to do.

I caught his wrist. "Wait."

He looked at my hand and then back at me, eyes wide.

"Stay." It wasn't the wrong thing to say. I knew it wasn't. We'd turned a corner.

He pushed a hand through his damp hair, straightening the

t-shirt that clung to him. He had taken a shower at some point between the punching bag and carrying me to bed. He cleared his throat. Swallowed hard. "Jacklyn…"

I didn't give him the chance to hurt my pride. "You're not going to be able to sleep alone. I'm not suggesting anything but you sleeping on that side of the bed while I sleep on this one, so neither of us is alone."

His eyes searched mine for a moment before shaking off my hand and walking around the bed. He settled onto the other side, the mattress creaking a little under his added weight. He shifted and squirmed, as if struggling to get comfortable. He wouldn't be able to, because he held himself ramrod straight.

We'd been so good with each other all day. Maybe a bit solemn, but I thought I'd helped him break out of it. And just by asking him to say, I'd wound him up again. I needed to break the tension.

"Aren't you going to say goodnight to me again?" I teased. It had been what had woken me. That and the gentle kiss to my forehead.

He didn't say a word.

"Do I have to actually make the effort of turning toward you and staring knowingly, or do you have the idea?"

"You were asleep…" he trailed off.

"So it doesn't count?" I was a little too smug about this, but if I could focus on one good thing in my life, then I was grateful to have this bit of progress between us. "Oh fine, if no goodnight, do

I at least get a little kiss on my forehead?"

He stifled a chuckle, and I counted that as a victory. "Not talking. Sleeping. So shut up already."

"Oh, come on, it was sweet."

He rolled over toward me, sighing that frustrated sigh of his, like I had annoyed him once again. But when I turned to face him, his eyes were dancing with mischief. He looped his arm around my neck and squashed me against his chest—a playful hug.

"This isn't a kiss good night. This is suffocation." But I settled in, my hand coming to rest on his chest, feeling the wild thumping of his heart beneath my fingertips. I hoped I was causing that. I hoped it was a good thing.

"You'll live." He grinned. "You always do."

I smacked him hard in the chest. When had our senses of humor gotten so dark? Must be the continuous trauma.

His legs tangled with mine and he pulled me closer. "You can't hit me like that." He ran his fingers through my hair. "It actually hurts."

"You'll live," I mocked. "You always do."

Another chuckle escaped him. His fingers slid from my hair, trailing along my chin, nudging my face upwards so I was looking at him. The soft pad of his thumb ran across my lower lip in a whisper light touch and I watched his eyes follow, watched him trying not to kiss me, and my heart leapt in my chest.

"Did you know if you polish an ancient sword that has been used in battle, it bleeds the blood of the people it killed? Even after thousands of years."

You had to love Kyp and his ability to share the most random factoid at the strangest of times. "That can't be true."

He waved a hand at me. "Well, it doesn't bleed like a wound, but the grinding water goes deep brownish red and it smells like..."

"I don't remotely want to know."

He chuckled. "My point" —he brushed his fingers through my hair again— "is that even ancient swords bleed from their past battles. Didn't I say you were a weapon?"

"You did."

"An exquisite weapon, though."

"You're no different, Kyp Franklin." I wasn't sure if he heard me; I was pretty sure he wasn't listening.

But I hoped he was.

His lips pressed to mine, soft, slow, and more than a little hesitant, like he half-expected me to punch him for it.

As if.

"Okay?" he breathed.

"Shut up." This time, I kissed him, deepening the kiss and pulling him even closer.

Whenever I was with him, it felt like I couldn't get him close enough, like I would gladly breathe him in and let his soul mingle with mine. It was addictive, energizing, exactly what I needed.

After all, we'd done a Ritual. As far as Arvokians were concerned, we were married. And if the Ritual book I'd read cover to cover when I'd first come to the brownstone was any indication, that vow made us soulmates.

No wonder I'd felt so empty when we were apart.

I still did. A part of me would never heal. There was still so much to tackle. Still, so much that had been wrong and would be wrong in both our lives, but as we finally reunited, whispering *I love yous* against each other's lips, one wound finally healed.

And eventually, when we parted for the good of our sleep schedule, Kyp fell asleep with me on my pillow, wrapped in my arms.

I hoped it was as much of a comfort to him as it was to me.

TWENTY FOUR

KYP

The sun streamed its warmth on Kyp's face and, for a moment, he waited for Jainey to kick him in the back. But she wasn't the person sharing his bed this time, and it made the entire terrible day and difficult night rush back into his mind.

He turned over to find Jacklyn asleep beside him in those silly strawberry pajamas. They'd shared more than a few passionate kisses and a renewed exchange of their love last night. They'd bared their souls to each other.

Her hair was a messy strawberry-scented cloud, fanned out over the pillow. Her eyes were puffy and red, her face a little tear-swollen, and she pouted in her sleep. She was beautiful.

Did her heart stutter like his did when she looked at him?

She shifted in her sleep, eyelids fluttering open. "Hey."

"Hey." The quiver in his voice betrayed him, so he jumped in with both feet. "Any second thoughts?"

Jacklyn tensed. "You?"

"You didn't answer me." His heart decided now would be a pleasant time to climb out through his mouth and make an escape.

"You didn't answer *me*." Fear sketched its way across her face, and it was an odd source of comfort to him.

"None. You?"

She smiled. "Not at all."

"Good." He leaned forward, pressing a quick peck to her lips. "In that case, we should get dressed and get moving. We've got work to do."

"Yeah?" she asked, excited. "What's our first step?"

He couldn't believe they were doing this.

"Kyp." Zane's eyes were about ready to pop free from her skull. "What in the *hell*?"

They had returned to the sitting room, but this time, Jacklyn and Kyp weren't gaping at the others. This time, the positions had been reversed. The team—*their* team—was gaping at Jacklyn, Kyp, and Cxarana.

He had not visited her intending to take her with them, but when Cxarana did not greet Kyp and Jacklyn at the entrance of the temple, not with mocking verbal barbs, nor amiable salutations, he'd found her in her main workshop hastily packing herbs into a satchel.

She was running away from her role as the Arvokian Liaison. And Kyp found he could not let her do it alone. Before he knew it, he was helping her pack.

"Do you just take in any stray these days?" Kylie scowled.

"Careful, sweetie." Jacklyn smiled. "You're one of those strays."

"Mom?" Jordan asked. "That looks like one of the people that experimented on me."

"I assure you, young Mr. Franklin, that was not me," Cxarana said.

"It wasn't," Rennie agreed. "The one that worked on us had a deeper voice."

"So, what?" Austin asked. "An Arvokian pissed you off, so you kidnapped the Arvokian Liaison?"

"Have you completely lost the plot?" Drew chimed in.

"Enough!" Kyp called out over the noise. "We can argue about this all night and let Ross's sacrifice and what will by that point be the sacrifices of Ray and Jainey be for naught, or we can listen to each other and make a plan. Can we get started now?"

Silence.

"We've all had some time to recuperate. I know Zane and Cass were going to search through the files from Livingston's home. We went to question Cxarana, but we found her running away from home. So, I suppose we should all compare notes."

When this was done, when they were all back home safely, Kyp was going to float the idea of electing the next leader of the Order. He was certain they would elect someone, anyone, other than him, and he was perfectly content to be nothing more than the finances behind the organization.

"I'm not saying a word until she tells us what the hell she's doing here." Austin jabbed a finger at Cxarana.

Rennie stepped through the mess of people and rested a hand on Cxarana's arm. "Tell us. It's okay. Don't be scared."

Cxarana turned to the girl, then back to the room. "I suppose I should begin by stating that I am not privy to much more information than you are. I'm a mere trainee. When a Council appoints a liaison, it means only that they are historians of the relationship the Arvokians and humanity have pursued over the ages. I was born within the pocket dimension that rests between the Dusk and your world, the Dawn."

"She's got nothing more than we do," Kylie said. "Which means she's a waste of time standing between me and the moment I suck the air out of Lavinia's lungs."

"Lavinia is mine," Jacklyn growled.

"I understand, Cxarana." Rennie spoke over Jacklyn and Kylie's bickering. "Tell me more. Why were you running away?"

Cxarana emitted a clacking noise Kyp had come to understand was her clearing her throat. "Kyp Franklin was the first human I pledged as a Key. I found that, as I aged into my role, I became more and more uncomfortable with what I was tasked to do. There were... inconsistencies in behavior. Things I was taught that do not properly mesh with the orders of the Council. I found myself in much the same position as Kyp Franklin once did."

"Oh?" Kyp fought a smile. He'd always felt a kinship with her. It was nice to see it wasn't one-sided.

"I needed to defy their rules. There has never been a time without an Arvokian Liaison in the temple, but I packed all the herbs I could carry, took the bowl and the knife, and as many books as I could manage. I planned on fleeing but did not know where to find you. If Mr. Franklin and Ms. Madison had come any later, the temple would have been empty."

Rennie removed her hand from Cxarana's arm and shrugged her tan sweater up from where it had slid off her shoulders. "She's telling the truth. She's terrified and angry. Furious. But she feels safe here."

"Child," Cxarana gasped. "I didn't even sense you probing."

"Yeah," Rennie said. "That's what happens when you surgically implant an Aegis gland in a body that doesn't know how to regulate an Aegis."

Cxarana grunted her displeasure. "When our Council used my pocket dimension to smuggle Raymond and young Jaina through, allowed foul Sirins to march through *my* home as a shortcut to escape from you, I could no longer sit back and do nothing."

"The leaders of the Arvokians are plotting against us," Jacklyn said.

"This is a declaration of war," Cass said. Tears shone in her eyes. "The Dawn against the Dusk."

Zane plucked at a tear in her jeans. "I knew I never should have picked a side. This will be a bloody massacre."

"No. You do not view this from the correct perspective. There are allies in the Dusk," Cxarana said. "Beings that rebel against the Council's rule and defend others there against them."

"We need to reach out to them," Jacklyn said. "Cxarana, can you connect us to these allies?"

"Nothing like that has ever been done before."

"Because clone Skeleton Keys and surgically created Guardians were a regular practice in the Order back in the dark ages? I'm through with tradition. Tradition is just peer pressure from spirits, anyway." Jacklyn smirked. "I'm not going to sit and wallow. I'd like to burn this whole thing to the ground."

Too much, Jacks. Too much.

"You should not need to do so!" Cxarana argued. "If you'd been allowed to serve your purpose and seal the rifts properly, that would end things."

"Yeah, that doesn't look like it's gonna happen," Austin said. "So those allies in the Dusk? We're probably gonna need them. How do we bring them here?"

"Better yet, why haven't those allies already taken down the Arvokian Council?"

Cxarana shook her head. "Our abilities are different in the Dusk. The pocket dimension makes us stronger. In order to fight on the same level, we would need to bring the Arvokian Council to the Dusk."

"Or bring the rebels of the Dusk here," Jacklyn said. "Arvokian abilities still seem pretty strong here in the Dawn."

"Wait! I think I have an idea." Zane launched herself to her feet. "What happens to the interdimensionals if the rifts close?"

"They... We will survive, but we will be frail," Cxarana said.

"Then we need to close the rifts."

"If you close the rifts, I request asylum." Cxarana's voice went shrill.

Jacklyn turned her hazel eyes on Kyp. They shared a nod.

"You'll have it. We'll protect you here, even after our Aegis is gone," Jacklyn vowed.

"Wait!" Zane said. "Shut up, everybody! The papers we lifted from Livingston included a load of research documents. Lavinia and the others are planning to open something they call a MacroRift," Zane said.

"Yeah, I spotted that before everything went to shit," Jacklyn said.

"Exactly. If Cxarana hadn't shown up, this was supposed to be my first order of business. They intend to siphon energy from the rifts and pull them together into one rift the Skeleton Key must open. They need a large location for it, and they need to wait until nightfall. Something about the Ritual they'll use. They have to give Jainey some kind of treatment. There's a note on it taking a couple of hours to take hold in her blood."

"Why would they want that?" Kyp asked. "What's the endgame?"

"It doesn't matter," Zane said. "That's the rift we've gotta seal."

"Opening a MacroRift would have to be done slowly." Her bruise-colored skin looked less vivid. In fact, Kyp guessed she might have gone pale. "The child would bleed out before they could finish."

"A slow drip? Like blood donation?" Kyp asked, gritting his teeth against the thought of anyone daring to harm his baby.

"Yes," Jordan said. "They've tested that on us before. If we open a rift any larger than normal, we have to keep bleeding into it to open it. They hook us up to all kinds of machines."

"Which means we have time," Zane said. "This is going to sound awful, but what we want is for Jainey to open that MacroRift. Once it's open, if we close that one rift, we close them all. And this nightmare is over. Permanently."

Kyp turned to Cxarana. "And once that MacroRift is closed, we all lose any special abilities we got from the Dusk?"

Cxarana nodded. "To my knowledge, yes."

"Once the MacroRift opens, how will we know when the other rifts close?" Cass asked.

"The Ritual performed to even force a rift open that far would need to channel the energy of the other rifts to do so. It will close the others the moment the MacroRift opens," Cxarana said.

Kyp hated this. He could tell the others did, too. The plan was to let Jainey bleed, just not enough to kill her. His heart twisted.

"We can't do this," Jacklyn whispered.

"Do you have any better ideas?" Kylie asked. When Jacklyn didn't answer, she continued. "And what about the kids that don't belong to the 'Golden Couple?' What are we gonna do about them?"

"Caleb has chosen the wrong side," Kyp said. "He shot Jacklyn."

"I wouldn't exactly say that's the wrong side, but go on," Kylie said.

Kyp resisted the urge to bite back. "He helped Livingston escape. Does that work better for you?"

"We still have to save him." Rennie's voice shook as she spoke. "We can't just leave him there. We can't leave any of them. I mean, Caleb's mom is right here, but the other two are like me. Their parents died, and they were left alone. Street kids. They may be siding with the others because they won't have a home if they go against them. We can help them. We just need to reach them."

"Let me talk to Caleb," Jordan said. "I know I could stop him. He's my best friend. He can't be okay with them hurting Jainey."

"Okay, but to do any of that, we need to know where they are first," Cass said. "We've got a lot of things we want to do—"

"—and we want to do them right away," Drew cut in.

"Yes, but we won't be able to do anything unless we know *where*." The last word came out strangled, and Cass's eyes began to glow. "Hey, guys!" An abrupt wave, and Cass was no longer in control. "Sorry, Cassie." Gana winced. "It's just that I got this idea, and I need confirmation." She bounced on her toes.

"Gana." Kyp smiled warmly. They didn't have a great relationship when she was alive, but he had wanted one. He'd always found Gana to be a fun sparring partner. "Your ideas are always welcome."

She ducked her head, a small smile on her face, and Kyp worried he'd embarrassed her, but he didn't have time to worry for long.

"The warehouse in Trenton, New Jersey," Gana said. "It was licensed to Lifestone Pharmaceuticals, but the Order was paying huge sums of money for shipping costs to that address. At first, we thought the payments were for supplies, although the amounts were too high. So high that we went there to investigate."

Jacklyn's solemn eyes met Kyp's, and he understood. This was the battle that had led Jacklyn's mother to her death. The battle that had destroyed the Order's resistance. The battle Kyp had instigated.

"You're right," Kyp said, impressed. "With everything that had happened, I never went back. We never investigated it further. The attack from the interdimensionals made it seem like they were gunning for Lavinia as much as they were for us. Hell, they killed Jacklyn *and* Kylie. I thought..."

Crap. Such a foolish decision. The answer was staring him in the face.

"Zane, have we looked into any more of Livingston's or Lifestone Pharmaceuticals properties?"

"There aren't many. I can see if I can narrow it down."

"In the meantime, I say we start at the warehouse," Jacklyn said. "Gana's right. They may have been planning this already and guarded the warehouse so strongly because they didn't want us to put an end to it. It may be abandoned, or it could be exactly what we're looking for. At least we cross one off the list."

"Be ready to go. Seven thirty tonight, we take the fight to them," Kyp said. "And Gana?"

She hummed in response, but a smile played at the edges of her lips.

"Thank you," Kyp said. "We've missed your input."

A pleased nod before she fled from Cass, and Cass' eyes returned to their normal shade of brown.

"Flatterer." Jacklyn grinned, leaning into Kyp's side.

He shrugged, holding up a finger to show Jacklyn he needed a minute. Kylie sat in the middle of the group, as they gathered their things and prepared for battle. Her hair hung lank and lifeless around her porcelain face. She'd borrowed a blue button-down from Cass the night before, and she fiddled with its buttons. Her legs were crossed and one booted foot tapped on the floor in an erratic pattern. She looked lost.

He knelt in front of her, seeking out eye contact. "Hey."

She glanced up for a moment, then returned her attention to the shirt button. "What are you doing here, mingling with the lowlifes? Aren't you the big cheese now? Shouldn't you be busy... doing Jacklyn or something?"

He was not going to dignify that with a response.

"This isn't Lavinia's Order anymore, and that's not how I run things."

This time, she did meet his eyes. "Is this what you wanted? When you wanted to steal the Order from her? Did you imagine this mess?" She threw her hands up in the air.

For a moment, Kyp didn't answer.

"What?" Kylie snarled. "Did you want me to lie to you? To protect poor mentally fragile Kyp? Because this whole Order is disorganized and unstructured. You've taken a regimented army and turned it into a collection of strays and nobodies. Half of these people don't even have an Order pedigree."

"I know. You think I care about any of that?"

"You never did. You're a bleeding heart. Disgusting." She tore her eyes away from him, her nose scrunched.

"I came here to find out if Ross had made any progress." He ignored her comments.

She stilled. "No. No change." She twisted a button. "So, know-it-all, what do you think? Is he *dead* dead?"

Kyp scratched his head.

"Yeah, you think he is," Kylie said. "You don't have to answer."

Kyp brushed a gentle hand over her hair. She shuddered and leaned forward, a choked cry escaping from her tightly clamped lips. He pulled her into a hug. "I'm sorry. I'm sorry for all of it. We let her pit us against each other. Let's not do that anymore."

Kylie's hands shook, but she hugged him back. "I still hate you."

"Yeah, I know. I'm truly sorry about Ross."

"Don't be." She pulled back and swiped at her eyes. "He did it for the kids. He really loved them."

Kyp nodded. "They loved him too."

"I know." She gave herself a firm shake. "Okay, that's enough. Get back to work before someone starts believing I have feelings or something."

Kyp stood up, tapping her ankle with his foot. "Wouldn't want that." He moved back through the room to find Jacklyn standing at the door, watching him. "What?"

"You're too kind." She gestured for him to follow her. "Armory trip. I want to prepare."

He followed her warily. "I'm not kind."

She marched down the stairs. "You're a horrible human, forgiving Kylie, who helped torture you all your life."

"She needed forgiveness. We were raised to believe our success, our very survival, depended on the destruction of anybody who stood in our way. Maybe we have a chance to change things now. Besides, we need to be a unified presence. We can't risk Kylie deciding to help Lavinia at the last minute. Not this time."

"And you don't think she will?"

"I think she sees the monsters pretty clearly now." He glanced around the hall. "Where's Cxarana?"

"Cass and Drew are getting her settled."

"And the others?" He narrowed his eyes at her.

"Austin and Zane are organizing the armory for us. Rennie and Jordan are like Kylie and Cxarana. They need time. Without it, they'll take a toll on the mission."

"How magnanimous of you," Kyp commented.

"Shut up." She grinned. "You're trying to keep us both from diving all the way into how badly this can go."

"Myself more than you. If we're right, and I hope we are, I'll be coming face to face with Lavinia tonight. That never goes well."

They walked for a few seconds before he stopped her outside the armory. "You know, you scare the hell out of me."

"Pfft. Nothing scares you."

Kyp shot her a meaningful look. "You know that's not true."

She sighed. "What did I do now?"

"You didn't do anything. I just tell you things I don't even mean to say. I tell you things I don't even really know until they're spilling into your ears."

She laughed, but it was rife with bitterness. "I scare you because I keep you honest? I think I kind of like that."

With a hand on her hip, he tugged her toward him, the other hand reaching up to cup her cheek. "You know, things are different this time. I don't look at you and see an angel or a hero. I look at you and I see this dangerously flawed person I want to spend every damn waking minute of my life with and it's positively infuriating, but what can I do about it?"

She narrowed her eyes. "One, you're dangerously flawed too." She waited a beat, dramatic as usual, before her face lit up. "Two, I think that's the most romantic thing you've ever said to me."

Kyp rolled his eyes and offered her a wry smile. "Right. You know I'm not good at this stuff."

She kissed him, a soft lingering brush of her lips against his. "I'm serious. I'm not being sarcastic."

He raised an eyebrow. "Not sarcastic? Are you okay?"

"You're funny. Are *you* okay?"

With a sigh and one more kiss, they turned toward the armory to prepare for their next attack.

TWENTY FIVE

JACKLYN

"What if we can't save him? What if he's already gone?" I'd never seen Zane look so concerned. She chewed at her lower lip and held the steering wheel in a white-knuckled grip.

We were on our way to the warehouse. Our plan was simple—get in, save the kids and Ray, kill the hell out of everyone else, and close the rift. And hopefully, we would all get out alive.

Zane wasn't helping my confidence.

"We can't think like that." I glanced back to make sure Rennie and Jordan weren't listening. Austin had launched into a story of an epic battle from his past, and had them both spellbound. The last thing I needed was Zane chipping away at their confidence, too.

"This is why I never wanted to pick a side," she continued, calmer this time.

I breathed in deep and released it through my mouth in a

whistle. "It's a little late to be singing that song, Zane. You made a choice. Trust yourself to have made the right one."

Zane frowned and slumped in her seat. "Is it the right choice if it means someone you love suffers for it?"

It didn't take a licensed psychologist to dissect her meaning. I wasn't here to give her a psychiatric evaluation, though. "I understand, Z. I do. But you know damn well Ray would have been in this mess whether you joined in or not. Hell, if you weren't involved, it probably would have happened sooner."

Zane huffed a laugh.

"Now I need you to get your head in the damn game. This isn't the time to explore your emotional connections. This is the time to channel them. You know that."

Zane didn't take her eyes off the road, but a smile tilted her lips as she nodded.

Not eager to jump the gun, we parked down the street from our location, found a tall office building and climbed up its window ledges and drain pipes until we reached the roof. Some were more adept than others, but thankfully, Jordan and Kyp were capable of telekinetic lifts when necessary.

Zane crouched near the ledge and raised her binoculars. Her straight black hair whipped around her as the wind began to pick up, the night growing frigid.

I joined her, zeroing in on the site without any visual aid. Would seeing our target stem the tide of my emotions? Put an end to the way they churned and crashed against the shore of my mind like a wild current? No. It just reminded me that my father and my child were close.

We couldn't stay there waiting and planning. We had to get in there.

The warehouse was one of many in the district. The flood lights of the loading dock lit our target up like a spotlight.

"Okay, everyone," I said as I took the lead. "I know this feels like the end of the world, but we can face it. We can handle it."

"We can?" Jordan squeaked.

"Sure we can. This may be your first rodeo, but it isn't ours. We're used to fighting for our lives."

"And winning," Kyp added. "We usually win those."

Except for the times we didn't. But we wouldn't mention those during a pep talk.

"See." I hitched a thumb in Kyp's direction. "He knows what I mean."

Jordan snorted, but made a face. "Do you guys smell that?" He sniffed the air. "Is something burning?"

A deep inhale revealed an odd mix of burning candles and ozone. I was about to confirm, but Austin did it for me.

"Air smells nasty. What is that?"

"You smell it too?" I thought Jordan and I had only caught the scent thanks to our enhanced senses. But if Austin could smell it…

"Did anyone listen to the weather report today?" Drew glanced around him.

"A little cold for you, pipsqueak?" Kylie snarled.

Austin stepped in between them. "I'll show you cold."

"Guys!" Rennie raised her voice. She pointed at the sky. "He's asking because it's snowing. I don't remember anything about snow being predicted for today. Do you?"

We followed her line of sight and found what she was looking at. It was hard to see at first, but as the volume increased, it suddenly became clear—this was not snow.

A warm, wet drop hit my cheek. I swiped at it and my hand came away black with soot and ash. My heart hardened like a stone.

Austin swiped a speck of the stuff from Drew's shoulder. "Shit." He rubbed the filth between his fingers. "It's the end of the damn world."

Drew nodded slowly. "Is that a... dimensional bleed?"

Jordan gasped. "The MacroRift."

Kyp's voice was a hoarse whisper. "It's open."

We glanced at our son as he bounced on the balls of his feet. Itching for a fight. This boy with his father's dark hair and eyes like my mother's. He wasn't ready for this. Neither was Rennie.

They were still so young and innocent.

Hell, so were the rest of us.

"They're already bleeding Jainey out," Kyp said. "We have to go. Now."

It wasn't easy sneaking into a warehouse. The loading dock was well lit, despite the late hour. Most of the loading bays were already sealed. There was only one open.

It wasn't like we could sneak through those rolling metal doors; they were too loud when they opened. We could try to drop into a window, but the windows were all very visible from inside the warehouse. There would be eyes on us the moment we entered.

The most ingenious plan I could think of was to split up—two to the windows on the street side of the warehouse, two to the back entrance, and one to the rooftop entrance. But before anyone else made their entrance, I would be making mine with Kyp. Right through the one open door.

It was a gutsy move. Probably too damn gutsy. But the bottom line was, Jainey was the star of the show right now. We wouldn't be able to get close to her without the others seeing us. So we decided to cause some trouble. Create a distraction.

Our move was probably expected. There wasn't even a pair of guards at the doors. It didn't matter. They were sitting pretty on their thrones, relishing their last victory over us, the victory they believed would end the war, permanently defeating us. I intended to oust them from those thrones.

A pile of boxes created a wall at the entry, blocking off our view of anything happening beyond them.

"*Our view is blocked,*" Kyp said telepathically. We were all mentally linked through him and Jordan, though we also wore earpieces to conserve their Aegis when possible.

"Ours isn't," Drew whispered. "Jainey and Ray are in our sights. They're farthest from you. Closer to the back door."

"We have to get back there," I said to Kyp. *"And we have to do it quick."*

I focused my Aegis so I could better hear the muttered discussions happening around Jainey and Ray.

"The rift must be wider!" Lavinia.

"I'm trying! I'm just sleepy," Jainey whimpered.

My heart shattered, along with the last of my restraint and caution.

"Fuck. This. Shit." I shoved a crate as hard as I could, sending the wall of boxes crashing down, chunks of crates scattering like Jenga pieces. "I'm going in."

Kyp shouted in my mind, but I couldn't be brought to care. Dust flew into the air. Debris settled in front of me. My eyes locked on Jainey as soon as it all cleared.

Beautiful brown eyes that had likely been drooping from exhaustion now gazed at me with shock. My baby girl.

Ray lay beside her, connected to Jainey by a tube in his side. He was strapped to a stretcher by strips of metal clasped around his chest, waist, and legs. His eyes were clouded, like he was sedated, but a small smile flickered across his lips. I imagined he was happy to see his baby girl, too.

The concrete flooring of the warehouse had shattered into chunks, which writhed and skittered over the pulsating red scar that had been torn through the earth below.

I yanked my daggers from my hip holsters and rushed ahead, leaping over debris and sailing forward. There was no amicable way to resolve this. We weren't about to sneak in, and we weren't about to negotiate. This was an attack. We'd either get Jainey back and save the world, or we would die trying.

I landed on the edge of the MacroRift. Sirins swamped me from either side and I stabbed them with the daggers, yanking my weapons free and moving on.

Shouts and roars sounded around me, but I was single-minded in my pursuit.

A claw, large and misshapen, crashed into the floor in front of me, tearing the cement further apart, and I leapt back, careful to avoid the edge of the rift.

I swore. The claw was nearly my height, and mustard yellow, bespeckled with geometric patterns. And it was jutting from the tear in the earth.

I wasn't sure when he had caught up to me, let alone gotten ahead, but Kyp was beside Caleb, where the boy stood guard, protecting Livingston. "Do you see? Look at what they're bringing here!"

There was a hint of fear in the child's eyes. Had Kyp gotten through to him?

Jainey's whimper carried through the space between us.

"Now!" I commanded the rest of the group through their entrances. I dashed around the giant claw, grabbing at the floor. If I could free Jainey, I could stop this. Unfortunately, she was guarded by Zelnick.

The Order exploded from their various entrance points and

into a warehouse crawling with interdimensionals.

Zelnick watched me as I approached. "Jacklyn Madison! I'd hoped we would meet again."

I sneered. "I was counting on it."

"All bark and no bite," Zelnick said. "Disappointing."

I hurled a knife directly at him, the dagger slipping from my fingers end over end. Zelnick brought his hand up in front of his chest just in time to block the knife, but it slammed through his hand, pinning it to his body.

"Arf, arf, bitch." I tossed my other dagger up in the air and roundhouse kicked the handle, redirecting it toward his throat.

The knife froze in mid-air. Flipping directions, it sailed back my way until Kyp stepped up beside me, freezing it yet again.

"Mother," Kyp said with a sneer.

"You will not destroy this for me!" Lavinia approached us.

Kyp redirected the knife and sent it sailing into the nearest Gorvhan. It bought him enough time to draw his sword. "I'll take her. You free Jainey and Ray."

"And Zelnick?" I asked.

"Master Zelnick!" Cxarana's raspy voice boomed through the warehouse, echoing off the walls and drawing the attention of everyone in the warehouse. "You have betrayed everything the Keys of the Dusk stand for. And for that, you must face retribution."

"Keys of the Dusk?" I mouthed to Kyp.

He shrugged and raced at Lavinia, sword in hand.

Lavinia shook her head. "You never learn, do you?"

I wanted to help him. I wanted to shoot her right in the head and end this. But I knew she would deflect it, and the battle was only beginning. I couldn't afford to risk wasting bullets. If I needed them, I'd use them. I wanted my revenge. But freeing Ray and Jainey right then was the better choice.

As Kyp advanced and Lavinia expertly parried, as Cxarana's hands glowed and she dodged a fireball thrown by Zelnick, I scanned the crowd.

Austin, Drew, Jordan, and Rennie alternated between fighting the new kids and begging them to understand what the world would become if this was allowed to continue. Zane, Cass, and Kylie battled Sirins and Gorvhans while guarding the MacroRift.

And right between Jainey and Ray, guarding the medical tubing that connected them, was Marcelo.

"A mother's love knows no bounds," Marcelo purred, a smile pulling at the corners of his mouth as I made my way toward him. "I've heard a shotgun shell doesn't either. The buckshot goes everywhere. Is that true?"

"True enough. Do you come back from bullets?" I yanked my guns out of their holsters. This time, I could justify using them. Marcelo couldn't stop bullets, and we were at war.

I fired once, twice. Marcelo dodged and dove for Jainey's bed. I barrel rolled toward him, guns up. "Step the hell away from my child."

Marcelo held up both hands. "Little lost Key. Please, you have to understand. I tried to help you and your friends. I even kept your boy Kyp from getting killed. And in return, you had your assassin kill my brother, Crelius." He jerked his chin to where Cass stood, fighting with her sai. "I recognized the wounds. And I'm not a fool."

"Your brother took my son away from me. And you knew where he was all along. You were never going to tell us, so your earlier assistance was irrelevant. Whatever deal you had with Liv mattered more to you." I stepped forward, my eyes darting around to examine the beds Jainey and Ray were strapped to. A control panel on their sides likely manipulated the restraints, but I couldn't get to them from this far back.

"What can I say?" His voice was like moist gravel. "I *am* a businessman."

"An unscrupulous one," I said. "Although business-monster might be a better fit."

Wind picked up around the warehouse, droplets of water hitting my cheeks. Behind me, Gorvhans hissed and screeched. Sirins roared and fired guns.

Good luck, Kylie.

Words I never thought I'd think.

"You could have helped my kids. You could have saved them."

Marcelo laughed. "You think that matters now? There is no saving them. Not anymore."

"You can start by unhooking them from those beds."

"It's too late for that. It won't save her."

My blood froze. "What do you mean?" He said nothing. "You're such a good guy, aren't you? An honest business-monster trying to get by. It's not like you're dealing in addiction. You're just trying to provide for your people. But you're not a bad guy. So unhook the kid. That's what a good guy would do."

"I would if I could, but like I said, it's too late for that." Marcelo backed away.

"Oh, would you quit your nattering?" Ray. His voice was brittle, his head barely lifting from the bed, but he was conscious.

I guessed it was a good sign. If he didn't wake up in this racket, he could well be gone.

Marcelo reached into his jacket, where I spotted a holster.

I ran for the wall, using speed and momentum to run up the side, pushing off and kicking the gun right out of his hand as soon as he had pulled it free. It flew from his hand and right into the back of Zelnick's head.

I couldn't have planned that.

Cxarana took the upper hand in her battle, wrapping a hand around Zelnick's neck the moment he whirled around to see what hit him.

And that was when Marcelo made a colossal mistake. He reached for Jainey.

The bullet exploded through his skull faster than I could blink. No time to consider another option.

Marcelo had been trying to make himself out to be a friend, at least to Kyp. A year ago, I might have believed in that possibility, believed that if I tried hard enough, I could work with him, that we could find a way to work together without anyone getting hurt.

But he had lied. He had known where our children were the entire time. He had perpetuated the harm that had come to them and never said a word. That wasn't kindness. And whatever reason he'd just reached for her, it wasn't to set her loose.

But this was. I aimed the gun at the control panel on the side of Jainey's bed as I stepped forward. Then another shot aimed at the panel on Ray's side.

With the coast clear between us, I raced for them, eager to free them from their bonds and keep them safe. My heart soared as I got closer; my pride at an accomplished victory didn't even hold a candle to the relief at seeing Ray and Jainey alive. They looked weak, but that was fixable.

"No!" Livingston shouted as the floor trembled beneath my feet. I tumbled onto my knees as the concrete cracked and shattered.

I whipped my head toward him, ready to take him down, but Kylie rushed at him from the other direction. I hesitated. I couldn't take Kylie out along with him.

I had trouble processing that. I was usually on board with hurting Kylie.

Kylie whipped a gust of air at him, and Livingston fought back with a stream of flame. Should I help? Or should I protect Jainey?

I pushed to my feet, wobbling as the floor pitched beneath me.

I had to do something. A power drain? It could help me to heal Jainey's and Ray's wounds.

As if sensing my plan, Ray began undoing his bonds. I reached out my hand and focused on draining Livingston.

But I couldn't. My Aegis just... stopped. I stared at my hands. The feeling was all too familiar. That moment when I'd struggled to heal Gana, but I couldn't. My breath hitched. I couldn't lose my Aegis now. We'd all die here.

"No," a voice commanded from the center of the battle, deep and determined, thunderous enough to rumble the floor.

Kyp?

I sought him out, only to find he and Lavinia had stopped fighting, turning to watch the source of that attention-drawing tone.

The entire battle backed away from the figure.

"I can't do this anymore." The voice lost all of its commanding nature and returned to the voice of a little boy out of his element. Jordan's voice. His hand was held out toward where Livingston stood, his brow furrowed.

Jainey sat up, and the fluid in the tube connecting Ray and Jainey began speeding through the connection, sending Ray back down onto the bed.

"Damn it all!" Ray said. "She's draining me."

Jainey raised her hand and added her energy to the force building from Jordan. I stumbled closer, but Jainey glared in my direction, stopping me in my tracks.

"Jordan." Livingston turned to face him, his expression tense. "What are you doing?"

"Refusing." His voice hardened. "You tortured us. You kept us from our parents. You don't get to demand anything else from me, or my sister, or from any of us." The growls of the Senefestrian and a low static hum from the rift were the only sounds in the room, aside from Jordan speaking.

Beside me, Jainey's face contorted. How much of this was Jordan and how much of it was Jainey feeding her abilities into him? Jordan had never shown this level of control before.

"Jordan—" Lavinia started.

Jordan waved a hand in her direction. "Don't talk. You lied to me. I'm done listening to you."

Lavinia gaped, mouth opening and closing uselessly.

"I didn't come here for you. I came here for my sister. But I'll take it." His voice remained steady as he returned his attention to Livingston. "You lied to us about everything. You said you created us for a reason, but you forgot to tell us there were perfectly good people already doing the job you told us we were created for. You didn't tell us we were freaking abominations designed to destroy this world. Ross loved Caleb, so he took him on as his son, even if Kylie and Lavinia are his biological parents. He loved Caleb like he was his own." He looked at the other kids before he spoke again. "Livingston had Ross killed."

"Ross is dead?" the redhead kid cried.

The kid with braids turned toward Livingston. "You killed

Ross?"

"Ross couldn't be trusted. He's the reason we lost Jainey to begin with. He placed her in the hands of the enemy!" Livingston was starting to sound desperate.

"The enemy you told us about was a lie," Rennie shouted. "These people are good people. You only kept us away from them because you knew how the truth would make you seem. Like a mad scientist playing God."

"Using us as sacrifices," Jordan added, jabbing a finger at where his sister lay.

"We need you," Livingston argued. "You're alive for a reason. How many people can say they have a purpose? A true purpose, a goal they were born to complete? You can still do that. You can meet your potential."

Caleb walked steadily toward Jordan, expression blank, eyes unfocused.

I tensed. I'd never get to them in time.

Jordan looked at Caleb casually. "I'm sorry, bro."

Caleb nodded, eyes on Livingston. "Why?"

"Jordan, Jainey. Caleb. *Please*," Livingston begged. "I am just like you. I'm one of you!"

Caleb wrinkled his nose, his gaze dropping away, swooping toward the MacroRift, and the one solitary claw embedded into the floor of the warehouse, trapped half in and half out of our world. There was space for more of it to come through. Yet another barrier to the end of this nightmare.

"He gave himself our abilities, but he isn't one of us," Jordan murmured.

"That's right," Cxarana's voice rang out. She stood behind Zelnick as though he were a shield. His shoulders were hitched up to his ears, his mouth hung open and his eyes were questioning. "The Ritual that ties a Key to the world for as long as it takes to serve their purpose requires intent to accomplish it. It requires, from either the child themselves or their parents, an ardent desire to protect others." She pulled back, a jagged piece of metal I hadn't noticed before sliding free from the base of Zelnick's brain.

He crumpled to the floor, and Cxarana stepped around him calmly. "Dyraxion knows, had Raymond Madison not come along for Kyp Franklin's Ritual, and it had just been Lavinia Franklin, I may not have been able to accomplish it." She glared at Lavinia. "Don't believe for a second that I don't understand exactly what you've done to *my* children. Make no mistake. *All* those I have bound are my children. And all have suffered from your presence in their lives."

Lavinia raised her chin as though accepting a challenge.

She addressed Jordan. "Every one of the Keys is bound to the world to accomplish a purpose. A noble one. You and your like are well-intentioned, but you have been lied to. However, I can still see the good in you, that same ardent passion. And though Livingston may have lied to you about your mission, he didn't change the intent within you. This is why our dearly departed Zelnick could accomplish the Ritual. It's why you needed to believe the members of the Order to be the villains." Her rounded eyes flicked to Livingston. "He could not have accomplished anything close with this one."

"Meaning," Jordan said, "you are nothing like the rest of us."

"I am as powerful as any Key! The plan has already been set into motion. It cannot be stopped!" Livingston's voice broke and his head flew back as Jordan and Jainey's fists tightened in the air.

"Maybe not," Jordan said. "But you *can* die."

Caleb's fists joined theirs, held out toward Livingston, tightening.

Livingston's eyes bulged, blood spilling from them like tears. His hands thrust out, fingers twisting in the air, searching for salvation. He clenched his bared teeth, a low thrum emitting from him.

"You're torturing him," Lavinia said, eyes wide with wonder.

"He tortured us first," Jordan said.

Together, all three Skeleton Keys twisted their fists, and Livingston tore apart, a rain of meat and blood and bones showering through the air.

The Mind Key can move things apart and the Body Key can manipulate every atom of the body. I did it every time I drained power from others or blocked their hearing.

And the power of the Skeleton Keys decimated everything that was R.D. Livingston.

Jainey slumped forward. I barely caught her before she tumbled right off the bed. I took the opportunity to disconnect the tubing flowing from Ray to Jainey. A mustard yellow fluid, like viscous bile, spilled from the tube. I gagged, but kept moving, healing the wounds in both of their sides.

And then the creature whose claw had made it through the rift tightened its grip on the ground below and pulled, breaking into the concrete beneath it, and I realized I had been a fool.

I wanted to run. Run because I was good at it. Run because I didn't want to see what happened next.

But my whole life was here. Where would I run?

Where could I even go, when the chunks of concrete the creature tore from the floor revealed a rift much larger than the size of the warehouse? A thin level of concrete was all that stood between the Dawn and the Dusk.

The creature could easily destroy that barrier.

But it wasn't trying to tear it apart.

It was trying to pull itself through.

And it was succeeding.

TWENTY SIX

KYP

Kyp hadn't found himself and his mother on the same side of a battle in over a year, but there they were, together behind a wall of crates, analyzing the spreading cracks in the concrete.

Kyp glanced to where he'd last seen Jacklyn. She had fully detached Jainey from the machines, and was guarding her and Raymond. They were, blessedly, alive and well.

"What the hell have you done, Mother?" Kyp asked.

The giant creature's triangular head and torso burst through the concrete beside Jordan, making the boy look almost lilliputian in comparison. The creature was gargantuan, its body covered in a thick carapace. It was larger than any animal in their reality. It appeared almost prehistoric. For all he knew, it may have been. After all, it came through from the Dusk, and they knew nothing about how anything evolved there.

"We were running short on Senefestrian blood," Lavinia

answered blithely. "So we found a Senefestrian. The plan was to hold it here, imprison it. Zelnick knew how to control it. With the blood from one, we could have made an army of Skeleton Keys."

The mustard-yellow skull crashed down at Jordan, teeth gnashing, and he dove clear.

Lavinia winced. "Without Zelnick alive, fighting and imprisoning it might be more difficult than I'd assumed."

Kyp had believed he could no longer be surprised by his mother, but he was wrong. "Of all the shady, knavish, corrupt plans you've come up with in the past, this was, by far, the most foolish."

A spotted back claw burst through the pavement, swatting into Cass and Zane and sending them flying backward.

Kyp leapt to his feet. He needed to find a way to help, but Lavinia grabbed his jacket, holding him still. In that time, Jordan and Caleb used their telekinesis to catch Cass and Zane in the air and safely lower them onto a stack of packing supplies.

Their power was stunning.

"He's stronger than you." Lavinia marveled at the sight.

"Yeah, well, he's stronger than you, too." Kyp grimaced. She always knew how to push his buttons. He may as well push hers back. "Look what you've done to yourself. I'd bet you hadn't intended on creating something that could destroy you as easily as do your bidding."

The creature turned its face toward Jacklyn, Ray, and Jainey. Jordan tensed, readying an attack.

She pursed her lips. "I was fairly certain I'd already done that with you. I'd set out to create a protégé and instead got a six-foot thorn in my side."

He probably shouldn't be nearly as pleased as he was. "Well, the good thing is, I did learn something from you."

She side-eyed him. "Oh?"

He allowed his smile to grow, a calculated movement. "Betrayal." Harnessing his Aegis, he shoved her up and over the boxes they were hidden behind, sending her sprawling on the floor in front of the creature as a distraction.

He expected to feel pain or doubt at his actions, which caused the creature to stab at her with one of its pointed legs. But he felt only serenity. This was balance. Justice paid in full.

"Mother!" The shout tore through the air, and Caleb came right after it, diving between the creature and Lavinia.

"Caleb!" Kylie screamed after him, head twisting back and forth to watch over him, even as she held off a half-dozen Gorvhans from attacking the Guardians Lavinia had artificially created. Then her eyes met Kyp's.

"Please," she whispered in his mind, before she returned her attention to protecting the Guardians.

This time, when faced with the choice to protect herself from pain or others, she chose to protect the Guardians who meant absolutely nothing to her. And because of that, Kyp found himself sliding Caleb *and* Lavinia away from the direct path of the Senefestrian.

There was no avoiding it. This would be a full-on battle if they were going to force that creature back through the rift. And how would they seal it once they did?

Kyp took stock of the battle as it raged around him. Austin and Drew fought the remaining Gorvhans and Sirins, while Kylie, Rennie, and the other new Guardians focused on the Gorvhans that snuck through the opening created by the Senefestrian. Jordan joined Jacklyn in protecting Ray and Jainey while they recovered. Cxarana helped Cass and Zane up from where they'd landed. Caleb protected Lavinia.

Kyp knew what he had to do. He had to drive the beast back through the MacroRift.

He hadn't been able to kill Lavinia. He hadn't been the one to save Jainey or Ray. He didn't stop Zelnick. He didn't even need to protect Jordan.

This part had to be on him.

He picked his way over the shattered crates and searched for a weapon. Any weapon.

And then Jordan was in front of the creature, his hands held out, hair soaked in sweat. Jordan mentally pushed the creature back toward the rift. It wasn't enough, and even if it was, as long as it still lived and the rift remained open, it would come back through once his concentration faltered.

Still, Kyp wasn't going to turn away from helping him. Maybe if they threw it in, they could gather their forces and find a new mode of attack.

He rounded the creature, pulling it back and away from Jordan and closer to the rift as he side-stepped around the edge, saying a silent prayer to anyone who would listen that the weapons he and Lavinia had been using hadn't been swallowed up by the scar in the ground.

Speak of the devil and she shall arrive.

Lavinia leapt onto the creature and plunged her sword toward the space between its front and back legs. The sword clanged and snapped off in its carapace, and the Senefestrian pushed harder against their hold, reared back, and then snapped forward.

It threw Lavinia from its back, the power of her Aegis flailing out wildly to help cushion her fall.

It swatted Jordan aside.

Kyp redirected his Aegis, but wasn't fast enough, and his son crashed down on the warehouse floor with a jarring boom. Before he could even blink, Jacklyn dropped to her knees beside him as the creature turned its massive head toward them. Its gaping maw opened, revealing dual rows of broad, sharp teeth.

"Jacks! Above you!" He screamed it every way he could, with his voice, with his mind, with his body language as he jolted forward.

Jacklyn nearly blurred as she yanked her guns free from their holsters and shot upward.

"Avoid its blood splatter!" Kyp shouted. "It's poisonous!"

Cxarana had told him in the temple when he'd brought Jainey. *"Senefestrian blood can do two things, depending on how it is treated after harvest. In its raw form, it can do untold damage to the cells of a Key. Damage that no Ritual could reverse.*" A Key killer.

The *bang bang bang* of Jacklyn's guns as they fired into the creature's face rang in Kyp's ears. Black ichor spouted from wounds where its facial armor cracked. She rolled out of the way of the splashing liquid, taking Jordan with her.

The creature growled and stumbled, and a horrible screeching rent the air. But it lived on. Shot in its face. Stabbed in its side. How could they kill it?

Boom.

His head whipped around just in time to see Austin reload and pump his shotgun.

Boom.

The armor protecting its legs cracked and flew from it in chunks.

Jacklyn lifted Jordan into her arms and scurried backwards, cradling her precious cargo as she took off toward Jainey and Ray, where they were safely in a corner, hiding under the beds.

They needed to get that Senefestrian through the MacroRift, even if it would change everything. And it would. It would cut them off from the other side.

Cut them off from everything that made them Keys.

But it would save the world.

Boom.

Zane approached from the back, on the other side from Austin, firing an identical shotgun. When the second shot hit, the creature tumbled forward, nearly crashing face first.

That's when he saw it.

Doubt flooded him. The creature was suspended over the MacroRift, its soft underbelly exposed and hovering over the opening. A dozen other horrors, much more common to him, rushed through the rift, delighted to take advantage of the opportunity to feast on the humans whose every secretion intoxicated them.

Kyp fought the panic building in his chest. On one side of the creature, Jacklyn hid with their kids and her father, protecting their family. Cxarana stood before them and erected a splatter shield around the Order members to protect them from the creature's blood. Near them, Austin still fired on the creature with whatever he had on hand as it swiped at him.

On the other side, Zane took Austin's approach, while Rennie, Caleb, Kylie, Cass, Drew, and the newbie Guardians continued to fight the remaining interdimensionals.

Uneasiness flared when he realized he had no idea where Lavinia was. He was still searching for her when the dagger skimmed along his side, slicing into his flesh.

The answer, it turned out, was right behind him.

Hissing in pain, he whirled on her, swinging a fist in her direction. She jumped back. Once again, they squared off.

"You tried to stab me in the back? Metaphorically doing it wasn't enough?" Kyp asked. "I took you for a lot of things, Mother, but never a coward."

She laughed, and it almost sounded good-natured, almost like the laughter she'd occasionally allowed to slip out in his childhood. A chill slithered along his spine. "You realize you can't win this battle, don't you? The only person who can win here is me. I'm going to save the day. Even if we could get control of the Senefestrian or kill it, we'd still need to close the MacroRift, and I know you don't have the gumption."

His eyes flitted left and right, searching for a weapon he could use against her as she flipped the dagger in her hands, eyes intent on his.

"How do you win, Mother?" He stressed the last word, some deeply buried part of him struggling to remind her of what he was to her.

He was a father now, despite how impossible and improbable it was. He'd read about it in books and seen it in movies—when you had kids of your own, the sins of your parents were supposed to make more sense. But they didn't. In fact, the further he invested himself in Jordan and Jainey's lives, the less he comprehended the unbridled evil of the way he'd been treated by his own parents. By his mother.

The easier it became to want to punish her for it.

"Because you can't close the MacroRift." A devious smile slid across her face. "You don't know how. Only I do. And the answer is more of a punishment than I could ever give you with my own two hands."

"It doesn't matter." His gaze lit on a sword behind her. "We've won. You're hardly capable of running this operation yourself, and your existing science experiments will fight you if you try. Once we close this rift, you won't open any more. Nobody will. And this entire Order of the Key nightmare will be over. You'll have no choice but to let go of your power."

"Perhaps. But you were never burdened with humility. Do you know what you need to close a MacroRift?" Lavinia scoffed. "The lifeblood of the person who opened it. Do you know who opened this one?"

Jainey.

The battle around him went silent, his ears ringing. His throat dried up, his heart twisting within him. "You're lying."

"It's a price you are unwilling to pay," Lavinia said. "But I have no such issue."

"You'd never be able to open another rift if you did," Kyp said hoarsely. "Jordan and Caleb wouldn't help you if you harmed her. It would still be over for you."

It was a superficial argument. If Jainey's blood could seal the MacroRift, it would close the only entry between here and the Dusk. Jainey would not come back. This would be her final death.

Even if they reopened the rifts after, would she come back? Would it be over? It didn't matter. He wouldn't hurt her. Even if it meant the MacroRift continued to spit out Senefestrian after Senefestrian, he was too selfish to lose the child that had stomped up to his front door such a short time ago and had blown his entire life down around his ankles.

It was anathema to everything he lived for. He'd sooner die.

But Lavinia didn't need to know that.

He allowed himself a smile. Some of that wild faith Jacklyn had given him back before he realized everything good crumbled to dust. "First problem first."

If Lavinia got her hands on the Senefestrian blood she wanted, perhaps she could find a way to clone another Key. If there were any remaining tissue samples or tests to use with it... He needed to keep the Senefestrian blood out of her hands.

It would be a hollow victory, but it would be a victory. And they needed a damn victory.

He dove at her, feigning a tackle that she easily ducked away from. He took the opportunity to chop her in the throat.

She choked, her hand coming up, and he spun, snatching the dagger from her hand and plunging the blade into her chest. She jerked away just enough that his aim wasn't true. The dagger buried closer to her clavicle than the heart he was aiming for, but it wouldn't be pleasant either way. It would slow her down, even if it didn't kill her.

And if it didn't kill her, he'd be back for her.

He called out with his mind to the one person he could trust to do what he needed without question. It wasn't who he'd expected to count on, but he needed her, and he knew she'd come through.

"Kylie! Let's ensure Ross's death won't be in vain."

She whirled to face him, her blonde hair cutting through the air. With a nod, she waved the red-headed Guardian girl over, and she seamlessly slid into her space in the battle against the Gorvhans and Sirins.

They'd had their issues. They'd hated each other at times. But Kylie was a true warrior. She'd been raised with and trained among the rest of them. She crackled with fury and moved like silk. And he could count on her in a fight again.

It felt good. Like going back to basics.

He channeled his Aegis into telekinesis, drawing the sword he'd spotted earlier into his hand. It flew to him; the handle slapping against his hand with a jolt.

"*Use your wind,*" he said. "*Fly me out under the Senefestrian.*"

Her incredulousness cut through their connection. "*Idiotic.*"

"*Weak spot.*" He tried to send her the mental equivalent of a reassuring grin. "*I'll stab, and you whip me back. Easy breezy—*"

"*—you're so cheesy.*" The eyeroll was clear. "*Fine. It will be quick. I'm not gonna be responsible for dropping your ass.*"

Wind whipped up around him, blowing his hair back from his face and pulling at his clothing, building until it was almost like a hand pushing into his back.

"*Well?*" Kylie grumbled. "*Move with it and it will carry you. Don't expect me to do all the work!*"

He had truly lost his mind. He was trusting Kylie Robertson—not just with his life, but with the entire world. It wasn't a good plan. It wasn't even a *satisfactory* plan. But it was the only plan he had.

And after that, he'd deal with how to seal the MacroRift.

He pushed forward, and the wind wrapped around him, moving with him, picking up the speed of his steps. He lifted into the air; the wind pushing up from underneath him, guiding him into place under the Senefestrian.

He took a closer look at what he'd spotted earlier. Perfect. A soft, sensitive opening in the creature's natural armor.

He reared back, and the wind went with him, propelling him forward and helping him to stab through the creature with maximum force. The thing reared up, and Kyp gripped his sword with both hands, the blade buried in it up to the hilt. It tottered on its feet for a moment, wounded as they were by Austin and Zane's gunfire. The movement brought Kyp into full view of everyone else.

Black blood spilled from the wound, flowing over his hand and down his arm.

His eyes met Jacklyn's for a fraction of a second before the wind disappeared beneath him and he tore his gaze away to seek out Kylie, apprehension spreading through his chest like a stain.

Kylie still reached for him, but her head was twisted to the side at an unhealthy angle. Holding her up by a fistful of her hair was Lavinia, blood smeared across teeth bared in a vicious grin.

So much for the poise she always tried to exhibit. She looked downright barbaric.

"No." The plea spilled from his lips, and he gripped the sword with everything he had, even as he felt Lavinia tug at his fingers, using her telekinesis to peel them back, one by one.

A pool of red and black rippled beneath him. He looked into the churning evil of the MacroRift and found it exerted gravity over him, dragging him toward the tear. Sulfur wafted into his nose.

Blood oozed over his fingers. He struggled to keep them on the sword. Every finger Lavinia peeled off meant him pushing two more back on, and the sword was beginning to slip from his grasp despite his efforts. The cut in his side burned horribly.

How long had he been hanging there? Minutes? Probably mere seconds.

He'd been foolish. He should have made sure Lavinia was dead.

He looked to Jacklyn one last time, projecting his words to her as his grip failed.

"I love you. Keep her the hell away from the kids. She'll kill them."

He plummeted into the black to the sound of Jainey's screams in his ears and Jacklyn's screams in his mind.

Twenty Seven

Into the Rift

Jacklyn

"*I love you. Keep her the hell away from the kids. She'll kill them.*"

My eyes darted to Lavinia, who was focused solely on Kyp. It was a look Kyp had inherited and one I knew well—she was using her Aegis.

Kyp slipped into the rift, disappearing into its tarry surface, even as the creature staggered, struggling to stay conscious.

I looked back at the family I'd hid. Jainey and Jordan and Ray, all recovering from their injuries. All dazed-looking and half-broken.

"I love you, kids," I said. "Ray, take care of them until I get back."

"Birdie, what—" he called after me, but I didn't have time to stop.

I darted around behind Cxarana and under the still flailing claws of the creature. I had only seconds to nail this plan, but I had to do it.

Like hell was I gonna leave Kyp for dead in the Dusk. And like hell was I gonna allow Lavinia to be around my kids when I wasn't there to protect them.

Only one way to solve both problems before that creature fell and blocked the entryway.

I used my Aegis to block sound from exiting the space surrounding me. Then I rushed around Lavinia from behind, the bang of my boots against the concrete hidden from her. She was trying to treat her wounds from the battle, but she must've spotted me from the corner of her eyes, because she whirled to face me just as I collided with her.

Before I could get cold feet, before she could try to stop me, I slid her under the creature's body and followed after her.

We made it to the rift only seconds ahead of the creature crashing down, covering most of it.

For a moment, there was just space. Nothingness.

And then there was the chill of the thin membrane between us and the Dusk.

Then there was falling.

I wrapped my arms tightly around Lavinia's waist as I fell. If I was going to fall into the Dusk, I was gonna use Lavinia to cushion my fall.

A faint sucking sensation pulled me through the tear, and down became up and up became down, and I was propelled into the air like I was shot out of a cannon. The shift in gravity ripped my human cushion from my hands, sending Lavinia flailing into the air beside me.

I twisted my body in the air, landing just like I'd been taught, not by the teacher beside me, but by the father she'd forced to hide from me for most of my life. When I landed, I bent with it, rolling over my shoulder and back onto my feet to burn off some of the momentum.

Lavinia's landing was much rougher than mine. She already bled from several wounds inflicted during her battle with Kyp, and while she tried to stop herself, she hit the ground with a crack. If it was anybody else, I would have winced in sympathy. But it was Lavinia, so I didn't.

A storm of Sirins marched in the direction of the rift, dressed in leather and armor, chest plates and gauntlets that appeared to be made of something similar to chain mail. The rift, despite all laws of physics, was cut into the ground of this place, too. The Sirins carried torches, a blessing since the sky in the Dusk was an immaculate, silken black uninterrupted by starlight or any other blemish. Gorvhans loped behind them. And through it all, there was not a single sign of Kyp as far as my eyes could see.

What if he hadn't been able to get away from all the interdimensionals? He couldn't have been fully eaten, could he? In that short of a time?

My heart pounded. I was lucky to even be alive. What if it was like space here? What if I couldn't breathe, if the air was toxic?

I cut myself off before the panic took hold. I'd already made my choice, and it had been the right one, no matter how risky.

I had to get out of there before the interdimensionals got any closer. A quick glance around revealed a dark shape to the left. The outline looked like a shelter of some kind. I could hide behind it.

Dropping to my hands and feet, I tried to mimic the way a Gorvhan ran. If the darkness didn't cover me, perhaps it would at least help camouflage me for one of them.

One problem? Moving away from the fire made it increasingly difficult to make out my surroundings. No matter how good my vision was, it didn't work in the absence of light. And that's what the Dusk was—a complete absence of natural light.

As I got closer to where I thought the shape was, I held my hand out to try to determine my surroundings. My palm connected with something that had softness and give. My fingertips skimmed along it to find sharp points and lines. Whatever it was, it smelled like petrichor, and rustled when I touched it.

A bush! Holding my hand out, I crawled forward, the rough uneven ground scraping along my knees and elbows. I followed the line of what had to be branches and leaves until it ended. Hopefully, that break in the leaves meant I could crawl behind it and hide.

I turned, and my hand landed on what felt like a pebble. I barely suppressed a hiss of pain as it nearly broke the skin of my palm. Silence was key. If I could manage not to draw any attention to myself, I could put enough distance between myself and the army of interdimensionals, and I'd have time to regroup.

Don't breathe too loud. Dammit heart, don't beat so loud.

Finally, I made my way around the bush, and kept crawling, my hand in front of me, putting every other sense to work to make up for my lack of vision. I kept going until my hand brushed what had to be cool stone.

I leaned my back against it, half expecting it to be the carapace of another Senefestrian, because that was my luck, really. It wasn't growling, and it wasn't drooling on me, so it was as safe a bet as any.

Channeling my Aegis, I warmed my hand to a simple glow. Or that's what I intended. Instead, my hand flared in a full flame. I doused it quickly, but winced. That would attract unwanted attention if anyone happened to be looking.

My Aegis felt stronger here. I readjusted and tried for the warm glow again.

I could see! I was in the center of a rock structure.

A man hid further along the outcropping, a little closer to the action. He was too tall to be Kyp. An Arvokian? I squinted to make out his features. The light helped when coupled with my Aegis. It was still difficult, but it was getting easier. This area of the world had a strange spattering of star-like gashes in the canopy of sky. How that could be, given it was the same sky here as it had been over there? I had no idea, but that wasn't a mystery I was going to figure out right now.

Maybe it was part of the dimensional bleed.

I leaned out a little farther. Hopefully, he wouldn't be able to see me any better than I could see him.

A hooded cloak hung heavy across his shoulders. It was a chocolate brown, like the rock formations around him. He turned, scanning the distance. His eyes glowed an ominous gold, probably an evolutionary advantage needed to live here. Or a disadvantage. I would imagine he would be pretty easy to catch with eyes like that.

And then his eyes lit on me.

He yanked something from his pocket, and I took off. I wasn't waiting around for him to catch up with me. Who knew what side this guy was on?

The ground here was spongy, and it took me a minute to get the traction I needed to build momentum. I'd barely gotten a few dozen feet before something jerked my feet out from under me. I hurtled forward and landed in a field of pink and yellow flowers that almost looked like chrysanthemums. I flipped to face the man, fire blasting from my palms.

He struggled to catch up with me. He'd closed the distance by catching my feet with some kind of makeshift bolas. I set the rope aflame, freeing myself before turning my palms back in the stranger's direction.

"Halt your flames!" A rough voice sounded within my mind, and I flinched. With no real effort, this man had nudged aside the protections I had erected in my mind. *"Have you and yours not already done enough? You're destroying the Rannic blooms!"*

"I'll stop burning shit when you get the hell out of my head."

I held a flaming hand to the blooms.

"This is the only way we can understand each other. We do not speak each other's languages. And I'm not asking you to stop burning... fecal matter." His thin lips twisted. *"I'm asking you not to burn the Rannic blooms."*

Right. I supposed that made sense.

Up close, I could see much more of the man. He had the purpling skin of Cxarana and Zelnick, the same eggshell white hair tucked beneath his cloak. His eyes were different, like a cat's—pronounced darkened lids and slitted pupils. His forehead was high like Cxarana's, but his cheekbones were not as sharp. His chin was rounded, and his physique was larger, broader than the Arvokians I was familiar with. He was cut, the body of a soldier, and his chest was bare aside from the leather sash across his shoulder with pockets sewn into it. His pants were a strange mix of the same brown and yellow geometric patterns that marked the Senefestrian.

He blinked. *"Are you looking for the other?"*

"Technically, two others came through. A woman and a man. I'm looking for the man. But I should find the woman. She is dangerous." I accompanied each mentioned person with an image, in case genders differed in this world.

"You bring us your dangers?"

"You're one to talk." I projected images of Gorvhans, Sirins, and the Senefestrian.

"That was not our doing."

"And this was not ours. The woman is our enemy. She harmed the man. I injured her and followed them in to save him."

Sure, it was a little fib, but Lavinia had created the situation that brought her here, so it was also a little true.

Semantics.

His cat-like eyes narrowed. He probably knew exactly what I was thinking.

"I helped the man. Kehp."

"Kyp." I smiled so as not to offend him. Something struck me. How could he have already helped Kyp? I'd only come in a minute or two after him. *"Does time move differently here?"*

He frowned. *"I have never ventured to your world. How would I have that knowledge?"*

He had a point. *"Can you take me to him?"*

"I will." He returned the smile, but it looked uncomfortable on him. He motioned for me to follow him.

"No funny business though."

"Funny business?"

I really should have known better. *"Betrayal, traps. You know?"*

He nodded sharply, and we continued on our way. I followed him along the rocks.

"I'm Jacklyn. You?"

"Dahmyan." He ducked under a low-hanging branch and led me into a cavern. *"Here. Speak to your Kehp. I will continue scouting and inform you when there is safe passage back to the*

Dawn."

With a nod, I stepped into the cave. And there he was. My Kyp. A few feet into the cave, lit only by a small fire hidden behind a curve in the wall. The fire smelled sulfuric, like it was from the pits of hell. Kyp bent over it, using its light to wrap a grody wound in his side. His hair hung forward, blocking his view.

I knelt beside him. "Kyp."

He flinched, and crab-walked away. His eyes met mine, and he slumped down. "Jacklyn." A beat. "No, wait, what the hell are you doing here?"

"I jumped in right after you." Perhaps the shrug after wasn't my brightest idea.

He returned to wrapping his wound. "So casual."

"If it makes you feel better, I used Lavinia as a crash pad."

His head shot back up. "She's here, too?"

"Yes, but I left her for dead by the entrance where all the interdimensionals were trying to get into our world."

He chuckled. "Well, she shouldn't be alive much longer, in that case." He leaned forward again to wrap the wound.

"Kyp."

"It's nearly been an hour. Are you sure you jumped in right after me?"

"Kyp?"

"Dahmyan thinks they'll stop going through, eventually. They're having a harder and harder time getting in. But I don't believe that. The bleed is happening here too. Did you see the stars? That's not supposed to happen—"

"Kyp." I pushed his hair out of his eyes and cupped his face in my hands. "Let me heal you."

"Wait!" He took my hands in his and flipped them back and forth. "No open wounds, that's good. Be careful. Senefestrian blood got into one of mine. Dahmyan washed it out with what little water he had, but it's still burning."

I shook his hands away and pressed mine against his wound. I let the stronger force of my Aegis flow through me, using the very first ability Kyp had taught me, healing him with my fingertips.

The warmth flowed through me and spilled out through his wound. And yet, nothing happened. It didn't heal.

It wouldn't heal.

My stomach churned. "Maybe my Aegis works differently in the Dusk?"

He shrugged. "Could be..."

"Or?" I'd known him long enough to know his 'but' voice.

"Senefestrian blood is poisonous. It could be keeping the wound from closing."

My throat tightened. "No, that's... no. That would kill you."

"It would."

"Okay, then we can't close the MacroRift."

"We can't anyway," Kyp admitted.

"No, we can't," I agreed. "Not if it will kill you. We don't close it now, then we can save Kylie, and we can save you."

"If Lavinia's dead, we can save her, too?" Kyp rolled his

eyes and then shook off his own question. "That's not the point. Lavinia told me something when we were fighting. We can't close the rift, anyway."

I stepped back, unnerved. "Can't or won't?" He couldn't be falling for her crap again, could he? "Since when do we believe intel Lavinia tells us?" I glanced down at his hands. They were covered in dried blood, the substance nestling deep in the whorls of his fingerprints, like a thin layer of candle wax.

"Can't." He shifted so he sat up straighter, the pain evident on his face. "She said it will take Jainey's lifeblood to close it. Meaning—"

"—all of it." Tears sprang to my eyes. "We'd have to kill her. No, we can't do that. What can we do instead? Maybe we can block the entrance? The Senefestrian is partially blocking it already. How can we replicate that? Can we get another Senefestrian? Or can we get that Senefestrian better placed? It's not like we could lift it. I mean, I'm strong but I'm not that strong."

"He's stronger than you." Kyp stared out over my shoulder.

"Who? Who's stronger than me?"

"Jordan. Jainey, too."

"Well, yeah." I waited, but Kyp just kept staring. "We could try to build something to cover it, but anything strong enough would take time, and we would need to monitor the MacroRift at the same time. Have some people monitor it while others do the building. Where would we be able to find any material strong enough to keep a Senefestrian from coming through the—"

"We're stronger together!" He grabbed my hands in his. "Remember?"

His gaze went manic, like it always did when the pieces fell into place, when he solved an important puzzle. It was a particular look, the reward of the solution, coupled with the horror of the revelation.

And somehow, the revelation was always horrible.

I gulped and nodded. "Stronger together."

"Why are Jainey and Jordan stronger?" he asked, leading me along as he always did, showing me the path he took to get where he'd already ended up.

"Because they're Skeleton Keys."

"And how are those made?"

I smirked. "Well, their mother and father loved each other very much."

He snort-laughed, but he still grabbed me by my shoulders. "Yes. Your blood, my blood. What else?"

"Senefestrian blood," I said. "That's why they were trying to bring one over. They wanted more blood so they could create more Skeleton Keys."

"Right." He brushed his hands through my hair, a patient smile on his face. "And I poisoned myself, albeit accidentally, with Senefestrian blood. Which means, Senefestrian blood now runs in my bloodstream."

"Wait." I grabbed him by his forearms, a giggle escaping. "Wait, do you mean together we can close the MacroRift?"

"Yes," Kyp answered soberly. The pain of the poison must have really been getting to him.

"But how would we heal you if the MacroRift is closed?" I swiped my hand over the sweat breaking out on his brow. "Is there an antidote for Senefestrian poison?" His face, already pale, continued its slide toward the color of chalk.

"No, but it doesn't matter. She said closing the rift would require lifeblood. She happily told me the truth, because she knew I would be devastated. Because the truth is devastating. Lifeblood isn't like any regular blood. Arvokians use it in Rituals, although rarely. If a Ritual requires lifeblood... I would have to die."

He leaned back against the cave wall for support.

I couldn't... He was lying. There was no way.

"Why yours? Wouldn't it need mine, too?"

"What?" he asked, winded.

"What about my lifeblood? If it needs yours, why wouldn't it need mine? It's the combination of our blood that would do it. It would have to be both..." I trailed off as my thoughts caught up with my mouth.

"No. We don't know that." His eyes filled with tears.

"Don't you lie to me, Kyp Franklin," I hissed. "You can't afford to lie. We won't get another chance, and I am not risking the children's lives on you trying to protect me."

Kyp swore and took both my hands in his. "You're right. It could just be mine, but it could be both of us." His hands slid up my arms, up to my face, and he cradled me there, like I was precious. "Baby, this can't be... There has to be another way." He pulled me into a tight embrace.

"Is there any other way you can think of that will protect them?" I kissed his ear, his neck, and squeezed him back, my hands pushing into his hair. I held him as close as I could and prayed for him to find another way.

"Not for the long term. It would only be a matter of time before something broke through." He pulled back and met my eyes. "But we can end this. We can save them."

"And if it fails?" My heart raced, and I breathed like I'd just run a race, but inside, I was oddly calm.

"Then we die, come back, and figure out what comes next."

"And if it doesn't, safety. For them. Forever."

"And all it will cost us…"

"…is our lives."

TWENTY EIGHT

KYP

"*H*as your condition worsened?" Dahmyan's head tilted curiously toward Kyp.

Kyp peeled himself away from Jacklyn's tight hold, managing a weak smile for his new, surprising ally. "*No. But it has not gotten better. She tried to heal me, but even that didn't work.*"

Dahmyan bared his teeth. "*That is unfortunate. I am sorry.*"

Kyp turned to Jacklyn. "Help me up?"

She swiped aside the tears in her eyes and on the point of her nose. Pulling his arm over her shoulder, she helped him to his feet.

"*Tell me, Dahmyan,*" Kyp asked. "*How do you feel about the rifts between the worlds?*"

"*There is a civil war among our people. There are those that intend to permanently tear rifts between our worlds to hide from the creatures here. There are others, like myself, that believe the rifts must be closed. We ran from our problems and brought death and destruction to another world. Now the creatures flee the Dusk.*"

Our people should handle our own problems and seal the rifts. But only the Keys of the Dusk can seal a rift. And there are very few of them on our side." He straightened, pride settling in the set of his shoulders. "*I am one of the few.*"

Kyp smiled, resting a hand on his shoulder. "*In that case, new friend, we have a gift for you. All you have to do is get us to that rift.*"

The cavalry was already on its way. With a sound similar to a bullhorn, Dahmyan had summoned an entire battalion of warriors to the MacroRift before Jacklyn had made it through.

Dahmyan returned to the cave to let them know the battalion had arrived and was ready to lead Kyp and Jacklyn back to the rift.

A glance outside the cave revealed a battle had broken out between Sirins and Gorvhans, and other Gorvhans, these used as beasts of burden, being ridden by Arvokians. It was chaos, chaos Dahmyan planned to utilize, but that would take time. Until then, he gave the couple privacy.

"We need to tell them," Kyp said.

"How can we?"

"We could try... I could try with my mind." He offered her a reassuring smile, or at least the closest he could manage. "We're stronger together, and we're stronger here. Maybe we can reach across?"

"They're close to the rift." She grabbed both of his hands in hers and let them swing between them, brushing her thumbs across his knuckles. "What do you need from me?"

"Share your Aegis with me. If I can reach Jordan and Jainey, they should be able to help."

"Okay." She closed her eyes. They snapped back open. "Wait. What are we gonna say?"

Kyp's heart trembled. "I don't know. We'll just come up with the best we can."

"You're right. It's impossible to get it right anyway." She closed her eyes again and took a deep breath, digging her heels into the dirt floor. "Let's do this."

He mirrored her stance, closing his eyes and reaching out with his Aegis, pulling what he needed from Jacklyn to get the necessary power boost to send a message through the connection he had previously created with Jordan.

The power within him zinged through the air until it landed in a familiar landscape. Jordan. The warm welcome of his mind told him Jordan was searching for a sign of Kyp and was grateful to discover one. The joy in Jordan's mindscape twisted Kyp's heart even tighter.

He hated to have to burden him with this.

"Jordan," Kyp said. "Your mother and I are together in the Dusk. We have to tell the team important information. Can you project this message to the others?"

"But we were about to come get you out of there!" Jordan argued.

"We don't have a lot of time, kid. Please," Jacklyn said.

A pause. "Okay." A surge of Aegis power like he'd never felt before brought them before their team within Jordan's mindscape. It seemed that being so close to the MacroRift intensified their abilities. They looked beaten and bruised, but they had survived. He couldn't feel Caleb or any of the other new kids. And Kylie— Kylie was still gone.

"Business first," Jacklyn began. "We know how to close the MacroRift."

"Awesome!" Rennie grinned. It was a nice, friendly grin. She was a welcoming personality. Kyp would miss her.

"What do we do?" Jainey's head was cushioned on Drew's shoulder, her eyes half-lidded.

"The thing is, *you* don't do anything," Kyp said, quickly dispelling anything they may be considering. "You certainly don't do anything crazy like drop yourself into this rift. We have everything we need here."

Austin's expression turned to consternation far quicker than the others, and Kyp regretted how much of a pain in the ass he'd been for Tex in the beginning. He was more than valuable. He was a good man.

"But if you close the MacroRift from the Dusk, how would you get back from…" Cass trailed off. "*No.* Unacceptable."

"We don't have time to fight with you about this." Jacklyn was shaky, but her tone brooked no argument. "The alternative is unthinkable. This is the only way we found to seal it. And it will be sealed."

Fear was a living thing on the faces of their team. This family Jacklyn and Kyp had formed together. These people they loved more than anything.

"You'll die," Ray said, voice strained.

"No." Jordan moved to storm away, but Kyp pulled back on the mental reins, holding him there. "What are you doing?"

Kyp's control over the connection flickered, and Jordan instantly stopped trying to fight and brought the connection back to full strength.

"We have to do this," Jacklyn said. "And you have to let us."

"Kyp is bein' awful quiet over there," Austin said, accent thickening with worry.

"There's only one way to seal a rift that enormous," Kyp said.

Cxarana turned to Drew and Zane. "The lifeblood of the person who opened it."

"And *that* is not gonna happen." Jacklyn's eyes flashed with ferocity.

Drew held Jainey even tighter, and Ray let out a deep, mournful sound.

Pain lanced through Kyp's side and into his head. He'd be lucky if he didn't lose consciousness before they could enact their plan.

Their world-saving plan. Because saving the world meant ending theirs.

Despite all his courage, his knees wobbled.

Jacklyn explained the plan to the others while Kyp took in

their family. Watched Cass, his best friend, mouth "No" and lean against Zane. Watched Zane swallow hard, fighting emotions she never enjoyed showing. Watched Cxarana block access to the rift, all the while maintaining what felt like eye contact with Kyp. Watched Austin hold Rennie up with one arm, and Jordan with the other. Watched Ray drop to his knees and cover his face with his hands. Watched Jainey cry on Drew's shoulder, while Drew buried his face in her hair. Watched all the color drain from Jordan's face. His jaw hardened, eyes fierce.

Kyp knew that face. Jacklyn made it all the time, and he knew what would come next before the kid opened his mouth.

"Sorry, kid," Kyp cut him off. "This is a sacrifice you won't be making."

Jacklyn nodded. "This is our play. You don't save us. We're your parents. We save you."

Jordan shook his head, his eyes dull with losses he had yet to experience. Would it hurt him that terribly to lose them?

"No. You can't. This was made for me. I have to do this. If I don't, what kind of hero does that make me?"

Kyp had never considered Jordan to be the combative type. This was a new side of him. So many sides of him Kyp had yet to see. Would never see.

"A hero for the future, son."

"A hero *with* a future," Jacklyn added.

Jordan was still shaking his head, vehement. "It's *my* duty. What you're proposing won't even work. It needs me."

"Actually, it needs her," Jacklyn said, never the type to pull punches. "Would you rather we chose that?"

"Jacklyn and I have always been stronger together. Because together, we made you. Both of you."

"It's not going to work. It's sweet, but it's poetic nonsense," Jordan cried.

Jainey clung to Drew's neck desperately, her lip wobbling as she finally looked up. "Jordan."

Jacklyn's fists clenched. Kyp could feel her struggling to hold her heart together.

"If it doesn't work, we'll come right back," Kyp said.

"And then you'll get your opportunity to kill yourself."

Kyp flinched and looked at Jacklyn. She was sad. Heartbreakingly sad. But also angry.

"No!" Jordan cried. "It isn't like that. You've all taken me in and treated me like a real person. But I'm not real. I was created. For this. To save the world. I can protect Jainey, Rennie, you. I can make sure it never happens again."

"No, kiddo." Kyp's vision blurred, his voice breaking as he spoke. "The world is magnificent. And you are no less real than any of us. There are so many incredible things you can do. You don't have to be a soldier. You don't *have* to be anything. Which means you can be *anything*."

Jacklyn nodded, her voice thick. "You've been locked up; you deserve the chance at life. You take Jainey. You get out there and you *live*." Her face dripped with tears. "Ray'll show you around, right?"

Ray stood, stepping forward and rubbing Jainey's back. "I'll be the da I shoulda been to ya both. I swear it."

"Thank you," Kyp said.

"You better," Jacklyn said. "I'll haunt your ass if you don't."

Ray laughed, something between a hiccup and a cry. "You can count on it, Birdie."

Jainey reached forward and Jordan took her from Drew and held her tightly.

"We love you guys," Jacklyn said.

"We do," Kyp said. "All of you."

"And we love you," Jacklyn said.

"Both of you," Kyp said.

Jordan sniffled. "Mom. Dad." His voice sounded so small.

"Nooooo," Jainey cried. "Mama! Papa!"

Kyp's heart tore in two.

"We've only had you for a second and you're already going," Jordan said.

"Remember what Cass can do," Jacklyn said.

"Could do," Jainey said. "She won't be able to when you close the rift!"

"No." Kyp kept his tone gentle for his baby girl, despite the strain. "But Gana, Jaina, Mari, they were always watching over us, even before they reached out for Cass. And we'll be there too." He hoped it would be a comfort to Jacklyn, too.

"Besides, you'll remember us. Learn from our successes and

failures, and you'll stay with our family," Jacklyn added.

"And we'll always be here. Right here next to you."

Jordan swiped at his eyes, cleared his throat. "Just come back through here first so we can hug goodbye, and—"

"—and you forget how well I know your mother," Kyp cut him off. "The genes did *not* skip a generation. You'd take our place in a heartbeat. Besides, there's a whole army of Arvokians, Sirins, and Gorvhans at war here. We're using it as a distraction with some help from the locals."

"*Excuse me.*" Dahmyan. This was it. "*We're out of time.*"

"Dahmyan?" Cxarana glanced around her. "I'm coming through. That is my home. If the doorway is to close forever, I should go back. Defend my world as you have yours." She stepped closer to the rift. "I will help you accomplish your final mission."

"We have to go. We love you. All of you. We love you so much," Jacklyn shouted.

"We love you too!" they shouted back, a mismatched chorus of love falling upon them like raindrops.

That was as good a way as any to end the connection.

There was no good way to end the connection.

Kyp dropped to his knees, his side now an inferno. Jacklyn dropped beside him. He looked into her eyes and saw his own pain reflected there.

"They will be okay," she said. "They have the others. They have each other."

Kyp nodded, and Jacklyn helped him to his feet.

"You ready?" he asked.

"Not really," she said, and then she flashed him one of her characteristic grins, eyes sparkling with mischief. "You know, the thought of losing you always did scare me to death."

He glared at her. "Shut. Up." But he couldn't help but crack a smile.

"This is just another mission. Let's do this."

"Let's."

They moved toward where Dahmyan waited for them.

"*I will get you to the rift. Follow me.*"

With his arm wrapped around Jacklyn, they headed through the cave entrance.

"*Did I hear Cxarana?*" Dhamyan asked.

Jacklyn smirked at Kyp. "*Could be, she's coming through the rift to help.*"

Dahmyan looked pleased. At least they had made someone happy today.

TWENTY NINE

KYP

In the end, it wasn't at all what he expected. As a child, he decided he'd defeat his mother or die trying. If he'd managed to accomplish this goal, his next would be to seal the rifts, so he could live a peaceful, normal life. As it was, he wasn't sure his mother was dead; he was about to seal the final rift, and that was it.

An ending he hadn't foreseen.

His throat was scratchy, uncomfortable from crying and from screaming during the battle. His eyes were swollen with tears. His side burned so intensely he couldn't straighten himself out. The only thing keeping him moving forward was knowing he only needed to fight for a little while longer.

He dropped to his knees before the rift.

Dahmyan had led them there, around the back from where the battle was taking place. Dahmyan's team had fought the others back, giving them space to work. The guttural screams, the clangs of metal meeting metal, the bloody rips and tears of battle—that was the soundtrack to this moment.

He and Jacklyn couldn't do it themselves. They'd tried to steel themselves to do it, to themselves, to each other, and they hadn't been able to go through with it. Dahmyan had offered, but when Cxarana came through the rift, it was she they chose.

She was, in her own offbeat way, family to Kyp, and though she and Jacklyn had never had a chance to become close, family to Jacklyn by extension.

Cxarana did her duty with no malice and with quite a bit of reluctance, but she made the necessary cuts, trusting them and their choice.

And then they waited.

And while they waited, Kyp thought about the whys.

He'd gotten what he'd always wished for. And while he didn't get the chance to live out his dream of a normal life, at least Jainey and Jordan would have that chance.

After all, he'd learned the lesson a year ago.

Love is sacrifice.

When he closed his eyes, she was there—the times they laughed together, the challenging lean of her body during an argument, the curl of her lips. That wide toothy smile of hers, the light of her eyes when excitement coursed through her, the way her hair tumbled over her shoulders in waves, how she didn't walk as much as strut, how she poked fun at him endlessly, the taste of her kiss, the sound of her laugh, the many different ways she said his name (a warning, a welcome, a prayer, a breath), the way she told him she loved him and the look in her eyes when she said it, her voice in his ears, always in his ears.

He opened his eyes. She offered him a weak smile.

There were worse ways to go.

JACKLYN

In the end, it wasn't at all what I'd expected. When I first discovered I was a Key, I'd feared I would eventually die a bloody death, but I don't think I ever really believed I would die. I was always more afraid for Mom and Gana. And I'd been right about that fear.

After that, I'd been certain I would die in battle, either in my quest for vengeance or afterward, but I'd definitely go down fighting.

This wasn't fighting. This was slow. And it sucked. But it had a purpose. It was for a greater good. Saving the world. Saving my kids. Just like Mom had done. Sacrificing for those I was meant to protect, the way Gana had.

If meeting Cass had taught me anything, it was that there was something after this. Even if I couldn't communicate with the kids once the rifts were closed, I could see how they were. How the Guardians were. How my father was.

I had always intended to be there for my children the way my parents couldn't be. But my father would be with them instead. I meant what I said. I would haunt the hell out of Ray if he didn't take good care of everyone. This was his chance to redeem himself.

If I had to do this, at least I wasn't alone the way the others had been. At least I had Kyp. The love of my life. The pain in my ass. My best friend and my foil. I'd rather he got the chance to have a real family, to live in peacetime. I'd had that opportunity, even if it hadn't been real.

But if we both had to go, at least we were side by side.

We were sprawled out over the edge of the scar on the ground, pouring our blood into the red-black pool beneath. The scar on the earth was healing. Gradually, it was working.

I grabbed Kyp's hand and gripped it tightly. He didn't look good. His skin was pale, and there were dark circles beneath his eyes. He squeezed my hand, but his grip was loose, his strength waning. Mine wasn't far behind.

He flashed me a blissful smile, and I wondered if his thoughts had gone in the same direction as mine had.

In the middle of the battlefield, with the tint of the red glow reflecting off our faces, we were committing the ultimate act of love. After all, love was sacrifice. Sacrificing time. Sacrificing quiet. Sacrificing space.

And sometimes, it meant sacrificing your life.

It hadn't been easy. None of my life had been easy. A lot of choices had been taken out of my hands. This choice? This choice was mine. I didn't have to do this. Neither did Kyp. But this was a gift.

The comics I spent most of my life reading flickered through my mind. Tales of heroes I always wished I could be. So many died for their cause. And they became even more than a hero.

I closed my eyes and became a legend.

Epilogue

Jordan

Jordan knelt in front of the carved wooden memorial archway. The one-time Order of the Key had worked together to build it, placing it over the stump of a weeping willow. Ray said it was from a tree his mother and father used to meet under.

Jordan wished he'd seen the tree itself, rather than this monument to their death.

This was stupid. He could probably speak to them anywhere and they'd hear him as well as they would here. But all of the movies, the books, the television shows they'd used at the facility to keep them pacified said you went to the grave to speak to the dead. They didn't have an actual burial site, so he'd have to work with the memorial.

It had taken some time before they'd returned to his father's home. And it had taken more time for him to sneak off on his own.

He lowered himself in front of the memorial and sat on the

dampened earth. He cleared his throat.

"Hi, Mom. Hi, Dad."

He rolled his eyes at himself. He'd start by catching them up. Then he'd get to the point.

"We're all still living together. Zane used her hacking skills to get us all legit identities. Rennie and I are in high school. Jainey is in kindergarten. Caleb... left. He was angry—at us, at what Lavinia and the others had done. He was angry at everything. Nothing I said could get him to stay. He said he didn't belong here and—"

He sighed.

"Ray is a stay-at-home grandpa. Totally focused on us. Cass, Drew, and Austin are all in college. Cass wants to be a grief counselor. Go figure. Drew's looking to be a teacher. Austin's gonna be a cop. Wants to keep helping the world, even without his abilities. Rennie's kinda terrified he's going to get hurt because he's used to being invulnerable."

He took a deep breath.

"I guess I should get to why I'm here. You see, we're all moving on without having our Aegis."

Birdsong filled the air, and Jordan let his attention drift with it. Mom and Dad would be patient as he struggled to get his words out. He dug his fingers into the dirt beneath him, felt the soil under his fingernails, and wished he could somehow uncover the courage to say the words out loud.

It was silly, this secret of his. It wasn't like his mom and dad could do anything about it, even if they could hear him. Saying it out loud wouldn't make it any different.

"Everyone is... well, they aren't overjoyed. You're gone and we feel your loss every day. But we're moving on. We're living life. And I don't want to mess that up."

Tears sprang to his eyes. "You gave your lives closing the rifts so we would lose our abilities, so the monsters would go away. You died so we could live normal lives."

He held out his hand in front of him, pulling the leaves from a nearby tree with barely a thought. Fire flickered in the palm of his hand, ready and waiting to turn the leaves into ash the instant they made it to him.

"So why can I still do that?"

ACKNOWLEDGEMENTS:

So, I may have edited and published my other books during a pandemic, but this was the first book I wrote dming one. I'm so thankful for the communities that made this possible.

Though this is the second edition of this book, I would like to thank Laynie Bynum and MB Dalto for discoveling my writing and giving me my first true publishing shot. And thank you to the rest of the Sword & Silk team and authors who stood behind this release and me from stalt to finish: Nicole Bezanson, E.M. Wright, Haleigh Wenger, Amanda Pavlov, Amelia Loken, and Ann Miller. I'm so lucky to have shared in this journey with each and every one of you ladies. Jellllia Henold D'Lima, my editor extraordinaire, thank you for taking the time to understand these characters and this world, no matter how bizane it got. You always manage to pull my sculpture out of the stone, and I'm so grateful to you and your suppolt. Celin Chen, the creator of my beautiful covers, thank you for giving my babies the presentation they deserve. They're wrapped in your goodness, and I'm so grateful to have you working with us. Kristin Jacques, blog maven, and the woman I go to whenever someone tells me I have to do promotion. You somehow know exactly what I should be talking about, even when I'm burnt out and out of ideas. You make me shine.

To the Minners and Manzano families at large, thank you for sending continuous support our way, and for understanding..,us. All of us, quirks and all. Our little corner of the family is grateful to you.

To my siblings Melissa and Jon and their wives Dorothy and Kristy, thanks for listening to me ramble on about all my publishing woes now and all my weirdly elaborate stories then. You played your part in growing the storyteller I am, the force of nature I've become, and the dark sense of humor I've amassed. Thank you.

To my mom, Doris Minners, you've always been my number one fan. Even when I thought my writing was crap, you encouraged me. You ask me about my edits more than anyone else in the world, even my editors. You care about every weird little step in the process of my growth, and I truly appreciate it.

To my outrageous number of nieces: Millie, Wynnie M., Moira, Wynnie F., Kaitlyn, and Chloe. You and Logan do an amazing job at keeping me a child at heart. Never be afraid to push Aunt Justine to keep thinking weirder and weirder. It's good for my career, and for my sanity.

To my circle of IRL friends who are family, Allegra, Fruh, Jennine, Anthony, Julian, Heather, J'vania, Carlos, Christopher and Victor. Though writing this was a process that occurred largely without your in person presence, I appreciate your check-ins, your shows of support, and your virtual hugs. And I'm grateful that, by this point I've hugged most of you in person once again. Your presence in my life is beyond value. Thank you for making me a part of your family as well.

To my writing groups, WriteHive, The Teacup Dragons, Writer in Motion, Pages Promotions, and the Pitch to Publication 2016 crew: Your support has been invaluable. From 'what am I going to do' questions to imposter syndrome uplifts, to 'is this a viable career path' leaps, I don't think I would have had the confidence to try half the things I have without you all at my back. I'm taking more risks and I'm proud of it, and I owe it all to you lovely people.

To my writing students and my editing clients, you teach me as much as I teach you. We're in this together and I love every minute of working with you. I wish you all the success.

To Jeni Chappelle and Kaitlyn Johnson, though neither of you worked on The Skeleton Key, you both did so much for The Order of the Key that there would be no sequel without you. Thank you so much.

Jeni, thank you for being my teammate, my friend, and sometimes...my conscience. I'm a lot to wrangle, so I appreciate you trying. I'll keep making it difficult for you, so you know I haven't changed.

To KJ Harrowick, thank you for your beautiful graphics, the gorgeous website you've built me, and your general awesomeness. You're a great friend and I'm thankful I get to keep you.

Hannah Kates, Jerusha Renee, Lauren Persons, Dakota Rayne, and S Kaeth, thank you for being my guards against imposter syndrome. You're all incredible humans and I'm so blessed to know and love you all.

To Maria Tureaud, my writing sister, my critique partner, the person who talks me down off every writing ledge. I've been so blessed to share my stories, both fiction and non-fiction, with you and to have the opportunity to learn yours in return. I'm so incredibly eager to see how your career continues to grow and change. You keep kicking ass, and so will I. Who knows where will be in five years?

To Joy Garcia, I don't know who I would be if I hadn't met you. Your support in all things and your constant momentum pushes me to keep growing, to keep doing, to keep trying, and I'm so lucky to have you cheering in my corner. We're doing it, girl. We're making things happen. And it's only going to get better.

To Megan Manzano, thank you for being there for my various anxiety and anger outbursts, to share stories about the things we love and despise about everything we share in common. We're different in so many ways but similar in all the ones that matter. I'm lucky to have gained you in the marriage to your brother. He's pretty cool too.

To Ismael Manzano, thank you for continually being the real life version of "get you a man who'll…" Your endless support and love is invaluable. Your understanding of the days when I have to take up residence in my office and the days I blow off domesticity or gatherings because of edits and deadlines and career life...you have no idea how much it all means. The freedom you give me to keep working on the things I enjoy is priceless. And you are amazing. You've read every single rough-as-hell version of all of my work, and you read it again when I need you to. Thank you for all that you do to keep me in a place where I can pursue my dreams. You are more than you'll ever know.

To my wonderful son Logan. This time has been hard for you, but I've gotten lucky. The last two years home with you working while you went to school remotely has been such a blessing. Getting to spend my days as an integral part of your life, getting to directly witness your triumphs, daily for that long, built an even greater bond between us than we already had (and the one before wasn't too shabby). You're twelve when I'm writing this, and I can't wait to see the man you'll become. I am eternally in awe of you, from your strength to overcome your obstacles, to the immense empathy in your heart, to the fact that you can sing the same song over and over under your breath and not even realize it. Your imagination is a thing to behold and keeps me thinking outside the box. You are an inspiration to me, and the light in my heart. Never change, kiddo.

And lastly, and perhaps most importantly, to my readers. Thank you for taking this journey with me, and thank you for showing up again for Jacklyn and Kyp and the Order. Have faith in this story...you don't want to miss how it ends. And it's not over yet.

About Justine Manzano

Justine Manzano is the geeky author of the geeky YA series *Keys & Guardians,* and geeky YA novel *Never Say Never.* Known as a Professional-Life-Ruiner-By-Antagonist, Justine's fiction is tough on the outside and sweet on the inside, like an M&M or a hard candy with a gooey center, delivered with sass and snark. A freelance editor, she also serves as an Editor-in-Residence at WriteHive. She lives in Bronx, NY with her husband, teenage son, and new puppy! She can usually be found at her website, www.justinemanzano.com or all the usual social media haunts. If you've looked in all these places and can't find her, she's probably off reading fanfiction. She'll be back soon.

Also By Justine Manzano:

Never Say Never

Brynn Stark swore off love forever.

Her friend Val is determined to change her mind, no matter the consequences.

Prickly and cynical, Brynn tries to avoid Val's attempts at setting her up, until Val reveals her true identity--Aphrodite, goddess of love, who promises to show Brynn why she shouldn't lose faith Skeptical at first, Brynn soon realizes she's falling for Adam, Val's boyfriend. So she throws herself full-force into dating Val's picks, hoping one can lure her away.

When even that doesn't work, Brynn's forced to decide if she'll choose her goddess-given fate, or risk it all for the wrong-but-right guy.

One thing's for sure.

Love sucks.

And it's all about to blow up in their faces.

Also By Justine Manzano:

The Order of the Key
Keys & Guardians, Book 1

Jacklyn Madison never expected to be attacked by a beast on an evening
snack run.

Add a rescue mission enacted by a trained regiment of teenaged warriors,
and her night officially becomes just like a scene from one of her beloved
comic books. Turns out, her parents were once members of the Order of
the Key, gifted humans that protect humanity from creatures spilling
through inter-dimensional rifts. Unable to control her newfound abilities,
Jacklyn and her family rejoin the Order.

After an attack on their headquarters leaves Jacklyn questioning their
leadership, Kyp—the boy who led her initial rescue—reveals a darker
secret. The Order's leader may be corrupt, and Jacklyn's questions could
put her family in danger. Drawn into the search for proof, Jacklyn must
use her guts and magical brawn to protect her family, her friends, and
herself from the monsters spilling from rifts, and those hiding within the
Order.

www.ingramcontent.com/pod-product-compliance
Lightning Source LLC
Chambersburg PA
CBHW060423310726

48977CB00001B/24